Praise for *A Distant Melody*

"The first book in the Wings of Glory series is an intriguing story of love, loss, and second chances. Sundin places the reader in the middle of the action as her complex, believable characters are forced to make difficult decisions."

—*RT Book Reviews*

"Sarah Sundin writes a poignant love story and includes some interesting facts and anecdotes to make her debut novel a must-read."

—ChristianBook.com

"*A Distant Melody* reads like the work of an experienced and talented writer, capturing my attention from the first page until the final word."

—TitleTrakk.com

"I loved *A Distant Melody*! Sarah Sundin is a master at lyrical writing, and she has that rare talent of being able to combine humor with heart-pounding action. I couldn't stop turning the pages, and I don't think I'll ever forget Sarah's compelling characters or their poignant story about honesty, redemption, and grace."

—Melanie Dobson, author, *Love Finds You in Liberty, Indiana* and *Refuge on Crescent Hill*

Praise for *A Memory Between Us*

"An exceptional read."
—*Booklist*

"A gripping tale of war, intrigue, and love."
—*RT Book Reviews*

BLUE SKIES TOMORROW

Books by Sarah Sundin

WINGS OF GLORY SERIES

A Distant Melody
A Memory Between Us
Blue Skies Tomorrow

WINGS *of* GLORY
BOOK THREE

BLUE SKIES TOMORROW

A Novel

SARAH SUNDIN

Revell
a division of Baker Publishing Group
Grand Rapids, Michigan

© 2011 by Sarah Sundin

Published by Revell
a division of Baker Publishing Group
P.O. Box 6287, Grand Rapids, MI 49516-6287
www.revellbooks.com

Printed in the United States of America

Library of Congress Cataloging-in-Publication Data
Sundin, Sarah.
    Blue skies tomorrow : a novel / Sarah Sundin.
        p.   cm. — (Wings of glory ; bk. 3)
    ISBN 978-0-8007-3423-7 (pbk.)
    1. World War, 1939–1945—Aerial operations, American—Fiction. 2. Air pilots, Military—Fiction. 3. Americans—Great Britain—Fiction. 4. B-17 bomber—Fiction. I. Title.
PS3619.U5626B57 2011
813'.6—dc22   2011011733

Published in association with the Books & Such Literary Agency
52 Mission Circle, Suite 122
PMB 170
Santa Rosa, CA 95409-5370
www.booksandsuch.biz

11   12   13   14   15   16   17   7   6   5   4   3   2   1

In loving memory of my grandparents. Frederick Stewart served as a pharmacist's mate in the U.S. Navy during World War II, and Lucille Stewart raised my infant father on the home front without a washing machine or clothes dryer. They are two reasons why the Greatest Generation was great.

1

Antioch, California
Wednesday, March 1, 1944

Helen Carlisle strolled up G Street, careful to keep a pained expression. Some days the performance of grief was easier than others, but it was always necessary for her son's sake.

She shifted two-year-old Jay-Jay higher on her hip and inhaled the Delta breeze, flowing fresh from the San Francisco Bay into the Sacramento River Delta, rain-scrubbed and scented by new grass on the hills.

With a bump of her hip, Helen opened the door of Della's Dress Shop and set her notebooks on the table by the door.

From a picture frame on the table, Jim Carlisle smiled up at her—long, lean, and handsome in his Navy blues. The hometown hero. Was he wearing that uniform when a Japanese torpedo slammed into his destroyer off Guadalcanal?

She pressed her fingers to her lips and then to the cold glass over Jim's cold face. But a scan of the shop revealed no sign of her in-laws. Footsteps came from the back room, and the curtain swished open, so Helen repeated the performance, laid another kiss on the portrait, and lifted it for her son. "Give Daddy a kiss."

Jay-Jay mashed his palm over his mouth, making a crunching sound, and passed the kiss to the father he couldn't remember.

A crunching sound? Jay-Jay's cheeks stretched rounder than usual. "Sweetie, what do you have in your mouth?"

He shook his blond curls, his mouth clamped shut.

"Let Mama see." Helen dropped to her knees, pinned the boy on her lap, and pried open his mouth. He howled and flapped his arms at her.

"Please, sweetie?" Nausea billowed through her. Chunks of slimy gray shell lay in her son's mouth. She'd set him down for a minute, only a minute while she hung the thermometer poster in the window of the Red Cross Branch Office to monitor the War Fund Campaign.

"What are you doing to my grandson?" Della Carlisle's voice fluttered down in waves.

"He—he has a snail in his mouth." Helen whipped a handkerchief from her dress pocket and scooped out the mess, dodging sharp white teeth.

"A snail? Heavens above. Didn't your mommy feed you lunch?"

"Of course, I did. A deviled ham sandwich, an apple, milk."

Jay-Jay squirmed out of her arms. "Gamma!"

Mrs. Carlisle swept him up. "Let's see if Grandma has something that little boys like to eat."

Helen winced and got to her feet. Mrs. Carlisle seemed to be present for any mistake on her part. She wadded up the handkerchief. She'd rinse it out after her shift.

"Oh ho, here's my boy." James Carlisle strode in from the stockroom with the same powerful gait his son used to have. In one fluid motion, he snatched Jay-Jay from Mrs. Carlisle's arms and swung him around for a piggyback ride. "'Snips and snails and puppy-dog tails,' don't you know? It's good for him. Make a man of him."

Mrs. Carlisle eased back into the stockroom.

Jay-Jay squealed as his grandfather galloped and whinnied around a dress rack.

Helen smiled at the affection between the man and his namesake. "Mrs. Carlisle can go home for lunch now. I'll be here until one."

"Three."

The notebooks by the door sang out her lovely plans. "I can only stay an hour. I need to discuss the spring tea with Mrs. Novak, deposit Red Cross funds, take knitting patterns to Dorothy so she can make socks for soldiers, the Junior Red Cross meeting at 3:30—"

He laughed. "And I have to collect rent from my tenants and attend the bank board of directors' meeting. Three o'clock. Family first." He let out a horsy snort and trotted off.

How could she complain? Her father-in-law owned her house and let her live there rent free in exchange for a few hours at the store each week. Besides, she had a cute wardrobe at a deep discount. She opened the cash register and rearranged her schedule in her head. This evening she could see Dorothy and Mrs. Novak. The plans for the tea couldn't wait.

Jay-Jay's curls bounced as his grandfather galloped around, just as they bounced when he danced with Helen. Tonight she and Jay-Jay wouldn't have time to dance or read stories or cuddle for bedtime prayers.

A sigh drained from her chest. Why did everything good get taken from her life?

"Mama, look." Jay-Jay's peals of laughter blended with the bells on the front door.

"I thought I saw you come in, Helen." Victor Llewellyn walked to the counter with his clipped stride, although the Navy had driven the stoop from his shoulders, thank goodness.

"Hi, Vic. I heard you were in town." She stretched her hands over the counter.

He took them, leaned forward, and kissed her on the cheek. "How's my future wife?"

"I wouldn't know. Haven't met her." Oh dear. Why did he have to start this again? She didn't want a repeat of his peevish behavior in high school. "I heard the Navy sent you to Port Chicago."

"The Judge Advocate's office made me a liaison officer. Not much of a position, but a start."

"They load ammunition there, right?"

"Right. My job is to iron out tension. All the men are colored and all the officers are white. I've received lots of justifiable complaints—lack of recreation, poor working conditions, inappropriate placement. They have a college grad loading ammo. If he were white, he'd be an officer. That's the Navy for you."

Helen smiled at Vic, whose hair and eyes were the same shade of brown as iodine.

"But I tell you, it's boring." He folded his arms on the counter and winked. "Could use a murder to liven things up."

She laughed. College, law school, and the Navy had given him more confidence.

"Or a secretary," he said.

"Excuse me?"

"I'm authorized to hire a civilian. Interested?"

"Oh yes. I'm only involved with the Red Cross, Women's Club, Ladies' Circle, the Junior Red Cross, and my home. Plenty of time."

"Too bad." His face grew serious. "Did Mr. Carlisle tell you we had a talk?"

"A talk?" Helen sought out her father-in-law's silvery blond head above the dress racks.

★ 12 ★

Mr. Carlisle approached without Jay-Jay. "Did you ask her?"

"Not yet." Vic's mouth twisted. "Didn't you tell her?"

"I thought you—"

Helen huffed. "Tell me what? Ask me what?"

The men looked at her, then at each other. Vic gave Mr. Carlisle a nod. "You should tell her first."

Mr. Carlisle gazed down his slim nose at Helen, with his jaw edged forward. "Yes. For Jay-Jay's sake, it's time to think about your future. Of course, you'll never stop mourning Jim . . ."

Helen heard her cue, ducked her head, sifted through pennies in the cash register, and willed up wet eyes.

"Of course not," he said, voice husky and firm. "But it's been over a year. You have to think of the boy. He needs a man in the house. It's time for you to date."

Helen snapped her gaze to her father-in-law. What made him think a twenty-two-year-old woman needed permission? Then she had a strange sensation, like refugees from Hitler's Europe must have felt, the joy of freedom and the fear of an unfamiliar world.

"I'm sorry, Helen." Vic's forehead bore a V to match his name. "I wanted to give you time to think about this."

"It's all right." Of all the stupid things to say. Yes, she needed time.

"How's Friday night?"

Helen darted to the rack of new spring dresses. Her left foot drooped, the polio-ruined weakling, and she used her ballet training to make it behave. "I—I can't, Vic. I can't."

He nodded as if he understood, but he rolled his lips between his teeth. Sulking, as he had when she dated Jim.

Mrs. Carlisle bustled in from the back room. "Helen, look what I found the other—oh! Lieutenant Llewellyn, what a pleasant surprise."

"Thank you, Mrs. Carlisle. I came by to see Helen."

"I should send that fabric sample for your mother. You can give it to her, can't you? Oh dear." She glanced between the back room and the object in her hand. "Oh dear."

"I can wait." Vic straightened his blue uniform jacket. "What do you have for Helen?"

"It's for Jay-Jay's Daddy book." She stroked the item in her hand. "I—I cleaned Jimmy's room yesterday. I found this behind the desk drawer. You know how impulsive Jimmy could be. He forgot about it, never had me sew it on his sash."

"Yes?" Helen wavered her voice to match her mother-in-law's.

Mrs. Carlisle lifted her chin and gave the item to Helen. "His Boy Scout badge. Camping or campfires or some such."

On the cloth disc, yellow and orange and red threads curled in flames. Helen's fingers coiled around the smooth silver-dollar scar on her right palm, and her eyes watered.

"Such a good little Scout, always active, always—always—you have a picture of Jimmy in his Boy Scout uniform, don't you, in the scrapbook?"

Helen nodded. Why didn't the tears quench the fiery pain? Work—she needed to work, the only cure for weakness, the only cure for pain. "I—I need to—"

"I'll be going," Vic said. "Port Chicago's close. I'll see you around."

Helen looked up with blurry vision to his resigned face. Would a new romance help? She wanted to find out, but not with Vic. "I'll see you."

Pyote Army Air Base
Pyote, Texas

Lt. Raymond Novak gazed out the right cockpit window of

the B-17 Flying Fortress to the sleek aluminum wing knifing through the air. "Engine three's on fire."

"What?" Lieutenant Flynn leaned forward in the pilot's seat to look around Ray. "A fire? I don't see anything."

"It's a training flight."

Flynn's head drooped back. "Come on, I passed this part. This is a high-altitude bombing flight. Go out, drop the 'blue pickle,' go home."

The blue-painted practice bomb had splattered one hundred pounds of sand and smoke on the desert floor 15,000 feet below, but Ray's job wasn't done. He smiled at his trainee. "Expected a milk run, huh? No flak, no fighters, no problems?"

Flynn's eyelashes fluttered. "We're in Texas."

"Yeah, and engine three's on fire."

Flynn filled his green rubber oxygen mask with curses. "I know how to handle a fire."

"Good. You'll have no problems today." He put steel in his voice. "You're off to combat soon. My job is to get you ready."

The roar of the Fort's four engines didn't conceal Flynn's muttering: "Blind leading the blind."

Ray's gloved hands tightened around the wheel. A coward. That's what Flynn thought, what everyone thought.

He should have joined the chaplaincy like he wanted. A pilot's silver wings no longer carried prestige without combat ribbons. For four years Ray had put off his dream of being a pastor. He'd worn the uniform of the Army Air Forces, trained hundreds of pilots, and watched fellow instructors die fiery deaths. But he was a coward because he didn't go to combat. Baloney.

Still, what kind of man trained people to face a situation he hadn't faced himself? How many men had he trained to kill, to die?

Ray expelled a deep breath. For every man in combat, dozens toiled behind the scenes. Were their jobs less important? Were they all cowards? No, and neither was he.

He shook his head to rid himself of the niggling feeling, but it remained. It always remained. "Fire in engine three, Flynn. You'll lose the wing. What do you do?"

★

"At ease, Lieutenant Novak."

"Yes, sir." Ray sat facing the desk of his commanding officer, Colonel Beckett.

The CO tugged down his olive drab uniform jacket, temporarily closing the gaps between brass buttons. He cleared his throat and shuffled papers.

Ray unzipped his leather flight jacket and studied the officer, the thinning dark hair, the loose jowls, the unreadable expression. Why had he summoned Ray? Perhaps he wanted his opinion of Lieutenant Flynn. The other instructors had lost patience with him.

Colonel Beckett lifted a smile, wide mouthed and wide eyed. "I have good news for you."

Good news? Not with that face. Dr. Jamison had worn that face when he told Ray he could get out of junior high gym—because his leg was broken. Dolores Eaton had worn that face when she said Ray wouldn't have to support her expensive tastes—because she was returning his ring.

Ray slid his hands down his thighs to grip his knees. "News?"

"You know what things are like in the Training Command lately. You've been an instructor a long time, haven't you?"

"Yes, sir. Over four years."

"Four years. Four years." Colonel Beckett flipped through papers with thick fingers. "Yes, advanced training at Kelly

SARAH SUNDIN

Field, B-17 transition training, now here at the Replacement Training Unit. Say, you must be ready to get out of this instructor assignment."

Out? Until the war ended, the only way out was gross misconduct, medical discharge, or death. As much as he hated military life, Ray would rather stay in for the duration.

The colonel tapped the papers on edge to neaten the stack. "Thousands of pilots have returned stateside after combat tours. We want to use their valuable experience."

"Yes, sir. Some of them make excellent instructors." And some didn't.

"I'm glad you see things our way." The phony grin returned. "You can understand why the Training Command now requires that all pilot instructors have combat experience."

Ray pulled up handfuls of olive drab wool over his knees. "All?"

"You're from California. Antioch—had to look that up on the map. I found you a plum assignment at the Sacramento Air Depot. I convinced your new CO to grant you full weekend passes. How would you like that? Home-cooked meals, fishing, the girl next door?"

The girl next door was nine. "What would I—the air depot?"

"Supply officer. Can't beat that. No dangerous flights, no cocky—"

"No flying? Sir, I love flying. I love teaching. I know nothing about supply."

"You'll be trained. Fully trained. Plum new assignment."

"Supply?" A warehouse of crates, forms to type in triplicate, a mountain of paperwork—what could be worse?

Beckett tucked Ray's papers in a manila folder. "Let's be realistic. You can only return to the Training Command if you fly a combat tour. And you're—what?—thirty-one? You don't want to go to combat."

"No, sir," Ray said through clenched teeth. Combat would indeed be worse than a warehouse.

"The Training Command has become the reward for heroes. Can't all of us be heroes."

"No, sir." Ray braced himself against the sting. He was the only Novak brother who wasn't a hero. His younger brother, Jack, flew a B-17 into Pearl Harbor during the attack and now flew with the Eighth Air Force in England. His baby brother, Walt, had lost an arm to Nazi bullets in an air battle over Germany. But Ray? Ray hid in an instructor position. No, in supply.

Colonel Beckett set Ray's file on the corner of the desk, his fate decided.

Ray stood, turned on his heel, and headed outside. He pulled his little black leather notebook from his shirt pocket and jotted down "Never smile when giving bad news." Maybe he could use the story in a sermon someday.

He lifted his head to the sky he'd been shot out of, without a parachute. High above, cirrus clouds streaked tire treads across the crisp blue.

"Lord, help me see the good in this." He needed to find the lining to this cloud, but right now it looked more gray than silver.

2

Antioch
Friday, March 10, 1944

Helen pedaled down Sixth Street, harder with the left leg than the right, punishing the left leg for its weakness, as she'd learned on the polio ward and in Madame Ivanova's ballet studio.

She'd already visited the bank, the grocery, and the Red Cross office. Antioch had only raised one thousand dollars for this month's War Fund Campaign—a long way from the ten-thousand-dollar goal, and Helen needed to motivate the ladies. First she had to pick up those socks from Dorothy Wayne and review the Ladies' Circle agenda with Mrs. Novak before picking up Jay-Jay at her sister's house.

A gust of Delta wind blew plum blossoms from the Fergusons' tree, which billowed about Helen in a pale pink blizzard. At the risk of looking as callous as Scarlett O'Hara tapping her dancing feet in her widow's weeds, Helen let laughter bubble from deep inside. With the Carlisles' permission to date, someday she might shed the heavy restraints of widowhood as she had her old leg braces.

Of course, wartime pickings were slim. As the song said,

"They're Either Too Young or Too Old." Or they were Victor Llewellyn.

Petals brushed her cheek. She coasted down a slight incline, kicked her feet off the pedals, and laughed again. Why not? No one could hear her.

"Beautiful day."

Helen jerked back her attention. On the other side of the street, an Army officer walked down the sidewalk.

Ray Novak tipped his cap over his black hair. "Hi, Helen."

"Hi." She raised one hand from the handlebars. Should she wave? Salute?

The bike wheel wobbled. No, she should steer.

Helen groped for the pedals and handlebars, but sky and branches and asphalt rushed around. Her left leg gave out under her, the traitor, then the left wrist, and she crumpled to the ground. Many years' experience restrained her cry.

> Clumsy cripple Helen,
> Ugly as a melon.
> Trips on hairs, falls down stairs,
> Clumsy cripple Helen.

She groaned, shoved blonde hair from her eyes, and tugged her skirt into place.

Footsteps ran to her rescue. "Are you all right?" Ray pulled the bike away and offered his hand.

"I'm fine." When she took his broad hand, warmth rushed down her arm from that silly childhood crush.

Back on her feet, she stumbled, her shoe halfway off.

Ray caught her by the elbow. "Careful there."

"Thanks." She worked her heel back into her espadrille and looked up into his face. What a kind face with unusual gray eyes, soft as a rain cloud.

Those eyes narrowed. "Are you hurt?"

The soreness in her left ankle indicated a bruise, while her left wrist throbbed. She wiggled her fingers—good range of motion. "My foot's fine. My wrist is sprained, not broken."

He chuckled. "Spoken as Dr. Jamison's daughter."

"Spoken as his perennial patient." Goodness, she stood too close to him. No one was around, but she stepped back anyway.

"We should get you to his office. Wait, he got drafted into the Medical Corps, didn't he?"

"Mm-hmm. Washington DC. Mama went with him."

"Dr. Dozier or Dr. Libbey?"

"Oh, I'm fine. Besides, I need to finish my errands, pick up my son at Betty's house, and get these groceries home."

"We've had this conversation before." He tipped a smile. "How old were you? Ten?"

Helen's mouth drifted open at the memory of the handsome college man carrying her, with her sprained ankle, to her father's office after another bike accident. No wonder she'd had a crush on him. "Oh no. You don't remember that, do you?"

"Of course. How could I forget taking the doctor's daughter to a doctor?" He plucked plum blossoms from her hair. "And how can I forget helping a pretty girl with flowers in her hair?"

Her shoulders went limp. He was so romantic, and she was a clumsy fool. She hadn't hurt herself in ages, not since the night of George and Betty's wedding. Jim's last furlough.

She brushed off the sleeves and skirt of her brown suit. "I'm a mess."

"You look fine."

Now to brush off the attention. "Your mother told me about your transfer. You must be pleased."

Ray grimaced and twisted his head to one side. "Afraid

not. I've been put out in the most boring pasture in the world. No flying, no preaching. Still looking for that silver lining."

Helen had always liked how Ray talked to her as an adult, even when she was six. "You'll find it. If you don't, I'll knit you one."

Barks and growls sounded behind her.

She whirled around. A beagle and a mangy gray terrier played tug-of-war with a paper-wrapped package. "My pork chops!"

"Hey!" Ray rushed them, stomped his feet, and flailed his arms. "Drop that."

A yelp, and the terrier took off with the meat, the beagle nipping at his heels.

"Stupid mutts." Ray sprinted after them.

"Ray, stop." Helen laughed despite the loss of two ration points. At least the point value for pork had dropped that month. "Even if they listened, I wouldn't want it."

He turned back, his chin dipped in laughter. "Guess not."

"Thanks for trying."

He returned, wagging his head. "I've always prided myself on my peacemaking skills, but dogs don't listen to reason."

Helen laughed and picked up her scattered groceries. She held up a square tin. "At least they left the Spam."

"Quiet. They'll be back." He lifted her bike and swung down the kickstand. "Say, too bad about the meat."

Helen picked up her Ladies' Circle notebook. "Just as well. Jay-Jay and I don't like pork chops."

Ray fetched a can of soup from the middle of the street. "Why did you buy them?"

"It's Friday."

"Friday?"

"Friday's pork chop night for the Carlisles."

Ray walked over to the bike, tossing the can up and down

like a baseball, his mouth pursed. "Routine's comforting, isn't it?"

She gazed into his understanding face. "Well, yes, it is."

He took the Spam and the notebook from her and arranged them in the basket. "You may not like pork chops, but you like eating pork chops on Friday nights."

"I suppose so. I never thought about it."

"Where to?" He took the handlebars. "I'll walk the bike. You can't ride with that wrist. Besides, I need to knock these handlebars into position."

"Again?" A little smile rolled up her lips.

"At least you won't get in trouble with your dad this time."

"No, thank goodness."

"Where to?"

Helen massaged her sore wrist. "Home, please." She couldn't bother him with her errands. She'd finish later on foot. Dorothy, Betty, Mrs. Novak. Oh dear. How could she visit Mrs. Novak? Wouldn't it look as if she'd followed Ray?

"And home is . . . ?"

She laughed. "Sorry. I forgot you haven't been around. I'm at Seventh and D."

He pushed the bike down Sixth Street. "Any other routines?"

She crossed a strip of grass and headed down the sidewalk. "Where do I start? Routines, schedules, lists. I couldn't get anything done without them."

"You're well-disciplined."

Helen shrugged. "Betty says I overdo it. She says I'm Martha and she's Mary."

Ray grinned at her. "Is she right?"

"Perhaps. But without Marthas in this world, nothing would get done."

"True. If we were all like Betty . . . She's always struck me as sort of . . ." He gazed up as if searching for the right word among the clouds.

"A flibbertigibbet."

Ray laughed. "Boy, you two are tough on each other."

"We're sisters. We love each other."

"That's the key, isn't it? Connection. Love." His eyes darted about, and then he rested the bike against his side and reached into the pocket of his khaki uniform shirt. "Excuse me. I have to write something down."

"I didn't realize I was quotable."

He glanced at her from under dark eyebrows, flashed a smile, and scribbled in his notebook. "Sorry. Bad habit."

"Why? If you have an idea, it's best to write it down before you forget."

"Sermon ideas. It's stupid. The way this war's going, I won't be able to give a sermon for years."

Helen rose up and down on her toes, little ballet exercises called *relevés* to strengthen her calves. "All the more reason to take notes. You have experiences in the Army you'd never have as a civilian. When the war's over, you'll have a treasure trove."

He raised a long, steady gaze and caught her in full *relevé*. She lowered her heels. His gaze didn't budge as he tucked away his notebook. "Dolores didn't share your view."

Dolores. Helen knew that name and didn't like it. How could any woman break an engagement, break the heart of this sweet man? "I don't understand. You're a pastor. Even as a teenager, you were a pastor. You visited me when I—I was sick, cheered me on as I learned to—to walk again, and besides, you have to keep up your skills, right?"

He guided the bike around the corner onto D Street. "My skills? That's part of it, but it's more than that, deeper than that. Sometimes I think if I can't put pen to paper each day, a part of me will shrivel and die." He chuckled. "Sounds strange, I guess."

"No. It's your heart's work."

"My heart's work." He gazed up through the tree branches. "That fits."

"You can't deny your heart's work. I denied mine for years."

He gave her a quizzical look.

Helen chewed on her lips. "Jim—well, he liked to keep me to himself, so I gave up volunteer work. But I missed it. I wasn't myself without meetings and committees and something to give my life purpose. Not that being a wife and mother wasn't—"

"But you weren't doing your heart's work."

She released her breath. "No, I wasn't. Then when Jim died, I went back to what I enjoy." Oh no, her voice didn't quaver, not one bit.

Ray didn't look shocked. "Good thing. Mom tells me how much you do for the church, the Red Cross—I'm sure I missed something."

Helen stopped on the driveway beside her little cream bungalow. "Only my house. Here we are." She led him up the driveway to the garage set back from the house.

Ray propped up the bike and raised the garage door. "Just need a wrench."

"Oh, leave it. I'll have my brother-in-law—"

"Won't take long." He poked around in the mess on the tool bench.

Helen unbuckled her bike basket to take her groceries into the house.

"Let me get that," he said. "You shouldn't carry anything."

"I'm fine. It doesn't hurt anymore." The pain in her wrist had dulled to warmth, nothing to speak of.

Without a word, Ray unbuckled the last strap and carried the basket toward the kitchen door on the side of the house.

"No, really. I'll do it." She followed as fast as her sore ankle allowed. What if someone saw? "Please, Ray. Please let me."

"Don't you know the Novaks are a stubborn lot?" He climbed three steps and crossed the threshold of her home.

Helen clutched the stair railing, unable to breathe. Did anyone see him go in? Mrs. Llewellyn across the street could never keep her mouth shut.

"On the counter okay?"

Helen pumped air into her lungs, hitched up a smile, and entered the kitchen. "Sure."

Ray pulled groceries out of the basket. "Anything need to go in the icebox?"

"Not anymore," she said, pleased at her breezy tone. Why worry? The kitchen window faced the backyard.

"Dumb dogs." He settled his gaze on her. "Say, what'll you do for dinner?"

She picked up the Spam and the tomato soup with a flourish and a cheesy smile. If she wore her ruffled apron, she'd be ready for an ad in *Good Housekeeping*. "Why, I'm all set."

Ray stepped closer and took the cans in a move strangely and wonderfully intimate. "I have a better idea."

3

Savory steam wafted from pots on the stove, and red gingham curtains framed the window. Outside, the budded branches of the nectarine tree bobbed in the wind. This year Ray would be home for the crop.

"Guests on your first night home." Mom clucked her tongue and peeled an extra potato, but her cheeks jutted out in a smile.

Ray leaned against the cupboard. "Dogs ran off with her main course. Seemed the right thing to do."

Mom murmured her agreement. Potato shavings leaped from the edge of her paring knife and did acrobatic flips into the garbage.

Ray reached into a blue glass bowl and popped a strawberry into his mouth. His tongue savored the contrast between smooth skin and rough seeds until he couldn't stand the temptation any longer. He smashed the berry against the roof of his mouth, and the perfect blend of sweetness and acidity seeped out.

Mom sliced the potato into quarters and tossed it into a pot. "Helen said she had something to discuss?"

He reluctantly swallowed the pulp. "Some Ladies' Circle thing."

"She's such a dedicated worker." Mom rinsed asparagus in

the sink and shot Ray a mischievous glance over her shoulder. "Not to mention attractive and available."

He smiled and poked around in the strawberry bowl. "I'm above such superficial considerations."

Mom gasped and scooted the bowl away from him. "Leave some berries if you want to impress the widow Carlisle."

Ray laughed. "You make her sound like an old lady."

"No, she's young. Very young. But she's a widow, and you mustn't forget. Helen and Jim—you weren't around, but they were so wrapped up in each other. You know how exclusive the Carlisles can be. Helen still mourns him."

In his trouser pocket, Ray fingered the blossoms he'd plucked from Helen's golden hair. That lovely young woman laughing in a flurry of flowers was no longer in mourning.

Mom turned to the sink and snapped off the base of an asparagus stalk. A lot of gray streaked her black hair now. "She puts up a brave front with her activity, but only to cover her pain."

Ray snagged another berry. His mother hadn't seen the glow in Helen's tea-colored eyes when she talked about her work, her heart's work.

Crisp, wet snaps, and Mom tossed woody stems in the garbage. "Be careful. I know how you get swept away."

Careful? Ray had known Helen all her life, mostly as a little girl, but today he'd seen her in a new light. She was attractive and available, and Mom couldn't spoil the thrill of discovery.

"Ray?" She gave him that "you didn't answer me" look.

He stuffed the berry into his cheek. "I'm always careful." His voice came out muffled.

Her gaze penetrated deeper.

He smiled around the berry and reminded himself not to swallow.

She broke out in a laugh. "You boys always thought I

didn't know you sneaked fruit. I knew. But I couldn't resist those smiles."

Ray chewed, swallowed, and flashed his most innocent smile.

Her mouth and eyes curved, and she walked over and placed a water-cooled hand on Ray's cheek. "I'm glad you're home, dear," she said, her voice thick. "I'm glad you're safe, glad you'll never see the things your brothers have seen. I don't know if . . ."

The truth stung, but Ray refused to wince. Mom didn't think he could handle it.

Neither did Ray.

★

"Interest is flagging, donations are down. It's hard to recruit volunteers." Helen sat at the dining room table, proper and professional in a brown suit and cream-colored blouse.

Ray held up his glass of iced tea. What a perfect comparison to Helen's eyes. Not only the color, but the clarity, the translucence, and the golden glow within. And her blonde hair glistened like honey. He had always liked tea with honey.

"We Americans are impatient." Dad ladled a second helping onto his plate. "Casualties are high. We haven't set foot on French or German soil, we're bogged down in Italy, and progress in the Pacific is slow. How do we keep our sense of urgency?"

"I've been thinking. I'd like to put on a children's pageant. I wouldn't be able to organize it in time to help with this War Fund Campaign, but it's never too late to help with the cause." Helen sliced the chicken on her son's plate.

"No! My do." Jay-Jay swatted her arm.

"Sweetie, please." Helen swept a nervous glance around the table.

Ray gave her a reassuring smile. He didn't envy her duty to enforce manners while keeping the peace.

Dad picked up a drumstick and leaned closer to Jay-Jay. "It's fried chicken, son. Finger food. Pick it up and gnaw at it." He growled at the chicken.

Jay-Jay let out a wet chortle and screwed up his round face. "Grr."

"John, you're a horrible influence," Mom said with a laugh.

Ray picked up a chicken wing, gave his mother a pointed look, and added to the growling.

Helen laughed. "Sounds like feeding time at the zoo."

"Always. Always around here. I'm sorry, Helen." Mom's forehead bunched up, but her thin shoulders shook in laughter. "Boys never grow up."

Ray let out a rumbling good snarl.

"So I see." Helen gave him a look, half-stern, half-playful.

Something hot stirred in his chest. Mom was definitely wrong. Helen was ready. And didn't the growling prove she needed a man in her life? Every little boy needed a firm hand, but he also needed someone to teach him how to make armpit noises. And wouldn't Helen like a shoulder to lean on, a strong back to carry her burdens?

Ray took a deep breath to fill the width of his chest. Nora, Ann, and Dolores had all loved his solid build. Of course, they'd all broken up with him. And Jim had been built like a string bean. His chest deflated. Yeah, he did tend to get swept away.

Helen's laughter pulled him back. Sunny, lemony laughter to go with the tea.

"I agree," she said. "The pageant doesn't have to be fancy. Red, white, and blue sashes, paper hats. They could wave flags they colored themselves. Wouldn't that be charming? Songs, patriotic poems, maybe a skit."

Mom cut her chicken with a knife and fork, always the lady. "How touching."

"That's the idea." Helen rocked forward. "Remind everyone we're fighting for the children, for the future. Then we pass sign-ups for the blood drive, sell War Bonds, recruit hostesses for the Soldiers' Hospitality Center."

Ray smiled. Her energy, compassion, and organizational ability would make her the perfect pastor's wife. Getting ahead of himself, but maybe he needed to. Nora, Ann, and Dolores hadn't been suited to life in the parsonage. If he'd considered that earlier, he wouldn't have racked up three broken hearts and two broken engagements.

"No! Daff!" Jay-Jay cried.

Ray startled.

"Sweetie, please. Please don't." Helen's voice strained. She pulled her son onto her lap and kissed his forehead.

"No! Mama, daff."

"Daff?" Ray said above the boy's grunts.

"Dance," she said. "It's something we do."

"One of your routines?"

A glimmer of a smile. "Every night after dinner, we dance to the radio. It's nothing, really."

Nothing? Not to the little boy writhing on the lap of his mother, who looked ready to go home far too early.

"Jay-Jay," he said in a tone just low enough to attract attention. "Would you like me to play the piano for you?"

Jay-Jay faced Ray with two fingers in his mouth and interest in his blue eyes.

"Oh goodness," Helen said. "I couldn't ask—"

"You didn't ask. I offered. You lost your pork chop dinner. You shouldn't have to lose your evening of dancing."

Mom stood and gathered dishes. "Ray will play all night anyway. He'd rather have an audience. And I'll be reading in the study to keep Pastor Novak company while he polishes his sermon."

"I don't want to impose," Helen said.

Ray leaned forward. "Jay-Jay, what's your favorite song?"

"Moo," he said around his fingers.

"Moo?"

Helen stroked her son's curls. " 'In the Mood.' He likes anything fast and bouncy."

"All right, then." Ray tossed his napkin onto the table and headed for the parlor.

"I should help with—"

"You'd be the greatest help," Mom said, "if you entertained Ray so I don't have to listen to him whine."

"Little boys." But Helen's scold held laughter, and chair legs scraped over the floor.

In the parlor Ray shoved back the coffee table and rug, shed his olive drab uniform jacket, and sat at the piano in his khakis.

Jay-Jay ran into the room. "Daff. Moo."

"Coming right up." A few scales, and Ray started the song. When Helen sidled into the parlor, Ray jerked his head toward the dance floor behind him. "Daff."

"I'll just sit and watch."

"No, Mama, daff."

"Go ahead, Helen. I'm not watching." Not yet anyway.

She gave a self-conscious laugh, and soon two sets of feet shuffled and squeaked and tapped the hardwood floor. Jay-Jay's squeals rose high in the air and low to the floor.

Ray built up to the finale and glanced behind him. Helen held her son on her hip and twirled around, her hair a golden wing behind her. She moved gracefully, without a trace of her old limp.

Ray remembered her tiny body lying paralyzed on the bed

in the Jamisons' living room, remembered her struggling to walk in steel-and-leather braces, shedding one brace and then the other with a determined set to her chin. He couldn't believe she remembered his visits. It didn't seem like much, but he couldn't stand how Betty Jamison ran around the neighborhood on healthy legs with Dorothy Carlisle, who had been Helen's best friend. A teenage boy couldn't substitute for a sister or a girlfriend, but Ray could read a storybook or play a game of checkers.

Helen gasped. "You said you wouldn't watch."

"Nope. I said I wasn't watching, not that I wouldn't." Ray drummed the final chord and grinned. "What's next?"

She rolled her eyes. "How about 'Don't Be That Way'?"

He laughed. "Come on, we need fast and bouncy, right, Jay-Jay?" He launched into "Beat Me, Daddy, Eight to the Bar."

The pace demanded Ray's attention, but he popped occasional glances to watch mother and son jitterbug, squeal, and grow red in the face. Finally, Jay-Jay spun into a giggling heap on the floor.

"Uncle! Uncle! We can't take it." Helen lurched, laughing, to the wall and leaned her arms on the piano top. "Ray, that's amazing, but please let us rest."

He smiled at her rosy cheeks and tousled hair, and made a quick musical transition to "Taking a Chance on Love." Not subtle, but he was in no mood for subtle.

"Oh dear, what's this?" She poked between the threads of the doily on the piano top.

"You've discovered the Novaks' deepest, darkest secret," he said in his deepest, darkest voice.

"Looks like an ink spot."

"Yep. Very deep. Very dark."

"I imagine one of you boys had something to do with it."

"Jack, of course."

"He always got in trouble, didn't he?"

Ray ran through an intricate run. "This time we all got in trouble."

A scar on her cheek gave her smile a cute little tilt. "How'd that happen?"

"Let's see. Jack was about five. I hated to see him get another spanking, so I told Mom I did it. But I didn't know Jack had talked little Walt into confessing."

"Typical. Walt lying, Jack manipulating, and you being nice."

"I lied too."

Her gaze pulled like a fishing line. "That's different."

The heat returned to his chest. How stupid to offer to play piano when he wanted to dance. "Jay-Jay, want to play the piano?"

"My?"

"Ray, he'll just pound the keys."

"How's that different from what I do?" He put his hands around the boy's solid middle and lifted him to the bench.

Jay-Jay slammed both hands on the keyboard.

"How's that different?" Helen covered her ears. "Oh, I don't know. Melody? Rhythm?"

Ray took a little hand and separated out one plump finger. "Like this. One finger at a time." He walked Jay-Jay through "Mary Had a Little Lamb."

The boy started his own discordant composition.

Ray leaned down to his ear. "May I ask your mother to dance?"

Jay-Jay nodded and grinned at the keys while two fingers tapped like a pair of demented woodpeckers.

Helen stood straight, her lips parted, her elbows still on the piano top.

Ray got to his feet and bowed. "May I have this dance?"

She gave a small laugh, high and nervous. "Sure, but doesn't that require music?"

He took her hand, so small and warm, and twirled her under his arm. "Sounds like 'The Woodpecker Song.'"

Her laugh rang lower and more natural. "It does, doesn't it? And we may not have a tune, but we have a beat."

Ray grinned and worked that beat. He hadn't danced for over a year, but it came back to him, and Helen kept up, the perfect partner. All that spinning, wiggling, laughing femininity drove the heat from his chest into every muscle of his body.

His cloud had a lining, all right, but gold instead of silver. This golden young woman.

4

Saturday, March 18, 1944

Helen clipped her white cotton nightgown to the clothesline and fumbled in her apron pocket. Only two clothespins remained, locked in mortal combat. Helen groaned. She needed both hands to separate them. As soon as she let go of the nightgown, the wind snatched it, and the gown billowed onto the lawn like a ghost.

"Every—single—time." With each word, Helen snapped the gown, which hurt her wrist, but she had to work out the injury. She couldn't do anything right, especially laundry. The Delta breeze blew from the San Francisco Bay, funneled down the valley where the Sacramento and San Joaquin rivers met, and blasted Antioch and Helen's wash.

What a lousy weekend. How silly to hope Ray would visit or call on Friday. Last week she thought he might be sweet on her, but he was just sweet to her. Honestly, what did she expect?

She secured the nightgown with all three clothespins, then headed to the garage for more. On the lawn, Jay-Jay rocked back and forth in the old wicker laundry basket Mama had left when she and Papa moved to Washington DC in November.

"Oh no! A storm at sea." Helen plucked up her son, plopped him on the grass, and set the basket over his head. He roared in delight. Mama was right—an extra basket came in handy.

The garage smelled of dust and oil and Jim. Helen grabbed a pocketful of clothespins and got out as fast as possible.

"Hi there." At the foot of the driveway, Ray Novak tipped his garrison cap to her.

"Oh. Hi." Helen's heart tumbled like the load in the washing machine. She freed her hand from her bulging pocket to wave, and a clothespin fell to the asphalt. Stupid, clumsy girl. She picked it up. "Out for a walk?"

"Mm-hmm. Nice day." Handsome in crisp khakis, he strolled up the driveway.

And Helen wore an old brown gingham dress and a ratty gray cardigan, with her hair up in a kerchief. She hadn't even bothered with lipstick.

Ray smiled as if oblivious to her appearance. "Thought of you last night."

"You did?"

"Death by pork chops."

Helen gave him a smile. "Yet you abandoned me to my fate."

"No choice. At the Air Depot I'm Laurel and Hardy rolled into one, and I couldn't get the shipment out in time to catch my bus. Just got in this morning."

"That's too bad." In the warmth of his smile, her disappointment evaporated. If only she didn't look like Ma Joad in *The Grapes of Wrath*.

Ray peered into the backyard. "Um, your basket's moving."

The basket inched across the grass like a headless turtle. "It's probably giggling too."

"Yeah?" Ray walked over and squatted. "Say, what a big, strong tank. What's a tank doing around here?"

A smiling face peeked out. "No. Day-Day."

"It's not a tank? It's Jay-Jay? Whew. Thought I'd have to call in the Army."

Jay-Jay poked a finger through a hole in the basket. "Bang!"

Helen went to the good basket and pulled out Jay-Jay's blue striped shirt. "Ray, would you like one too, so you can have a tank battle?"

"Sounds great." He sat cross-legged in the grass. "You survived the pork chops."

Helen clipped the shirt to the line. "Only to suffer an after-dinner visit from Vic and Jeannie."

"The Llewellyn kids? I thought you were friends."

Helen shook out her yellow gingham peasant skirt. "We are. Jeannie and I have been friends since . . . since I was sick. We love competing against each other. But you know the Llewellyns. Vic pesters me to work for him at Port Chicago, and Jeannie drops French phrases then covers her mouth and says, '*Pardon, chérie.* I forgot you only had high school French.'"

"Does she? I should teach you obscure phrases in German, Hebrew, Latin, or ancient Greek."

"You speak all those?"

"Read them, yes. Speak them, barely."

Helen set clothespins like birds on a branch huddling from the rain. "Jeannie graduates from Mills College in June. We were supposed to graduate together."

"You didn't go."

"Jim wouldn't have it." She sucked in her breath. Where did that come from? "We wanted to get married."

"Young love is impatient."

"Yes." She wrestled a sheet in place, and it wrapped her in a clammy embrace.

Ray stood and helped her stretch out the sheet on the line. "Any regrets?"

She stared across the clothesline into those knowing eyes. "Not when I look at my son."

Jay-Jay dug in the dirt under the hedges Mr. Carlisle had planted, oleander hedges that threatened the view of the outside world. Stupid things refused to die, no matter how much Helen deprived them of water.

"He's a great kid," Ray said. "A budding musician and a swell daffer."

Helen smiled and dug in her pocket for more pins.

"Last night," he said, eyes warm as gray flannel. "I'd rather have been daffing than sitting in my barracks worrying about you and pork chops. I didn't even know about the scourge of the Llewellyns."

She experimented with a playful look, but she was out of practice. "Some knight in shining armor you are."

"I'm no knight."

"Sure you are. Twice now you've rescued me after bike accidents." She pinned up a bobby sock, so childish, but with stockings unavailable she had no choice.

Ray frowned at the sky. "Knights go to combat and slay dragons. Not me. If I met a dragon, I'd talk him into using his fire for good instead of evil."

Helen laughed and added the sock's mate. "I hope you never meet a dragon who won't listen to reason."

"Yeah." His voice sounded tight, but he turned before Helen could read his expression. "How about I deal with this little dragon?"

The wind puffed out the sheet, and Jay-Jay chased it with dirty hands.

Ray grabbed him around the middle, swung him overhead, then glanced at Helen. "Before I get him wound up, does he still take—is it almost time . . . ?"

She nodded. Impressive for a man to remember about naps, especially a bachelor. "Half an hour."

He gazed up at the giggling boy he held with nice thick arms. "Say, munchkin, how about a story?"

Helen pointed to the back porch. "I have books on the table."

"Books. Your mommy knows what I like." Ray flew Jay-Jay like an airplane, sat down with him, and thumbed through the books. "What would you like? *Make Way for Ducklings? The Color Kittens?*"

"Da boo."

Ray looked at Helen, eyebrows twisted in comical shapes.

"His Daddy book." She made her voice sober. "The brown scrapbook."

Ray settled back and flipped through black pages while Jay-Jay pointed and jabbered. Helen whipped out piece after piece of laundry and focused hard on how many clothespins each required.

"Did you do this all yourself, Helen? It's a lot of work."

"That's what I needed." When the telegram arrived, Helen had laughed. Papa told everyone she was mad with grief. For the next month she sequestered herself, pasted photo corners with rubber cement, and mounted photos and mementoes to present Jim as everyone remembered him, as Jay-Jay needed to know him. Meanwhile, Helen learned how to act like a proper widow.

"For Jay-Jay's sake," she said.

"It's a fine thing you did."

Helen ducked to the laundry basket to shake out two socks. How much longer would she have to endure sympathy and admiration for her bravery? Would she ever get to be herself again? Could she even remember who she was?

★

"So . . . ?" Betty Jamison Anello stretched the word in twenty directions. "Tell me everything."

Helen sliced celery at an even pace. "Tell you what?"

"Tell me why Ray Novak's in my living room."

"George invited him." Helen scraped the celery into the mixing bowl while her older sister did nothing. Everyone loved her for being Betty. She didn't have to work for it as Helen did. "The bread, Betts."

She heaved a sigh and crumbled bread into the bowl. "Yes, but why did my husband find Ray all cozy on your back porch?"

Helen opened the cupboard and rummaged through a jumble of spice tins. "He went for a walk."

"Out of his way, don't you think?"

Several blocks out of his way. Helen shrugged, glad the open door hid her smile. Finally she found the sage. "How can you work in this kitchen?"

"This is so sweet, so right." Betty leaned her plump hip against the cupboard, hands idle. "Does he know you made up stories about Sir Raymond the Valiant?"

Helen gasped and brandished a wooden spoon in her sister's face. "Don't breathe a word or I'll . . . I'll . . ."

"You'll stir me until thoroughly mixed?"

"I'll swat you like Papa used to do."

Betty laughed her tinkling laugh. "And break my good spoon? You'd better not."

Instead, Helen applied the spoon to the stuffing mixture. "Slice the Spam."

"Well, he's awfully good-looking and sweet, and here you are with the Carlisle stamp of approval." Betty ducked her chin to deepen her voice. "I have decided, in my masculine superiority, to permit you to date. Honestly."

"Slice the Spam." Helen studied the recipe Betty clipped from George's *National Geographic* for Spam-birds, slices of Spam rolled around stuffing and fastened with toothpicks.

"The Carlisles think it's 1844, not 1944. First the insurance, now this."

Helen lined up the mixing bowl, baking pan, and toothpicks. Jim had made his parents the beneficiaries of his ten thousand dollar GI life insurance policy, which rankled, but the Carlisles did provide a generous allowance and a house to live in rent free.

The kitchen door swung open. "Doo doo?" Jay-Jay asked.

Betty laughed. "I hope he learns to say his cousin's name right."

Helen stooped to her son's level. "Judy's asleep, sweetie. She's just a baby, not a big boy like you."

His moist pink lower lip rounded out. "Pay."

"I know you want to play, but don't wake her, okay?"

Betty handed Jay-Jay two old tin mixing bowls of Mama's. "Judy has the Jamison sleep-through-a-major-earthquake trait."

Same as Jay-Jay. Helen grinned. "Go play music for Uncle George and Lieutenant Novak."

Jay-Jay banged the pans together and ran off.

The sisters laughed and got to work rolling Spam-birds, and Helen arranged them in the baking pan.

"Got any spoons we can borrow?" Ray stepped into the kitchen with light in his eyes.

"Spoons?" Despite her flipping heart, Helen slid the pan into the oven without mishap.

George crossed the kitchen, tall and lanky, with his uneven gait. "That drawer on the left. Darling, where do you keep the empty jelly jars?"

"Jelly jars?" Betty asked. "What are you two up to?"

In the doorway, Jay-Jay hopped up and down. "Pay! Pay!"

"We're forming a band." Ray gave Helen a lightning bolt of a wink and left the kitchen.

Electricity tingled down to Helen's fingertips.

Betty opened the icebox and gave the Jell-O mold a shake. "I was going to suggest bridge tonight, but I changed my mind. A little 'Stardust' on the phonograph, a little dancing, a little romance in the air."

The utensil drawer lay open. Helen grabbed a spoon and swatted her sister's backside.

✹

Helen tried not to watch Ray as they walked down D Street, but he held Jay-Jay asleep on his shoulder and hummed "Stardust" as he studied the night sky. How could she not watch? But did his silence mean contentment, fatigue—or did he dislike the company? "I hope we didn't wear you out tonight."

"Hmm?"

Helen scrunched up the pocket lining of her spring coat. "Betty and George talked so much, you barely had a chance to speak."

"Don't need it. I had a great time, especially dancing." He pulled the blanket higher over Jay-Jay's shoulders, but it slipped.

Helen tucked the blanket around her sleeping son. "Good music, wasn't it?"

"Good partner." A rumble in his voice played havoc with her heart. Then his smile edged into place. "You're a great dancer."

For some reason, she struck a ballet pose straight from *Swan Lake*, with fluttering hands crossed over her chest. "Thanks to eight summers of torture in Madame Ivanova's ballet studio."

Jim would have been disgusted by her display, but Ray's smile grew fuller. "That's right. You went away every summer, didn't you?"

"Off to Aunt Olive's musty Victorian in cold, foggy San Francisco." An appropriate place to banish a cripple girl.

"No fond memories, huh?"

Helen strolled down the sidewalk. "I loved the dancing, the music, Aunt Olive, but I hated being away from my friends and I hated the weather and Madame's switch."

"Switch?"

"That's how she corrected us." She imitated the smarting, flicking lashes. "You are weak, Helena. You must work harder. Deeper *plié*, more turnout, point those toes. You are weak."

"You're kidding."

Helen swung her gaze to Ray. She must have sounded crazy. "Well, she was right. If I worked harder and did it correctly, she wouldn't have needed to switch me."

His lips set in a hard line. "Did that ever happen? Was there ever a day she didn't switch you?"

"I was never good enough. Not with this . . . this foot."

Embers flared in Ray's charcoal eyes.

Helen stepped back.

"That's not right." His neck muscles stood out. "Children should be punished for disobedience, not imperfection. What does that teach a child? The only way to salvation, to approval, is to be good enough, do the right things."

Helen turned up the walkway to her house, away from the tension. "It wasn't that bad."

"Did you tell your aunt?" His voice cooled down.

"She told me not to complain and to try harder. So I did." She smiled over her shoulder at Ray. "That's just the way of things. Besides, I got stronger and walked better, so everyone was happy."

"Except you."

She climbed her front steps and put on a bigger smile. "Honestly, it was fine."

SARAH SUNDIN

"What should I do with the munchkin?"

"Here." She lifted her son from Ray's chest, which involved pleasant brushing of arms and shoulders. Jay-Jay's hands trembled midair. He lifted his head, brought his eyes to focus on Helen, and relaxed into her arms.

Ray leaned against the door frame and crossed his arms over his waist-length olive drab "Ike" jacket. "Are you happy now?"

"I am. I have a sweet boy, friends and family nearby, and plenty of time to volunteer."

Ray had a delicious way of studying her for a long moment before he spoke. "You looked happy tonight."

She leaned her cheek on Jay-Jay's curls and returned Ray's intense gaze. "Good company."

5

Sacramento Air Depot
Monday, March 27, 1944

At the typewriter, Ray could almost convince himself he was writing a sermon and doing something useful. Nope, another stupid requisition form.

He returned the carriage, savored the "ding," and typed, "GLOVES, FLYING, UNLINED SUMMER, MEDIUM, B-3A, CASE, 1 EA." The *M* key was weak. Ray struck extra hard to press through the carbon paper.

He gazed around his closet-sized office with its file cabinets and shelves full of forms. His winepress. In the Bible, Gideon threshed his wheat in a winepress, hidden from the Midianite invaders. Was Ray any different? The War Department had stepped up the draft, reclassifying fathers and taking one of every twenty men in civilian war work or farm work. While fathers went to combat, Ray hid.

He grumbled and fetched another form, the last in the pile. Swell, he needed to reorder. He leaned out the office door and scanned the warehouse for Corporal Shuster, his right-hand man. No, Ray needed to figure this out. There was a form, a special one, a requisition form for requisition forms.

He flipped through the stacks on the shelves. "If the Germans want to bring down the U.S. Army, all they have to do is cut off our paper supply."

Corporal Shuster entered the office. "The shipment is ready for inspection, sir."

Ray followed him out. The corporal reminded him of a mouse with his pointed face, bright eyes, and erratic movements. What kind of man was he? Maybe Ray's purpose here was to get to know the men.

"Where are you from, Corporal?"

"Originally, sir? Small town in Vermont." Shuster sneezed and wiped his nose with a wiggle that made him look even more mouselike.

Ray moved to the side to let a forklift pass. "How'd you end up here?"

"Joined up, sir." He led Ray down a canyon of crates. "Seems like yesterday I was riding the rails, just another hobo, and Uncle Sam gives me a test, says I'd be good in supply, puts me in a smart uniform, and feeds me regular. It's a good life."

Ray sighed. Too bad he didn't share the man's positive attitude.

Shuster's gaze skittered over the crates. He probably knew the contents and destination of each one. "This is good, orderly work," Shuster said. "When I do my job right, the boys on the front get what they need to fight."

"Yeah." Why did Ray let an avalanche of forms bury that truth? These supplies helped his brother Jack in England, his friend Bill Ferguson in the Pacific, and all the men on the front.

He stepped outside into the cool morning sunshine. Throbs of airplane engines filled the air. A C-47 cargo plane pointed its snub nose into the sky while another turned onto the downwind leg of the landing approach. Pain built in Ray's chest, and his fingers curled, missing the feel of the control wheel.

Ray had inquired into a position with the Air Transport Command, but ATC also served as a reward for returning combat pilots. For heroes.

"Lieutenant?" With a strained smile, Corporal Shuster held out a clipboard. How long had he been waiting?

"Sorry. Where do I sign?"

Shuster led him to a truck and pointed out crates and boxes and labels, and had Ray sign here and here and there, and initial here and here and—no, over here. Ray served as an officer's rubber stamp, a bureaucratic hurdle for Shuster, who could roll out shipments a lot faster without him.

"Ready to go, sir?" Shuster asked.

Ray chuckled. "You tell me."

Shuster flagged down the driver and pitched an imaginary fastball. "Move on out."

The truck rumbled away and revealed a clear view over the flat Sacramento Valley to Mount Diablo some fifty miles south. The Diablo hills slouched like lazy students in their desks, but Mount Diablo stood several thousand feet above the others, the only one in class who knew the answers.

Antioch snuggled at the base of the foothills, and somewhere in Antioch, Helen bustled around.

The weekend glimmered in his memory. He'd gotten his Friday shipment out on time, caught his bus, and whisked Helen and her son to his parents' for dinner and piano playing. When Jay-Jay fell asleep on the sofa, Ray and Helen danced to the radio.

Saturday she invited him to join George and Betty Anello at her place. After many long looks over dinner and too few dances, Ray tried to leave, but the Anellos left first. Ray and Helen talked past midnight on her porch swing under the rustling branches of a cherry tree. Every time he said he should go, a new wave of conversation carried them away.

He held her hand under the pretense of examining the fine scars from cooking accidents. He could have kissed those scars and those on her face, and he could have kissed her, but he had to be careful.

Jay-Jay needed stability. Before Ray crossed that threshold, he wanted to be rock-solid certain. Granite, not pumice.

"Lieutenant, where'd you want this pallet?"

Ray blinked at the forklift operator. He pointed to an open spot inside the door. "Park it there while I find out."

Shuster jogged up to the forklift and examined the invoice. "Nice fellow, the lieutenant," he said to the operator in a not-low-enough voice. "Real bright too, but his head's in the clouds."

All his life. Ray returned to his office and those mind-numbing forms. At least with his head in the clouds he could see that golden lining.

★

Antioch
Friday, March 31, 1944

"Excellent job, ladies." Helen smiled at the members of the Junior Red Cross in the classroom at Antioch High. The children's pageant, "Vaudeville for Victory," had energized them far more than preparing surgical dressings or collecting funds. However, the Antioch Branch had surpassed its goal in the War Fund Campaign—over twelve thousand dollars—thanks in part to a sizable donation from Carlisle's Furniture and Upholstery and Della's Dress Shop.

"Let's go over this again. Be at El Campanil Theatre no later than . . . ?"

"Nine o'clock," the girls chimed.

"Right." Helen scanned the list in Mary Jane Anello's rounded handwriting. "Nancy Jo, Rita, Anne, and Peggy will take tickets then pass clipboards and collection cups. Evelyn, Margie, Carol, and Gina will put the children in order, check costumes, and keep the children occupied backstage—quietly occupied—while Mary Jane and I run the program."

Evelyn Kramer raised her hand. Her strawberry-blonde pompadour rose higher than anything the Andrews Sisters attempted. "Mrs. Carlisle, may I bring a game?"

"Yes. Anything to keep them quiet."

"I know what I'm bringing," Margie Peters said. "Hand-cuffs and gags."

When the giggles died down, Helen turned to the president of the Junior Red Cross. "Thank you, Mary Jane. Excellent work."

Her round face lit up under her black curls tied back with a pink bow.

Helen dismissed the girls and checked her watch. An hour at the dress shop, a visit with Jim's sister, Dorothy Wayne, and her new baby girl, and then dinner with Ray and his parents.

Bubbles tickled her insides. She hadn't felt this way since the early years with Jim, but this felt different, a continual escalation without jagged peaks and valleys. Something steady in Ray gave her a sense of inevitability and rightness. This relationship wouldn't be passionate, but it also wouldn't have the undercurrent of desperation, the constant fear that if she messed up she'd lose him forever.

Helen headed down the hallway she'd walked four years ago as a senior agonizing over her decision. The acceptance letter from Mills College had hung on her bulletin board, but Jim's face grew darker each day. Mills might be a women's college, Jim said, but they had socials with men's colleges. Why should he wait for her, when he knew she wouldn't wait for him?

Helen opened the door, drank in cool air, turned the page

in her memory book to where it belonged, and pictured hand-some blond Jim Carlisle stopping her on these steps and asking her to the Winter Ball.

"You're kidding. Not our Mrs. Carlisle. She's old." Evelyn Kramer's voice floated around the corner of the building.

Old? Helen stood still. She'd never yet been called old.

"You ninny," Margie Peters said. "She's not old. My brother went to school with her."

"But she's a widow and a mother."

"So what?" Mary Jane Anello's laughter rang out. "I'm glad to see her happy for a change. Didn't she look radiant?"

Helen touched her cheek. Did she apply too much rouge?

"My brother George says they're sweet on each other," Mary Jane said. "And Pop says Ray Novak's a fine man. It's so romantic."

People were talking about them? Already? Gossip made it more real somehow. The bubbles inside rose to her head, and she grasped the staircase handrail. She wanted this relation-ship, didn't she?

So why did her hands shake?

☆

"Good afternoon, Mrs. Jeffries." Helen nodded and smiled to her next-door neighbor as she walked up G Street.

Two posters hung in the window of Molander Repairs. One showed a pilot gazing skyward—"Keep 'Em Flying." The second read "Vaudeville for Victory." Young Donald Fergu-son's crayon writing started bold, shrunk, and the T-O-R-Y dripped down the right side of the poster. Darling.

The next block boasted a neatly lettered sign for the pag-eant on the lawn of Holy Rosary, and a bit farther up, An-tioch Tire and Electric displayed little Linda Jeffries's sign proclaiming "Vauddeville for Victory" with a big X through the extra *D*. Helen smiled. The children's errors made the signs more winsome, just the angle she wanted.

"There you are, Helen." Victor Llewellyn ran across G Street on scissor legs like a quail. "I've been looking all over for you. Boy, you look swell."

"Thank you." She hoped Ray would agree. She loved her new caramel-colored suit with its asymmetric jacket and swingy box pleats in the skirt. One of the benefits of being a Carlisle.

"I like your hair up like that," Vic said. "It's perfect for tonight."

"Tonight?"

"We have reservations at Milan's at seven."

"What?" Helen stopped in front of the Women's Club, and a hard knot formed behind her sternum. "You can't make plans without asking me."

"I couldn't get hold of you. I decided to act first and ask later."

Typical Llewellyn arrogance. She strode down the street. "I'm sorry, but I have plans."

"What kind of plans?" His voice had an edge.

Helen crossed Fifth Street with the careful footing an edge required. "Mrs. Novak invited me for dinner. The children's pageant is two weeks from tomorrow."

"Will Ray be there?"

Her left foot caught on the curb. "I suppose so," she said in a light tone. "If he gets away from the Air Depot on time."

"You've been seeing a lot of each other, I've heard."

He'd heard? From his mother, no doubt. Why did the Carlisles buy Jim a house across the street from the town busybody? Too bad she never noticed anything that mattered.

"I thought you weren't ready to date."

"I'm not dating Ray. We're just friends." Helen shoved open the door to Della's.

"Good. Go out with me tonight. I know you like to dance."

"It's about time you two went out." Mr. Carlisle appeared from behind a dress rack.

Helen froze, too close to Vic, her breath trapped beneath a heavy load of expectations. Everyone expected her to pay homage to her fallen warrior husband and kiss his portrait. Mr. Carlisle expected her to be thrilled at Vic's overture. Ray would expect her to back away from Vic out of loyalty to him and the hope of a romance.

Vic grinned. "We have reservations at Milan's tonight."

"Very nice," Mr. Carlisle said.

Helen could play only one role with honesty. "I told you. I have plans."

"With the Novaks."

"Yes, for the pageant." Helen escaped behind the cash register.

Mr. Carlisle harrumphed and straightened the rack of spring blouses. "You spend too much time with them."

"I'm president of the Ladies' Circle."

Vic crossed his arms over his blue uniform jacket. "Ray Novak has his eyes on her."

Helen gasped. How childish of him.

Mr. Carlisle laughed and rearranged the blouses. "Don't let him get any ideas. I'd never let a Novak raise my grandson. Especially Ray. There's something soft about that boy. Weak."

Jim also talked like that about Ray, called him a coward. Helen fumbled with the stack of dollar bills and tried to laugh. "Goodness. All this fuss for nothing."

"Good. He'll end up like his father, you know. All boys do."

She couldn't count the bills. Why—why did boys have to end up like their fathers?

He slipped a blouse off a hanger, frowned at it, and slung it over his shoulder. "The Carlisles have belonged to our denomination for generations, and I won't let one meddlesome pastor drive me away, but the man needs to keep his nose out of people's business." He marched to the back room with the discarded blouse.

Helen stared at the swinging burgundy curtain. Pastor Novak meddlesome? What on earth had he said to Mr. Carlisle? And didn't Mr. Carlisle see the irony of pressuring her to date the son of the most meddlesome woman in town?

"It'd be a lot easier if you went out with me." Vic smiled and winked.

Helen set her jaw and bowed her head over the cash. "Good-bye, Vic."

6

Saturday, April 1, 1944

Ray leaned back against the fuselage of the Jenny biplane in his grandparents' barn and smiled. Grandpa and Grandma Novak knelt on a blanket with Helen and Jay-Jay while kittens scampered around with exclamation point tails.

"That's it, sweetie. Gently." Helen held an orange tabby and guided her son's hand over the fur. The night before, she'd seemed tired and jumpy over dinner, although she'd relaxed dancing in Ray's arms. Today she wore a yellow peasant blouse with a yellow and white checked skirt, and she glowed in the sunshine that slanted through the barn door. This day at the farm seemed to be what she needed after a long week.

Jay-Jay shrieked in delight, and a gray kitten made three stiff hops to the side. Jay-Jay lunged for her. "Kitty."

"Gently," Helen said. "She'll come if you're gentle."

"Look," Grandma said. "Here's the mommy cat. Time for a snack and a nap."

Helen let out a deep sigh. "For someone else too."

A nap? Ray hadn't thought about that. So much for his romantic afternoon plans.

"When you're ready," Grandma said to Helen, "I have the guest bed made up for the little dear."

Grandpa grunted as he stood. "We figured you two love-birds wanted time alone."

"Grandpa!" Ray gripped the rim of the cockpit beside him. "What?"

"It's not . . . it's not like that."

"You said you were bringing the girl you were interested in."

Ray groaned and grabbed a rag draped over the wing. Yep, those were his exact words.

"Goodness gracious, Jacob," Grandma said. "Let's leave before you put your other foot in your mouth. Now, Helen, you bring in that little angel whenever you're ready."

Ray rubbed hard at the dust on *Jenny*. The early stage of a relationship required painstaking balance to avoid revealing too much too soon. Grandpa tipped the scale.

"You miss flying, don't you?" Helen said.

She hadn't left? Ray resumed polishing. "Yeah, I do."

Footsteps crunched over the straw toward him. "Too bad you can't take the biplane up."

"No fuel." He gritted his teeth and scrubbed a stubborn spot near the cockpit.

"I'm glad I'm not the only one whose family embarrasses them."

Ray shot her a glance. "Your parents are in DC."

A smile curved her lips. "Don't you think Betty makes up for them?"

"Betty?"

"Remember how she teased me last week about the stories I wrote as a girl?"

"What's embarrassing about that?"

Helen ran her hand over the spot Ray had cleaned. "The stories were about you."

A fog filled his mind, then swirled away. Her revelation righted the balance. "Me?"

"Why don't you take Jay-Jay and me on that walk around the farm you promised, and I'll tell you."

"All right." Ray tossed the rag in the general direction of the wing. Maybe Grandpa had done him a favor.

Helen coaxed Jay-Jay out of the barn with the promise of more farm animals, and they sauntered along the pasture fence. Jay-Jay mooed at old Flossie the cow and hee-hawed at Sahara Sue, the black Arab donkey Jack had shipped back from a mission to Tunisia.

Ray scooped up Jay-Jay, arched an eyebrow at Helen, and ducked behind the little boy's head. "Tell me a story, Mommy."

She laughed. "Put him down so he can run off some energy."

He complied. "How'd I end up in your stories?"

"After the bike accident when I was ten, I had a crush on you." Her skirt swished around her knees as she walked.

More and more intriguing. Ray nudged her with his shoulder. "Story time."

She gave him a sidelong glance. "Nothing original. Sir Raymond rode to rescue Princess Helene from dragons, tall towers, and raging rivers. Typical schoolgirl drivel."

"A knight in shining armor." It always came to that. To please Dolores, Ray had joined the Army Air Corps rather than the chaplaincy, but the uniform wasn't enough. She wanted a dashing dogfighter. She'd had several.

"Come on, Ray. Rescue me." Helen climbed the pasture fence, sat on the top rail, and grinned through the blonde hair blowing in her face. "Just like Saint George rode in with his faithful lance to slay the dragon and save the princess."

Ray walked up to her. He thought she was different. If she didn't respect him as he was, he needed to know now.

She pushed the hair off her face, and her grin fell.

He stood in front of her. "I'm not a hero. I just want to

preach God's Word. If you're looking for a hero, I'm not your man."

Helen's eyes rounded. "I didn't mean—they're just stories. You—you were a hero to me. You were kind to me, talked to me like a person, not a cripple girl. That's why I fell for you."

Something in her eyes said she'd fall for him again if he didn't blow it. He sighed and set his hands on her waist. "Come on down. You don't need a hero to rescue you. A gentleman will do."

She draped her arms around his neck, a twinkle in her eye. "Any gentlemen around?"

He laughed and swung her down. Then he gathered her hand in his and led her over the shoulder of the hill separating the pasture from the orchard. "Any chance that crush will return?"

Helen gazed at their clasped hands, and her eyelashes fluttered. "Was your grandfather right? Are you . . . are you . . ."

"Very much." The rumble in his voice revealed more than his words.

She nodded and leaned into his shoulder.

Boy, did he want to pull her close and kiss her, but they'd already taken one big whopping step. He had to slow down. "How long did that crush last?" he asked in a teasing voice. "Until Jim stopped knocking you off your bike and knocked me off my trusty steed?"

Helen's gaze jerked up to him. "He never did that."

Ray chuckled. "I was there. I saw you beat him in that bike race, saw him thrust that stick into your spokes."

"He wouldn't. He didn't." Her hand stiffened. "It was an accident. I fell."

Ray frowned. He'd never forget the furious look on Jim's face. But then, love did funny things to your memory.

Helen's cheeks twitched, and she drew back her hand.

"Hey, now." Ray faced her, took her hand, and waited until she looked him in the eye. "I've been in love three times, three serious girlfriends. I was engaged twice. All three women dumped me. It's part of who I am, and I can't change that."

Her gaze softened.

"You loved Jim a long time. You married him, you bore him a son, you lost him, and you've mourned him. Jim is part of who you are. I can't change that and I don't want to. I won't make you deny your past in order to have a future."

Her eyes widened, warm tea speckled with gold. Hair blew across her face. With a nervous laugh, she tried to shake it off.

Ray dropped one of her hands and brushed back her hair. "We'll take this slowly. I need to make sure my past doesn't lead me into hasty decisions, and you have things to work through. Then there's the munchkin."

Helen's gaze darted about. "Oh my goodness."

"Speaking of the munchkin . . . where'd he go?"

★

Helen gasped and scanned the farm. What had she dressed Jay-Jay in this morning? Why couldn't she remember? What kind of mother was she? What kind of woman lost her only son?

"Jay-Jay!" She pressed her hand to her forehead. "Oh no, what have I done? Jay-Jay!"

"Jay-Jay!" Ray's deep voice carried farther than hers.

Helen ran toward the fence where she'd flirted, selfish girl, thinking only of herself as always. "I can't do anything right. Jay-Jay!"

The pasture. Oh no. What if he crawled under the fence and got kicked or trampled? She climbed the fence. "How could I? Oh goodness. Jay-Jay!"

"Helen." Ray set a firm hand on her arm, his face calm

and steady. "Let's think this through. We'll go to the house for my grandparents, for two more sets of eyes."

"My baby." Her vision blurred. "How could I lose my baby?"

"No cause for alarm." He eased her off the fence. "He probably went to the house for more pie. Or the kittens."

"The kittens." That thought cleared her sight.

"Come on." Ray grabbed her hand and ran toward the barn.

When he swung open the gate to the corral, Helen dashed through the open barn door and stopped short, peering into the darkness while her eyes adjusted. "Jay-Jay?"

There he was.

The mother cat lay on a brown blanket with five kittens attached like teeth on a comb. Jay-Jay curled up next to them, eyes shut, mouth in a circle, and the mother cat licked his face with vigor. All the tension drained from Helen's body.

Ray let out a hearty laugh.

She spun around, pressed her hand over Ray's mouth, marched him out the barn door, and backed him against the wall, her hand tight over his mouth. "Never, ever wake a sleeping baby. Ever. Unless there's a fire. And it'd better be a big fire."

"Yeff, ma'am," he mumbled, his eyes big. Then his chest heaved, and his eyes curved into crescents. "Did you see? The cat washing him?"

"Ssh. Ssh." But her own laughter broke free. "He had—he had tuna fish for lunch."

Ray erupted in laughter, so contagious, and Helen buried her face in his chest and pulled his head down to her shoulder to muffle the laughter.

"The Lord watched over him," he said between laughs. "Even made sure he got a bath."

"Tuna." She burrowed deeper into his chest, and her laughter bumped against his. What was lovelier—the safety of her son or the laughing embrace of this man who was interested in her? Very much, he'd said.

The laughter mellowed to chuckles and contented sighs. Still his arms circled her waist. Still her hand cupped the back of his head.

Ray nuzzled in her hair. "Mm. You smell like grass and sunshine."

She melted into his embrace, solid instead of sinewy. He was just the right height. She didn't have to strain to reach him. "I'm glad I don't have tuna breath."

He straightened up, his eyes smoky, and he inhaled. "Mm, nope. Strawberry pie."

Oh goodness, this was really happening. His own strawberry-scented breath wrapped around her, and she drew closer to cover her memories of gregarious charm with Ray's quiet strength.

Something flickered in the gray of his eyes, the battle of restraint, and she had to make sure he lost. She tipped up her face to his warmth.

Ray leaned his head back against the barn wall. "Helen, honey, we need to wait."

"Why?" She twisted her fingers into his soft black hair, dizzy from his nearness. "No one can see."

A smile twitched on his lips. "Five minutes ago I promised you I'd take things slowly."

"So kiss me slowly."

His eyes widened, the battle lost, and he pressed his lips to hers in a slow, luxurious kiss.

She wasn't prepared for the passion.

Passion?

Passion came from anger. She wanted to pull away, but he

drew her back in with this different, tender passion. Everything she knew of Ray's character came through in his kiss, and she yearned for more of his care and his strength, and someday, oh please, his love.

"Oh, Helen," he murmured and gathered her even closer.

This was what she'd wanted all along. This was what she should have waited for.

Ray eased back and raised an adorable lopsided grin. "I'd better take you out on our first date."

"A date?" The thought paralyzed her.

"Dad taught me never to kiss a woman until the third date, and we—unless you want to count those dinners."

"Of course. Of course, they count."

He rearranged his arms around her waist. "Next week a nice dinner out."

Out? Where everyone could see her, judge her, and talk about her? Helen forced a laugh. "What should we do? Go to the White Fountain, share an ice cream soda, and jitterbug to the jukebox? Aren't we a little mature for that?"

"Yeah. Milan's is more appropriate."

Heavens, no. Although everything within her tensed, she stroked his cheek. "You don't need to impress me. You already have. Besides, the point of a date is to get to know each other. Aren't we doing that?"

Ray rested a kiss on the tip of her nose. "Very well."

7

Saturday, April 8, 1944

Ray held open the door to Milan's Restaurant, and the group exited into the cool evening—George and Betty Anello, Ray's youngest brother, Walt, his fiancée, Allie Miller, and Helen.

A triple date seemed like a great idea when Walt and Allie arrived from Seattle the night before to surprise Dad and Mom for Easter. Ray was wrong. He came alongside Helen. "This was a bad idea."

"Bad? Nonsense. I'm having a wonderful time. Really, I am." The strain in her voice negated her words.

Ray gave an affirming grunt. He didn't want to call her a liar.

"Was I too quiet? I'm sorry, but goodness, with George and Walt catching up—they're best friends, you know. Of course, you know. Then Betty and Allie discussing college memories and wedding plans and—"

"It's all right. I shouldn't have surprised you."

"No, it's fine. I'm having fun."

If she'd had fun at dinner, why had she acted like a gangster's moll on the alert, her gaze skittering around the room? As if she were afraid to be caught.

"Hiya, Mr. Anello." A group of teenage boys ambled past them on Second Street.

"Say, shouldn't you be home studying?" George gave the boys a mock glare. He addressed Walt behind him. "Teaching gets harder each day. The class of '44 doesn't want to study history. They want to go out and make it."

Walt chuckled. "Let's hope they never get a chance."

"Yeah? I wish they'd give me a chance."

"Our loss. If they let you in, the war would already be over." Walt clapped George on the back with his left hand, his only hand.

Ray's fingers clenched in his trouser pockets. George and Walt wore civilian suits, but George had the heart of a warrior despite his gimpy leg, and Walt bore the mark of a hero in the steel hook on his right arm. Ray wore the uniform, but he was an imposter.

"I'm sorry." Helen slipped her gloved hand in the crook of Ray's arm, her eyes soft. "I'll be better company."

He sighed and smiled at her. Poor thing thought he was mad at her rather than at himself.

At El Campanil's box office, Ray bought six tickets, since the night on the town was his stupid idea. A few yards from the rest of the group, Helen chatted with Jeannie Llewellyn.

No one could miss Jeannie in a gigantic red hat perched on the side of her head, a hat Ray did not want to sit behind in the theater.

Helen looked classy in a suit the same golden tone as the hills around Antioch in the summer. Under her hat, her hair was rolled and pinned up somehow. Ray set his hand on her shoulder.

She jumped. "Goodness. You startled me."

"Sorry." What did she expect in a crowd like this?

Jeannie arched one pencil-thin eyebrow. "Are you two together?"

"We came in a group." Helen fluttered her hand toward the others. "George and Betty, Walt and his fiancée. Have you met Allie?"

"Yes, I have." But Jeannie eyed Ray.

"Well, come say hello." Helen took Jeannie's arm and wheeled her away.

Ray stood alone, his stomach a cold hard ball. Women were usually glad to be seen with him, but Helen acted like a married woman caught with a forbidden lover.

Why? Did she think people expected her to remain faithful to Jim a year and a half after his death? Or was she ashamed to be seen with Ray?

Walt glanced over with a grin lifting his full cheeks. "You got the tickets?"

Ray managed to smile back. "Six tickets for *Cover Girl*."

"Don't want to miss this," George said. "Rita Hayworth, Gene Kelly, and orchestration by an Antioch native."

"You went to school with Carmen Dragon, didn't you, Ray?" Walt asked.

He handed the tickets to the usherette. "I was a year ahead of him at Riverview High."

"Riverview?" Jeannie's voice floated over the group. "That closed ages ago. Antioch High's been open *depuis longtemps*."

"See what I mean?" Helen whispered.

Her confidential smile warmed him inside. "*Oui, oui*. She jabbed your education and my age in a single breath." He touched the small of her back to guide her through the ornate lobby and down the right aisle into the theater.

"Hi, Mrs. Carlisle." An usherette waved, and the pompoms on her miniature sombrero wiggled. Her gaze flicked to Ray, and she giggled.

"Hi, Evelyn." Helen's voice stiffened.

Ray sighed, followed Helen, and sat in a plush seat. In a

town of seven thousand, did she expect to keep their relationship secret? Why would she want to? How could she kiss him so fervently one week, then be standoffish the next? Did she regret those kisses?

He did. After his noble intentions, he'd moved too fast. She wasn't ready and he'd gotten swept away, just as Mom said. But oh boy, how could he resist the way she invited him?

After the lights dimmed and the curtains parted, Goofy demonstrated "How to Be a Sailor," and the newsreel showed the U.S. Eighth Air Force returning to English bases after a bombing raid on Nazi airfields.

Ray scanned for his brother Jack or any of his former students. One man shed flight gear and mugged for the camera. Did he grin because he loved his job, because he survived, or to put on a show for the other men and the folks back home? Deep inside, was that airman a coward?

If he was a coward, at least he'd faced his fears. Unlike Ray.

At last the movie started, the opening credits rolled, and when Carmen Dragon's name flashed on the screen in Technicolor, the crowd cheered and applauded the hometown boy.

Not Helen. Her eyelashes fanned over her cheeks, and her lips were parted.

Between her volunteer work and caring for her home and her son, she must have worn herself out. She was tired and overworked. That explained her behavior. Ray felt a rush of relief and protectiveness. He smiled and jiggled her arm.

Helen gasped and flung both hands in front of her face, as if a monster in her nightmare had come to life.

He sat back. "Bad dream?"

She blinked and patted her hair. Her chest rose and fell quickly. "Yes. A bad dream."

He gave her a warm smile in the flickering light from the screen. Next weekend he'd plan a quiet and early evening.

SARAH SUNDIN

✫

Ray hummed "Long Ago and Far Away" and twirled Helen under his arm as they turned onto D Street. "Too bad I don't sing like Gene Kelly."

"Or dance like him."

He swung her into his arms. "Hey, now. I'm not that bad."

In the moonlight, her eyes glowed. "No, you're just right."

Yeah, he could kiss her, but he'd wait until Mrs. Carlisle went home from babysitting duty, and then he and Helen could cuddle on the porch swing behind the shield of the cherry tree.

They climbed the steps, the front door swung open, and Jay-Jay ran out. "Mama!"

Helen scooped up her son. "Sweetie, what are you doing up? Goodness, it's 10:30."

"He wanted to wait for you." Mrs. Carlisle stood in the doorway and leveled a cool gaze at Ray.

He smiled and tipped his service cap. "Good evening, Mrs. Carlisle." It was none of his business why the Carlisles disliked the Novaks, but he suspected it had to do with the Great Choir Robe Debate of 1928.

Helen smoothed her son's curls. "He should be in bed. Tomorrow's Easter. We have church and dinner."

"He didn't want to go to bed."

"No bed," Jay-Jay said.

"Come on, sweetie. I really need you to go to bed."

"No!" Jay-Jay swatted at Helen's face.

She turned to the side. "Please, sweetie? Please?"

Ray frowned. Why didn't she discipline him for hitting? Why did she ask permission of a two-year-old? To avoid a scene in front of him?

Mrs. Carlisle crossed thin arms. "What's the harm in one late evening?"

✫ 67 ✫

Helen's face agitated, and Ray had to do something. He whispered in her ear, "Do you have a basket for him?"

She nodded and bounced the little boy.

Ray ducked down to him. "Say, munchkin, did you know the Easter bunny won't come till you're asleep?"

Blue eyes stretched wide.

Helen gave Ray a grateful look. "Goodness, Jay-Jay. If he sees you awake, he might hop away and never come back."

"Go bed." Jay-Jay slithered out of Helen's arms and scampered inside with his grandmother clucking behind him.

Ray gathered Helen's hand in his. "I'll wait out here. Take your time."

She glanced inside the house and backed through the door. "Thank you for walking me home, Lieutenant. Maybe I'll see you tomorrow in church."

Lieutenant? Maybe she'd see him? Heat expanded in his chest. "Yeah. Maybe I'll see you around sometime." He marched down the steps and flipped a wave over his shoulder.

"Ray . . ." Her voice reached to him in quiet, pleading waves, but no footsteps followed.

"Good night, Mrs. Carlisle." Steam filled his head. He hated steam. He had to put it out, and he knew the best place in the world to do so.

★

Ray's clothes stuck to his body, but the San Joaquin River had been cold, the air not much warmer, and if he air-dried, he ran the risk of arrest for indecent exposure.

He turned onto D Street. Most likely, Helen would be asleep already, but he had to make the effort.

A sliver of light shone around the blackout curtains in Helen's living room. Ray paused on the sidewalk. He'd rather wait and pray some more, but apparently the Lord wanted this done now.

He knocked. A moment later, the door opened a crack, then fully. "Ray? What are you doing here? Goodness, I'm a mess."

A mess? Not at all. She wore a long silky lavender robe over a matching nightgown, and her hair hung in waves to her shoulders. She'd removed her makeup, but a lack of lipstick didn't reduce the appeal of that mouth.

But that wasn't why he was there. "I'm surprised you're still up."

"I couldn't sleep. I was working on the children's pageant. It's next week." She brushed her hand over her hair, and her forehead puckered. "You came back."

"I needed to apologize."

"Whatever for?" Her gaze leaped over his shoulder. "You'd better come in before Mrs. Llewellyn sees me out like this." She motioned him inside.

Ray leaned back against the shut door and put his hands safely in his pockets. "I've got a lot to apologize for. First, you said you didn't want a date, then I conspired with Walt and George."

"I'm sorry I was bad company. I didn't mind. I enjoyed having the old gang together."

Ray tilted his head and smiled at her. Maybe she did, but not in public. "I moved too fast. Last weekend at the farm was amazing, but I moved too fast."

"Don't you remember?" Helen wrapped her arms around her middle. "I was an active participant."

Warmth rumbled in his chest. "I remember, all right, but today I went too far."

"No, you didn't. I'm sorry. I don't know what came over me. I just . . . it was the first time I'd been out for years, and I felt like . . ."

"Like everyone was talking about you?"

"Well, yes." She pulled her lips in between her teeth.

Ray gazed at the ceiling. "Maybe they were, but maybe they were happy for you."

She let out a loud sigh. "I'm sorry. I can't do anything right. Things were going so well. Why do I have to ruin everything?"

Ray frowned at the distress on her face. "Nothing's ruined. Just some growing pains. Understandable, don't you think?"

She pressed her hand over her eyes. "I'm such an idiot."

"An idiot?" He chuckled. "I win that award. Your son needed you, your former mother-in-law hovered over your shoulder, and I pouted because I couldn't have a good-night kiss."

Helen peeked from under her hand.

He nodded. "Yep, I pouted. You have one little boy in your life. You don't need two."

She smiled and lowered her hand. "Speaking of little boys, what happened to your shirt? The buttons . . . they weren't like that earlier."

Swell, he'd skipped a buttonhole.

She laughed. "Your tie . . . where is it? And your hair. What happened?"

"I went for a swim." He patted his rolled-up tie in his jacket pocket and smoothed his lumpy hair. "Left your place, took a dip, talked to God, and here I am."

"What did you wear?" She clapped her hand over her mouth and laughed. "You didn't."

He glanced into her living room with a sofa, a radio, and a card table piled with papers. "Name, rank, and serial number. That's all you'll get out of me, lady."

Her laughter reached inside him and tickled spots he'd forgotten about for over a year.

He winked at her. "Looks like you're stuck with another little boy."

"I like little boys." She chewed on her lower lip. "Do you still want that good-night kiss?"

Oh yeah, but how could he with her in that nightgown? He walked to her, kept his hands in his pockets, and leaned over to place a kiss on her lips.

"You may be a little boy, but I'm not your mother." She wrapped her arms around his neck. "And no one's watching."

Did she know? Did she know what she did to him? He pulled her close and sank into the longest, silkiest kiss. He might not be a hero, but he was a man. Every day the Army and society drained away his manhood, but with Helen Carlisle he gained it back.

However, she was too close, too silky, too willing. Even though she was almost a decade younger than he, she'd been married. She was used to more than kissing.

He disengaged himself. "I'd better go."

"Why? This is so nice."

"Too nice." He kissed her on the forehead and backed away. She looked even more alluring with her hair mussed up and her eyes all dreamy.

"I'm glad you came back." Her breathy voice made departure even more difficult.

Ray puffed out a breath. "Gotta go." He opened the door and trotted down the walkway to a safe distance. "I'll see you tomorrow at church."

"Have a nice dinner with your parents."

"I'd rather be with you."

She leaned against the doorjamb and sighed. "Me too."

That voice curled around him and pulled. He strode back up the steps and swung her—laughing and protesting about the neighbors—into his arms for another heated kiss.

Next Easter maybe they'd dine together as a family.

8

Sunday, April 9, 1944

"Egg!" Jay-Jay held his treasure high and ran to Helen.

She held out the basket. "Very good, sweetie. What color?"

"Ello." He ran off. "More egg."

Helen inhaled spring air only slightly tainted by the scent of the oleander hedges surrounding the Carlisles' backyard.

"Look over there," Mr. Carlisle said to his grandson. "But you'd better hurry. I lo-o-ove Easter eggs." He rubbed his belly and smacked his lips.

Jay-Jay laughed. "No. Mine."

Helen wiggled her toes inside her cream pumps. Ray said she'd looked pretty walking down the aisle in church this morning, prettier than ever, but then he thought that every time he saw her. She smoothed the side pocket of her dress containing the note with those words.

How romantic he was, asking if she needed an extra hymnal, then passing one back with the note peeking out the top.

Helen pirouetted in the middle of the lawn, twirling the skirt of her lilac-flowered dress. She laughed. What would everyone think? "Jay-Jay, where are you?" she called to cover up.

He plucked an egg from among the tomato seedlings in the Victory Garden. "Boo egg."

"You're so clever." And so darling in his gray suit with a light blue bow tie. Below his short pants, his round pink knees pumped as he ran the egg to Helen.

"That's the last one," she said.

Mr. Carlisle grabbed his head. "Oh no. I didn't find a single one. Jay-Jay beat me."

"He'll have competition next year." Helen smiled at her sister-in-law, Dorothy Wayne, who sat in a wicker chair with three-week-old Susie nestled under her chin.

Mr. Carlisle picked up Jay-Jay and swung him in a circle. "Oh ho. No one beats my boy."

"It's time to go home." Dorothy stood with a pinched look on her face. "I promised to help Mother Wayne in the kitchen. I'll say good-bye to Mom on the way out."

"I'll go with you. I'm needed on kitchen duty too." Helen followed her friend in the back door. "Don't worry, Dorothy. Men are no good with babies, but once Susie starts running around and batting those big brown eyes, watch Grandpa melt."

Dorothy gave her a thin smile and entered the kitchen. "Bye, Mom. I need to get Susie home."

Mrs. Carlisle kept mashing potatoes. She wore a blue floral dress in the latest fashion, which contrasted with the outdated way she wore her hair in mousy brown waves close to her head. "Thank you for coming, dear."

Helen smiled at Dorothy despite the sour feeling in her stomach. "I'll drop by tomorrow and pick up the sashes for the pageant. I appreciate your help."

A curt nod made brown curls bob, and Dorothy headed for the front door.

Helen sighed. Although her parents preferred Betty and her bounciness, Helen never felt unloved. Thank goodness the Waynes welcomed Dorothy into their family and their home, since her husband, Art, was bogged down in Italy with the U.S. Fifth Army.

Helen set the basket of eggs in the icebox. "How may I help?"

Mrs. Carlisle stood on tiptoes to get enough force from her tiny body to mash the potatoes. "I don't need your help."

Helen shivered from the cool tone. She didn't need help? The cooked ham sat out, the table hadn't been set, the cherry pie hadn't been put in the oven, and the pot of peas boiled over.

She turned off the burner, wrapped a towel around the handle, and lifted the pot until the bubbles died down. "I'm glad to help. I'm family, after all."

"No, you're not." Her voice quivered.

What on earth? Since her wedding day, the Carlisles had insisted she was a Carlisle, and the Jamisons agreed. She was never to come home begging. "Excuse me?"

"Not after what I heard. You'd better pray Mr. Carlisle doesn't hear." She mashed so hard, the bowl tipped with a glassy clank on the counter. "Oh dear. Oh dear."

An old, cold dread squeezed Helen's chest. "What do you mean?"

"Don't play innocent. Such carrying on. You ought to be ashamed."

Ashamed? She couldn't think of anything to be ashamed of. Unless . . .

Helen grabbed the lid and strode to the sink. "I can't imagine what you mean."

"With a Novak, no less. And with sweet little Jay-Jay in the next room. Have you no shame?" Mrs. Carlisle splashed milk in the bowl, far too much milk.

"I can't imagine." Helen's hands shook so hard, she spilled peas into the sink.

"Oh! You can't, can you? Mrs. Llewellyn saw Ray Novak go into your house and leave quite some time later. Quite some time. And you in your nightgown, a slinky thing like the pinup girls wear, kissing him for all the world to see."

"It wasn't like that." Helen walked around with the pan, searching for a bowl.

"What was it like? Tell me." She scraped potatoes into a bowl and sent pasty blobs onto the table.

Helen wiped steam from her forehead. "After—after you left, I couldn't sleep so I did some paperwork. He came back to apologize for something he said. We talked—maybe five minutes, right in the doorway. He never . . . we never—"

Mrs. Carlisle spun around, eyes in slits. "Did you seduce him?"

"Heavens, no!"

"Did you kiss him?"

Her mouth flapped open and shut. "Well, yes, but Mr. Carlisle said I could date."

"Victor! He said you could date Victor Llewellyn."

"I don't like Victor. Not that way."

"You're not supposed to. You said you loved my Jimmy."

"Of course I did." Helen whirled around and grabbed the first bowl she saw.

"If you truly loved Jimmy, you could never love another man. You wouldn't be in some torrid love affair. You'd marry for support and companionship, nothing more."

Helen dumped the peas into the bowl, and they turned into a green blur. She hadn't sought passion with Ray. It had just been a pleasant surprise. Was she supposed to turn down this delicious relationship for appearance's sake?

"I . . . I . . . " She turned and startled at the look in her mother-in-law's eyes—pure grief.

How would Helen feel if Jay-Jay died and his wife moved

on? It would be as if her son were dying all over again, as if even his memory were dying.

As long as Helen mourned Jim, a piece of him lived.

Mrs. Carlisle sniffled. "I won't breathe a word of this to Mr. Carlisle. I told Mrs. Llewellyn she was mistaken. But you—you need to act like a proper widow."

Helen wiped the back of her hand over her eyes. She'd acted like a proper widow for seventeen months, but now she had a new role, a bright and fresh role that didn't even require pretending. How long would she be expected to maintain the old role? How long before her mask cracked?

★

The aroma of roast chicken wrapped steamy tendrils around Ray and drew him to the kitchen, where he found Walt plucking skin from a drumstick.

Ray inspected the second bird and found a morsel in the pan juices.

Mom stepped in from the dining room and gasped. "Go away, you vultures."

"Can't leave the kitchen even to set the table, can we?" Allie Miller nudged Walt away from the poultry. "Shoo."

He pulled her into the dance position and sang out, " 'Shoo, shoo, shoo, baby.' "

Allie laughed, and her brown curls puffed out as he swung her.

Ray took advantage of the distraction and snagged a piece of chicken thigh.

Mom grabbed his arm and marched him to the doorway. "Out with you, both of you."

"I don't know how you manage, Mrs. Novak." Allie danced her fiancé to the door and pushed him out.

He puckered his lips at her. "Don't you love me?"

"With all my heart, darling. To show my love, I want to put dinner on the table—unmolested." She smiled and shut the door.

He frowned. A black curl hung over his forehead. "Almost nabbed a drumstick."

Ray licked his fingers now that Mom couldn't see. "You could have had it. We had Mom outnumbered, but then you had to bring in feminine reinforcements."

Walt grinned. "Isn't she swell?"

"Yeah, she is." Ray was amazed at the changes in Walt, partly due to Allie's love and partly due to—well, his experiences flying a B-17 over Nazi-occupied Europe. "Less than a month until the wedding. How are you holding up?"

"Can't wait." Walt headed for the dining room and flashed Ray a smile. "You thinking of joining us in matrimony?"

Ray laughed. "Helen and I have only been seeing each other about a month."

"Yeah, I guess you need to take things slowly after all she's been through."

"Yep." At the dining room table Ray burrowed in a towel-lined basket. "Hey, look, sourdough rolls. No butter to put on them, of course. Stupid rationing." He took out two and tossed one to Walt.

He bobbled it and trapped it against his chest.

Ray's stomach contracted. "Sorry about that."

"Don't be. I'm still learning to be a southpaw." He took a bite of the roll. "Was Helen okay last night? She seemed . . . high-strung."

Ray shrugged and pulled up a chair next to the basket. "Doesn't like nights on the town." He also spoke with his mouth full. Mom's sourdough rolls were the best, hot and chewy inside a crispy crust. And, oh, the tang of them.

"Mom had better teach Allie to make these." Walt used

his prosthesis to pull out a chair, sat down, and tipped the chair back. "That sounds right."

"The rolls?"

"No, Helen. She and Jim kept to themselves. They'd get together with the gang, but not often. They preferred privacy."

Ray chewed the last bite, and his chest felt as light as the roll. A love of privacy? Was that all it was? Seemed odd for an energetic young woman, but if she wanted privacy with Ray, he wouldn't argue.

Thank goodness last night's apology worked. Helen seemed relaxed at church. Those looks she gave him—boy, oh boy. And that note she returned with the hymnal, the note now tucked in his Bible: "How am I, you ask? I'm torn between the Pastors Novak. My mind tells me to watch the elder, but my heart longs to watch the younger. If only you were in the pulpit, both would be satisfied." To be back in the pulpit with that lovely face adoring him from the pews—what could be better?

Walt held up his hand. "Toss me another roll."

Ray coiled for the pitch. "Watch out. You know I've got a mean curve ball."

"Raymond Novak!" Mom stood in the doorway with a platter, Allie right behind her.

He twisted to face them. "Want one? Catch."

Mom's eyelashes fluttered. "Allie, dear, pray for daughters."

She laughed. "I do."

Mom set the platter of chicken on the table. "Boys, please call your father for dinner."

Ray and Walt grinned at each other and called out, "Your father for dinner!"

"For heaven's sake," Mom said. "Really, Allie, I did raise them with manners."

"I know. More importantly, you raised them with love."

She blinked her large green eyes and arranged the serving bowls at the head of the table.

Walt patted her lower back.

Ray sighed. If only he could sit down with Allie's parents and persuade them not to boycott the wedding because Walt wasn't the society gentleman they desired for their only child. Walt was a fine man. What could they have against him?

"The Distinguished Unit Citation," Dad said to Grandpa Novak as they entered the dining room. "And Jack flew the lead ship."

"A big honor." Grandpa held out a chair for Grandma.

"He won't take credit for the DUC, but it was his doing."

Walt chuckled. "The air exec flew with him. Jack didn't make the decisions."

Dad lifted the carving knife to punctuate his sentence. "If he was there, he had a say."

Ray nodded and stroked the glossy crust of the roll. Jack's pride would make sure he did.

Mom set a bowl of steamed asparagus on the table. "I wish he wasn't there. A second combat tour in England? After all those missions in the Pacific?"

"What was he supposed to do, Edie? Take a desk job?" Dad sank the knife into the first chicken.

Ray felt as if the knife plunged into him instead. Desk jobs were for men of no consequence.

Grandpa shook out his napkin. "A desk job would kill Jack faster than the Huns."

"Sap his vitality." Dad carved, and piece after piece dropped off, revealing pale bones.

The roll's crust cracked in Ray's grip. He identified with Gideon when he told the Lord, "I am the least in my father's house."

"It was more than that." Walt passed a full plate to Mom.

"He wanted to make up for his mistakes, make it up to the people he hurt."

"Make it up to himself also," Ray said. "Sometimes the hardest person to forgive is yourself."

"That's the truth, boy," Grandpa said. "No one can beat up a man harder than the man himself."

"Yep. Jack didn't like what he saw inside." Ray dug his fingers into the cracked golden sphere and ripped it open. "He wanted to make himself a better man, prove himself a better man."

Comments volleyed and plates passed, but Ray stared at the peaks of flavorful dough and the gaping holes.

What lay inside Ray Novak? Towering peaks of strength or gaping holes of cowardice? A tangy aroma or bland nothingness?

"Amen" sounded around the table.

Ray startled. Dad had said grace, and he'd missed it.

Mom sliced her asparagus. "I'll never understand why men feel they have to hurl themselves into danger to prove themselves, but thanks for trying to explain, Ray."

He gave her a wan smile.

"That's my brother," Walt said. "Always smoothing things out."

Dad gave Ray a stern look from under salt-and-pepper brows. "Can't always do that. Sometimes pastors have to be mean."

Ray swallowed a bite of chicken. " 'Speak the truth in *love*,' Dad."

"Yes, but speak the *truth*. As Jesus did."

"He came as the Prince of Peace."

"And the consuming fire."

" 'Blessed are the peacemakers: for they shall be called the children of God.' "

" 'Blessed are ye, when men shall revile you, and persecute you, and shall say all manner of evil against you falsely, for my sake.' " Dad leaned forward. "That means we'll make enemies. Jesus did."

"Goodness," Allie said. "In this house the Word of God truly is a sword."

Everyone laughed.

"Don't mind them," Walt said. "They love a debate."

Mom sent a soothing glance between Dad and Ray. "And they both know Jesus came as the Lion *and* the Lamb, full of grace *and* truth."

"Hear that wisdom?" Ray lifted an eyebrow at Allie. "I take after her."

She smiled back. In time, the prim heiress would get accustomed to this rough-and-tumble household.

"Raymond," Dad said in a low, solid voice. "Have you ever confronted a member of your congregation?"

He blinked a few times. "I only had two years in a church, and as the assistant pastor. I did sick calls, funerals—"

"A pastor must confront sin before it destroys the person and the church."

"I know that."

"You can't tiptoe around it. You have to face it head-on. When you do that, you don't always keep the peace. You create conflict. You make enemies."

"For crying out loud." Grandpa frowned at Dad. "Why do you try to make your sons your mirror image? Ray is Ray, just as the Good Lord made him. You be yourself, boy."

He gave a sharp nod and bit into some asparagus, a bad stalk, bitter as Dad's words and the knowledge that he needed a grandpa's protection. Both men thought he was weak.

Dad's neck muscles stood out. "Be himself, yes. But he needs to be willing to confront, to face opposition."

Ray's shoulders edged back, and he lifted his chin. If Dad's brusque ways were best, why did the Carlisles dislike him? Why couldn't he mend that rift? "So, Dad, how do these confrontations of yours work out?" His voice came out tight.

Dad poked his roast potatoes around like shells in a shell game. His cheeks twitched. "Some repent. Some don't. That's between them and the Lord and the people they hurt."

Just as Ray thought. He'd stick to the ways he knew best, the ways that worked for him. But an entire glass of water failed to remove the bitter taste.

9

Saturday, April 15, 1944

" 'Let freedom ring.' " The voices of the primary school students filled the high expanse of El Campanil Theatre, followed by a round of applause.

In the wings, Helen adjusted red bows at the tips of Connie Scala's French braids, then corralled Connie and her brother Alfie closer to the heavy curtains and beckoned to the children's choir. Thank goodness, the bustle of pageant preparations took her mind off her romance with Ray, the Carlisles' disapproval, and the black puffs of gossip in the air.

After Mary Jane Anello led the choir backstage, Helen smoothed her red skirt and navy and white linen jacket and walked to the microphone.

Over the stage lights, she smiled at the black blobs of the audience. "Next we have Alfredo and Constance Scala tap-dancing to 'Stars and Stripes Forever.' " She nodded to the Antioch High School band before her and retreated to the wings out of sight.

One of those faceless blobs was Ray, who made Helen feel like a giddy schoolgirl. Two were the Carlisles, who expected her to grieve for the rest of her life. On stage, under those blessed lights, Helen could be a competent, energetic Red Cross volunteer, the only performance that pleased everyone.

She scanned her clipboard. Right on schedule, Mary Jane brought Donald Ferguson from backstage. "Are you ready, Donald?" Helen whispered.

"I can't remember a word." The fifth-grader's freckles stood out stark under his red hair.

Helen brushed the shoulders of his suit. "With those lights, all you see is a bunch of black blobs. Pick one blob, way in the top row, pretend it's your mama, and recite as you've recited to her all week."

He cracked a smile. "Mother said if she heard it one more time, she'd go nuts."

She chuckled. "Then go make her nuts."

Helen turned to watch the last of Alfie and Connie's dance, and tapped her toes in her navy and white spectator pumps. The children ended with a flourish, then scurried offstage without waiting for their applause.

Helen patted Donald on the back, led him to the microphone, and returned to her post. "Mary Jane," she whispered. "Bring Jay-Jay up, please."

Donald recited Lincoln's Gettysburg Address in a firm and emotional voice, declaring the truths to the top row of the ornate theater.

What did Nora Ferguson think about Helen introducing her son? Nora had been awkward around her lately, and Helen pretended she was too young to know Ray and Nora had been high school sweethearts. And what did Ray think watching a boy who could have been his son?

Donald raised his hand high. " 'It is rather for us to be here dedicated to the great task remaining before us—that from these honored dead we take increased devotion to that cause for which they gave the last full measure of devotion.' "

Arms wrapped around Helen's knees. "Mama!"

"Ssh." She scooped up her son and burrowed a kiss in his soft cheek. "I missed you."

He flung his arms around her neck and gave her a smacking kiss. Was anything sweeter than a child's love?

Mary Jane straightened Jay-Jay's sailor hat. "He's so cute. I can't wait to be a mother."

"Wait." Helen locked her gaze on the girl. "Wait until you find a good man."

"As you did."

Helen nodded, all part of the performance. When Donald's applause receded, she gave him a handshake and faced the audience. Jay-Jay shielded his eyes and buried his face in Helen's shoulder, and the audience responded with "aahs."

Helen smiled. "The Lord has blessed us here in Antioch. Our land has never been trod by enemy boots, or pocked by enemy shells, or shadowed by enemy planes. Our children live in freedom because our men fight tyranny. Our children live without fear because our men face danger. Our children live because of the sacrifices our brave soldiers and sailors make."

She nudged Jay-Jay so he would look up. The hushed silence ran deeper than polite listening, and sniffles rose from a few spots. Helen's breath caught. To this community, she and Jay-Jay symbolized that sacrifice. Her role as mourning widow was essential to the war effort. The town needed her grief to motivate them to give and serve and fight. As long as the war lasted, she would never be free.

"The children," she choked out. "The children. They are the reason we must be 'dedicated to the great task remaining before us.' As in Lincoln's day, our war is far from over. We must not grow weary. I beg you to give generously of your time and effort, your money, and yes, even your lifeblood." She raised half a smile.

"For our final number, all the children will sing 'God Bless America,' but first Jay-Jay has a message for you."

He leaned forward so far, Helen grabbed at him. "Give!" he yelled.

"Use your manners, sweetie."

Amid the laughter, a ham was born. He grinned. "Pease."

If that didn't move this town, nothing would. Helen stepped to the side. The children trooped onstage, the boys with Sunday suits and slicked hair, the girls in curls and braids and starched crinolines. They all wore red, white, and blue sashes, one of many donations by the Carlisles to the pageant.

The audience joined in with throaty voices, and goose bumps shivered up Helen's arms. The show was a success, but would the emotional impact lead to action?

Once the pageant concluded, the parents came down to the stage to collect their children, the boys in the band packed their instruments, and the Junior Red Cross girls fell to work at sign-up tables or cleaning up.

Helen ticked into the final phase and rearranged papers on her clipboard.

"Mrs. Carlisle?" Peggy Lindstrom asked. "May I please play with Jay-Jay?"

Helen smiled at the tall blonde. "That would help immensely."

Peggy squealed and swung Jay-Jay onto her hip. "Let's go play."

Whatever would mothers do without teenage girls? Helen smiled and tapped Evelyn Kramer on the shoulder. "Wait about ten minutes before you get out the carpet sweeper."

Her face brightened. "I know where it is. I work here."

"That's why you signed up to do it."

"Hi, Helen." Ray stood at the foot of the stage stairs in dress uniform.

Her heart did a shimmy. "Hi there."

His parents stood behind him. "Excellent show," Pastor Novak said.

"A very moving speech. Not a dry eye in the house." Mrs. Novak chuckled and raised a wadded handkerchief.

"You're a gifted speaker." Ray smiled, but his eyelid twitched.

"Thank you." She swallowed hard. Her speech had wounded him, hadn't it? Did he think she didn't respect him because his contribution lay in the rear rather than on the front lines?

He set one foot on the bottom step. "Can I help?"

"Oh yes." She smiled at the chance to show how she appreciated him. "I could use some manly muscles to take down the set."

"You're looking in the wrong place, but I'll do what I can." He winked, unbuttoned his service jacket, and tossed it to his mother. "See you at home."

Helen said good-bye to the Novaks, pointed Ray to a ladder backstage, and glanced at the diminishing crowd. The Carlisles. The Llewellyns. A nervous flutter rose in her stomach. She needed to keep busy far from Ray, so she wouldn't feed the gossip.

She strode to the opposite side of the stage. "Carol and Gina, start on the bunting, please."

"Ah, I found my future wife."

Helen winced, faced Vic, and forced a smile. "I'm pleased to hear that. Have I met her?"

Ray approached with a ladder, Vic took her hand and kissed her cheek, and Helen's heart seized. What would Ray think of her?

"Hi, Vic." Ray set up the ladder and smiled as if he didn't see how Vic clutched her hand. "Come to help? This is a two-man job."

"If you can spare me." Vic gazed at Helen with the proprietary affection of a man for his girlfriend. How dare he? Ray would think she was cheating on him, just as Jim had thought.

"I'll manage fine." She tugged her hand free and marched down the steps, her cheeks hot. She needed to work and now.

She helped Carol and Gina fold the bunting draped over the front of the stage.

What was she going to do about Ray? She liked him so much, but now he'd think she was loose. And if he somehow forgave her, still the Carlisles and the town needed her to mourn. Could she have a romance in secret, or would she have to end things with Ray? Why did everything have to be so complicated?

He stood on the ladder unhooking the plywood backdrop, while Vic steadied the ladder. Despite Vic's stony countenance, Ray smiled and chatted.

He wasn't jealous. Was it because he didn't notice? Because he didn't care?

Helen's throat swelled. No, he cared. Too much evidence pointed to that. He wasn't jealous because he knew he had her heart. In that confidence, he reached out in friendship to Vic. How could she help but fall in love with such a kind and insightful man?

"Mrs. Carlisle?" Gina patted Helen's arm. "Where's the box go?"

"I'll take it." She hefted the box full of bunting and climbed the stage stairs.

"Fascinating," Ray said to Vic. "That's good work you're doing at Port Chicago."

"I try." Vic's face transformed from stony to neutral.

"Okay, Llewellyn, grab that corner." Ray lifted one side of the section of backdrop. "Where to, boss?" he called to Helen and sent her a wink.

"Follow me." She headed backstage, her heart as overflowing as the box. Oh yes, he cared.

"You know, Helen," Vic called. "I could still use a secretary."

She laughed and shifted the box in her arms. "So could I."

Ray grunted. "It's hard to believe, isn't it? California was always a free state, yet Port Chicago—all military bases—are as segregated as anything in the Deep South."

"Watch that curtain," Vic said. "Imagine what it's like for the Negroes from the North. They're not used to such blatant discrimination."

"It's wrong. Slavery ended eighty years ago."

"Yeah, and these men fight for freedom abroad when they don't have it at home."

Ray gave a wry chuckle and set his corner down. "'Liberty and justice for all'?"

"Not yet, but we're working on it." Vic led Ray back for another section.

Helen set down her box and laughed. Ray Novak indeed had a gift for peacemaking.

Over the next half hour, Helen checked duties off her list, directed her volunteers, and carted supplies. Up in the lobby, she collected the sign-up sheets and donations.

"Look how many ladies signed up to prepare bandages," Nancy Jo said. "Maybe we'll meet our quota. And we've never had this many people sign up for a blood drive."

Helen's memory went back further, to after Pearl Harbor, when they turned away blood donors after they ran out of refrigerator space. Still, her eyes misted over. The people had responded. She couldn't wait to write Papa—he took such pride in her accomplishments.

"We're done with the backdrop. Anything else?" Ray and Vic saluted Helen.

She laughed. Had Ray won over Vic? "That's all. Thanks for your help."

"Say, Helen," Ray said. "Would Betty mind if Vic joined us for dinner tonight?"

Her jaw dangled. With that question, Ray let Vic know where he stood with Helen, all while offering the olive branch. But she didn't want Vic spoiling her evening. Besides, Betty couldn't stand the Llewellyns. "She'd love it."

Vic lowered his chin, and his mouth shifted to one side. "Thanks, but I have plans."

"Another time then." Ray shook Vic's hand. "Great working with you."

Vic left, holding the door open for Nancy Jo and Rita.

Ray smiled at Helen. "Almost done?"

"Yes." She admired the neat row of checkmarks on her clipboard. "I just need to find my purse, my coat, my umbrella, and my son."

"I don't know about your purse, coat, or umbrella, but your son is racing down the aisles with the Lindstrom girl."

"He'll sleep well tonight." She headed down the right aisle, a high-walled tunnel leading into the theater.

Ray nudged her. "I enjoyed watching you do your heart's work. You shone."

She nudged him back. "So did you. You slew my dragon."

"Vic? He's no dragon, just a man with a crush. I understand why."

His smile made her legs go limp. "You're the sweetest man."

"Nah. But if you want me to slay dragons, maybe I should start with Vic's mother."

Helen groaned and squeezed her eyes shut. Had he heard the gossip too?

"I'm sorry." Ray took her hand. "Mom told me what she said. It's my fault."

"Yours? You didn't spread gossip."

"No, but I got carried away last week. I didn't think how things looked, and you paid the price."

She tucked her lips between her teeth. "I'm fine. I've been busy."

"I understand if you don't want to see me anymore." His face lengthened in resignation.

Her chest clenched. She didn't care what the Carlisles thought, what anyone thought. What she had with Ray was precious—the affection and yes, the passion. Was she supposed to turn him down because she was attracted to him? Nonsense.

In the privacy of the tunnel, she swayed toward Ray and rested her cheek on his shoulder. "You can't get out of our dinner plans that easily."

A sigh collapsed his chest, and he wrapped his arms around her shoulders. "I'll be more discreet."

She nodded and snuggled closer. Would discretion placate the Carlisles? Would it satisfy Ray?

10

Saturday, April 29, 1944

Ray slipped lower in the wicker chair on Helen's back porch, his feet propped on another chair. Cirrus clouds streaked high above, tails flipped as God signed his handiwork. Soon the sun would emerge from behind the almond tree and hit Ray smack in the eye, but now the scene glowed—the robin's egg blue sky, the green hedges, and Helen hanging laundry in a light blue dress, her hair curled.

Compared to how she dressed the last time he saw her do laundry, today she dressed up. For him. He smiled and traced shapes in the condensation on his water glass.

Helen chatted about her latest Red Cross project, and Ray made appropriate interjections. When alone with Ray, or with his family or hers, Helen bloomed.

A night on the town with her would be swell, but home-cooked meals suited him after a week of Army food, the noise of the Officers' Club, and the profane banter in Quarters.

Helen glanced over her shoulder at Ray. "What do you think?"

His finger stopped midstroke on the water glass. "Sounds great."

"Does it?" She faced him with the laundry basket on her

hip. A smile edged up. "Sounds great that Evelyn and Peggy's tiff over a boy threatens to tear apart the Junior Red Cross when I need them most?"

He pasted on an innocent smile. "Yeah, great. Your best idea yet."

She laughed. "You didn't listen to a word I said."

"Sure, I did. Not all, but some."

"Is that right?" She sauntered toward him, the basket swaying with her hips.

"I'm too entranced by the music of your voice to hear the words."

"Sweet talker." She nudged his legs with her knee, a smile playing on her lips. "Do I bore you?"

"Never." He scooted his feet to the side of the chair so she could sit. "Somehow you manage to both relax me and invigorate me."

"So I put you to sleep, then wake you up?"

He chuckled and tapped his foot against her hip. "I meant I can be myself with you. I don't have to be a pastor, always wise and deep. I can just be a man."

"A man who daydreams?"

"About you? Absolutely." He beckoned with one finger. "Forgive me?"

"I could never be mad at you." She took his hand and sat on his lap. The wicker chair squeaked in protest, but held. Ray and Helen laughed together.

He caressed the soft peach of her cheek and pulled her down for a kiss. She smelled of grass and fresh laundry, and he couldn't get enough.

He suppressed the urge to tell her he loved her, because his love was tied to his desire to marry her, and he wanted to propose in June after the excitement from Walt and Allie's wedding subsided.

He took her face between his hands, eased out of the kiss, and gazed into eyes of mouth-watering tea. No long engagement this time. He had to marry her soon, by Christmas at the latest.

"What are you thinking about?" she asked in a husky voice, a dangerous voice.

He grinned to break the spell. "Laundry detergent and tea."

"What?" She gave his shoulder a playful push. "Seriously, Ray."

"Seriously? You missed the point. I don't have to be serious with you. I like that."

"Because I'm a silly little girl?" Despite her light tone, a challenge sparked in her eyes.

"You? You were never silly, even as a little girl." He ran his thumbs over her cheekbones. "I don't have to be serious with you all the time because you're well adjusted. I love counseling people, but sometimes it's nice to be around someone who isn't broken."

Helen ducked her chin. "I—I think I hear Jay-Jay. He must be up from his nap."

The chair squeaked as she rose, and Ray sighed at how his lap cooled with her gone.

He took a long draft of water, no longer icy, but cold enough.

Next weekend they would take a good, easy step together. At Walt and Allie's wedding, Ray and Helen would be seen together, but not as a true date. Then she'd see everyone wanted happiness for her. And once they were engaged, the outflow of congratulations would help her accept their approval.

The Carlisles, on the other hand, would take work. Perhaps they saw the romance as a slap in the face of their son's memory. Regardless, they couldn't lock Helen in the graveyard forever. She was a young woman, full of life, with a son who needed a father figure.

With time and kindness, Ray would rise above the feud they had with his dad, show them he was a worthy man to raise their grandchild, and win them over.

Screams rose from inside the house. Apparently Jay-Jay didn't like what his mother told him to do. A woman's cry pierced through.

Ray jerked upright. Helen! Had she gotten in an accident?

"No! Please? Please, stop." More screams from Jay-Jay, a soft thud, and Helen cried out.

Someone was in the house! Ray's heart rate doubled. He'd have to be the hero. How could he? He scanned the porch for something to use as a weapon, but all he had were his fists.

Dear Lord, help me. He ran around the corner of the house toward the side door.

The last time, the only time he'd used his fists, he'd broken Bill Ferguson's nose, and Bill fell and smacked his head on the pavement. Bill was all right, but Ray could still see the blood dripping down his unconscious face and see the terror in the eyes of the other first-graders.

That day he'd vowed never to give in to anger again.

But today he had to protect the woman he loved.

Ray flung open the screen door and stopped short. Helen cowered against the wall, shielding her face, and Jay-Jay sat on the counter, screaming. No burglar. Just mother and son, a chair pulled up to the cupboard, and an open box of arrowroot biscuits.

Jay-Jay screeched and threw an apple at his mother.

She sobbed. "Stop. Please, stop."

What on earth? Who was in charge here?

Jay-Jay picked up another apple.

"No." Ray snatched it from his hand. "Don't treat your mother like that."

The boy stared up at him with wide, red eyes.

Ray grabbed him, marched him to his room, and plopped him on his bed. "Don't come out until your mother tells you." He shut the door and stood guard in the hall. But the child was silent, as if stunned, as if he'd never been disciplined like that before.

Maybe he hadn't.

Ray squirmed and crossed his arms. Sure, Helen gave in to her son in public to prevent a scene, but did she always give in? When he married her, he'd have his work cut out with the little fellow.

What was wrong with Helen? Why did she act threatened? Jay-Jay was two years old.

Another reason to marry her, the sooner the better. She needed help. The boy was acting his age, but if she didn't clamp down on this behavior, he'd never grow out of it.

In the kitchen, chair legs scraped and shoes shuffled on the floor.

Ray leaned closer to Jay-Jay's door. Silence. If the kid broke out, Ray would march him back. He headed to the kitchen, where Helen picked up an apple, pushed her hair back from her red face, and swallowed a sob.

She wouldn't meet Ray's eye.

He leaned against the doorjamb. "Did I overstep my bounds?"

"No, you helped. Thank you." She set the apple in the basket but tipped it over and sent apples thumping to the floor. Helen flattened both palms on the counter, lowered her head, and gulped back a sob. "I'm a horrible mother."

"Now, now." He stepped over apples and gathered her into his arms.

Her body shook, and she buried her face in his shoulder. "I'm a failure. I can't handle him anymore. I can't."

"Now, now. You're just tired. You work hard and you're doing this alone. No wonder you're overwhelmed. Yes, maybe you give in to him a bit much, but you'll get the hang of it."

"He's so . . . so violent sometimes . . . so much like—no!" She burrowed deeper.

Ray frowned at her overreaction. His collarbone hurt, and he shifted her to the side. "He's two. He's testing you. He'll push until he finds your limits. You have to push back, give him those limits, let him know who's boss."

"But he's—he's—I can't handle him."

"It's not that hard, honey. He's no more than thirty pounds. You pick him up, tuck him under your arm, and haul him away until he stops kicking and screaming. You speak to him with the authority God gave you, and don't let him get away with any disrespect. None."

She raised her tear-stained face. "Oh no. I'm one of the broken people. I'm sorry."

Ray wiped away her tears. Sometimes she acted with competence and vigor, and she seemed like the one person in the world who needed him least. Other times, like now, with fine white scars on her face and insecurity in her eyes, she seemed like the one person in the world who needed him most.

He liked that contradiction, her vulnerable strength.

She sniffled. "I'm sorry. You liked me because I wasn't—"

He settled a kiss on a scar along her cheekbone. "I can handle some brokenness."

"But I'm ruining—I always ruin—"

He silenced her with a kiss full on the lips, a salty kiss. "Darling, I'm crazy about you. Don't you know? It'll take more than a little tantrum to drive me away."

11

Saturday, May 6, 1944

Over the olive drab ridge of Ray's shoulder, Helen scanned the crowded reception hall in the Belshaw Building.

Although no one would call Walt handsome or Allie beautiful, they glowed dancing as man and wife. Due to the silk shortage, Allie wore Mrs. Novak's old wedding dress, restyled with Della Carlisle's expertise and creativity. Walt whispered something in Allie's ear, and she laughed and pressed her cheek to his.

George and Betty shared the dance floor with Ray and Helen and the newlyweds, but why didn't the wedding guests join them? Why did they have to stare?

"I like green eyes," Ray said. "But I prefer brown."

Helen pulled her attention to the gray eyes she preferred most of all. "Hmm?"

"The song. Aren't you listening?" His mouth bent, soft as his kisses and close enough to indulge in one.

She tuned her ears to the strains of "Green Eyes." She smiled. "Of course, I'm listening. I always do."

"Ouch. Got me right in the heart." He winced, but then gathered her close and nuzzled in her ear. "Yeah, you do. Right in the heart."

SARAH SUNDIN

Everything inside her softened and melted into him, but the entire town scrutinized her every move. At a nearby table, Mr. Carlisle jutted out his chin. Mrs. Carlisle's face agitated as much as Helen's emotions.

Shoved on stage, Helen was pummeled by multiple directors working from clashing scripts, shouting opposing stage directions. All her life, Helen had known her role—precocious child, determined polio survivor, energetic student leader, devoted wife, mourning widow. The only time her roles conflicted was when Jim demanded she give up her leadership positions.

At the time, her choice to obey him seemed clear, and she'd lived with her decision, defended it even as she regretted it, and shouldered the role as she had the role of cripple. No one knew how heavy the burden, a burden stripped away by a Japanese torpedo.

Ray's sigh puffed on her cheek. "I have to do my brotherly duty, but I'll be back."

She murmured her understanding and found herself dancing with Walt while Ray twirled Allie around. No one would mind if Helen danced with the groom, would they?

Partners switched, and she danced with George, and a twinge in her left arm reminded her what Jim had thought when she danced with the groom, her own brother-in-law.

But Ray didn't watch, didn't seem to mind. He never did. Maybe he wasn't the jealous sort, or maybe he didn't care. Was Jim right? Did jealousy prove the depth of love?

Helen forced herself to dance, to smile, and to breathe.

Vic tapped George's shoulder and swung Helen away as the band played "Perfidia." He snuggled too close. "The next wedding will be ours."

She pushed out a laugh. "Only if you fall asleep and dream it." Yet now the Carlisles smiled. Why did they try to control her?

The music changed, but Vic maintained his grip. Now the gossip would shift. Not only was Helen Carlisle carrying on with the pastor's son, but she was two-timing him, the little tart.

"May I cut in?" Ray laid his hand on Vic's shoulder.

Vic's lower lip poked out, but he stepped away as etiquette required.

Ray took her in his strong arms. "Missed you."

Her head swam. People would count how many dances they shared. What was a proper number for a widow? The reception was no place for a small child, but she wished she hadn't let Mary Jane Anello watch Jay-Jay and Judy at Betty's house overnight. Then she'd have an excuse to avoid this dance.

She backed out of Ray's embrace and almost lost her balance. "I've got to—got to help with the reception. I'm a bridesmaid, and things have to be done. Betty won't do them."

He cocked a smile and held out one hand. "Martha, Martha, come and dance."

"Later. I promise." Helen whirled away, and her long skirt caught on a chair leg, clumsy cripple girl. She made her way to the gift table. Work—she needed to work.

No one had thought to organize the gifts. She moved the large packages to the back, put boxes with bows on top of boxes without, and arranged gift tags to satisfy the guests' pride.

"*Bon soir, chérie.*" Jeannie Llewellyn leaned against the table in a smart cream suit with red trim. "I'm glad you could wear that yellow dress again."

Helen's shoulders tightened. She had no desire to patronize the black market in San Francisco. And she preferred to think of her dress as golden. "Doing my patriotic duty."

"How like you. Such a busy little beaver, aren't you?"

Helen suppressed a grimace. Their competition had been

balanced and fun in high school, but not since. How could she deal with her old friend right now? "Are you having a good time?"

Jeannie fingered the bow on a box from Clara Jeffries, which probably contained embroidered guest towels similar to the ones in Helen's bathroom. "I try, but *c'est très difficile*. The whole thing is so sad."

"Sad?"

Jeannie leaned close and brought a whiff of Chanel No. 5. "The Novaks had to invite half of Antioch because poor plain Allie has no friends."

Helen gritted her teeth. "Be fair. She comes from Riverside and she's lived in Seattle this past year, both hundreds of miles away, and with the restrictions on travel—"

"Mercy. No need to be offended. But don't you wonder why her parents didn't come or why she couldn't find one friend—just one—to balance the wedding party? I know you and Allie have never been close."

Helen stared at Jeannie's perfect makeup. Why hadn't she ever noticed how Jeannie resembled her mother, not just in looks but in character? "Dorothy couldn't stand up for her so soon after her daughter's arrival, and I was honored. I look forward to getting to know Allie better."

"As sisters-in-law?" Jeannie gave her a nudge and smile.

Helen's jaws clamped, and she adjusted a pile of packages.

Jeannie wrapped her arm around Helen's shoulder. "Don't listen to my mother, the fuddy-duddy. I think it's sweet. Ray Novak's too old and dull for my taste, but you seem happy, and you'd make a perfectly darling pastor's wife. Of course, I hoped you'd marry Vic so we could be true sisters."

"You want me to go through life as Helen Llewellyn?"

"*Terrible.*" Jeannie's mouth pursed in a pretty little way. "I suppose that would be selfish of me."

Helen gave her a simpering smile. "I wouldn't expect anything less. Now, if you'll excuse me, I need to help with the cake."

Jeannie smiled and motioned her away. Thank goodness her vaunted college education didn't help her detect Helen's true meaning.

Her skirt swished around her feet as she headed for the cake table past too many eyes focused on her. Why couldn't they watch the bride? Why couldn't they mind their own business? Why couldn't everyone leave her alone?

✫

When Walt and Allie sank a knife into their wedding cake, Ray joined in the applause, louder than necessary, to express the joy he should have felt at the marriage of his baby brother.

Ray should have been the first of the brothers to marry, not just because he was oldest, but because Jack preferred chasing girls to settling down, and Walt had always been struck dumb in the presence of a woman.

At the cake table, Helen stacked plates and lined up forks and got in the way of Mrs. Anello and Mrs. Lindstrom. No doubt about it—Helen was avoiding him.

Back at Pyote Army Air Base, one of his fellow instructors had dated a woman who acted hot in private and cold in public. Like Helen. Turned out the woman was married. His friend felt cheap and used.

Ray understood.

He had ignored Nora's vacuous letters to him at Cal while she fell in love with Bill Ferguson. He'd ignored Ann's snide jokes about life in the parsonage and Dolores's roving eye while she cheated on him with half his cadets.

He refused to ignore this.

Ray weaved a path among the guests. *Lord, help me be*

calm and diplomatic, but help me see the truth so I don't get duped again.

"Hi there." He set his hand in the small of Helen's back. "Why don't you take a break? Even Marthas need rest."

She faced him and stepped back, dislodging his hand from her waist. "Goodness, maybe later. There's so much to do."

He set a smile in place and looked at Mrs. Anello. "Do you have things under control? May I steal Helen away for a while?"

"Please do." Mrs. Anello's smile looked as fake as Ray's, but with a trace of gratitude around the eyes. She pressed plates into Ray's and Helen's hands. "Take a break, Helen dear. You deserve it."

"But . . ."

"We're fine. You young people go have fun."

Ray gripped Helen's free hand and led her toward a quiet table in the back corner.

"Ray, please." She wormed her hand free.

He faced her with the calmest expression he could muster. "Why not? The other couples are holding hands."

Her eyebrows sprang up, and Ray's chest tightened. He planned to marry her, and she didn't even think they were a couple?

She raised a twitchy smile. "We decided to be discreet, remember?"

He set his plate on the table, helped Helen to her seat, and leaned down to her ear. "Discretion I understand; secrecy I don't."

"Secrecy?"

"In private everything's great, but in public you treat me like an acquaintance at best."

Her shoulders squirmed in his grasp. "I don't . . . I just . . . it's so early."

Two months was too early? He drank in a deep breath, took his seat, and leaned his forearms on his knees. "You don't want anyone to know about us, but they already do."

She smashed a chunk of cake under her fork tines. "I know. Oh dear."

His throat hardened. How could he keep the stoniness from his voice? "Are you ashamed of me?"

She swung her gaze to him. "Ashamed? Oh goodness, no. I could never—"

"That's what it looks like. You were married to a hero, and now you're stuck with a cowardly supply clerk."

She sucked in her breath. "Oh, Ray, I never—"

"I need to know." He locked a firm gaze on her. "I'm serious about you, and I need to know whether I'm just someone to keep you company until this blasted war is over and the heroes come home."

Her mouth flew open as if he'd punched her in the gut. "I could never. I'm not like that."

"Why don't you want to be seen with me?"

Her head shook in tiny tremors. "It's not like that. Really, it isn't."

He held out open hands to her. "So let me show how much I care for you. Hold my hand. Dance with me two, three, four songs in a row."

She clapped her hand over her mouth and squeezed her eyes shut. "Please don't."

Ray stared at his hands. They'd always be empty, wouldn't they?

"I need to go." He got up and walked away, his mouth frozen in a polite smile to mask the steam roiling inside. He needed a swim as never before.

"Please don't go." Slender fingers clutched his arm. "Ray, please."

"I'm tired. I'm going home."

Redness rimmed Helen's lovely eyes. "I'm so sorry. I'm not ashamed of you. You're the most wonderful man I've ever known, but everyone's watching, and I—I don't know how to act anymore."

"How to act?"

She pressed her hand to her forehead. "I don't know anymore. Everyone in town wants me to be the brave little widow, and the Carlisles want me to mourn for the rest of my life, and you want me to . . ."

Ray curled one finger under her chin. "Stop worrying about everyone else. When you figure out what you want, come and tell me." He turned to go, but her grip tightened.

"I'm sorry. I want to be with you. I do."

"I'm sorry too—sorry I pushed too hard, but maybe we should—"

"Please. Would you please—please ask me to dance again? I really want to be in your arms right now. I'd be glad to, honored to dance with you, all night even."

Maybe Dad was right and Ray was weak, but the pleading look in those brown eyes got to him, and he led her to the dance floor and folded her in his arms.

However, heaviness weighed down his heart. What was going on under the pinned-up honey-blonde curls pressed to his cheek? Why did she let the Carlisles control her? She even let her son control her.

What on earth had he gotten himself into? Despite what Helen said, she didn't know what she wanted, did she?

In his mind, Ray shoved his plans into the rubbish can.

12

Tension coiled like a snake, and Helen treaded softly as Ray walked her home, a vital skill she'd learned in her marriage.

Sometimes the snake slithered away, and sometimes he struck.

At Helen's front door, moonlight illuminated the sympathy in Ray's eyes and the hurt behind it. He sighed. "I owe you an apology. I care about you a lot, but I rushed things. You're not ready for dating. I need to step back and give you time."

Her heart twisted. No, she couldn't lose him. Whatever it took, she had to hold on. "Nonsense. I told you I want to be with you and I meant it."

"But—"

"I'm sorry." She stepped closer, rolled her fingers around the lapel of his uniform jacket, and smiled through the panicky flutter in her lips. "I've been silly. Why shouldn't everyone know? Really. Jim is gone and the Carlisles will have to get used to it."

He ducked his head to the side. "That's not what I—"

"You want everything to be public. I understand. See?" She pulled him down into a deep and passionate kiss. He relented and let himself be pulled in, and if she kept him there, maybe he'd see how much she adored him, how much she needed him. Maybe if she pulled him in deep enough, he'd drive out all the darkness.

"Wow." He lifted a sloppy smile. "That was great, but by public I meant a night on the town, holding hands. This—this can stay private."

"So let's go inside." She gave him a flirtatious smile and opened the door. He hesitated but followed. Jim accused her of leading countless men over that threshold.

No, she wouldn't think about that.

She set her pocketbook on the mail table that caused the scar on her cheek, and she flipped on the lamp. The previous lamp had accidentally smashed over her head. Jim found out she'd had the plumber over to fix the sink.

No!

She spun around and twined her arms around Ray's neck. Black hair, not blond.

"Honey, are you all right?"

"Mm-hmm." She burrowed under his chin and brushed her lips over his roughness. She would not let Jim keep her from Ray.

"We should sit down and talk." His voice rumbled husky and irresistible, but he set his hands on her waist to keep her away.

"I'd rather not."

"Let's sit down." He led her across the entry where she'd accidentally broken her arm after Betty's wedding when Jim saw her dance with George.

No!

She hung back when they reached the sofa where she'd accidentally been pinned down and accidentally dislocated her shoulder. She wasn't home that day when Jim called.

"No!"

Ray turned, eyebrows raised. "What's the matter?"

"Nothing. Nothing." She attempted a smile and circled her arms around his waist. "I just don't feel like talking."

"I do." He gave her a fatherly look. He thought he knew best, didn't he? Because he was older, because he was a pastor, because he was a man.

Well, she knew things too. She knew more about love than he did.

Ray caressed her cheek. "Something wonderful has been happening between us. But we need to slow down. Sometimes I think you're the woman I've been waiting for and I—"

She kissed him so he wouldn't complete the thought. "So, what are you waiting for?"

He tipped a smile. "Clever."

"Hmm? What are you waiting for?" She worked her hands under his jacket and across the broad expanse of his back.

His eyes fluttered shut. "Can't remember."

Helen slid her lips along his jaw line until he moaned and met her and gathered her close. Nothing fatherly in his touch now.

She fell into his kiss, but she kept her eyes open and etched Ray into her mind—soft gray over biting blue, quiet humor over gregarious charm, gentle caresses over slaps.

No! She kissed him harder. She had to etch over the memories. Had to.

His shoulders stiffened under her hands, and he pulled back, breathing hard. "It's time—it's time for me to go."

"No, don't leave me." She clung to him and kissed him. She wasn't finished.

"Helen," he said against her lips. He took her face in his hands and stepped back. "Believe me, I don't want to go, which is exactly why I need to go."

"No, no, no." She shook her head in his grip. If he left,

she'd explode. Something would explode inside and kill her. "Don't go. Please, don't go. You have to stay."

"Are you . . . are you all right?"

"Stay. I need you. I need you to stay."

He ran his hand over his mouth. "Um, Helen, I need to go."

"Why?" A spark traveled up her fuse. He demanded so much of her. Why wouldn't he give her what she needed? "You said you wanted to kiss me in private. We're in private. Did you change your mind? Huh? Would you rather go back outside, kiss me for all the world to see?"

"What? That's not what I meant."

"You want everything public, don't you?"

His head swung from side to side, his forehead in knots. "I don't—I don't know what's going on here."

"Let me get this straight." She charged for the window and flung back the ruffled white curtains. "Out there I need to stay by your side, always by your side, only by your side, and hold your hand and gaze adoringly at you, but in here—that's where you can kiss me, where you can beat me up."

Ray's eyes, his whole face stretched long. "Beat . . . what?"

"No!" She clapped her hands over her ears, worked them up into her hair. "I didn't say that. I didn't."

Concern curved around his eyes. "Did Jim . . . did he hit you?"

"No! Don't say that. He couldn't. He didn't. He loved me."

"I know, but did he—"

"No!" She gathered her hair in fistfuls. "He was a hero. Everyone loved him."

Ray lifted his hand.

She flung out her arms to block him, but she deserved it. She started it.

No blow landed.

"Oh, Helen." His voice fell on her instead, his soothing voice.

She peeked between her arms.

"Oh, honey. How could he do that? What kind of man beats his wife?"

His sympathy sank deep into her soul, but the truth, voiced for the first time, plunged faster and harder, and shattered her. The shards exploded out—out at Ray.

Her hands closed into fists, coiled in front of her chest. "No. Don't say that. Jim was a hero. A hero!"

"But he hit—"

"No, he didn't. He never did. How dare you? You're ruining everything."

"I—I'm trying to figure it out. He hurt you, but you defend him?"

She pressed her arms down to her side, down on stiff, ratcheting gears. "I'm defending the truth. I'm defending the father of my son. And you're attacking him."

"Helen—"

"How dare you? You—you're a clerk, a coward. You are. Jim said so. Jim said you were soft, a coward. He was right. You won't fight, and now you're picking on Jim. He's dead and you're picking on him. That's what cowards do. They pick on the defenseless."

Ray's expression hardened. "As Jim picked on you?"

"No! He didn't." Her fists shook at her sides. "No one—no one stands in my house and insults my husband, the father of my child. You wanted to leave, didn't you? So, leave."

"Helen—"

"Get out!" Her voice hurt her ears. She had to get rid of Ray Novak, get him out of her life forever. She stamped her foot and pointed a shaking finger at the door. "Get out and don't come back."

Something flickered in those gray eyes. Fear. A woman's anger scared him. Jim was right. He was always right.

"You coward. Get out of my house now!"

He set his lips in a thin line and headed for the front door. "I'm leaving."

She followed to make sure he left. He retreated down her front steps, and she stanched the pain at the sight of his back, which had felt so strong under her hands only moments before. But she was wrong, always wrong. Ray was weak. "Don't ever come back."

He looked over his shoulder, his eyes narrowed to slits in the moonlight. "I won't."

Helen slammed the door, her knees wobbled, and a low moan rose in her throat.

She stood alone with her memories. They had lurked off-stage in the wings, ever present but never acknowledged. Now they slinked onstage and assaulted her.

She buried her face in her hands. "Oh Lord, take them away. Take them away."

★

"What on earth happened?" Ray marched home for his swim trunks and towel.

"She's crazy, Lord. Crazy. The woman's stark raving mad. To think I contemplated a life with her."

He puffed air into his cheeks and let it vibrate over his lips, as if he could blast off her kisses—first so passionate he thought he'd better marry her within the week, then something new, fierce, almost hostile.

He shrugged off his jacket and slung it over his shoulder.

Helen sounded desperate for him to stay, as if her sanity depended on it.

Ray expelled another puff of air. "Too late."

★

Helen picked up Jay-Jay's Daddy book from the coffee table and stumbled down the hallway, her left foot drooping. She had work to do.

Everyone thought the world of Jim Carlisle, and that's the way it had to be. Jay-Jay must never know what his father was like, and therefore, no one else could know, including Helen. She had to forget again.

Of course, Ray knew now. But he'd never tell and he'd never be back. A fresh shard pierced her heart, and she grasped the doorjamb to her room for support.

Even if he forgave her—and how could he?—she couldn't take him back. He knew. For Jay-Jay's sake, she could never have him.

She stripped off her dress, which smelled of Ray, slipped on the lilac silk nightgown Jim loved, and studied herself in the mirror. The gown fit as it had in the early days of their marriage. On Jim's last furlough in June of '42, it had been tight from weight remaining after Jay-Jay's birth. Jim rhapsodized over certain parts of her fuller figure and belittled her for others.

She slammed her eyes shut. No, she needed to chase Jim's dark side back to the wings where it belonged. For that, she needed light.

She pulled two candles and a box of matches from the top dresser drawer, and pressed the candles into the stupid Carlisle heirloom candlesticks, wobbly things. She twisted each candle for good measure.

Jim loved candles. He loved fire, didn't he? Loved to use it, loved to burn her, loved to slam her hand onto the stove burner if she messed up dinner or forgot to serve pork chops on a Friday night.

Helen whirled toward the bed. Only the good things. Only the good things.

She lay on her stomach on the bed, propped the Daddy book on pillows before her, and opened it to a picture of Jim in his sailor suit holding three-month-old Jay-Jay for the first time. His elbows stuck out at an awkward angle, and his face shone with wonder.

This was the Jim she needed to preserve, the man with the disarming grin and quick joke, the man who crooned love songs in her ear and died for his country.

Helen turned the pages and filled her mind with the chosen past, the sanitized past, the false past, but the memories refused to leave stage. They spewed vile lines at her and rehearsed every hit and kick.

"Lord, help me." She slumped to the pillow, her hand on the wedding photo, her scarred body curled around the book of lies, and she yielded to her grief.

★

"A coward?" Ray stomped across the deserted beach around a small cove on the San Joaquin River. The moon cast sparse light on the charcoal ripples.

After he stashed his clothes and towel under the willow tree, he took a running dive into the water. Boy, did that feel good. He slicked back his hair and washed off the feel of Helen's caresses.

"A coward?" He plunged forward and divided the water with strong strokes. *Lord, you said, "Blessed are the peacemakers," and that's what I am. How does that make me a coward?*

With powerful kicks, he propelled himself across the cove, faster than he'd ever swum. How many German or Japanese dragons did he have to slay to earn respect? He did his part. He wore the uniform and contributed to the war effort.

Cowards feared death and war, but not Ray.

His body drooped under the weight of the lie.

He surfaced to tread water.

He didn't fear death, but he did fear war. He didn't want to cause pain and destruction, to kill someone even by accident, to smell blood, to see death, to experience the adrenaline pressure of attack. What if he couldn't handle it? What if he was hiding behind his age and his pastoral calling and his supply position?

What if he *was* a coward?

On the far side of the river, a black band of hills separated the sky from its reflection. Before tonight, Ray's view of himself was as clear as the star-strewn sky, but now, mirrored over the blackness of Helen's accusation, his image wavered like the stars on the river.

"Lord, am I a coward if I don't confront my fears?"

He dunked his head and spat out river water, nauseated at who he was and what he had to do to change it.

13

Jim held Helen's hand over the candle on the dresser top, lower and lower.

She screamed and writhed, powerless to stop him. The flame seared the palm of her hand. How would she explain this wound? Another cooking mishap?

"Promise you'll stay home when I'm at work." Jim's cool voice contrasted with the heat enveloping her hand.

"I promise. I promise."

"No phone calls, no guests, and no visiting when I'm gone, you hear?"

"Yes! Yes!" With her scream, she blew out the candle.

Jim cussed and threw her onto the bed. Her shin cracked against the footboard. She curled up in pain, clutched her blackened hand to her chest, and screwed her eyes shut against the heat.

So much heat. An orange glow shone through her eyelids. A crackle, a crash.

Helen opened her eyes, panting. It was only a dream. Jim was dead. She uncurled her right hand to reveal the glossy silver-dollar scar. The heat remained, the orange glow, the pall of smoke.

Smoke?

Helen sat up and gasped. Flames licked up the wallpaper around the dresser and the door frame. One of the candles had fallen from its candlestick.

"Oh no!"

Despite the heat, a chill stopped her heart. "Jay-Jay!"

She sprang for the door, but the flames beat her to it.

"Jay-Jay, wake up! Get out of the house." She'd have to go around to rescue him. On the other side of the room, orange tentacles groped for the curtains.

"No!" She scrambled over the bed and tugged back the curtains. "Jay-Jay, get out of the house!"

Helen flipped open the window latch, coughed, and swatted away a cloud of acrid smoke. She pushed up on the sash with the heels of her hands, but it didn't budge. She screamed out her frustration. Jim never fixed the fool window, and he never let her hire anyone else to do it.

She grabbed the ceramic table lamp and heaved it at the window. The lamp shattered, but the window remained intact.

Helen screamed until a fit of coughing doubled her over.

"Lord, please." Her gaze ransacked the room for something, anything to break the window.

Nothing. Everything was too big, too little, or too soft.

Every breath burned. "Please, Lord. Please get me out. Save my baby."

☆

Ray toweled off and jiggled his legs to warm up. A dip usually soothed him, but he still reeled from Helen's outburst.

A shudder ran up his spine, and he slipped his trousers over his damp trunks. "Wow. What an outburst."

Tonight he'd seen a whole new side of Helen Jamison Carlisle. She'd never been angry at him before. She always forgave him easily, as if she'd do anything to avoid a fight.

His stomach constricted. Of course, she did. Jim beat her.

Was that why she cowered from Jay-Jay's tantrum? Sure, she overreacted, but when Jay-Jay acted like his dad, Helen might have been thrown back to the terror of her marriage.

Then tonight she flinched when he reached for her, not the first time she'd flinched.

Ray groaned. "Why didn't I put this together before?"

She showed classic signs of a battered wife—avoiding conflict, flinching from contact. And those scars didn't come from cooking accidents and clumsy spills but from a wife-beating jerk.

Did he restrict her activities? Sure. He didn't let her go to college, did he? She gave up her volunteer work when they married and picked it up after he died, not to keep herself busy but to return to her heart's work. Jim kept her away from it.

What about isolation from family and friends? Didn't everyone say Jim and Helen kept to themselves? That they loved privacy? Hardly. Jim just wanted to control her.

Ray shook sand off his shirt, harder than he had to. "I'm so blind. What kind of pastor am I? I was so intent on fitting her into my empty slot for a wife, I missed it all."

He punched his arm through the sleeve of his khaki shirt. His dream of a healthy marriage to a healthy woman lay in tatters.

Now what? She needed help, but Ray wasn't the man to help her and a romance wasn't the means. Romance made it worse.

He sighed and headed to town without buttoning his shirt.

A red light pulsated over the buildings and treetops in defiance of blackout regulations.

A fire.

Ray let out a low whistle. "Lord, get those people out. Send your protection over them."

✯

Thick black smoke roiled above Helen, and flames unfurled toward the window, her only exit.

"Lord, help me!" She hefted up the nightstand, but even in her panic, she didn't have the strength to raise it high enough, much less break the glass. Tears streamed down her cheeks, worsened by the stinging smoke.

She ducked below the smoke and filled her lungs with precious oxygen. The drawer!

"Please let this work." She yanked it out of the nightstand and dumped the contents. With both hands and all her might, she swung the drawer at the window. A crunch.

Again! Harder! The drawer broke through and jammed. Helen pried it free, put her face to the hole, and sucked in cool, sweet air.

"Fire!" she yelled. "Help! Fire!'"

She rammed the drawer at the triangles of glass until her arms shook. A jagged rim remained around the frame, but now was no time to fret about new cuts and scars. Grasping the sash overhead, she hoisted her hip onto the sill, swung her feet outside, and jumped.

Pain sliced into her bare feet, and she crumpled to the ground. She pulled out chunks of glass. "Not now."

Where was everyone? Where was the fire truck? Mrs. Llewellyn spent all her time spying on the neighbors. Why did she choose to sleep now when her nosiness would be useful?

Helen stood and winced at the pain in her feet. She ran and stumbled and screamed. "Fire! Help! My baby!"

Her cries sounded feeble against the crackle and roar. She rounded the corner of the house, ran up the stairs, and tugged open the door. Smoke filled the living room.

She charged ahead, but flames slunk down the hallway

and flicked into the living room. "No! Jay-Jay!" The scream seared her throat.

She'd have to get him out through his window. Helen spun for the door, past the mirror where she'd primped in another lifetime, before the wedding, before taking Jay-Jay to Betty's house.

Helen ground to a stop. Betty's house?

She pressed her fingers to her forehead. The wedding was tonight—yes, tonight, and Jay-Jay . . .

Yes! Jay-Jay was at Betty's.

"Thank you, Lord." She raised her eyes. Flames raced overhead.

"No!" She whirled around and stared into the mouth of a dragon descending on her with foul breath, longing to devour.

Helen lunged for the door. So did the dragon.

★

Ray jogged south down McElhenny Road toward the throbbing glow and the column of gray smoke drifting east. No fire truck clanged, no volunteer firemen shouted, no plumes of water shot through the air.

"Fire!" he bellowed. "Fire!"

He turned right on Sixth Street. He stubbed his toe on a crack but kept going. If someone remained inside, he could be a hero without going to combat.

Ray groaned. "Stop it, Novak."

He passed the little hospital at the corner of A Street, and his heart thumped harder. The fire seemed to be in his neighborhood. His family? His friends?

Not his parents' house. He tossed his towel and jacket on their lawn. "Fire! Fire!"

To the west, clangs and sirens broke the night's silence. Finally, someone had called.

The flames rose a bit south, close to Helen's house.

Although sweat ran down his temples, his insides turned to ice. He'd left her in an unbalanced state. Could she have burned down her house in a fit of madness?

He broke into an open run. "Helen!"

Each step churned up nausea. It was Helen's house, he knew it in his mind and his heart, and when he wheeled left onto D Street, his eyes confirmed it.

"Helen!" He sprinted down the street. Flames danced on the bungalow and taunted him. A roar, and a section of roof caved in, sending up a fountain of sparks and flames. Thank goodness Jay-Jay wasn't there.

"Lord, help me save her." He took the stairs in two steps, but the heat repelled him. Strange thing, fire—translucent. The doorknob sat in sight only three feet away, but might as well have been in the next county.

A creak overhead. Ray leaped down the stairs as a timber crashed to the porch.

"Helen!" How could he rescue her? Even if he got in, would she cooperate?

"Water." Maybe he could douse himself with a hose, cover his mouth with a wet cloth—his shirt. He ran for the house next door.

At the side of the house, a lady bent over the spigot.

"Helen!" In his joy he reached for her, but the memory of how they parted stopped him. "Thank goodness you're safe."

"Gotta—gotta." She fumbled with the hose. "Fire—there's a fire. Gotta get the—the faucet, hose, nozzle. The—the fire. Gotta—gotta."

"I'll help." The garden hose wouldn't do any good, but Helen was in shock. She needed to do something. He lifted the hose from the rack and turned on the water.

She tugged the hose to its full length and raised a limp stream of water. When she pressed her thumb over the end, the water sprang to life. The outermost drops sizzled in the flames.

In her futile effort Helen stood brave and determined, a black silhouette against the flames. Her hair hung in tangles to one shoulder while pinned up on the other side. The firelight glinted off her bare arms and around her curves in that dangerous nightgown.

Ray longed to take her in his arms, but she wouldn't let him.

"Need longer—longer." Helen dropped the hose and ran to her backyard.

He followed, but the fire truck pulled up, men scrambled out, and neighbors gathered in bathrobe-clad clusters.

Ray ran to the truck. "She's out. It's all right. Helen's out."

"Her baby!" Mrs. Jeffries sobbed.

"It's all right. Jay-Jay's at George and Betty Anello's tonight. He's safe."

"Thank you, Lord. Thank you, Jesus."

He left the crowd and ran behind the house to find Helen. Poor thing. What did she think she could do? The entire fire department couldn't save her house.

She staggered out of the garage. "No hose. No hose. Rubber drive."

"It's all right. The fire truck's here."

She passed him. "Gotta get the book."

Ray jogged alongside her. "The book?"

"Daddy book. Jay-Jay's."

"You can't." A section of wall collapsed, and he pulled her away from a burst of flame and hot air.

"No!" She shook him off and limped to the front yard. "I need it."

"You can't go inside. It's too late."

"No! It can't be." She ran faster, stumbling, face twisted. "Jay-Jay needs it. It's all we have of him. All we have."

Ray picked up his pace. Did she really think she could go inside? "Stop, Helen."

"I have to. I have to." She rounded the corner of her house. She wasn't going to stop.

"Helen, no!" He burst forward and flung his arms around her waist.

"No!" She flailed fists at his sides. "Don't! Don't stop me."

"It's too late. It's gone, honey. It's gone."

"No-o-o." Her voice and her beating trailed off, and she raised her face to her home and her life going up in flames. "No-o-o."

"I'm sorry, honey," he said in her ear. "I'm sorry."

"It's gone. All gone." Her body went limp.

He struggled to hold her in the silky nightgown, and he eased her down. She crumpled over her knees.

Ray knelt beside her and stroked her back. "I'm sorry, honey."

"It's all gone. All I have of him is gone. He's gone."

Giant plumes of water arched overhead, and droplets rained down on them, rained down the truth. The man beat her. He was dead. And he still controlled her.

Ray's hand settled on Helen's soot-streaked hair. He couldn't compete with a ghost. Not as he was.

14

Monday, May 15, 1944

Helen lugged the secondhand suitcase down Sixth Street with Dorothy Wayne alongside. The only good thing about losing her home and all her possessions was the work. She even had to apply to the Office of Price Administration for new ration books. So much work. But work kept her mind off the losses, the memories that refused to retreat, the shame of what she'd said to Ray, the pain of driving off the man she loved, and the worry of how she'd manage Jay-Jay and her volunteer duties while working.

Her life lay in ashes, as barren as the little lot at the corner of Seventh and D.

"Are you sure you want to move in with my parents?" Dorothy pushed baby Susie in her carriage.

"I don't have another option." Helen readjusted her grip on the suitcase full of donated clothes, some out of season, many unflattering, and most out of style.

Jay-Jay tugged her hand and stooped. "Tick."

"Yes, sweetie. Leave the stick."

"What about your parents?" Dorothy asked.

"In Washington DC? They're in military housing, a one-bedroom apartment, and Mama's working, so who would watch Jay-Jay?" Not to mention Papa's strong words when she married Jim over their objections: "Don't come back begging."

"Tick, tick, tick, tick, tick."

"No, sweetie, leave the stick."

Dorothy frowned. "You can't stay at Betty's?"

"You know they don't have room. They let me sleep on the couch last week while my feet healed, but I need to go."

"Nothing to rent?"

Helen sighed and turned right on C Street. Everyone else thought her plan was perfect. "My allowance from the life insurance covers living expenses, but I need to replace furniture, clothing, linens, pots, pans, dishes—everything. If I work for Vic three days a week for a few months and stay with the Carlisles, I can save up and buy those things."

Dorothy stopped in front of her childhood home, a two-storied Craftsman. "As long as it's only temporary."

Helen stared at her friend. Dorothy seemed happy to live with her in-laws, but perhaps she was having problems. "Why?"

"Oh, no reason." Dorothy shook back her brown curls and laughed. "Just because my parents drive me crazy doesn't mean you won't get along fine." She pushed the carriage up the street. "I've got to get Susie home for her bottle. Say hi to my mom. I'll see you later."

"Bye." She tried to smile at her friend, but this past week, smiling took as much effort as walking had during her recovery from polio. Find the muscles, feel the muscles, use all your will and strength to make them move.

"Tick." Jay-Jay giggled and swatted Helen's knee.

"Ow!" She pulled up her leg. "I told you to leave the stick."

"My tick." Storm clouds gathered on his face.

"Sweetie, please." But pleading never caused the storm to break, did it? Not with the father and not with the son.

Her stomach clenched. She leaned over and put on a firm face. As Ray said, she had to assert her authority. "Sweetie, give me the stick." But her voice betrayed her and faltered.

"No!"

"Oh, you poor baby." Mrs. Carlisle trotted down the walkway. "You lost your Daddy book, your toys, and now your mommy wants to take away your stick."

"He's hitting."

"He's a boy." Mrs. Carlisle swept up her grandson. "And he's a baby. He doesn't know better."

A chill raced through her. How would he learn better unless she taught him, and how could she teach him when his temper terrified her and the Carlisles spoiled him? Was that how they'd raised Jim?

"Let's find your room." Mrs. Carlisle bounced Jay-Jay on her hip and headed for the house. She chuckled as he tapped her arm with the stick. "Yes, a fine stick for a fine boy."

Helen picked up her suitcase and her sagging resolve, and followed her mother-in-law into the darkened house, the drapes drawn as always to control the temperature.

"You'll be in Dorothy's old room," Mrs. Carlisle said to Helen as she climbed the stairs.

Despite their childhood friendship, she couldn't recall what Dorothy's room looked like. Helen and Betty and Dorothy played at the Jamisons or out in the neighborhood.

Mrs. Carlisle swung open a door. "We brought up the furniture from the garage. We packed it last year when she got married."

Helen stepped inside the narrow room. A twin bed with a white chenille bedspread hugged one wall, and a dresser sat next to the closet on the opposite wall. A utilitarian room, which cried for a throw rug or a picture on the wall, but Helen smiled. "Thank you. It's lovely."

"Now, Jay-Jay, let's get you settled in. You'll be in your father's room." Mrs. Carlisle opened the next door.

The image assaulted Helen's eyes. On the wall hung pennants in Antioch High's black and gold, and Jim's jerseys for football, basketball, and baseball. Helen gripped the doorjamb. He had been a senior when she was a sophomore. Why would a handsome star athlete pay attention to a cripple girl? Helen worked hard and went to every game, memorized his every play, and flirted with him constantly.

If only she hadn't.

"Come on, baby boy. See what your daddy played with?" Mrs. Carlisle showed Jay-Jay model cars and a top and a wooden truck.

Helen glanced around, breathing hard. While Dorothy's room was bare, Jim's room was a shrine. True, many families preserved their dead sons' rooms, but Jim had married three years before Dorothy.

No wonder Dorothy never invited Helen over to play.

"I need—I need to fetch the other suitcase."

"All right. We'll be up here." Mrs. Carlisle pulled a book off the shelf. "This was your daddy's favorite."

Helen stared at her small son in his father's room, surrounded by his father's possessions, and dread gripped her heart.

This was where Jim learned to be who he was.

She whirled away and headed downstairs, clutching the banister because her left foot dragged.

Once outside, she filled her lungs with clean Delta air. "Lord, please don't let my son grow up to be like his father."

At the end of the block, a woman approached. Mrs. Novak.

Oh no. Helen hadn't talked to her since the fire. How much had Ray told her? Did she know the horrible things Helen had said? Did she blame her because Ray hadn't come home last weekend?

Ray's absence brought a mix of pain and relief. Someday Helen would have to face him, but how? And how could she face his mother today? But if she turned around or crossed the street, Mrs. Novak would know Helen was avoiding her.

Mrs. Novak waved. "There you are, Helen. Your sister said I'd find you at the Carlisles'."

"I just dropped off the first suitcase." She hefted up a smile.

Though her eyes were blue instead of gray, Mrs. Novak had the same soft gaze as Ray. "I'm sorry about the fire. I've been praying for you."

"Thank you." Her throat clamped shut. She didn't deserve sympathy.

Mrs. Novak opened her pocketbook, and her black eyelashes flitted against cheeks redder than usual—and blotchy. "I received a letter from Ray today."

"A letter?" Why would he write a letter when he was so close?

"He enclosed a note for you." She held out a piece of paper. "Please don't blame yourself."

Chill bumps ran down Helen's arms. "Blame myself?"

"You two had a—a quarrel after the wedding, didn't you?" Helen gave a sharp nod.

"So, please don't blame yourself." Mrs. Novak took Helen's hand and pressed the letter into it.

Her fingers could barely move, but somehow she unfolded the letter.

Dear Helen,   May 10, 1944

By the time you receive this, I'll be on my way overseas for a combat tour. While this may come as a surprise, I've debated this decision for some time. In my supply position I impede the war effort, but as a pilot I can do my country some good.

I need to make one thing perfectly clear—this decision comes from prayer and reflection over many months, and nothing you said prompted this in any way.

However, it's best for me to leave for a while. I pushed you into something you weren't ready for, and I apologize. I admire you greatly and care for you deeply, and I regret how things ended. Please accept my apologies.

I will be praying for Jesus' healing hand in your life. He will strengthen you and comfort you when you sit at his feet.

Helen's head felt full of molten lead. "Combat?"

"I know." Mrs. Novak swiped tears from her cheek. "In his heart, Ray isn't a soldier. He isn't cut out for this."

Helen scanned the letter. "Why?" she whispered, although her own accusing words screamed the answer.

"My father-in-law says he saw it at Easter, that Ray feels he needs to prove himself." Her voice broke. "I can't imagine why."

Helen could, and the shame of it crushed the wind out of her. "Oh no."

"I shouldn't be afraid for him, but I can't help it. Grandpa Novak says we have more to fear if Ray doesn't go. He says if Ray doesn't do this, he'll never be able to live with himself."

For the first time in years, Helen longed for her old leg braces to steady her. How could they say she wasn't to blame? Her rash words drove a gentle man to face grave horror and danger.

15

No. 1 Combat Crew Replacement Center
Bovingdon, Hertfordshire, England
Wednesday, June 7, 1944

Ray's eyes adjusted to the interior of the hut, a long tube of corrugated tin. A couple dozen cots lined the walls, and three potbellied coal stoves ran down the aisle.

"A Quonset hut," the officer next to Ray said, punctuated by cuss words.

"Rookies." A man lounging on a cot spoke from behind a girlie magazine. "You want to sound like a fool, go ahead and call them Quonset huts. Here they're Nissen huts."

Ray crunched over dirt clods on the concrete floor and tossed his duffel on a cot. "Better than a foxhole on the Normandy beaches."

Down came the girlie magazine. "Say, Pops, what are you doing over here? Need help setting up your rocking chair?"

Ray tipped him a smile. "Sure. Let me help you out of your high chair first."

The laughter said he'd passed his first test. If only the tests looming before him would be so easy.

"Captain's here, rookies. Line up outside."

Ray trooped outside under a pewter sky with the other eleven newcomers.

The captain, a compact man with thick features, looked familiar. "Welcome to the CCRC, men. I'm Captain Hawkins."

Ray smiled at the man's Maine accent. Only two years before, Cadet Hawkins had been one of his best students at Kelly Field.

"Guess what, men? Everything you learned in stateside training is dead wrong. You think you can fly on instruments, but you can't. You think you know how to fly in formation, but you don't. And you think you're ready to take on the Luftwaffe, but I'm here to tell you, you aren't. Understood?"

"Yes, sir!" But Ray stiffened in position. The Training Command did its best to adapt to suggestions from the combat theaters.

"My job is to get you ready before you're assigned to a bomb group." Hawkins tapped his cigarette between sausage-like fingers. "Yesterday was D-Day, boys, in case you're too stupid to know, and the Eighth Air Force dispatched over two thousand bombers. We lost only one due to enemy action. However, one crashed on takeoff, one on landing, two B-24s collided, and a rookie sliced his wing through the undercarriage of his squadron commander's B-17, forcing the major to ditch at sea after his crew bailed." He pointed his cigarette at the men, as if they'd caused the accidents. "Stupid rookie mistakes."

Ray started to frown but stopped himself since he stood at attention. Hawkins had been a friendly young man, but war had toughened him beyond recognition.

Hawkins's gaze hit each man like a schoolmaster whacking his pupils with a ruler. "You will not make similar mistakes. Understood?"

"Yes, sir!"

Hawkins squinted at Ray, and his eyebrows bounced.

Ray gave him a slight nod.

Hawkins flipped a page on his clipboard. "All right, boys. At ease. You have half an hour to settle in. Report to mess at 1200, then at 1300 you're due at the Link Trainer. All dismissed except Lieutenant Novak."

After the other men filed into the hut, Hawkins erupted in a grin and pumped Ray's hand. "Boy, it's good to see you. What on earth are you doing here?"

Ray chuckled at the familiar personality. "Always wanted to see England."

"Come on. You're the best instructor we've got."

"You need combat experience to be an instructor now. They transferred me to supply."

"You're kidding. No wonder you came here. You're born to fly."

"Yep." Although incomplete, his explanation satisfied everyone, except those who knew him well. Letters from home had caught up with him at the Preparation for Overseas Movement Center. Mom was scared, Dad incredulous. Grandpa's letter hit hard when he wrote, "I know you won't be able to live with yourself if you don't do this, but remember, you don't have to prove yourself to anyone."

Maybe, but he needed to prove it to himself.

"Say, Novak, why don't you join me for lunch so we can catch up?"

"Sounds great, but first I'd like to ask a favor, sir."

Hawkins laughed. "Sir?"

Ray raised a salute and a smile. "You outrank me."

"All right," he said with a roll of his eyes. "What's the favor?"

"My brother's with the 94th Bomb Group. Could we let him know I'm here?"

"Sure." Hawkins beckoned with a sweep of his hand. "We'll call Bury St. Edmunds."

They headed south down a muddy road away from the living sites and toward the airfield and the technical sites—the administrative buildings, supply stores, and maintenance shops.

Hawkins gave Ray a sheepish smile. "Sorry about what I said about stateside training. If I don't drive the cockiness out of these fellows, they'll never survive their first mission, much less a thirty-mission combat tour."

"Yep. You can work with ignorance but not cockiness." Ray smiled as a squadron of twelve Flying Fortresses emerged from the cloud cover. "Beautiful."

"Formation's too tight," Hawkins said over the throb of forty-eight Wright-Cyclone engines.

"Looks right to me."

"That's one of the differences between training and combat. We get turbulent weather over Europe, need to fly looser formations to avoid collisions, especially under fire."

Ray's lungs felt tight. If someone shot at him or a plane dived at him, his instinct would be to swerve, to collide.

Hawkins turned down a side road lined with more Nissen huts, and a jeep passed. "Last time I saw you, you got me in trouble for buzzing the tower after graduation. I think of that whenever I write up a fellow for buzzing. Least once a week."

Ray chuckled. "Hated to write you up. That was the only time, if I recall. Unlike that other fellow in your class—Rivers, wasn't it?"

"Yeah, Ted Rivers. Got his head blown off by a Luftwaffe shell."

Ray stopped in his tracks, unable to breathe.

Hawkins faced him, and his cheek twitched. "Sorry. Forgot you're a rookie. That's what it's like over here. You get used to it."

Ray nodded, but he never wanted to get used to violent deaths of promising young men.

Hawkins led him into a Nissen hut partitioned into offices. He shrugged off his flight jacket and hung it on a coatrack. "Have a seat. This may take a while. Your brother's name and position?"

"Maj. Jack Novak. He's a squadron commander, unless he's been promoted recently. He's due." The chill of the metal chair worked through his wool trousers.

Hawkins spoke to the operator, sandwiched the receiver between his ear and his shoulder, and flicked his cigarette lighter.

The yellow flame sparked Ray's memory. The fire at Helen's house had served as a sign for Ray, just as the Lord used fire to consume Gideon's offering, overcome his last reservations, and send him to war against the Midianites.

He tried to think of Helen as little as possible. Too painful. He prayed for her, but how could he help? If he hadn't raced into romance, he could have written to her and counseled her as a friend.

When he found out what Jim had done, Helen lashed out— not at Jim, but at Ray. She hated him for knowing the truth, because she couldn't face the truth herself.

Ray stood in the rubble of another failed romance, but for the first time, the failure was his fault.

"Novak?" Hawkins's forehead crinkled up. "You remember what I said about a Fort ditching at sea?"

Ray blinked away his memories. "Yeah?"

"It was your brother."

★

Ray leaned his elbows on his knees and ran his hands into his hair. Jack looked so small and pale on the hospital cot, not his usual daring self.

The doctor said he'd been pulled from the Channel in time but came close to dying. Dad and Mom would have been devastated, as well as Walt, and Ray himself.

"Lord, what am I doing here?" he whispered. His decision to fly a combat tour didn't affect just Ray but his whole family. Was it selfish to try to prove himself if the effort killed him and hurt those he loved? Or did this concern for safety show he was the worst kind of coward, only worried about his skin?

He puffed out a breath and pulled his black notebook and pen from his shirt pocket. "What is courage?" he scrawled. "What is cowardice?"

Fear didn't make a man a coward, but rather the inability to act due to fear. Could Ray find courage to take action when necessary? Did his faith run deeper than his seminary knowledge, deep enough to sustain him no matter what?

Life had never tested his courage, so he needed to test it himself. At the bottom of the page he wrote, "Will I pass, Lord?"

A groan rose from Jack's cot, and the pile of blankets shifted.

Ray stuffed his notebook back in his pocket. "Jack?"

His gaze swam in lazy circles until it settled on Ray.

"Jack?" He rubbed his brother's upper arm, which felt chilly. "Hi there. Think you can stay awake?"

"Awake?" Jack coughed so hard, his metal cot creaked.

"Look who woke up just in time for bed." The nurse, Lieutenant Taylor, scurried to the bed. "I can't give you anything for that cough, Major. You need to clear out that seawater, but would you like some more morphine?"

Jack's mouth twisted under his black mustache. "But I'm—didn't I?—I didn't die?"

Ray laughed softly. "You came mighty close. You were

unconscious when Air-Sea Rescue plucked you out of the water. You had a bad case of hypothermia."

Jack craned his neck and stared at his right leg up in traction, then broke into another coughing fit. "My foot?"

"Oh, you broke several bones." The nurse flipped her hand and laughed. "You'll be in a cast about six weeks, young man."

Jack squinted at the window. "What day is it?"

"The seventh," Ray said. "The invasion was a success. We're making progress."

"My crew—did they make it?"

"All safe. Startled a flock of sheep, but they're fine."

"Good." Jack frowned. "Where am I?"

The nurse popped a thermometer in his mouth. "You're at the 65th General Hospital. We just came to Redgrave Park in Botesdale in Suffolk. You wouldn't believe the quaint little villages we have around here. The nearest town of any size is Bury St. Edmunds, which is about—"

"I been 'ere b'fore," Jack grumbled around the thermometer.

Ray raised a smile to the nurse, not the first time he'd had to smooth his brother's rough edges. "Jack's based at Bury St. Edmunds."

Jack narrowed gray-blue eyes at Ray. "What're you doin' 'ere?"

"Took you long enough to notice."

"But what—where?"

"The Combat Crew Replacement Center in Bovingdon—training, waiting for assignment to a bomb group."

"Com'at . . ." Jack hitched himself up and spat the thermometer out onto the bed. "But—but you're an instructor. No, you're in that supply job. What happened?"

Explaining his decision required skill. If Jack sensed his real motive, he might use his rank to interfere. "I volunteered," Ray said.

"You what?"

"Major, I need your temperature." Lieutenant Taylor poked the thermometer at Jack's lips.

He glared at her. "Later."

She dashed away, chattering to herself. With Dad's forceful personality, Jack made an effective commander, but a less-than-pleasant patient.

His gaze bored into Ray. "You volunteered?"

"Yes." He set a determined expression on his face. "I need to be here."

"But why? And why now? I thought you and Helen . . . "

Jack might as well have punched him in the gut. "Long story. I'll tell you later."

"Women always make for long stories."

Ray gave him a sympathetic look. Jack had been pursuing a nurse for about a year. "Didn't work out with Ruth?"

"Nope. Category E, damaged beyond repair." He slid under the pile of blankets. "Remember those balsa wood planes Grandpa always put in our Christmas stockings?"

Ray leaned forward on his knees. "Sure do. Never lasted long, did they?"

"Kind of like macaroons."

Macaroons? Ray held up one hand to stop Lieutenant Taylor, who approached with a syringe. The last thing Jack needed was more morphine.

"Remember?" Jack said. "You'd get one or two flights out of them, then crack the horizontal stabilizer, glue it together. Next flight you'd snap the wing in half, glue it together. Chip the nose, more glue. Eventually the glue weighed it down so much it couldn't fly."

Ray murmured.

"That's what it's like with Ruth. Too many crashes, too many cracks, too much glue. Can't fly."

Somehow, under all that medication, Jack made sense. Even if Ray survived his combat tour and Helen worked through her problem and ignored the men sure to find her attractive, it was too late for them.

Helen Carlisle was the most wonderful woman Ray had met, he'd had his once-in-a-lifetime chance with her, and he'd blown it.

16

U.S. Naval Magazine, Port Chicago
Friday, June 9, 1944

"Don't worry, Helen. The ordnance isn't fused. It can't deto-
nate."

"I know." She gave Vic a smile even though he'd said the
same thing a dozen times in the two weeks she'd worked for
him.

Still, she held her breath as they drove from Vic's office to
the pier, as if a misdirected puff of air could cause an explosion. Hundreds of boxcars full of torpedoes and bombs and
depth charges hunkered behind high earthen revetments.

Vic parked the staff car and opened the door for Helen. She
stepped out in her new gray suit, holding her pad of paper as
if she knew what she was doing. She hadn't taken secretarial
classes since she planned to go to college with Jeannie, who
had just graduated from Mills and had a swanky job in San
Francisco. Helen didn't even know shorthand. However, she
typed at a fast clip, wrote businesslike letters, and took furious notes.

Vic stood in front of her in his blue service uniform. "I'm
glad you're here. You give me hope."

Helen sighed. For such a brilliant man, he sure repeated

himself. "You know I'm only here to earn enough money to set up house."

"Marry me, and we'll set up house together. You'll never have to work again."

"Are you going to ask me every single day?"

"Until you say yes."

Helen's stomach soured. But she only needed this job for three months. "We're here to see Petty Officer Carver Jones, right?"

Vic huffed at the change in subject. "Right. He's the one with a degree from Howard University."

"You mentioned that." Several times.

He led her to the pier, where a freighter docked in Suisun Bay. The water flowed deep here in the Delta, where the San Joaquin and Sacramento rivers merged into a bulge and gathered strength to finish the journey into San Francisco Bay.

"They finished widening the pier," Vic called over the noise of machinery and men. "Now we can load two ships at once, and we'll get—"

"Twice as much ordnance to the Pacific Theater."

He raised his eyebrows and grinned. "Yes."

At the base of the dock, Vic saluted an officer, who sent a seaman to find Petty Officer Jones. In the loading area, hundreds of men worked at a fast pace, carrying crates, rolling torpedoes, loading items in cargo nets, hooking up winches, and swinging booms. Marines stood on guard, and naval officers called out orders. All were white. All the sailors doing the hard labor were black.

Like the pictures of antebellum plantations in Helen's high school history book. Something inside her squirmed. Only the whips and dogs were missing from the scene.

A black man wearing a blue chambray shirt and dungarees approached and saluted Vic. "Good morning, Lieutenant."

"Stand easy. Mrs. Carlisle, this is Petty Officer Carver Jones. Jones, my new secretary."

She extended her hand. "How do you do?"

"How do you do, ma'am?" He shook her hand and dipped his square chin. He had the light build of a scholar, not a dockworker.

Vic clasped his hands behind his back. "So, Jones, are the men pleased with the new recreation facility?"

"Yes, sir, but they wonder why it took the Navy a year and a half to meet that need."

"Shameful. That's why I worked so hard to speed up the process." Vic gave Helen a quick look.

She uncapped her pen, ready to take notes.

"We appreciate that, sir, but the men still have complaints."

"Send the men my way."

Petty Officer Jones tucked in his lips and gazed along the length of the pier, which jutted upriver. "They're afraid of retaliation, sir. They prefer to have me present the complaints anonymously. They hope my pretty words will persuade you."

"Truth persuades me. Justice persuades me."

"Yes, sir. In time they may see, as I already have, that you're on our side."

Helen scratched her pen on the corner of the page to get the ink flowing, and shot Vic a glance. Despite his annoying traits, he was a good and fair man.

"Thank you, Jones." He lowered his chin. "I wish I could do something about pay levels, promotions, and segregation, but I can't. And I can't change the Navy's archaic policy keeping you men from combat. But is there anything else I can help with?"

"Two things, sir, which affect safety. First of all, the officers have stepped up the competition between shifts. We believe the officers are betting on us. We're concerned that safety has been sacrificed for speed."

Helen scribbled notes, but her gaze darted to the dock. What kind of men bet on such things? And did she really want to be close to the sloppy handling of munitions, fused or not?

"The second issue is training." Jones rubbed the back of his neck. "The men are on edge. None of us were trained in ammunition handling. We're learning on the job, and we haven't received a single lecture on safety. Someone's going to get hurt."

"I'll get on that immediately, see what I can do."

The men exchanged salutes and parted.

Vic opened the car door for Helen. "Good man, Jones. He'll be a leader in the Negro community someday. You know, I thought this was a losing assignment, but I've changed my mind. I have a chance to do some good, plus I'm making connections. Now, don't you want to marry a man with such a shining future?" he asked in a tongue-in-cheek tone.

"No, thank you." She lowered herself into the seat, and her jaw tightened. Why did the men in her life want to control her? Vic pestered her to marry him, Mr. Carlisle told her how to raise her son, and Jim—Jim still controlled her from his watery grave.

Vic drove away, and Helen doodled on the page as if rearranging her notes.

Jim controlled her most of all. No matter how she tried, she couldn't shove back the memories. Her façade lay in ashes, as did the Daddy book that had propped it up. Mrs. Carlisle wanted her to assemble a new scrapbook, but Helen couldn't paste the falsehoods back in place. The man beat her, burned her, and caused two miscarriages.

Babies he kicked out of her.

Grief swamped her, and she swung her gaze out the window to conceal the tears burning the backs of her eyes. The first time he beat her unconscious, the first time he killed a child inside her, she threatened to tell her father the truth when he examined her, but Jim cried. He actually cried, he was so sorry, he just loved her so much, that's why she made him angry when she didn't behave, and it would never happen again. Never.

She told Papa she slipped in the tub and had been bleeding anyway.

Jim got away with it. He always did.

Clumsy cripple Helen.

Vic parked the car by the wooden administration building.

"I need to use the ladies' room." Helen bolted from the car and dashed into the restroom.

Jim said no one would believe her anyway. Fun-loving, sunny, popular Jim. Who would believe he beat his wife?

Ray believed her.

Helen sobbed. She leaned against the bathroom wall and fumbled inside her pocketbook for a handkerchief.

Ray was the only one who had ever figured out the truth, the only one who believed the truth even as she denied it and spewed hateful insults, hateful because he did know the truth.

"Oh Lord." She pressed her handkerchief over her face. "Lord, the truth hurts so much." But the lie hurt too, in a different way, like a slow-acting poison.

She slipped to her knees, her cheek pressed to the rough painted wall, and the truth heaved through her like labor contractions. She couldn't bear it, couldn't bear the pain. No matter what she did, how hard she tried, how well she performed, Jim beat her.

He beat her. He beat her. He beat her.

Helen clutched her head and collapsed over her knees to shield herself, but the memories assaulted her mind as Jim had assaulted her body.

"Lord, help me. I can't bear it."

A whisper. The softest whisper in her ear. He knew. Jesus knew what she had endured. He'd endured it too. He was beaten and scarred. He understood.

For the first time, she yielded to his comfort. Jesus didn't take away her tears, he received them. He didn't take away the memories, he shared them. He didn't take away the hurts, he felt them. Somehow, with the Lord, she could bear it.

"Ten o'clock?" Betty set her hands on her hips. "Hasn't Vic heard familiarity breeds contempt?"

Helen scrunched her eyes shut and tried to rub the heaviness off her eyeballs. She was spent, dried out, every drop of moisture wrung from her soul. "He thinks the more hours I spend with him, the sooner I'll fall in love."

"Typical Llewellyn arrogance."

"Not tonight, Betts. I just want to pick up Jay-Jay and get some sleep." She stepped around her sister and into the house.

"Are you hungry? Do you want some dinner?"

"No, thanks. Vic had trays sent up from the mess, the gentleman." She passed her brother-in-law in his armchair. "Hi, George."

He flipped over a sheet of stationery on his lap. "Hiya, Helen."

She entered the nursery, where Jay-Jay lay on a makeshift bed, his rump in the air, his mouth in a soft circle. Sweet pain thumped behind Helen's breastbone, as it always did when she watched her baby sleep.

Such a tiny person, dependent on her alone. Had she made the right decision to go to work? She needed to provide a home for him so she could learn to discipline him away from his grandparents' spoiling. But in the process she spent so much time away. Was she helping or hurting?

"He looks innocent now," Betty said. "And yet . . ."

Sure, Betty could be smug. Judy's first birthday wasn't until next week. Jay-Jay hadn't thrown a tantrum at that age either.

Helen stooped and lifted her son. His sleepy muscles twitched until he snuggled against her. She stood slowly so she wouldn't fall.

Betty tucked Jay-Jay's blue blanket under his shoulders. "He sure has a temper."

Yes, he did. Helen shivered and hugged her son closer. Boys emulated their fathers. This was why she'd constructed her façade in the first place, so Jay-Jay would emulate the Jim she designed, not the real Jim.

But what if he carried his father's nature deep inside? What if she couldn't discipline it out of him?

Helen pressed her cheek against the soft little face on her shoulder. *Lord, please don't let him turn out like his father.*

✳

65th General Hospital; Botesdale, Suffolk
Saturday, June 24, 1944

Ray strode around the lake that snaked across Redgrave Park, the old manor the hospital camped on. If only he could dive in and swim off his anger. Ray had been assigned to the 94th Bomb Group, Jack's group. Jack had interfered, and he'd keep interfering and give Ray some safe ground job.

If that weren't enough, fresh anger pulsed hot inside— anger at himself.

On the train he'd read a letter from George Anello. According to George, Helen looked worse than after Jim died, distraught and frazzled.

Ray thought he'd done her a favor in leaving, but had he? His love sparked the fire that devastated her life, and he didn't even stick around to help sweep up the ashes.

What could he do? All he could offer was a letter, but would she want to hear from him?

He picked up a pebble and chucked it across the lake. As a minister, as a man who loved her, as the only person who knew about Jim, he had a duty. Tonight he'd write her. "Lord, tell me what to say."

The park spread around him, lush green rolling land. Jack's nurse said he and some friends had come down by the lake. Patients strolled among the trees in the sunshine, chatting and smoking. Under an ancient oak, a wheelchair stood empty, and a patient sat on a blanket necking with a redhead in a light blue suit.

Jack. Sure didn't take him long to get over Ruth.

"Ray? Is that you?" Jack's best friend, Maj. Charlie de Groot, jogged up behind him, holding the hand of a petite blonde in a uniform the same gray-blue as Jack's girl wore. "Glad I caught you. Why don't you give the skipper a bit more time?"

"Time? Looks as if he's making pretty good time."

The blonde laughed. "Over a year in the making."

A year? Of course. The blonde's uniform bore a caduceus and golden wings. She was a flight nurse . . . and so was Ruth. So Jack had glued things back together after all.

Charlie put his arm around her shoulder. "May, this is Jack's older and better brother. Ray, this is my girlfriend, Lt. May Jensen."

Ray saluted her. "Older, yes. Better, no."

"Definitely more humble." May's smile glowed against porcelain skin.

"Say, looks like they took a break," Charlie said.

They headed for the tree, where Jack gathered Ruth close for another kiss. But Ray couldn't wait. He had to be back at the CCRC by 1700 hours, and he needed to confront Jack. Now.

"Hi, Jack."

Jack looked up and lifted an enormous grin. "Hey! Hi, everyone. Guess what? We're getting married."

May squealed and knelt on the blanket to hug Ruth. Ray and Charlie shook Jack's hand and sat cross-legged on the brown Army blanket. Jack introduced his fiancée, Lt. Ruth Doherty, an auburn-haired beauty with a Chicago accent.

For the second time in as many months, Ray felt the ugly nip of jealousy. Both his brothers would beat him to the altar. But jealousy destroyed all it touched, and Ray refused to indulge. He put on a smile. "So, little brother, you found some more glue."

Ruth rearranged a sling over a cast in a protective, don't-ask-how-I-broke-my-arm sort of way. "We decided to build with something more permanent than glue."

Ray gave her an appreciative nod. At least his future sister-in-law wasn't empty-headed like that girl Jack had dated in seminary.

"So, Skipper, regret that transfer to the Pacific?" Charlie plucked a blade of grass and stuck it between his teeth.

"You bet. First thing Monday, I'll contact Colonel Dougher and cancel it." He squeezed Ruth's shoulder. "You're engaged to the new air executive of the 94th Bombardment Group."

Ray hated to add tension to a joyful day, but he needed to bring this up now. He leaned forward, his hands clasped, his elbows pressed into his knees. "We'll be spending lots of time together then."

Jack swung a grin to him. "You got your assignment."

"Your doing?" His voice came out tight.

"Dead right. Dougher will treat you well."

Ray gave his brother a steady, firm gaze. "Promise me one thing—no special treatment. I expect to fly the dangerous missions, same as the other pilots."

Jack's smile froze. "You realize we'll assign you where you'll serve best."

Ray pictured himself swimming leisurely laps in that cold lake. "If I wanted a noncombat position, I would have stayed stateside. I came here for one reason—to fly a combat tour."

"But you have skills and talents—"

"If I weren't your brother, what would you do? If you didn't know me?"

"But I do know you, and you'll do best—"

"I'm a qualified pilot. I've flown with the Army Air Force for four years, over a year and a half in a B-17, far more than those teenagers you send up every day without question. And I requested combat. Don't stop me."

Charlie stretched stocky legs in front of him. "Watch it, Jack. You're a changed man. Don't start manipulating again."

Jack closed his eyes and sighed. "I don't mean to manipulate. Really."

"So don't," Ray said. "I'd rather not talk to the CO about this."

Jack groaned and rolled his gaze away. "I won't interfere."

"Good." Ruth lifted her cast with a scribbled engagement ring on it. "I'd hate to return this, but I only agreed to marry the new, improved Jack Novak."

Laughter circled the group. Ray set his hands on the blanket behind him, leaned back, and gazed up through the branches. He'd won that battle.

But that was a battle of words, his forte, and required only a bit more backbone than his usual negotiations. What would he do when bullets came his way?

Ray chuckled. He couldn't believe he'd fought for the right to fight.

17

Antioch
Friday, June 30, 1944

Vic opened the car door for Helen. "Why don't you freshen up? Then we can get dinner, celebrate your first paycheck—and our engagement."

The only thing Helen wanted to celebrate was getting home at a decent hour. She raised a sweet smile. "Good night. See you Monday."

She headed up the walkway to the Carlisle home. In her last letter, Mama said the only way to deal with such persistence was to be firm and never encourage him.

Mama gave the same advice about dealing with Jay-Jay's temper—be firm and never give in, the way she'd dealt with Helen's tantrums. Helen had learned to control her temper. Jim hadn't.

Mr. Carlisle sat in his armchair with the *Ledger*, its headlines declaring, "Progress on Saipan" and "Asparagus Season at an End." He lowered the paper and smiled at Helen. "How was your day?"

"Great. Got my first paycheck. Not much, but a start." She headed for the kitchen and Jay-Jay's sweet giggles. On the days Helen worked, Mrs. Carlisle now picked up Jay-Jay at Betty's after the dress shop closed.

"Well?" Mr. Carlisle said.

"Well, what?"

He held out his hand. "The paycheck."

Her fingers curled around the precious piece of paper. "I'll open an account on Tuesday."

"You have Jim's account."

A chill crept down Helen's arms. "But he willed it to you. My name isn't on it. I can't even write a check."

"Yes, of course. A man should manage his family's finances."

"I can handle my own account."

He set the newspaper on the end table and gave her a soft smile. "How would it look if the daughter-in-law of a bank director was reduced to handling her own finances? As if I couldn't take care of you."

"But I—"

"Why would you need it anyway? I've always given you a generous allowance."

"Yes, but I need to buy household goods so I can get my own place."

Mr. Carlisle walked over with the tall, lean frame he'd passed to Jim. "I'll set aside a portion of your paycheck for that after you've settled your debt."

Her breath caught. "Debt?"

"You burned down my house. It'll cost a thousand dollars to rebuild. And I can't use Jim's money. There's just enough to support the two of you until Jay-Jay turns eighteen. See? This is why I need to make the financial decisions."

"Didn't the house insurance—"

"Insurance? Insurance is a scam that preys on men who don't trust God to provide."

Helen's face grew as cold as her arms. Yes, the Lord would provide—with her paycheck.

Mr. Carlisle plucked the check from her icicle fingers, and she turned to the kitchen. Vic paid her fifty dollars a month. How long would it take to pay off that debt? How long until she could get a place of her own? Almost two years. The thought suffocated her.

In the kitchen, Mrs. Carlisle stood at the stove, and Jay-Jay sat behind her, swatting her calves with a wooden spoon. She winced at each stroke but said nothing.

Helen gasped and dragged her son back. "Jay-Jay! Don't hit your grandmother."

He screamed in protest.

"He's fine." Mrs. Carlisle gave a limp smile. "He was playing drums, and I ran out of pans. It's my fault."

"Your fault? He's the one hitting." Helen snatched the spoon from her son.

"No! My poon." Jay-Jay smacked her in the shoulder.

Panic welled up, but she'd be firm and not give in. "No hitting."

Jay-Jay howled and flung himself to the floor.

"Oh dear." Mrs. Carlisle wrung her hands. "You'll ruin his spirit."

Helen cared less about his spirit than his character, but what could she do with those flailing limbs? Mama said she mustn't be afraid to discipline him. She *was* afraid, wasn't she? Because of Jim. But if she didn't overcome this fear, a greater fear would come to pass, and Jay-Jay would be as violent as his father.

Helen pried her son from the floor, restrained him, and pushed open the door with her backside.

"What are you doing with the boy?" Mr. Carlisle said.

"I'm putting him in his room until dinner," she said over

her son's screams, and she dodged a flying fist. She had lots of practice at that.

"It's dinnertime now."

"He can eat after he calms down."

"He needs dinner. He's a growing boy." Mr. Carlisle took away her son as easily as he'd taken her paycheck.

Jay-Jay clutched his grandfather around the neck and scowled at Helen.

She wrapped her arms around her middle to stop the queasiness. He was a growing boy, all right—growing to be like his father.

☆

Bury St. Edmunds Airfield, Suffolk
Saturday, July 8, 1944

Ray's vision strained through the darkness down the partially lit runway. He kept his foot on the brakes of *One O'Clock Jump*, his B-17G. *Jump* had sixty-eight bomb symbols painted on her nose, one for each mission. Rookies never received brand-new Forts.

Jump's four Wright-Cyclone R-1820 engines ran against the brakes at full throttle, rumbling the length of the plane, and Ray's heart throbbed in unison with the engines. He pulled a deep breath, expanding his chest under heavy layers of flight gear—undershirt, wool shirt, Mae West life preserver, parachute harness, and a new alpaca-lined duck cloth flight jacket.

"Tail wheel locked?" he asked.

"Check." Lt. Leo Goldman, the copilot, shot him a glance.

Yep, Ray had already asked twice, but he couldn't afford to have anything go wrong on his first mission, especially with his younger brother in the control tower.

At 0337, thirty seconds after the previous plane took off, a green flare shot from the control van at the head of the runway.

Ray's heart slammed into his throat. When the Lord had sent Gideon to battle, he'd said, "Go in this thy might." But was Ray's might enough?

He released the brakes, and the Flying Fortress lumbered down the runway, bouncing and shivering, heavy with a load of bombs for the German supply installation at Méry-sur-Oise in the northern outskirts of Paris.

At 115 miles per hour, he eased back the control wheel, and *Jump* lifted from the ground. He gave the brakes a little press to stop the spin on the wheels. "Wheels up."

Goldman flipped the switch on the control panel. "Check."

Ray reduced the throttles until he reached a speed of 150 miles per hour and a rate of climb of 300 feet per minute.

"Tail gunner to pilot. Can we go back?" Staff Sgt. Harland Burgess's voice whined in Ray's earphones. "I've gotta pee."

Ray smiled. He wasn't alone in his fears. "Should have thought of that before we left."

"I did. I went eight times."

"Use the relief tube, but do it now, before it gets too cold."

Goldman laughed. "Yeah. I heard of a fellow got frozen to the tube. They had to amputate. Now he's joining the WACs."

Ray tried to give his copilot a stern look, but he laughed. "Don't believe him, Burgess. You know they tell those stories just to frighten us rookies."

Two minutes had passed since takeoff, so Ray made a half-needle-width turn to the left. He scanned the black sky for the Aldis lamps that flashed in each plane's tail to aid in assembly. The night was clear over England, although the weather officer predicted clouds over France. If they couldn't bomb visually, they'd go for a secondary target.

By the time the sun rose, Ray would be over enemy territory.

Would he live to see the sun set? He huffed into his oxygen mask. *Lord, take away these thoughts.*

Over the next half hour, he climbed in a rectangular pattern. With each turn, the Forts closed ranks. First, Ray joined his V-shaped three-plane element, then the twelve-plane *A* group with Colonel Dougher in the lead, and finally the 36-plane combat box.

The group made a dogleg turn and headed for the English coast. The forty bomb groups of the Eighth Air Force were dividing forces to hit multiple transportation and supply targets throughout France.

"Ten thousand feet, Goldman," Ray said. "Start oxygen checks every fifteen minutes."

The copilot called on the interphone to the ten crew members stationed throughout the plane. They'd been on oxygen the entire flight to improve night vision, but at higher altitudes it became essential for life.

Ray gazed through the window in the ceiling of the cockpit. To his left above, Draco the dragon coiled his starry body. Today Ray would face the Nazi dragon belching fiery bullets and shells, but could he handle it? Could he bury his sword in the dragon of cowardice lurking in his heart? Did he even have a sword?

"Tail gunner to pilot," Burgess called on the interphone. "Pops, I don't feel so good. I don't think I'm getting enough oxygen."

The nickname had stuck, but Ray didn't mind. Only one of these boys was over twenty-one. They weren't even old enough to vote. "Did you get a good shave, Burge? Is your mask tight enough?"

"Yes, sir."

"He shaved last week," Goldman said. "He's good till September."

Ray smiled. "Check the connection, the regulator."

"I did. Everything looks fine, but I feel woozy."

Classic case of nerves. "Take deep breaths, relax, and pray."

"Yes, sir. 'Hail, Mary, full of grace—' "

"Keep the interphone clear, please."

"That's right, sir. No chatter."

Yes, they needed to keep the interphone clear, but prayer was more than chatter. As the corrugated hose on Ray's mask connected him to oxygen, prayer connected him to the only source of life and power.

He'd spent lots of time at the Lord's feet in preparation for today. Was Helen finding comfort and strength in his presence as well?

He couldn't stop thinking about her and loving her. Had she received any of his letters yet? He planned to send one or two each week until she responded or until George said she didn't welcome his correspondence.

" 'There'll be bluebirds over the white cliffs of Dover,' " sang out Technical Sgt. Hank Hewett, the flight engineer, in the cockpit behind Ray.

Yeah, those cliffs rose above the Channel fifteen thousand feet below, but it was still too dark to see them.

"Tomorrow, cats and something orange," Hewett sang. "Ooh, look at the pretty stars."

What on earth? Ray glanced behind him.

Although they were over friendly territory, Hewett stood on the platform for the top gun turret, his forearms draped over the handles, and he spun the turret around. "Whee!"

"Hewett?"

"Stars, stars, so many stars."

Was he hysterical, or was this the first sign of anoxia? "Goldman, get him down before he shoots somebody. Hook him up to a portable oxygen bottle. Buffo, do an oxygen check," Ray called to the bombardier down in the nose section. "Buffo?"

Ray and Goldman exchanged a worried glance. "Radovich, what's Buffo doing?" he asked the navigator.

"Something's wrong. He's staring into space."

"Get him on oxygen. Burgess, how are you doing?"

"My lips are tingling, Pops."

"Get on oxygen." Feeling light-headed himself, he flipped the radio switch overhead to command mode and informed Dougher he was turning back.

Ray put the Fort into a gentle dive and glanced up to Draco with a sick feeling in his stomach. His dragon would live to see another day, but what choice did Ray have? At twenty thousand feet without oxygen, a man could pass out in three minutes and die in twenty, and the portable bottles held only a fifteen-minute supply.

Once clear of the formation, he throttled back and pushed the control wheel forward so he could get below ten thousand feet as soon as possible.

Facing combat might be easier than returning to base. An abort on his first mission would look bad. Especially to Jack.

★

"Nothing wrong with this bird." Technical Sergeant Bodey, Ray's ground crew chief, dropped to the ground from *Jump*'s nose hatch.

Ray groaned. "The regulator? The valves? The tanks?"

Bodey bowed his head of silver hair and rubbed his chin with the blackened fingers of a lifelong mechanic. "Listen, son. The B-17 has eighteen G-1 cylinders in four separate systems to limit the effects of battle damage. What you described would be the failure of three of these systems without a single bullet hitting her."

Ray's gaze flicked to his brother, who leaned on crutches beside him. "All I know is three of my crewmembers showed signs of anoxia, and several others felt light-headed or nauseated."

Bodey ambled past Jack and toward the ground crew's repair shack. "First mission."

"Yep," Jack said in a clipped voice.

Ray blew out a puff of air. Did they think his crew suffered mass hysteria? Mass cowardice?

"Changed your mind about flying combat?"

"Of course not. There must be something he didn't check."

"Bodey's our most experienced chief. He's been working with planes since before I was born. Besides, *One O'Clock Jump* just came back from a complete overhaul at the Strategic Air Depot at Troston. She's in A-1 shape."

Ray gazed down the length of the plane, from her Plexiglas-capped nose to her bell-shaped tail fin. "I didn't chicken out. I was ready."

Jack's crutches shuffled on the tarmac. "We could use a good instructor here. Fellows always need brushing up—"

"I'll do fine next time, I promise."

"There won't be a next time."

"Jack—"

"Do you know how much an abort costs? Not just fuel and time and effort, but the cost to the group? The 94th went to enemy territory without your bombs, without your defensive firepower, and with a dangerous hole in the formation."

"It won't happen again."

Jack glanced toward the control tower. "Don't you see? If I let you fly, they'll think I gave you leeway because you're my brother."

Ray waited, his chest tight, until Jack looked him in the eye. "What would you do if another pilot aborted?"

"It was your first mission."

"Exactly. Would you pull a pilot for a single aborted mission after all the Army Air Force invested in training?"

Jack let out a long, low sigh.

"One more chance, Jack. One more. If I abort again, I'll pull myself."

He hobbled away on his crutches. "Fine. But this isn't some baseball game. This is war."

Ray nodded. Some wars were internal.

18

Antioch
Tuesday, July 11, 1944

Her throat tight, Helen examined the letter under the lamp on her nightstand. Ray was the sweetest man she knew, and she'd shoved him away.

When George handed her the sheet of airmail stationery after work the night before, she couldn't believe Ray had written her. But that was her name in the salutation.

Helen ran her finger over the ink. He must have gotten excellent marks in penmanship—so handsome, with a neat slant and even loops. She liked the way her name looked in his hand.

A breeze fluttered the curtains, but too warm to cool down her room. She sat on her bed in a cotton nightgown with her hair piled up, the pillow hot behind her back. Perspiration prickled her neck and sides, and dampness clung to her eyes as she studied Ray's letter.

All day long, while at Ladies' Circle and while running errands with Jay-Jay, she'd pondered how to respond. Now that Jay-Jay was tucked in bed, she could do so.

Once again, she read Ray's first sentence: "I'll understand if this letter isn't welcome or if you don't want to respond, but I enjoyed our friendship and would like to correspond with you."

This was no overture to a romantic second act, but a pastor

reaching out to a broken person. In her brokenness, Helen placed a sheet of stationery on the box propped on her knees. Perhaps she could sort out the mess of her life through this correspondence, not only from Ray's wisdom, but also the very act of writing.

She uncapped her pen. "Lord, help me know what to say and what not to."

> Dear Ray,
> Thank you so much for your letter. I'm pleased to hear you're doing well at the training center. What a joy for you to fly again and to see your brother. I know the Lord will be with you and keep you safe, and that you'll do well in your new position.

Helen huffed out a sigh. If only she could write, "Please, please forgive me for calling you a coward. I spoke in anger—rash, unthinking words, and I love you as you are, gentle and kind and thoughtful." Instead she wrote:

> My job is going well, although the hours are long and I'm falling behind in my volunteer work. The town proved it can function without me and raised $440,000 in the Fifth War Loan, 126 percent of our goal, while northern California came in at only 39 percent of its goal. However, our Red Cross branch is far behind in preparing surgical dressings, and I long to help. Most of all, I miss my heart's work, what I do best and serves the Lord most.
> I remind myself this is necessary so I can

get my own place. I try to be firm with Jay-Jay,
but it's hard with doting grandparents in the
house.

Helen leaned her head back against the wall. That ran deeper than she could reveal. Over dinner, Mr. Carlisle called his wife stupid for forgetting the pepper in the meatloaf, and she'd agreed with effusive apologies.

Jim used to belittle Helen like that, and she'd learned to apologize for her failings, hoping to stave off a beating. Sometimes it worked. Sometimes it didn't.

Did Mr. Carlisle beat his wife? Was that why she was such a shrunken, pathetic thing?

Even in the summer heat, Helen shivered. If Jim had lived, would she have shrunk as well? They'd only been married three and a half years, the last blessed year apart thanks to the institution of the draft. Helen had nudged Jim to patriotism. Wasn't it better to volunteer and pick his service than to let Uncle Sam draft him and make the decision? He chose the Navy, and Helen told him what a hero he was, her brave husband, she said, swinging the Grim Reaper's scythe, longing to be widowed, to be released.

She clenched her arms around her middle, and the sweat on her stomach soaked through to her bare arms. Some words could never be written.

✦

Over France
Friday, July 14, 1944

"There's the next bonfire," Lt. Earl Radovich called from the navigator's desk down in *One O'Clock Jump*'s nose compartment. "Right on course."

"Check," Ray said. Two thousand feet below in the darkness, an orange dot throbbed on French soil, as if imitating the sliver of rising sun ahead on the horizon.

He nudged the control wheel forward to descend to five hundred feet for the supply drop to French resistance fighters. Instead of using radio navigational aids that might tip off the Germans, the 94th Bomb Group had only the ancient glow of bonfires to guide them.

The long black shapes of the thirty-three other B-17s stood out against the reddening sky.

This mission was a test for Ray, and he knew it. The medium-altitude approach meant no oxygen and no excuse to abort. Not that he needed it—no odd singing from Hewett, no trance from Buffo, no tingling lips from Burgess. And no fear in Ray. None. Nothing but peace.

What Jack couldn't have known was how the nature of the mission removed Ray's concern about killing people. Unless a supply canister hit someone on the head.

"Excuse me, kind sirs." Between the pilots' seats, Lt. John Buffo, the bombardier, wiggled his large frame out of the passageway from the nose compartment. "Perhaps the Army Air Force wasn't the most appropriate choice for a man of my delicate constitution."

"Who else would take you, Proffo?" Goldman said.

Ray grinned at the juxtaposition of an English professor's brain with the name and body of a football lineman.

Buffo squeezed past Hewett's top gun turret to check on the supply canisters in the bomb bay. "Curse my keen mind and love of all things aerial."

By the time Buffo returned, the day had brightened to yellow, the planes to silver, and the lead Forts sprouted wheels beneath them like birds poised to grab a telephone wire.

Ray checked the altimeter. "Thousand feet. Lower the landing gear."

Beside him, Leo Goldman flipped the switch. "Check."

"Bomb bay doors open," Buffo said.

The grinding of the undercarriage added to the engine noise, and *Jump*'s speed fell as planned to increase the accuracy of the drop.

The land below beckoned with wooded hills and wide green meadows. The French Maquis had chosen a sparsely populated area in the Rhône Valley for the drop, while the rest of the Third Bombardment Division delivered supplies in six other regions, and the B-24 Liberators of Second Division hit airfields as a diversion.

Eight hundred feet, seven hundred, and the flying grew tricky even at the reduced speed of 130 miles per hour. Ray kept a close eye on the formation and the terrain. Five hundred feet wasn't quite buzzing, but close.

"We're approaching Area 5-A." Radovich used the code for the classified area. If shot down and interrogated, they could compromise the resistance if they knew too much.

"I see them." Buffo had the best view from the clear conical nose.

The lead plane released its load, and the others followed suit as they crossed the target area.

"Canisters away." Buffo released twelve 300-pound containers of food, medical supplies, and ammunition, and tiny parachutes blossomed in red, white, and blue for Bastille Day.

"They're waving," Buffo said. "I think—yes, they're giving us the V for Victory."

Ray stole a quick glance below, where miniature people waved and blew kisses. He snapped his gaze back to the formation, the altimeter, and the airspeed indicator. His throat and heart felt full. Those men and women had lived under the fist of Nazi tyranny for four years. They risked their lives to aid fugitives, commit sabotage, and gather intelligence. True heroes.

They couldn't see him, but he saluted anyway. "May you celebrate next Bastille Day in freedom."

Ray thought he was so brave flying a plane over enemy territory, but he was high above, not down there making hard decisions. What was best? To submit to authority as the Bible taught? Or to resist evil schemes as the Bible also taught?

With the landing gear tucked in place, Ray gained speed and altitude and wheeled away with the group. The Germans hadn't sent up the Luftwaffe or any antiaircraft fire—yet. He busied himself with the hard work of flying a four-engine bomber in formation, glad his crewmates would handle the shooting if it came.

"Say, fellows, keep an eye on that cloud at two o'clock high," Hewett said, his head in the Plexiglas bubble in the roof behind Ray. "I saw flashes."

"Buffo, Hewett, watch that area," Goldman said. "The rest of you watch your sectors."

One O'Clock Jump had twelve guns. Buffo had twin .50 caliber machine guns in the chin turret, while Radovich manned a single in each cheek, and Hewett had twin guns in the top turret. Back in the waist compartment, Tucker and Paladino worked .50s in each window, and Finley curled around two guns in the ball turret hanging below the fuselage. Off by himself, Burgess operated the two stingers in the tail.

Ray glanced up to the right. The silver flashes grew bigger, and Ray's stomach twisted around itself. The seat-pack parachute felt reassuring under his backside, but he didn't feel like practicing his German today. *Lord, please get me through this. Don't let me do something stupid.*

Hewett spun the top turret. "Okay, boys, bogies at two o'clock high."

Ray drew a deep breath, which caught on his dry throat. Stay in formation. No evasive maneuvers. Concentrate on flying, let the gunners do their jobs. Keep calm. Keep steady. Keep praying.

The flashes took shape—eight little single-engine Messerschmitt 109s, fast and nimble.

"Reminds me of a poem," Buffo said on the interphone. " 'Storm'd at with shot and shell, boldly they rode and well, into the jaws of Death.' "

" 'Charge of the Light Brigade,' " Ray said.

"That it is. Alfred, Lord Tennyson."

"They all died."

"Not all."

"Leave it to the prof to cheer us up," Goldman said. "Why don't you assign a twenty-page term paper while you're at it?"

As the fighters zoomed in, Ray understood the brigadiers better. Their courage took a different form than that of the Maquis, to charge forward into danger when they had no other option.

" 'Theirs not to make reply, theirs not to reason why, theirs but to do and die, into the valley of Death rode the Six Hundred.' "

Goldman hunched his shoulders and groaned. "Thanks, Proffo. Now you've got Pops spouting doom and gloom."

Right. He shouldn't be chattering in the first place, and as a pastor, he should speak words of comfort, but how could he when the lead Me 109 tipped and dived, spitting death at the high squadron?

Some men liked adrenaline, even longed for it, but Ray disliked the tinny taste of it, the erratic heartbeat, the tightened muscles, and the way it addled his brain.

Another Me 109 peeled off for the low squadron, but *Jump* was in the high element, to the inside of the combat box. The fighter zipped past the Forts to Ray's right, the fire of tracers crossing midair.

Burgess whooped from the tail. "They got him. He's going down."

Less than a second. It all took less than a second. The adrenaline chilled in a bilious pool in Ray's stomach. "Is there a chute?"

"Oh yeah, there is. Too bad. He'll come back up tomorrow."

Ray breathed out an unpatriotic sigh.

"Eyes open, boys," Goldman said. "Here come some more."

Six fighters swooped down like hornets, every which way, but Ray kept his hands steady on the controls and throttles. He had no choice but to forge ahead. Into the valley of Death. *"Yea, though I walk through the valley of the shadow of death, I will fear no evil: for thou art with me." Thou art with me. Thou art with me.*

Jump's guns opened in an ear-splitting staccato that jiggled the plane. German bullets frayed the trailing end of the right wing, but not the flaps or ailerons, nor any of the hydraulic lines, fuel lines, and control cables that ran through the wing. And Ray pressed on.

Then the fighters broke off the attack, and no one was injured, and not one bomber had fallen in the 94th, and they entered Normandy—Allied territory.

"Good job, men. Good job." Ray clapped Goldman on the shoulder. His cheeks hurt, his smile was so adrenaline-wide.

He couldn't wait to tell Helen, even if she never read the letter. He couldn't wait to see Jack's face. And for the first time ever, he wanted to buzz the tower.

19

Naval Magazine, Port Chicago
Monday, July 17, 1944

Vic had never kept Helen this late.

She leaned her elbows on the desk, pressed her fingers over bleary eyes, then fanned her hands out to the side. Yes, the clock actually read 10:10. A new record.

She closed her eyes. *Lord, I can't keep up like this. I need more time with Jay-Jay, more time with you. Please give me courage to speak up and wisdom to know what to say.*

Ray had both courage and wisdom.

In his last letter, he said God would give courage for Ray to get through combat and for Helen to face her battles.

A rush of warmth turned up her sleepy lips. He had sent three letters even though he hadn't received her replies. Sometimes, in censor-pleasing vagueness, he described the beauty of a sunrise from above the clouds or the quirks of the men at his base or the quaint villages in the area, and other times he delved deep and opened up about his fears and concerns.

When she wrote him the day before, she declared Sir Raymond the Valiant would slay his dragon as surely as Saint George had in olden days.

Helen headed into Vic's office. She had some slaying of her own to do. "It's late. I want to go home."

"Sure." Vic grinned and snapped shut the latches on his briefcase. "We got a lot done today."

Did they? It seemed like busywork to her. Papers passed back and forth, but the men's complaints never changed. Did the Navy send Vic only for appearance's sake?

He held the door open. "After you, my dear."

Helen looped her shoulder bag over her head and across her chest, and headed out the door. She stumbled over the threshold.

"Careful," he said. "Why don't you hold my arm?"

She marched down the hall and out into the cool night air. "I don't need your arm. I need to go home. It's late and I'm tired."

"See, if you married me, we wouldn't have to stay late. We could finish our work cuddled on the couch together."

Something solidified in Helen's mind. If it was courage, she'd grab hold of it. She stopped beside the car and faced Vic under the moonless sky. "Vic, this has to stop. I'm not going to marry you. Ever. I like you. I've always liked you as a friend, but if you keep up this nonsense with these late hours in the mistaken notion that I'll fall in love with you—well, I'm finding it hard to even like you."

The only light in the sky, the floodlights a mile away to help the night shift load two freighters, showed the droop in his eyes and the tightening of his cheeks.

She'd hurt him, but he wouldn't hurt her, not that way. Besides, she had to do this, and subtlety never worked with him. "I'm sorry, but I miss my little boy. I want to read him a story every night, and dance with him, and listen to his prayers, and tell him I love him. I haven't even seen him today."

Vic shifted his jaw to one side. "I'll take you home now."

She gripped her purse strap as if the Lord could use it to infuse her with strength. "I'll work from nine to six as we agreed. If you're not ready, I'll catch a bus. The Greyhound stops here in town, and it drops me a few blocks from home."

His chin lifted. "I won't have you riding the bus. I'll take you—"

An orange flash down by the river, blinding, as if the floodlights had turned into the sun.

Sound crashed into her ears, knocked her to the ground, like a door slamming, the doors of heaven slamming shut.

"What on earth?" Vic lay crumpled on the ground beside her.

The sky glowed yellow. Helen pushed herself up to her feet, and she winced. Broken glass from the car window poked her bare feet.

Bare? Where were her shoes?

There by the car. She'd been blown right out of them.

Thunder cracked, crashed, resounded, pitched her to the ground again. Sharp pain warmed her right cheek.

"We're under attack!" Vic scrambled to his feet. "The Japanese—they're bombing us."

All the air rushed from Helen's chest. A carrier strike? How did the Navy let a carrier so close? And the coastal defenses? No warning? None at all?

She ignored Vic's outstretched hand and reached for her shoes. "I need my shoes."

"Forget the stupid shoes. We've got to get to shelter."

"The glass. I need them." She slipped them on.

"Good God in heaven, help us." Vic stood still, hatless, his eyes enormous and directed north to the river.

Helen pulled herself up. The sight filled her eyes and paralyzed her heart.

White smoke towered thousands of feet in the air and

foamed over at the top. Red lines shot out in a horrid fire-works display.

"They must have . . ." Vic's voice came out raspy. "They must have hit the ship—one of the ships. The ordnance. Oh no, the men."

"How . . . how many?"

"Two shifts. Three hundred men."

The bottom dropped out of her heart. "We've got to get down there and help."

"Are you insane? We're under attack." He grabbed her arm and pulled her toward the building, but he stopped short.

One wall of the administration building was buckled, the roof sat at a crazy angle, and all the windows were blown out.

Whistles above. Thumps shook the earth.

Vic threw her to the ground and flung himself on top of her.

Under his weight, Helen turned her chin to look out. A glowing red chunk of metal the size of a door plunged into the ground and shook her. She cried out and tucked her face into the space between Vic's chest and the sidewalk. So this was what it was like for those poor people in Europe and Asia during air raids. Such helpless fear.

Where else were they bombing? Antioch didn't have any military targets except a small shipyard, but did the Japanese know? Did they care? "Oh Lord, Jay-Jay. Keep my baby safe."

Silence returned. And darkness. Such darkness.

"I think they're gone," Vic said.

"I never heard any planes."

"Me neither. Strange." He helped her up. "Let's get you someplace safe."

She shoved tangled hair off her face. "I need to help. The men on the docks, the ships, the barracks. Look at the admin-istration building. Imagine the barracks, right by the river."

"Don't be silly. It isn't safe."

"Safe?" She crossed her arms and felt rips in the sleeves of her suit. "It's war. There is no safe. I'm a trained Red Cross volunteer, I'm a doctor's daughter, and I have more than my share of experience with injuries."

"Helen—"

"Let's get to work." She headed back to the car. "We'll drive to the dispensary, pick up supplies—gauze, iodine, splints. Do you have a flashlight?"

"In the glove compart—Helen, this is crazy."

She set her hands on her hips. "Doing nothing would be crazy. If you won't drive me, I'll walk, but that'll waste precious time. Men are injured down there, bleeding, dying."

He paused. "Fine. I don't have time to argue. I've got to get down there myself."

After they brushed broken glass from the car seats, they drove to the dispensary. Aided by car headlights, a bucket brigade of men shuttled supplies from the partially collapsed building. One man called out instructions, a heavyset man wearing a navy blue service jacket, pajama pants, and a stethoscope.

Helen approached him. "Sir, my name's Helen Carlisle. I'm a Red Cross volunteer trained in first aid. I need gauze, iodine, splints, scissors, whatever you can spare."

He frowned and looked her up and down.

"She's with me, Dr. Thompson," Vic said. "And her father's a physician."

Dr. Thompson nodded. "Ever use a morphine syrette, young lady?"

"No, sir, but I've seen the training film, and I've watched my father give injections."

The doctor headed for a stack of boxes. "Take care of what you can down there. Send the serious cases here. They're setting up work gangs. Try to get those Negroes working for once."

Helen winced. From what she'd seen, the Negroes did all the work at Port Chicago.

With the car packed full of supplies and sailors, Vic drove down the dark road.

At the fork in the road, a Marine guard pointed them to the left. "Head to the barracks. That's where you're needed."

"Lots of bomb damage?" Vic asked.

"Bomb? That was no bomb. An accident, sabotage, I don't know, but the *E. A. Bryan* blew to smithereens. Not a bit left of her. Few seconds later, the *Quinault Victory* blew straight out of the water, broke to bits. Dock's gone, train's gone. Ain't nothing, nobody left down there. Ain't nothing you can do." He waved them down the road to the left.

Helen hunched in the seat behind the box of gauze bandages on her lap, squished between Vic and a pajama-clad officer who apologized in a Southern accent every time he bumped her. Nothing left? Nobody left? How many had been killed? And what would the barracks be like?

In silhouette, Vic's jaw jutted forward. "An explosion. Carver Jones warned them. He said this would happen." He pounded his fist on the steering wheel.

"Was he—was he working tonight?"

Vic's lips pulled tight. "We'll find out."

The barracks still stood—eighteen long, two-storied wooden buildings. The headlights showed window frames knocked out, collapsed roofs, and rubble all around. Men staggered out, supported buddies, or ran inside with flashlights and crowbars.

Vic parked the car so the headlights illuminated a dark doorway. "Okay, men, you four in the backseat, you're with me. You two in the front, stay with Mrs. Carlisle, set up a first aid station."

Helen spread blankets in the yellow wedge of light, and

the men piled up the boxes and gathered scraps of lumber for splints.

"Ma'am? You a nurse?" A man restrained another man as if he were under arrest. "My buddy—he got glass in his eye, keeps trying to rub it. He'll make it worse, I tell him."

"Your friend's right." Helen set her hands on the struggling shoulders, although the blue work shirt was splattered with blood and glass. "Please sit down, sir. Keep holding his hands," she said to his friend.

Her patient eased himself down, writhing and cursing.

"Sir, I need you to be calm and still." Helen knelt in front of him. She gently pulled down his lower right eyelid and used a square of gauze to lift loose glass particles. "Very still, sir."

His good eye honed in on her. "Ain't never had no white woman call me sir before."

She gave him a slight smile. "Then it's a night of firsts for both of us. I've never removed glass from a man's eye before."

She folded back his upper eyelid and repeated the process. Dr. Thompson would have to take care of the glass that had already penetrated the eye. By the time she'd placed a loose bandage around her patient's head, a dozen men stood in line for care. The Southerner in pajamas rinsed wounds with water from a bucket, and the other officer loaded seriously wounded men onto a truck. Helen sent her patient with him.

"Helen! Helen!" Vic ran up, supporting a man in torn work clothes. "It's Carver. I pulled him from under some timbers. He's cut up. I think his arm's broken. I gave him some morphine." He helped Jones lie down on the blanket, and then he ran off on his scissor legs.

Helen pulled her lipstick from her shoulder bag. "Pardon the indignity, Mr. Jones, but Dr. Thompson needs to know about the morphine." She wrote "MS 10:45" in red on his forehead, glad she knew the abbreviation for morphine sulfate from helping Papa in his office.

Jones groaned and clutched his arm to his stomach. Bloody gashes ran across his chest.

"All right. I'm going to look at that arm." Helen snipped open his shirtsleeve.

In the slanted, shadowy light, red blood glistened on blue fabric.

Jim had worn the same uniform.

How much had he bled before he died? How much pain did he bear? Did he die instantly or agonize for hours? Even after all he'd done, he didn't deserve to suffer like that. No one did.

Helen gasped from the pain of it and turned away for supplies. She arranged two lumber scraps on either side of Jones's broken arm and secured them with gauze.

She shivered in the cool air. *Oh Lord, forgive me. I wanted Jim to suffer as I did.*

What kind of woman wished her own husband dead?

20

**Over Germany
Tuesday, July 18, 1944**

Ray stroked the control wheel between gloved fingers. Black puffs from exploding antiaircraft shells dirtied the blue sky and the thick white clouds below, and *One O'Clock Jump* trembled whenever one burst too near. The men hated flak more than fighters because they couldn't shoot back. Ray felt the opposite. The fighter pilot looked a man in the eye and vowed to kill, but the antiaircraft gunners twenty thousand feet below aimed at radar blips, protecting their homeland.

Could Ray blame them? *Jump* carried four tons of bombs to destroy an oil refinery at Kiel. Without oil, Germany would perish.

Ray's vision darkened again, and he drew a rubbery-tasting draft through his oxygen mask. Despite what Sergeant Bodey said, something was wrong. "Oxygen check, Goldman."

The copilot waved a hand in loose circles. His dark eyelashes fluttered.

Ray shook Goldman's arm. "Goldman! Leo! Wake up. Hewett, get a portable on him. Radovich, how much longer to the target?"

"About ten minutes."

"Left waist to pilot. Paladino passed out. I've got him on oxygen."

"Thanks, Tucker." He flew through a spent shell. Black smoke snaked over the windscreen, shrapnel pinged against the fuselage, and Ray blinked.

He couldn't turn back with a full bomb rack when the flak was picking up. After the first abort, someone painted "Chicken Coop" on *Jump*'s nose. Even after the successful supply drop, Jack would want him pulled if he failed to complete this mission.

Or was he endangering ten lives—for what reason? To prove himself a man? To win Dad's respect? To earn God's favor? What a bunch of baloney. Had he lost his mind? People were shooting at him, his men were passing out, and for what? For what?

"Novak!" Someone tugged at his mask.

Ray blinked at Hewett's pale, freckled, frightened face. "What?"

"You nodded off. Take a deep breath. I hooked you to portable oxygen."

He'd passed out? For how long?

Goldman, wide-awake, manned the wheel. "Okay, fellows, listen up. We've got to finish this mission. No one calls us chicken. Everyone get a portable and keep an eye on your buddies. Take turns refilling from the main oxygen system."

Ray settled the yellow oxygen tank on his lap and studied the controls. "How much farther, Radovich?"

"We should be there. Don't know why the lead hasn't dropped."

"Radio to pilot. I know why. The wing command ship says the H2X isn't working. Head for the secondary."

The radar failed. Swell. The secondary target at Cuxhaven lay a hundred miles behind them, forty minutes plus time for the complex act of turning in formation. How long would the portables hold out? What if he and Goldman passed out at the same time?

Ray groaned. He flipped the radio switch overhead to command mode and informed his squadron commander he was returning to base.

"Again?" The major's sarcastic tone drove like a corkscrew into Ray's head.

He lowered the plane from her slot in the formation. The group would turn right, so Ray turned left to cross the Jutland peninsula just south of the Danish border. Aiming for the layer of altostratus below, he let *Jump* build to 200 miles per hour. "Radovich, got a new course plotted?"

"Highly unlikely," Buffo said. "He was drawing bunnies on the map. Yes, I put him on oxygen."

Jump plunged into the milky pool of clouds, and Ray kept a close eye on the panel. Pilots sometimes succumbed to vertigo and found themselves upside down. As long as he trusted his instruments rather than his instincts, he'd be glad to snuggle in the cloud's protection.

But at 12,000 feet, the clouds broke up. Below him stretched German land in neat squares of green with clusters of red-roofed buildings.

Ray had never felt so exposed, even when he'd forgotten his towel and had to air-dry after swimming in the San Joaquin. He could still see Helen's amused shock and feel her kiss.

He shook his head hard. "Boys, keep an eye out for fighters."

"Excellent idea," Buffo said. "There's a Nazi airfield about ten miles ahead."

"Can we skirt it?"

"They'll still see us."

"Say, Pops." Goldman's grin pushed up his cheeks. "Still got our bombs. Can't let them go to waste."

Ray shifted in his seat. He didn't like the idea, but his duty was to seek a target of opportunity. Perhaps they could destroy planes on the ground and keep them from the air.

"All right. Buffo, you can use that Norden bombsight for once." With radar-bearing Pathfinder Force planes in the lead, most of the bombardiers had nothing to do but flip the toggle switch when the PFF plane dropped.

"Nine thousand feet. Leveling off for the bomb run." Ray ripped off his oxygen mask and activated the Automatic Flight Control Equipment. With the AFCE and the bombsight, Buffo adjusted *Jump*'s course to line up the target.

In a few minutes, the airfield came into sight with crossing runways, blocky hangars, and flecks of planes. Flak burst in ugly black polka dots about a thousand feet too high.

"Strangest-looking planes," Buffo said. "Almost triangular."

Ray frowned. At the Eighth Air Force bases, rumors festered about experimental Luftwaffe planes. "Schmidt, make sure the strike camera's on."

"Yes, sir," the radio operator said. "We want proof of this. I don't want to hear any more clucking in the Nissen hut. We're no chickens."

"True," Buffo said. "But we're laying some eggs. Bombs away."

Jump bounced higher, relieved of her load.

"Oh no," Burgess whined from the tail. "Three fighters. Five o'clock high."

Ray groaned and shoved the wheel forward. A fighter could outdive a heavy bomber, but any extra speed would help, and the changing altitude would throw off the aim of the flak gunners.

"Okay, boys," Goldman said. "Remember your training. No chatter. Don't forget to lead. Fire in short bursts so you don't burn out your gun barrels."

The airspeed indicator read 270, the maximum according

to the manual, but Ray aimed for 310, knowing pilots had pushed it to 350 or above. The higher the speed, the longer it would take the fighters to close the gap, and the better fix his gunners could get.

"They're firing," Burgess cried. "Ha! Look at that. The tracers aren't even close."

Too far away. Good. Perhaps they were young and inexperienced. Perhaps they'd use up their ammo and fuel before they did any damage.

Ray's ears popped. The seat belt cut into his thigh.

"They're coming," Burgess said. "One at six o'clock level, one at five, one at four."

Six o'clock? Didn't every Luftwaffe pilot know a rear attack on a Fort was suicidal?

"Got one in my sights," Paladino called from the right waist. "Hewett, Finley, be ready for the break."

Ray glued his gaze to the controls. His heart whapped against his ribcage.

Guns chattered, pops rang out on the fuselage, Hewett swung his guns overhead, and a shadow flashed over the cockpit. Hewett cursed. "Missed."

"Damage?" Ray said.

"Took a shot at me," Paladino said. "Just added some ventilation holes."

"He's coming right at me," Burgess cried. "Oh no, oh no, oh no."

"Well, shoot, you dimwit," Goldman said.

"I am. I am." Then he whooped so loudly, Ray cringed from the volume in his earphones.

"Well, I'll be," Finley said from down in the ball turret. "The dimwit got the first kill. Look at him tumble. Woo! He exploded."

Ray's stomach contracted. A man had died a fiery death,

and everyone rejoiced. But the next fighter made a pass and laid a row of bullets across the wing. The only way for his ten men to survive was for the other two men to die or decide to leave.

What a horrible thing war was. But Ray had chosen it.

The ground zoomed closer. When he leveled off, he'd lose speed and bear the worst of the attack. What altitude should he pick?

The deck. He'd hit the deck.

He laughed at the thought. He took her down to fifty feet and buzzed white houses with red roofs. People on the ground held their hats against the propwash and gaped at the sight.

Ray kicked the rudder to slip to the side around a church spire. He'd always wanted to see Germany, but he didn't think he'd see it so close until after the war.

"The fighters are staying away," Tucker said from the waist.

Of course. They wouldn't fire on their own people.

Once out of town, Ray went down to twenty feet, even though Goldman cussed and wiped his hand over his mouth. The low altitude would limit the fighters' maneuverability.

Ray scanned the landscape. He tipped his wing over a tree, and let *Jump* live up to her name to cross a power line.

"Me 109 coming in," Tucker said. "Steep dive, four o'clock high."

Bullets and cuss words flew from the top turret behind Ray. *Jump* rocked hard and leaped ten feet.

"Who's the dimwit?" Burgess said. "Stupid Jerry didn't pull up in time."

Ray's chest crushed. A second man had died, a boy like those in the back of his plane. *Lord, please make this stop.*

"Ha! Now who's the chicken?" Burgess called. "He's leaving. *Auf wiedersehen*, you chicken. Bawk, bawk, bawk. Anyone know how to say 'chicken' in German?"

"*Huhn*," Ray said. "*Feiges Huhn* means 'cowardly chicken.'" But the pilot was no coward for turning away. Not at all.

A herd of cows scattered in front of him, and a blue haze glimmered ahead. The ocean.

A bittersweet smile spread over Ray's face. "We made it, boys."

★

Antioch

The sunrise illuminated jagged rims of glass around the Carlisles' living room window. Fifteen miles hadn't protected Antioch from blast damage.

Was Jay-Jay all right? Helen hustled up the front walk despite the fatigue gluing her left foot to the ground. Vic held her elbow to steady her.

Mrs. Carlisle flung open the front door and wrapped twiggy arms around Helen. "Thank goodness, you're all right. I was so worried."

Helen glanced over Mrs. Carlisle's shoulder. Fine time for her mother-in-law to get affectionate. "How's Jay-Jay? Is he all right?"

"He's fine. Barely even woke up. You know what a heavy sleeper he is."

Helen nodded with a gulping laugh. "Yes. Yes, he is."

Mrs. Carlisle raised red-rimmed eyes. "The first blast nearly knocked Mr. Carlisle out of his armchair. We thought it was an earthquake, but then the second blast shattered the windows. We ran upstairs, and there's our little angel, sitting up in bed. He frowned at me, said, 'No wake up,' and dove under the covers."

"Where is he? Where's my little boy?"

He stepped into the doorway in his blue and white striped pajamas. Helen scooped him up and kissed his sleep-warmed face and tousled curls. "My baby. Thank you, Lord."

"Lieutenant, thank you for keeping Helen safe." Mrs. Carlisle lifted her arms as if to hug Vic, then lowered them. "The radio didn't report what happened until after midnight, the phones are out of service, and you two weren't home. We were so worried. When they said it was at Port Chicago—oh dear. We thought poor little Jay-Jay was an orphan."

Helen sank to the porch step and clutched her son. She never thought her job would endanger her life.

"Where's Mr. Carlisle?" Vic asked.

"Checking the damage at his furniture store, the dress shop, and with his tenants."

Vic took Mrs. Carlisle by the shoulders. "Make sure Helen gets plenty of rest. And send a telegram to her parents. This will be national news."

"Oh yes, could you?" Helen asked.

"Of course."

"I'm going to my parents' to get a few hours sleep. I'll stop by George and Betty's on my way. As for the rest of town, when my mother hears the news, so will all of Contra Costa County."

Helen rested her cheek on Jay-Jay's soft head. "Thank you, Vic."

Only Ray remained to be notified, but that letter would have to wait until evening, because Helen's eyelids felt as heavy as blackout curtains.

☆

Bury St. Edmunds Airfield

Ray leaned back in the upholstered chair in the Officers' Club and cradled a cup of coffee. Someone pounded "One O'Clock Jump" on the piano with more enthusiasm than skill.

His smile rose with the steam from his coffee. Later tonight he'd write Helen about today's experience. He had faced his fears, and the Lord got him through. No matter what else life threw at him, he knew he was no *feiges Huhn.*

"There he is, the talk of Bury St. Edmunds." Jack sat in a chair across from Ray. A smile tilted his mustache.

"Guess I could do it."

Jack dipped his chin. "Sorry I doubted you."

"It's all right. I doubted myself."

"No one doubts you now. I tell you, the Eighth Air Force had a banner day. First Division took out a station where the Nazis build those robot buzz bombs, Second Division helped British ground troops break out of Caen, and Third Division hit oil targets, but everyone's talking about the photos you fellows took."

"Good?"

"Outstanding."

Ray nodded. Intelligence must have seen something useful.

Jack unwrapped a canvas bundle on his lap and pulled out a corrugated rubber hose. "Bodey was right. The oxygen equipment is sound. But you're right too. Look close." He stretched out the hose, and minute cracks appeared.

"Wow."

"Plane's older. All that exposure to cold broke down the rubber, gave you slow leaks."

Ray sipped his coffee. "Apology accepted."

"Oh, you're not out of the woods yet—literally." Jack chuckled and pulled a mangled leafy branch from the canvas. "We found this wrapped around the radio direction finder antenna."

The football-shaped device was mounted on the belly of the plane. Ray reached for the branch.

"I can't believe—" Jack's laugh sputtered out. "I can't believe you buzzed Germany."

Ray smiled at his trophy. "A souvenir of Deutschland."

✦

Antioch

Although it was two o'clock in the afternoon, it looked as if it were two in the morning with the living room windows boarded up.

"How can I help?" Helen asked.

On the couch under a lamp, Mrs. Carlisle glanced over the top of *McCall's* magazine. "Oh, I'm all done. I'm just taking a break during Jay-Jay's nap. They have meatless recipes in here this month."

Helen glanced around. Expecting work, she'd tied up her hair in a scarf and put on an old red gingham blouse from the charity donations after the fire. Now she had nothing to do, and for once, her agendas and committee plans didn't entice her.

"I'll see if Betty needs help."

"Good idea. She'll be relieved to see you."

Helen walked down C Street, past her childhood home. Her parents had rented it to a man from Philadelphia working at the Fibreboard Paper Products research facility at the old Riverview Union High School, Ray's alma mater.

She gazed up at her old bedroom window, still framed by creamy ruffled curtains. If only she and Jay-Jay could live there instead.

Her heaviness deepened and shoved her right on Sixth Street—away from her sister's house. Her hands opened and closed, her heartbeat skittered about, and her foot caught on a crack in the sidewalk.

Now that she didn't have to be brave, the trauma of the night before was catching up to her. So much death. So much pain. So much blood. She'd see Betty later. Not now.

Pastor Novak swept up a pile of broken glass on his front porch. He waved to Helen. "Glad you weren't there last night."

"Thank you." She would explain later. But perhaps, like his parents, Ray wouldn't worry if he heard how late at night the explosion occurred.

She turned left on D Street, a familiar route to a familiar place. The rubble from the fire had been cleared, and all that remained of her former home was the garage and the oleander hedges.

Helen walked the blackened outline of the house. She traced the boundary of the kitchen, as black as the burns Jim had inflicted on her. Then around the bedroom—the source of the fire, as Jim's abuse was the source of the chaos in her life. She kicked at the dirt where their bed once stood. "Why? Why did you do it?"

Those stupid, poisonous oleander hedges. They served one purpose, to screen the house so no one could see and no one would know.

Helen grabbed a bush close to the ground and yanked. "You wanted to conceal it, didn't you? You said I deserved it and it was your right as a husband, yet you hid it. You told everyone clumsy Helen got in another accident, the poor little cripple, because you knew it was wrong. You knew, but you did it anyway."

The bush didn't loosen, although Helen had starved it and trimmed it low.

She marched to the garage, tugged open the door, and grabbed a shovel. She sank the shovel into the earth, jammed it deeper with her foot, again and again until the bush tipped. Helen grabbed it with both hands and wrestled it out of the earth.

"I won't. I won't keep it inside anymore. I can't."

She kicked the bush aside and stomped on it.

"Helen?" Mrs. Llewellyn peered around the hedges. "Are you all right?"

Despite her sudden drop in blood pressure, she managed to smile and wipe her brow. "I—I never liked oleander."

Mrs. Llewellyn's forehead smoothed out. "I'm glad to hear that. I wondered why you had poisonous plants with a small child around."

"Not my choice." Helen turned, waited for her neighbor to leave, and then attacked the next bush. She had to tear it down, tear down her façade, but she had to be discreet. Jay-Jay needed to look up to his father, and the community needed its war hero.

But Helen had needs too. She needed to get her demons out and deal with them.

She tossed the next bush aside. God had provided for her need with a sweet man who knew part of the truth. Ray would listen. He could help her work through it.

Helen ducked her face to wipe her stinging eyes on her shoulder. A sob hiccupped out. "Thank you, Lord."

21

Bury St. Edmunds
Thursday, July 27, 1944

Ray inhaled the ancient scent of the square Norman-style Abbey Gate Tower, and stepped into its recess with Jack. California, with all its beauty, lacked this connection with centuries past he felt in England. He'd already seen Cambridge and couldn't wait to see London.

"This is what I like." Jack pointed at the long arrow slits penetrating the massive walls. "Back then they shot arrows through holes in stone. Now we shoot .50 caliber bullets through holes in Plexiglas."

"Yeah." Ray wandered through to the gardens surrounding the abbey ruins. He preferred to think of monks chanting their worship and transcribing Scripture in illuminated manuscripts.

"Got a letter from Dad yesterday." Jack grumbled and stuffed his hands in the pockets of his A-2 leather flight jacket. "He got my letter about staying in the military and not being a pastor."

"We knew he wouldn't be pleased."

Jack snorted. "I hope he's happier with my choice of a wife."

"He will be. Ruth's a fine woman." He entered a neat circular garden in full summer color. "Is this the first time Dad hasn't been proud of you?"

Jack leveled a gaze at him. "Have you forgotten how much trouble I got into as a boy?"

Ray chuckled. "Have you forgotten? He'd spank you and leave snickering under his breath. You know he did the same stuff when he was a boy. He took pride in your mischief."

"Pride." Jack shook his head. "The same pride that made him push all three sons to be pastors. Now he only has one."

Ray shrugged. "You're doing God's will for your life, so is Walt, and so am I. If Dad has a problem with our career choices, he can take it up with the Almighty."

"You tell him that. I'd rather face a squadron of those new little German fighters."

"Not me." On his last mission, a triangular plane zipped past at over five hundred miles per hour—without any propellers. Now he knew how Grandpa must have felt the first time he saw a carriage rumble down the street without a horse.

"Wouldn't Walt like a look at those jets?" Jack whispered.

Ray also had a hunch Walt's classified engineering work at Boeing involved jet engines.

They turned right toward the ruins and passed a trio of British soldiers singing "Hang out the Washing on the Siegfried Line." The Tommies and the Yanks exchanged salutes.

"Jets," Jack said. "All the more reason to smash Nazi aircraft factories, oil refineries, synthetic oil plants. We worked long and hard for air superiority, thousands of good men died for it, and our troops on French soil rely on it. We can't lose it now."

Ray clamped down on a smile. That sounded like the speeches Jack gave at mission briefings. He might not be a pastor, but he certainly could preach.

When they reached the abbey, Jack sat on a low wall of medieval rubble. "That's why I needed to talk to you today."

"Huh?" What on earth did he have to do with air superiority?

"I need to select crews to train in radar-guided bombing and serve in the 333rd Squadron as the Pathfinder Force for our wing. You're a logical choice. You're an excellent pilot and well respected by your crew—and by the whole group after your buzzing adventure. I wanted to ask your opinion."

"My opinion." Ray sat a few feet from his brother and ran his hand over the smooth stones embedded in the rough mortar. In the lead position, Pathfinder planes bore the brunt of Luftwaffe attacks, while "Tail-End Charlie" in the rear took the worst of the flak as the antiaircraft gunners found their range. The Eighth Air Force had increased combat tours to thirty-five missions, and most men finished within three months. Pathfinder crews only had to fly thirty missions, but they didn't fly as often and took twice as long to complete a tour.

Ray studied the jagged wall of what had once been a grand cathedral. Helen's first letter rested in the inside pocket of his flight jacket, an impersonal letter one would write an acquaintance, the rubble of what had promised to be a grand relationship.

Although his initial purpose in coming to England had been accomplished, he was in no hurry to go home. Besides, the accuracy of radar-guided bombing might decrease civilian casualties and bring a quicker end to the war.

He turned to his brother. "You always ask a man's opinion before making assignments?"

Jack grinned. "Never."

"Then sign me up."

★

Antioch
Thursday, August 10, 1944

Helen stood waist deep in the San Joaquin River with Jay-Jay on her hip. "Ready? One, two, three." She squatted until the water covered his shoulders.

He squealed in delighted terror and dug his hands into her shoulders.

She straightened up, and the evaporating water cooled her skin. "What a brave boy you are."

"Again! Again!"

Up and down she hopped, and she and Jay-Jay laughed together.

"Martha, Martha," Betty said. "You said you didn't have time for a fun day out."

"I don't. I'm behind in my volunteer work, I have laundry and errands, but my baby lives on the river, and he needs to know how to swim." The week before, a ten-year-old boy had slipped off the municipal pier and drowned. If only he'd known how to swim.

"My swim," Jay-Jay said.

"Yes, you will learn how to swim." Helen placed one arm under his shoulders and one under his round tummy, and glided him through the water. He craned his head up with a grin dimpling his cheeks.

Betty cupped a handful of water and poured it over little Judy's tummy. "Vic's not keeping his agreement."

"Last night was an exception. We had to drive up to Vallejo to find out what was going on at Mare Island."

"Can you tell me now?"

Helen swung Jay-Jay in a circle. The story would be in the newspaper anyway. "I told you they took the survivors of the explosion up to the Naval Ammunition Depot at Mare Island. They can't load at Port Chicago until they rebuild."

"Right."

"Well, yesterday they took the men out to work for the first time. When the men found out they were loading ammo, 258 of them refused to work. They said they were afraid to do their jobs."

"Goodness. What did the Navy do?" Betty held Judy under the armpits and dipped her feet in the water. Judy squawked and drew up her knees.

"They locked them on a barge. The brig isn't big enough. They're trying to talk sense into them."

"Is that what Vic did?"

"I had to stay on the dock, but Vic took their side."

"You're kidding. Didn't those men grumble that the Navy wouldn't send them to combat? Now they refuse to do dangerous work?"

"That's what I thought, but Vic disagrees." Her arms grew tired. She headed for the beach and set Jay-Jay in water a few inches deep. "Here, sweetie, splash around."

"Has he forgotten there's a war on?"

Helen sat in the water near her son and kicked to strengthen her feet and legs. "He says they saw 322 of their friends die, and they're shaken. I can understand—I'm shaken too. And I didn't have to clean up like those men did."

"I know, but still." Betty plunked down next to Helen and set Judy on her knees. "Men on the front lines see horrible things, and they have to plug on even when they're shaken. Jim did."

Helen nodded and made her lips waver. "They say they want survivor's leave. To be fair, the white survivors got leave, but still, men at sea don't have that luxury."

"And Vic took their side?"

"He says they have a point. They still don't know what caused the explosion. They're working under the same officers, and nothing's been done to improve safety."

Jay-Jay stood in water to his chest. Helen scrambled over and scooped him up. "Oh no, you don't, my little fishy. Not without your mama."

He howled, but Helen whirled him in the water and made him laugh.

"Apricot canning time," Betty said.

"Mm-hmm." The sweet smell of apricots from the Hickmott Cannery filled the air.

Betty smiled at the clear sky. "I love it here in the summer. What happy memories."

"Not for me." Helen plunged down so the water lapped Jay-Jay's chin. "My summer memories involve Aunt Olive's old house, a tyrannical ballet teacher, and San Francisco fog."

"You made up for it the last two years of high school when you begged off. I know you just wanted to flirt with Jim." She winked. "It worked."

Helen managed to smile. She'd only exchanged Madame Ivanova's abuse for Jim's. But then she buried her face in Jay-Jay's damp curls. A torturous marriage, but what sweet reward.

"Is it hard living with the Carlisles?"

Helen jerked her head up. "What?"

Betty laughed. "I didn't mean like that. They're wonderful people. They may be old-fashioned, but he's so funny, and they're so devoted to each other—and generous. Not just with charity. Goodness, you have the most darling wardrobe. They spoil you rotten."

"Sure." But Mr. Carlisle talked to his wife the same way Jim had talked to Helen—the wounded tone when she disappointed him, the dismissive tone when she expressed an opinion, the cutting tone when she made a mistake.

The corners of Betty's eyes tugged down. "I meant it must be hard living where Jim grew up. Everything must remind you of him."

For once, Helen didn't have to fake a pained expression.

Betty stood and walked to her towel under a willow tree. "I rushed you, didn't I? With Ray. You two seemed perfect for each other, and I thought you were ready. But then if, God forbid, anything happened to George, I wouldn't be ready for years, if ever."

Helen dragged her feet out of the water. Part of her longed to tell Betty the real reason she wasn't ready, but she'd only hurt Jay-Jay. And what would Betty think of a girl too stupid to follow her family's advice to postpone marriage, stupid enough to marry a wife beater? Jim tried to control her, even when they were dating. Wasn't that a clue?

Betty toweled off Judy's dark curls. "Maybe you'll be ready when Ray comes home."

"It's not like that. Not anymore."

Betty flipped a hand. "I see how often he writes. Oh! Almost forgot. I brought you his latest letter. George feels like a secret agent delivering your letters. He wants to buy a trench coat." She dug around in her bag.

Helen tried to look casual as she dried off the little boy Ray called "munchkin." Ray had such a gentle way with Jay-Jay. And firm. He'd never been more attractive than on the day he hauled Jay-Jay off and shut him in his room.

Betty swung an envelope between thumb and forefinger. "In an envelope this time. Ooh, a love letter."

"Oh, brother." Helen snatched away the letter and opened it. "See, it's not for privacy. There's something loose in here. A leaf?"

"A leaf? That's not very romantic."

"I told you." Helen pulled out a dried-up leaf and frowned at it. "Why a leaf?"

"For goodness' sake, read the letter and find out."

"Bossy, bossy, bossy." But Helen read.

Dear Helen,   July 18, 1944

As of today, I haven't heard whether you wish to correspond, and so I write. I pray often that the Lord will bring you peace and strength to help you through your difficult times.

You're probably wondering about the leaf. It's a tradition for soldiers to send home battle souvenirs, and this is mine. I can't disclose details, but on today's mission, under fighter attack, I flew at rooftop level over the homeland of our enemy.

As a girl, you wrote stories about a knight with a ridiculous name. Improbable as it sounds, today I put on my shining armor—all right, my flak vest—and smote the dragon of cowardice with the lance of the Lord's strength.

Now, fair princess, I present you this token of my esteem.

"Why did he send a leaf?" Betty asked.

Helen fingered the gift, her heart warm and woozy. "This is no leaf. It's the scale of a dragon."

22

Bury St. Edmunds Airfield
Friday, August 18, 1944

Ray sat on an overturned crate facing the woods behind his Nissen hut, a luxury awarded by shirtsleeve weather and a late-afternoon training mission.

He glanced down to the small Bible he always carried in his pocket, open to Psalm 19:9–10. "The fear of the LORD is clean, enduring for ever: the judgments of the LORD are true and righteous altogether. More to be desired are they than gold, yea, than much fine gold: sweeter also than honey and the honeycomb."

Ray fingered the plum blossoms he'd pressed in those pages in March, the blossoms he'd plucked from Helen's hair. At the time it seemed appropriate for the references to gold and honey, but now the truth of the verse rang out. "I had it wrong, Lord. You're the only thing that matters, for me and for Helen too. Forgive me for putting my selfish goals first." Deep inside, hadn't he hoped Helen's love would prove his manhood?

He sighed, closed the pages, and exchanged the Bible for her last letter. He leaned his elbows on his knees to reread the third page:

Tonight over dinner, Mrs. Carlisle mentioned
Jim, and I willed up wet eyes and a quivering
chin. I'm tired of it. You'll think I'm horrible,
but I'm tired of acting as if I were mourning
when I'm not.

What if my marriage wasn't idyllic? What
if Jim was a less-than-perfect husband? What if
my grief was never as deep as everyone thinks?

I'm ashamed to admit I'm an excellent
actress. My grief is necessary for Jay-Jay to
admire his father as a boy should, and for
Antioch to have a hero to rally around. So I keep
on acting, faking, lying.

You've already seen the worst side of me,
and you've invited me to write openly to you.
Perhaps you'll regret the offer, but if I don't
let the truth out, all of it, what's left of me will
crumble and crack.

"This is good, honey," Ray whispered. "This is good."
Her revelation of Jim's abuse, the fire, and the explosion
at Port Chicago had burned up her pretenses, and now truth
glowed like an ember among the ashes.

Ray uncapped his pen and added to the letter he'd started
the night before.

I agree you shouldn't reveal everything
to Jay-Jay or the community. Honesty is
important, but so is discretion. Your concern for
their needs is kind and reasonable.

What you've chosen—honesty with a

confidant—is the best course, and I'm honored
to be selected. Please know I'll respect your
privacy. Please also remember the Lord is your
best, wisest, and most loving confidant, and he
already knows every detail.

A rustle in the brush caught his attention. A small brown
bird hopped out and pecked at seeds.

To Ray's left, a cat flattened itself to the ground, a white
cat with large black blotches, as if young Jack had spilled
ink on the cat as well as on Mom's piano top.

The cat fixed gun-sight eyes on the bird, whapped his tail
back and forth as if adjusting for range, and chattered, "Ack,
ack, ack, ack, ack."

Ray grinned. The British word for flak was *ack-ack*, and
this cat sure considered himself an antiaircraft gunner.

The cat wiggled his backside and sprang. The bird darted
away. After a few seconds of frantic search, the cat sat on his
haunches and washed his hind leg.

That would be a cute story to put in his letter for Helen to
tell Jay-Jay. The cat looked about the same age as Grandma's
kittens would be now, the ones Jay-Jay loved.

"There you are, Ray." John Buffo ambled up, and the little
cat skittered away.

"Hi, John. What's up?" He scooted to make room for his
bombardier.

Buffo perched his large frame on the edge of the crate,
pulled off his garrison cap, and ran his hand through his
wiry brown hair. "Being a man of intellect and sentiment is
a liability in this profession."

Ray folded his letter. "Second thoughts about what we do
over here?"

"Second, third, millionth. We bomb from twenty thousand

feet, and the brass is thrilled if we hit within two thousand feet of the aiming point. That's half a mile, Ray. How many civilians do we kill down there?"

Ray looked into Buffo's deep-set brown eyes. He had the same thoughts and discussed it often with William Miller, the base chaplain. "After every mission, I ask God to forgive me for hurting or killing anyone. But I get in my Fort the next day and do it again. I wonder how genuine my remorse is, if I'm as callous as the others."

Buffo shifted his weight, and the crate creaked. "Sometimes I wish I were a dullard who could quaff a few beers and say, 'They started it.'"

Ray's gaze traced the border between verdant trees and blue sky. "Perhaps that's enough reason after all."

"What? That's nothing but simplistic training film propaganda."

"Is it?" He turned his pen in his fingers. "This is one conflict in which negotiation failed. Germany overran continental Europe and keeps attacking Britain. They aim for nothing and hope to kill civilians. Couldn't a rational man argue the Allies act in self-defense?"

"Yes, but we're attacking, not defending."

"If we stopped attacking, they would grow stronger until they ran over our defenses."

Buffo squinted and twisted his lips. "There must be a better way."

"Maybe someday there will be, but now the only path to peace is through the land of conflict." Ray tapped his pen on his knee. Hadn't Gideon noted the irony too? When the Lord called him to war, Gideon built an altar called Jehovah-shalom—"The Lord is peace." That was true not only for Gideon and for the Allies, but for Helen and for Ray.

They had to fight to find peace.

Treasure Island Naval Station, Yerba Buena Island
Wednesday, September 13, 1944

"Mutiny! How can they charge my husband with mutiny?" A black woman slammed the door of Vic's office in an old Marines' barracks. She wore a nicely cut dark blue suit with sleeves and trim of butter yellow, and when she marched to Helen's desk, the same yellow flashed in kick pleats in her skirt. She glared at Helen. "Mutiny?"

Helen gave her a reassuring smile. "Remember, Lieutenant Llewellyn is on the defense team. He's on your husband's side, Mrs. . . . ?"

She sighed and held out a gloved hand. "Jones. Mrs. Carver Jones."

Helen stood and shook her hand. "I'm Mrs. Carlisle. I'll let the lieutenant know—"

"Esther, what a pleasure to meet you." Vic popped out of his office. "I'm a great admirer of your husband. Please come in."

Helen took a legal pad and led Mrs. Jones into Vic's office.

"What's going on with my husband?" Mrs. Jones sat with her butter yellow pocketbook on her lap.

"Well, Esther, everything's going to be fine."

"He's been charged with mutiny. That carries the death penalty."

"Nothing to worry about. None of these men will be convicted, especially not Carver. He has a medical excuse for refusing to work."

"How did he get mixed up in this in the first place?"

Vic slid his fingers along his pen as if stretching it. "On August 9, when the men were told to load ammo, 258 of them refused. Two days later, they were asked again under threat of a charge of mutiny, and 50 men still refused."

"But Carver—"

"I know. But when asked whether he was willing to load ammo, he refused."

Mrs. Jones turned to Helen with indignation all over her face. "His arm's broken. He's wearing a cast."

Helen nodded. She remembered his injuries too well.

"This will all come out in the trial tomorrow," Vic said. "All we need is the documentation from Dr. Thompson at Port Chicago."

Mrs. Jones sat up even taller. "I talked to him. He says he'll get it out when he has time. He used the most condescending tone, as if I didn't speak English, much less major in it."

Vic turned to Helen. "Carver and Esther both have degrees from Howard."

Helen, the only one in the room without a college degree, gave a thin smile.

"He's been subpoenaed, hasn't he?" Mrs. Jones said. "He has no choice."

"Correct." He tapped his pencil on a stack of paperwork. "I need to warn you this trial won't be pleasant. The Navy wants to make an example of these men. But justice will prevail. Carver's case will be dismissed, as will those of two others with medical excuses. And the rest will be acquitted. At worst, they're guilty of insubordination, not mutiny. There was no conspiracy, no attempt to overthrow the officers. All seven of us on the defense team have worked hard, and the men will be freed and cleared."

"I pray you're right, Lieutenant." Mrs. Jones stood. "Thank you for your help."

"My duty and honor. That's my motto over there." He nodded to a cross-stitched sampler on the wall that read, "Let justice be done though the world perish—Saint Augustine."

Mrs. Jones shook his hand. "A fine motto."

Helen saw Mrs. Jones to the door, then returned and leaned against the doorjamb to Vic's office. The sampler had been stitched in blue and red—blue for the truth Vic would bring to light in the trial, and red for the courage he'd need to stand for justice.

He had been assigned to defend ten of the accused mutineers, and his desk teemed with thick file folders. He leaned over an open folder and scratched down notes.

"You're doing a good thing," she said.

"Hmm?" He took a few seconds to focus on her.

"I appreciate what you're doing. It takes courage to stand up for what's right, even when it's unpopular."

Vic's gaze honed in on her, and he opened his mouth. But then he squeezed his lips shut and returned to his notes. "Thanks."

She smiled. He hadn't proposed once since the explosion. Back at her desk, she straightened a pile of papers in Vic's compact script to type up.

"Say, Helen," he called. "How do you know I'm not like my dad, angling for connections and currying favor in the black community?"

She laughed and rolled a form into the typewriter. "At the risk of losing favor in the white community? I don't think so. I'm afraid your motives might be pure."

"Yeah." His voice was quiet and distracted. Buried in his work.

Something Helen knew well. She pecked at the typewriter keys, the kind of loud busywork she used to love to keep her memories at bay.

Work didn't comfort her the way it used to, not even her volunteer work.

Oddly, what comforted her most was what she'd avoided for years—confronting the truth. In each letter to Ray, she opened her memory bin a little further, released a few more ugly memories, and stilled their demonic dance by pinning their leathery wings to paper.

She swung the carriage return, flipped the paper release, and aligned the next part of the form.

In increments, Ray was receiving a catalog of Jim's abuse, but he encouraged her disclosure and reciprocated by telling of his own fears and doubts. The distance between them provided safety, as did his confidentiality as a pastor. He'd even promised to have Jack return her letters if anything happened to him.

A chill scurried up her spine. But with the Allies on the Siegfried Line at the German border, the war in Europe promised to wrap up by the end of the year. Even if it didn't, Ray would finish his tour and come home with his compassionate eyes and strong arms and sweet kisses.

No. Not for her. Helen zipped the paper out of the typewriter, set it to her right, and picked up the next form.

She drew an uneven breath. The deeper their correspondence grew, the more she loved him, but the more she had to be scaring him away.

23

Bury St. Edmunds Airfield
Friday, September 15, 1944

Glenn Miller's orchestra blasted out the opening chords of "In the Mood," and three thousand men in Hangar One whistled and cheered.

Ray had heard the song many times on the radio and phonograph, but it had never sounded as clear, crisp, and vibrant as it did live at the party celebrating the 94th Bomb Group's 200th mission.

In olive drabs, Maj. Glenn Miller played his trombone to the side of the stage—a musician, not a showman. Ray admired the humility that led him to give up his popular civilian orchestra and enlist in the Army Air Force to entertain troops abroad.

England was no safe haven, what with rumors of a pending poison gas attack and with V-1 buzz bombs flying overhead with fiery tails.

Still, Walt came as well. Ray glanced out the corner of his eye at his youngest brother, the only man in civilian clothes. No one grumbled about the presence of the air executive's brother, a veteran of the Eighth Air Force before the 94th Bomb Group even arrived.

Boeing had sent Walt as an engineering advisor to some classified unit of the U.S. Strategic Air Forces, most likely analyzing intelligence on German jet fighters.

After the applause for "In the Mood" died down, the orchestra played "Moonlight Serenade," Miller's signature number.

"Allie loves this song," Walt whispered.

Ray murmured his understanding. Playing with engines and visiting his brothers wouldn't compensate Walt for missing his wife, especially now that she was expecting.

When the concert concluded, Ray and the other officers rose to leave. The enlisted men would stay for a dance led by Glenn Miller's orchestra, but the officers' dance was in the Theater Building with the Griffiss Airacobras, the band of the U.S. Strategic Air Forces.

Ray looked in vain for Jack among the top brass, and then he and Walt walked out into the damp night, careful to stay on the path and out of the mud.

"Amazing." Walt glanced around. "When I flew, we had no more than six bomb groups, and we were glad to dispatch a hundred planes for a mission. Now we have forty groups and can put up two thousand planes. Can't fathom it."

"Is it hard to be back here?"

Walt tipped his head to one side. "Difficult memories, yeah. But some good ones. Nothing like the camaraderie from going through rugged times together."

"Hiya, Pops." Leo Goldman jogged past with Buffo, Radovich, and Sig Werner, the new radar operator on the crew. "Free drinks. You'd better hurry if you want good bar position."

Ray grinned. "Pick me up a cup of coffee, would you?"

Buffo clapped meaty hands to his chest. "A dagger to my heart. This grand celebration calls for the imbibing of a copious volume of liquid cheer."

"All right, all right. Make it two cups of coffee."

Ray's officers groaned, waved him off, and continued on their way.

He nudged Walt in the arm. "You miss that?"

"Sure do. My men called me Preach."

The brothers passed a truck filled with local girls brought in to dance, and entered the Theater Building. The band sat on a stage draped with red, white, and blue bunting. Overhead hung a banner emblazoned with "200" and the image of a squadron of B-17s.

"There's Jack." Walt pointed to a table not far away.

"Good, Ruth made it," Ray said. "Say, so did Charlie and May."

Everyone greeted each other. Walt had met Charlie and Ruth on his tour, but not May.

While May wore a subtle pink gown, Ruth turned heads in peacock blue. Most women seemed to resent Ruth's type of knockout beauty, but May didn't.

When Walt leaned his elbows on the table, his prosthesis thumped. "So, Charlie, Jack told me you were shot down over the Netherlands. You must have stories."

"Not many," Jack said. "Most of his experience is classified to protect the Dutch Maquis."

Charlie sipped his coffee. "Once we liberate Holland, I'll bore you to death."

"What was the hardest part?" Ray asked.

Charlie stuck a coffee spoon in his mouth, gazed at the ceiling, and made the spoon bob up and down. "The helplessness. Everyone at home thought I was dead, and I couldn't do anything. I couldn't even help the Resistance. If I got caught as a downed airman, I'd be a POW in a Stalag Luft, but if I committed sabotage, I'd be shot as a spy."

May snuggled close to her boyfriend. "You made the right choice."

"Make another good choice," Jack said. "Give up testing radar and come back as the best bombardier in the Eighth."

"Jack Novak!" Ruth's eyes flashed fire. "Don't you dare meddle."

He grinned and sang "Pistol Packin' Mama" with a western twang.

She laughed and whacked him lightly in the arm. "You goon."

Jack turned to his brothers. "Mind if Charlie and I take the ladies out for a dance?"

"Not at all."

But when they left the table, a dark blanket settled over Ray's mind. Dancing held no appeal, partly so he wouldn't abandon Walt, but mostly because of memories of his last dance—with Helen at Walt's wedding. If only he could dance with her now, let her cry her hurts onto his shoulder, kiss her honeyed hair, and speak words of comfort rather than writing impotent letters that took weeks to arrive.

Her bridesmaid's dress had been yellow, a rich golden yellow.

"Too bad things didn't work out with you and Helen."

Ray blinked and glanced at Walt. "The man gets married and suddenly he's a mind reader."

"It's a survival skill." Walt nodded sagely. "I was right?"

Ray sighed. "Yeah."

"Are you in love with her?"

"Marriage made you bold too."

"Well, are you?"

Ray gazed at the dance floor, where dozens of couples swayed to "Stardust."

"Does she know you love her?"

Ray stared at Walt. "I didn't say—"

"Mind reader, remember?" He tapped his temple.

Ray smiled. "She doesn't know."

Walt leaned closer, his hazel eyes serious. "Learn from my mistakes. Tell her."

The band changed key and played "Long Ago and Far Away," as cruel a choice as "Stardust." He raised half a smile. "Mind reading, boldness, and great wisdom—marriage has been good for you."

"Sure has. Heed my wisdom, gained at great cost."

"Why don't we get some coffee?" Ray stood, shrugged off his service jacket, and draped it over his chair to reserve it.

He had no intention of following his baby brother's advice. Helen had made progress as she chronicled Jim's appalling abuse. In the unlikely case that she had romantic feelings for Ray, a confession of love would distract her from this progress. And if her interest was platonic, his confession would end the correspondence and undermine months of healing.

Ray weaved through the crowd toward the bar and smiled at the irony. He loved Helen too much to tell her he loved her.

✭

Naval Magazine, Port Chicago
Wednesday, October 4, 1944

The Navy corpsman stared at Helen, but then how many female civilians entered the dispensary at Port Chicago?

Vic was busy with the trial, but why did he have to send Helen for a confrontation? Despite her flipping stomach, she smiled. "I'm here to see Dr. Thompson on official business for the Judge Advocate's office."

"Sure, ma'am. I'll see if he's in with a patient."

"Thank you." Four men in dungarees sat in the waiting room—two black, two white. To ease public outrage, the Navy had rotated in two white divisions to load ammunition.

A window framed in raw unpainted wood showed a view past buildings in various states of repair down to a newly built pier, where a freighter docked for loading.

Helen's breath caught. What if the Navy's promise to improve safety conditions was as hollow as the promise of a fair trial for the accused mutineers? Many of the written testimonies had been transcribed inaccurately, and Vic was disgusted by the prejudice and intimidation in the prosecution's questioning. The NAACP was even sending their chief counsel, Thurgood Marshall, to watch the trial and report the racism.

The corpsman ushered Helen into an office, where Dr. Thompson stood beside a desk.

Helen extended her hand. "Good afternoon. I'm Helen Carlisle. It's good to see you again under better circumstances."

A smile creased his pudgy face, and he shook her hand. "Why, yes. You helped after the explosion. A doctor's daughter, aren't you?"

"Yes, sir. My father's in the Army Medical Corps."

"Army? Not Navy? I may forgive you, my dear." He showed her a chair across from a dented metal desk. "How may I help?"

She couldn't avoid this, not with a man's freedom at stake. "My boss, Lt. Victor Llewellyn, serves on the defense team for the mutiny trial. One of his defendants, Petty Officer George Washington Carver Jones, was treated for a broken arm after the explosion."

His face hardened. "I sent my written testimony."

A single clinical sentence describing the injury, but nothing about how he was unable to work. Helen drew a deep breath and studied the battleship-gray desk covered with stacks of papers, medical books, and prescription pads. "Sir, I know how busy you are, but the defense is on the stand. The prosecution stated that 'there are plenty of things a one-armed man could do on the ammunition dock.' A statement from you could protect an innocent man."

"Innocent? They're a bunch of shiftless, lazy . . ." He gave her a sheepish smile. "My apologies. I've been away from feminine company too long."

Helen's stomach turned. However, his condescension gave her an idea. "Isn't it a shame the name of the Navy is being dragged through the mud because of this case? I—I'm a Navy widow myself." She blinked. She quivered her lips.

"Oh, Mrs. Carlisle. I'm so sorry."

A shameless act, but for a worthy cause. She raised her head and gave it a little shake. "For my husband's sake, for the sake of our son, I hate to see the Navy defamed. If even one innocent man can be acquitted—and such a good man— perhaps . . . perhaps . . ." She opened her pocketbook and fished out a handkerchief.

"Well, of course, of course. Let me write out a statement."

A few minutes later, Helen stepped out into the sunshine and showed the paper to Esther Jones. "The man's a disgrace to his profession."

Mrs. Jones raised eyes the color of coffee beans. "You did it."

Helen groaned and headed for the train depot. "Only after I waved my handkerchief and invoked the memory of my dead husband."

"Oh dear. I hope that wasn't too painful for you."

"He's been dead almost two years, and I don't miss him one bit." Her honesty slapped her across the face and stopped her in her tracks.

Mrs. Jones's eyebrows shot up, but then her mouth softened, and she settled a hand on Helen's elbow. "For every bad man, God made plenty of good ones."

The thought of a good man on a bomber base in England and another in the brig brought true tears to her eyes. "Men like Carver."

"And Lieutenant Llewellyn." Mrs. Jones guided Helen to the depot. "He's very fond of you."

Helen blinked her eyes clear. "Let's get him this testimony."

"I owe you."

"No, I owe you for being part of a world that tolerates this nonsense. I didn't see—I didn't know how bad it was until I started this job. The horrible things people say, the way you're treated. Oh, it makes my blood boil."

"Maybe that's the purpose. I knew the Lord would use Carver's trials for good, and now I see how. This case is showing the ugly underbelly of this nation, and if enough people take notice, something can be done. May the Lord raise up his people against injustice."

"Mrs. Jones, you'd make a fine preacher."

She turned with a gaze warmer than coffee. "Call me Esther."

Helen hoped her smile was just as warm. "Only if you call me Helen."

Antioch
Tuesday, October 24, 1944

Connie Scala and Linda Jeffries sat cross-legged on the sidewalk, playing jacks, and Jay-Jay tugged Helen's hand. "My watt."

"Yes, you may watch, but only for a few minutes." She was early for her meeting, and Ray's letter called to her from her pocketbook. She scanned for her favorite part.

Last night at the party, my brothers and I discussed the ink spot you discovered on the

piano and how it embodies our weaknesses—
Walt's for lying, Jack's for manipulation, and
mine for misguided peacemaking. Yes, Jesus
calls us to be peacemakers, but he doesn't want
peace at the cost of truth. My primary goal
shouldn't be the absence of conflict but doing
God's will.

A pastor needs to stand up for truth in ways
that may shatter the peace. I don't know if I can
do that. If I had known what Jim was doing to
you, would I have had the guts to confront him?

Courage comes in many forms, but I don't
know if I have the right form.

Helen pressed her lips to the paper. "Oh, darling. I know you do."

A little girl giggled, and Helen glanced down to Connie's grinning face. Helen gave her short black braid a playful tug. "I'm sure you also talk to yourself at times. Come on, Jay-Jay. Mrs. Novak said she'd have cookies."

"Cookie!" Jay-Jay scampered down Sixth Street and up the Novaks' front walk.

Mrs. Novak greeted him with a hug and then ushered them into the parlor. "I'll be right back with those cookies I promised. Look, I brought down my boys' old tin soldiers."

Jay-Jay flopped to his stomach on the hardwood floor. In his baby hands, two soldiers leaped to life and proceeded to kill each other.

Helen was drawn to the upright piano where she had spent romantic evenings with Ray, to the concealed ink spot, and to the portrait of Ray. She didn't have a picture of him, so every time she came, she drank him in—the kind eyes under the service cap, the tilt of his smile, and the angle of his jaw. Her chest ached missing him. His tour would be up by the end of the year, and he'd be home, but not hers.

"I never thought I'd have all three boys in harm's way. Not after Walt was discharged." Mrs. Novak held a plate of cookies and a glass of milk. "At least I have a daughter in the house for the first time."

"I'm so thankful you took me in." Allie Novak walked in and set a tray on the coffee table. "Would you care for tea, Helen?"

"Yes, please." Helen sat in a wing chair and forced a smile at her sister's best friend. One of several. Betty always did like quiet little things who wouldn't outshine her.

"Thank you for coming, Helen." Mrs. Novak handed Jay-Jay a cookie and set a half-filled glass of milk on a coaster on the piano bench. "I wanted to talk to you about something."

Helen opened the top notebook on her lap. "Oh yes. October's almost over, and we need to plan the Christmas party for the servicemen's children."

Mrs. Novak sat on the couch and took the teacup Allie offered. "I had something else in mind." She traced her finger around the china rim of the cup.

"The scrap metal drive? The blood drive?" Helen flipped through her notebooks.

"In a way, all of it." She pursed her lips. "I'm concerned about you."

"About me?"

"You seem tired lately, and I wondered if we could help. Allie has decided not to take a job with the baby coming, and she could lighten your load."

"It's not a load. I love this work. I do."

"Please let me help." Allie's large eyes stretched wide. "For the past two years, I've had a purpose, first with the Red

Cross in Riverside, then at Boeing. Walt wanted me here so I could be with family, but I feel useless. If I could help in any way . . ."

Helen stroked her notebook. How could she give up her heart's work?

Jay-Jay lined up soldiers for an assault on the coffee table, and Helen's heart crumpled. He needed more of her. The job with Vic took so much, and that wouldn't change until she could move out. But how could she please the Lord without service?

She groaned softly. Just that morning she'd read Galatians 3:2–3: "Received ye the Spirit by the works of the law, or by the hearing of faith? Are ye so foolish? having begun in the Spirit, are ye now made perfect by the flesh?"

Like the Galatians, was she trying to earn God's love, earn grace, earn forgiveness for killing her husband?

"Helen? You don't have to decide today."

"Yes, I do." Her voice came out ragged. "You're right."

The phone rang, and Mrs. Novak gave her an apologetic look. "Excuse me. I'm expecting a call."

Allie lifted a shy smile. "I don't have your talent for leadership, but I'd love to help."

Helen transferred to the sofa and smiled, although she doubted how much a society girl could help. "Let's see what you can do."

"I can run errands, make phone calls, type, anything you need."

Giving up any task would be like chopping off a finger, but Helen nodded and opened a notebook, her throat tight. If she was mistakenly relying on work to earn God's favor, perhaps it would be best to chop off some fingers.

"Helen?" Mrs. Novak leaned into the parlor. "The call is for you. It's Victor Llewellyn."

"Victor?"

"Mrs. Carlisle told him you were here."

Helen went to the hallway and picked up the shiny black receiver. "Vic?"

"I thought you'd want to know," he said in a heavy voice. "The verdict came in."

"Already? But you said they'd start deliberations today."

"They did. They finished eighty minutes later."

"Eighty? But—"

"Less than two minutes per defendant. But why deliberate if you've already made up your mind?"

Helen's mind thickened like syrup. "You don't mean—"

"Guilty. The court found all fifty of them guilty of mutiny. Fifteen years each. It's a travesty. They don't meet the legal definition of mutiny. No conspiracy. No attempt to overthrow officers. The Navy just wants to make an example of them so no one else considers insubordination. The trial was a farce, and they dragged us in and made fools of us."

She leaned against the wall and untangled her finger from the phone cord. "All fifty? Not—"

"Even Carver."

Helen pressed the heel of her hand against her forehead. "Oh no. Poor Carver. Poor Esther."

24

Bury St. Edmunds Airfield
Friday, November 10, 1944

Rubber squeaked on the tarmac, and Ray savored the sound after the intense flak they'd encountered over the Luftwaffe airfield at Wiesbaden.

His brand-new Pathfinder plane, an H2X radar-equipped B-17G, whizzed down the runway. Ray had named her *Ascalon* after the lance Saint George used to slay the dragon. With foot firm on the brakes, he flipped the levers on the center console to turn off the superchargers, while Goldman raised the wing flaps.

When the speed dropped to thirty miles per hour, Ray said, "Unlock tail wheel."

Goldman leaned down to the floor and swung the bar over. "Tail wheel unlocked."

Ray turned onto the perimeter track that circled the runways, and he joined the rumbling procession of silver B-17s, each tail fin bearing the 94th Bomb Group's *A* on a black square. They'd taken damage, and four of the group's thirty-eight bombers had slipped out of formation. At least France and Belgium were liberated, so a damaged plane had more places to put down.

When Ray reached the spoon-shaped hardstand for *Ascalon*, the ground crew motioned him in and showed him where to stop.

Ray and Goldman ran through the process of stopping the engines—idling them until cylinder temperature dropped and running at high rpm for thirty seconds before moving each mixture control lever to "engine off."

The engines' thunder died away for the first time in six hours. Ray tugged off his leather flight helmet. "Say, boys, do you know what's playing at the base theater tonight?"

"*Cover Girl* with Rita Hayworth." Goldman closed his eyes. "Mm, mm, mm. What I wouldn't give to get my hands on that redhead."

"Not if I saw her first." Hewett wrestled the machine gun out of the top turret with the help of the armorer. "I sing better than Gene Kelly." He broke into "Long Ago and Far Away."

Maybe Ray wasn't in the mood for a movie after all. He didn't need a reminder of his failed date with Helen. Their romance was long ago, and she was far away.

While his crew escalated their argument over who could win the Hollywood bombshell, Ray turned off a legion of switches on the control panel.

Sometimes hope flickered that he stood a chance with Helen, like after her last letter. She believed in him. She believed he possessed courage for anything he faced, and her belief strengthened him. If only he could keep her by his side to squash his self-doubts.

And to squash hers as well. Her letters showed such growth. She had shoved off the self-blame Jim taught her, and righteous anger had taken its place. Someday Ray hoped to guide her to forgiveness and peace, but first she had to work through the anger and betrayal.

Ray swung his legs to the side, stepped over the passageway that led down to the nose compartment, and stood behind his seat. He raised fists to ear level and pressed his elbows back, as good a stretch as he could get in the cockpit, but boy, it felt good.

After he picked up the flak vest and steel flak helmet he'd tossed aside when they were over the Channel, he followed Goldman and Hewett through the bomb bay and the radio room.

In the waist compartment, one man remained behind—Lt. Sig Werner, the H2X radar operator. He caught Ray's eye and waited for Goldman and Hewett to leave. "Say, Pops, I wanted to talk to you."

"Sure, Sig, what's up?"

Werner rubbed his close-cropped sandy hair. With his wide-set blue eyes and square jaw, he could blend in if they were shot down over Germany—if he could get the right uniform. "Thanks for talking to me last week. Sure, I was mad at you, but I needed to hear it."

Ray smiled and unclamped his parachute harness. On the October 7 mission to an oil refinery at Bohlen, the 94th lost eight bombers, one of which held Werner's former crew. He hit the bottle hard every night after that, which affected his work. "You're doing well this week."

"I haven't had a drop since. I thought the pain would kill me if I didn't drown it, but you made me see a man could also die by drowning."

"I see a lot of that around here." He also saw men try to slough off their sorrows in the arms of London prostitutes. Those men kept the base dispensary busy treating venereal disease.

Werner massaged the back of his neck, and his cheeks reddened. "I said some awful things to you."

Yep. Things like "self-righteous, know-it-all Puritan." Ray shrugged off his parachute harness. "No harm done."

Werner fixed his light blue eyes on Ray. "You're the only man around here with the guts to take me on. I owe you."

Ray clapped him on the back. "How about a cup of coffee in the Officers' Club?"

Werner strolled to the door, jumped out, and grinned at Ray. "*After* the movie. I'll give up booze, but I won't give up Rita."

Ray laughed and hopped out. The tarmac jarred his feet, and a thought jarred his soul. Helen was right. He'd stirred up conflict with Werner to bring peace in the long run.

He ambled down the length of his plane and ran his hand down Saint George's lance painted on the nose. Another dragon slain.

✶

Naval Magazine, Port Chicago
Wednesday, November 15, 1944

Helen tapped her fingers on her desk, mimicking the rain on the roof of the repaired administration building. Now that his assignment for the trial was over, Vic had been reassigned to Port Chicago, his punishment for being on the wrong side, he insisted. But Helen knew he had a purpose. His presence had a soothing effect on the men, since they knew he fought for them.

With no surviving witnesses, the Naval Court of Inquiry couldn't find a conclusive cause of the explosion but decided it was due to the presence of fused ammunition, rough handling, or the failure of a boom.

Helen had finished her typing and filing and had nothing to do until Vic returned from the clemency hearing with Admiral Wright. She hated to use work time for personal correspondence, but she couldn't stare into space for an hour.

She slid open the bottom desk drawer and removed her letter to Ray. She scanned the page, puffed her cheeks full of air, then blew it out. If any letter would scare him away forever, this was it, but she had to get out the last ugly scrap of truth.

Both Madame Ivanova and Jim blamed me for their abuse. Madame said if I were a better dancer, she wouldn't have to switch me. Jim said if I were a better wife, he wouldn't have to beat me. In public he blamed my injuries on polio-induced clumsiness. Even my father believed my clumsiness was to blame. Well, not one of those injuries was my fault.

But Jim's death is my fault. Oh, Ray, I prayed to be released. I actually prayed for it. When the war started, I saw my chance to be free for the duration. I appealed to Jim's patriotism, I gushed over the uniforms, and I fretted over what would happen if Uncle Sam assigned him in the draft.

If I hadn't influenced him, he never would have been on the USS Laffey on November 13, 1942. I killed him as surely as if I'd fired that torpedo myself. And I laughed in relief when I received the telegram—I laughed! Jim deserved to be punished, but he didn't deserve to die. He deserved the chance to repent, to change, to be forgiven by God and by me, but I never gave him that chance.

A drop of water smudged the ink, and Helen glanced up. Was the new roof leaking? She blinked away haze, and tears dribbled down her cheeks.

Never—not once in the two years and two days since Jim died—had she cried for him.

She stuffed the letter in her pocketbook and pulled out a handkerchief. "Lord, how can you forgive me for murder? Please, please forgive me."

She stood so fast her chair wobbled. She had to find work. In Vic's office she straightened his diploma from Boalt Law School and the cross-stitch of Augustine's quote, then whirled to his desk and sorted pencils. Didn't even one of them need sharpening?

There! On the corner of his desk, a stack of papers. Why wait until he asked her to file? She clutched them to her chest, went to her desk, and sorted them into piles.

She frowned. She recognized that paper—the medical form for Carver Jones signed by Dr. Thompson, the pig. Shouldn't that have gone to the admiral for the hearing?

The door creaked open. Vic marched past, gave Helen a nod, and entered his office. He'd been quiet and distracted since the conviction.

Helen went to the doorway. "Um, Vic, I found this while filing."

He sat down, flopped his briefcase on the desk, and held out his hand for the paper.

She gave it to him. "It's Carver Jones's medical form. Didn't you need that today?"

Vic pursed his lips. "No. They—they'd already seen it. Helped some. Admiral Wright reduced the sentences to twelve years for most of the men, and to eight for Carver and a few others."

Helen's chest crushed and forced out the words. "Eight

years? But he didn't do anything wrong. He should be acquitted."

"Yeah. Well, he wasn't." He opened his briefcase with a snap that matched his voice.

"You're appealing, aren't you?"

"I'll file an individual appeal as soon as possible."

Helen sighed and glanced at the sampler as she returned to her desk. "Let justice be done though the world perish." What if the world turned its back on justice?

25

Bury St. Edmunds Airfield
Sunday, December 24, 1944

"Finally finished our tours." Leo Goldman dipped his brush in blue paint and wrote "30" on Ray's forehead.

He winced as the paint froze on his skin, and he hiked his scarf over his mouth.

"Too cold for you, California boy?" Sig Werner unzipped his flight jacket and puffed out his chest. "This would be a fine spring day in North Dakota. Real winters make real men."

"Yeah? Well, this fake man wants hot coffee." Ray motioned to the GMC truck. "Let's take our celebration indoors."

The men lugged their flight gear to the truck, jostling each other and erupting in the loud laughter of men who had cheated death.

Ray lagged behind and gazed at *Ascalon*, to be passed to another crew when he returned stateside. Where was his joy at beating the odds, proving himself, and going home?

Vague uneasiness wormed inside, as it had since December 16, when the Germans launched a surprise offensive in the Ardennes, and heavy fog and ice had grounded the strategic Eighth Air Force, the tactical Ninth Air Force, and the RAF, leaving the Allies without air cover.

His discomfort lifted with the weather on the twenty-third when he could fly again. The Battle of the Bulge proved the war was far from over—but Ray was going home. The uneasiness returned to squirm in his stomach and twitch in his muscles.

"Come on, Pops. Your chariot awaits." Buffo beckoned from the back of the truck.

Ray sent an acknowledging wave. His flying boots crunched through the snow, and his breath left icy prickles on his scarf. Light fog hovered over the airfield, pewter gray in the twilight. Over an hour ago, *Ascalon* had landed with the fifty planes the 94th had dispatched for the maximum-effort mission, and still, dozens of engines droned overhead. Since First Division's fields lay farther inland, socked in by heavy fog, most of their planes were landing at Third Division fields in East Anglia.

Landing lights circled the field, haloed by fog, as close to Christmas lights as Ray would see this year.

He slung his flight gear into the truck and climbed in.

"Lousy Krauts," Goldman said as the truck pulled away. "Did you hear they dropped spies behind our lines in GI uniforms, speaking perfect American English?"

"Yeah, but we caught some of them," Radovich said. "Shot the stinking sons of Satan."

"Summary execution." Buffo shook a cigarette from his pack. "Fitting punishment for espionage and sabotage. However, I disagree that there is such a thing as perfect American English."

Ray massaged the sore spot on his cheek where the strap for his oxygen mask rubbed. "At least the Battle of the Bulge shows something good."

Nine pairs of eyes swiveled to Ray.

"Good?" Werner said. "They railroaded us, pushed us

back fifty miles, surrounded the 101st Airborne at Bastogne, killed or captured who knows how many."

"Yes, but why did they do that?" Ray said. "Remember what Colonel Dougher said at briefing? The Germans are driving for oil. They're desperate for it. Those rugged missions we flew to oil targets at Merseburg, Magdeburg, Bohlen—they worked."

"What a cost though." Werner's voice dipped low.

An explosion boomed in Ray's ears. He craned his head out the back of the truck. At the end of the main runway, a fiery plume rose in the darkening sky, eerie in the fog.

He let out a deep sigh. "Fort crashed on landing."

Quiet curses filled the back of the truck. In such weather conditions, the crash could have been anyone, even a crew on their last mission.

The truck came to a stop. After the men turned in flight gear and picked up coffee and corned beef sandwiches from the Red Cross girls, they entered the smoke-filled briefing room. *Ascalon*'s crew crammed around a table with Captain Winchell, an intelligence officer and one of Jack's friends.

Winchell poured shots of whiskey to relax the men and facilitate information gathering.

Goldman held up the flask. "Say, Pops. You wanted to warm up, didn't you?"

Ray smiled and sipped his coffee, letting his lips defrost on the rim of the mug. At 23,000 feet the thermometer read fifty degrees below zero. *Ascalon*'s aluminum skin, a pathetic cabin heater, and layers of flight gear only took the edge off cold like that.

Over the next half hour Winchell extracted mission details. Me 109s had attacked over Liège but were driven off by the "Little Friends," P-51 Mustangs escorting the heavy bombers. Low visibility over the target airfield at Babenhausen led to

H2X bombing, but flak was light and the Luftwaffe didn't reappear. No Forts from the 94th were lost.

"Good job, boys." From behind, Jack set his hands on Ray's shoulders. "Congratulations on finishing your tour. Can I talk you into a second tour?"

The men groaned, cussed, and waved him off.

Jack laughed. A thin laugh.

Ray glanced up. Jack's cheeks—usually ruddy from cold after a mission—were pale, and a tic shuttered one eye.

"Are you done, Winch?" Jack asked.

"Done with the interrogation." A smile crossed Winchell's square face. "But the party's just beginning."

"Ray, can I speak with you alone?" Jack asked in a low voice.

"Sure." He stood and sent his crew to the mess. Then he frowned at Jack. The uneasiness coiled into a hard lump in his stomach. Had a buzz bomb hit Walt's station? Had Jack received a telegram from home? Grandpa and Grandma were getting on in years.

"Let's go to my quarters." Jack led the way out of the packed room. As air executive, he enjoyed a private room, while Ray and the others slept twenty-four to a Nissen hut.

They stepped out into the frosty evening, and Ray snugged his scarf up around his mouth.

"New scarf?" Jack asked.

"Christmas present." Ray's smile rubbed against the soft gray wool, the silver lining Helen said she'd promised to knit for him. "What's up?"

Jack gazed at the men passing by. "Let's wait. They'll know soon enough, but . . ."

The knot in Ray's stomach shifted position. It was war news, not family news.

"Can't take long," Jack said. "Seventy extra planes are

landing here tonight, even a squadron of RAF Lancasters. We'll have seven hundred extra men to feed and house. Poor fellows will have to sleep in the briefing room, officers' club, the Aeroclub."

"Guess we'll share our turkey dinner tomorrow."

"Mm." Jack's eyes took on a focused look.

They turned down a road cleared of snow by hundreds of boots. They passed under trees frosted white and draped with icicles, beauty too great for words, but he'd try for Helen's sake.

Jack entered the hut shared by the other top brass and opened the door to his room, luxurious by military standards with a cot, desk, wash basin, and coal stove. He punched a finger through the ice in the wash basin. "I'll start a fire."

While he chucked a bucket of coal into the potbellied stove and lit it, Ray pulled out the desk chair and straddled it backward. "Bad news?"

"Times two." He brushed coal dust off his hands and sat on the bed. "Both will hit the men hard."

Ray pulled down his scarf and gave a slow nod.

"Glenn Miller flew out on the fifteenth to give a concert for the troops in France. His plane never landed. We don't know if it was shot down over the Channel or went down in the weather. The men will find out tonight."

"Oh no." Ray's eyes drooped shut. Although he'd never met the man, he felt as if he'd lost a friend, and he wouldn't be alone. Glenn Miller was more than a celebrity, he was one of their own.

"And Colonel Castle—I mean, General Castle." Jack raked his hand through his hair. "I can't believe it. He was only promoted a week—no, ten days ago. Ten days."

Brig. Gen. Frederick Castle, former CO of the 94th, commanded the Fourth Combat Bomb Wing and led the wing that day to Babenhausen. "What happened to Castle?"

"His plane went down. Seven chutes."

"Oh no." Like the captain of a naval ship, a pilot never left until all his men did.

"Looks like he leveled off to let the men bail, but then— then he didn't have time. The plane exploded."

A crushing sensation in Ray's chest. "Oh no. I'm so sorry."

Jack leaned his elbows on his knees and gripped his hair in fists. "When he first came to Bury, I didn't think much of him. He was a supply officer, for heaven's sake, no combat experience, soft-spoken, not what a commander should be. But then . . . he's the best man I've ever worked for. Ever. Intelligent, firm, caring, courageous. He flew all the toughest missions, all of them, made good changes around here. He disciplined me when I needed it, but he never, never gave up on me."

The only other time Ray had seen Jack this devastated was the previous Christmas when he thought Charlie was dead.

He got up, sat next to his brother, and draped his arm across slumped shoulders. "Lord, we know you have a purpose in everything, but sometimes we can't see it. We hurt. Please comfort my brother. Hold him tight and help him be strong for the men. We need you, Lord. Help us rest in your sovereignty, in the knowledge that you are good."

Jack raised haggard eyes. "Thanks. I needed that. I hate to ask—I know you're eager to go home, but could you wait a week or so? The men rely on you. Chaplain Miller—he thinks of you as an extra chaplain around here."

Ray's hand dropped onto his lap. The uneasiness had a name—incompletion. His work over here wasn't done yet.

Sure, the ground troops needed the air campaign to succeed, but it ran deeper than that. The war had kept him from the pulpit but not the ministry. This was where he was needed, to help men in their grief, sin, and moral dilemmas.

And Helen's healing had progressed, but right now she needed him as a counselor from afar. A tiny sapling of hope poked green against the snow. A few more months and she'd be ready for him in person, maybe even ready for the fullness of his love.

Ray gazed into the glowing red embers in the stove. "I'll be here longer than a week. I'm flying a second tour."

"What?"

"I'm a trained Pathfinder pilot. If I leave, you'll have to pull another man from combat for a month to train."

"Oh no. Oh no, you don't." Jack jumped to his feet and glared at Ray. "Everyone will think I talked you into it, that I'm up to my old manipulative tricks again."

"I'll tell them you tried to talk me out of it. But it didn't work."

Jack huffed and glanced at the ceiling. "Mom will kill me if anything happens to you."

"I'm in God's hands, not yours."

"Yeah, as if Mom would see it that way." He gave the stove a little kick. Then he turned to Ray with a trace of a smile. "Say, if you fly a second tour, you'll be promoted to captain."

"So?"

"And you'll get a thirty-day furlough at home first."

"I won't take it. The more planes we have over here, the sooner we finish this war and go home for good."

Jack rubbed his hand over his mouth and regarded Ray for a long moment. "All my life I thought you were the least stubborn of the Novak boys."

Ray lifted an eyebrow. "Guess again."

26

Antioch
Monday, December 25, 1944

"For my Della, my beautiful princess." Mr. Carlisle set another gift on his wife's lap and kissed her on the mouth.

"Oh, James, you shouldn't have." Her adoring smile was blocked by a welt on her cheek. Heavy makeup disguised any redness, but not the swelling.

Helen's stomach churned. Two nights ago she'd heard yelling and crying, and now the profusion of gifts and compliments sealed it—Mr. Carlisle beat his wife. Helen had once been foolish enough to fall for Jim's apologies and gifts and flattery after a burst of violence.

"Hold it up, son," Mr. Carlisle said. "Show us what Santa brought you."

Jay-Jay shredded paper, frowned, and held up two black pumps.

Helen dashed to his side, forced a laugh, and searched for the tag. "Goodness, sweetie, those are for Mama. See—*H* for Helen. That's Mama."

His lower lip pushed out and quivered.

"Lookie here." Mr. Carlisle waved a box wrapped in green paper. "This is for my boy."

Helen returned to the side chair and opened the box from Papa and Mama, which held brand-new black leather pumps and a chic suit in wool the color of wine.

Tears pooled in her eyes. Since rationing only provided two pairs of leather shoes per person each year, Helen used her portion on Jay-Jay's growing feet. This gift meant Papa and Mama had sacrificed for her. She missed them so much. Papa got mad at Mama sometimes, and he growled and slammed doors, but he never raised a finger against her.

But Papa was Helen's physician. Didn't he wonder why Helen's accidents increased after her marriage, ceased when Jim enlisted, and returned on Jim's furlough? Didn't he see? Didn't he care?

Granted, most of her injuries didn't require medical care, some weren't visible, and all were easily explained away. But still, why didn't he see?

Or did Papa think she deserved it too? He'd never truly forgiven her for catching polio, as if the doctor's daughter should have been immune, should have been healthy and strong like Betty, should never have stooped to wearing braces. Some parents coddled their invalids, but not Papa. He'd been harder on her, required more of her. And it was never enough.

The doorbell rang. Helen sprang to her feet, composed herself, and opened the door.

Dorothy Wayne stood on the porch. "Merry Christmas. I brought gifts."

"Come on in. Where's Susie?"

"I didn't bring her. I can't stay." She leaned in and waved to her parents. "Merry Christmas."

The Carlisles came over, kissed their daughter, exchanged bags of gifts, and returned to the living room.

Helen stared at them and then at Dorothy. That was all

they had to say to each other on Christmas Day? What was wrong with this family?

"Bye, Helen."

"Wait. I want to talk to you." Helen closed the door behind her and led Dorothy under the bare sticks of the nectarine tree in front of the kitchen window. Despite the chilled air, heat rose in her chest as she looked into her friend's puzzled face. "Did he beat you too?"

"Excuse me?"

"Your father beats your mother. Did he beat you too?"

Dorothy crossed her arms and looked away. "I don't know what you're talking about."

The heat prickled up the back of her neck. "Oh yes, you do. It's why you have so little to do with them."

Dorothy's brown eyes flashed as if Helen had done the beating. "I thought it was normal. I thought that was how men were supposed to treat women."

"Did he beat you? Tell me. Did he?"

"No." Her shoulders hunched up, and her voice shrank. "That was Jim's job."

"Jim?" So he'd practiced on his little sister. What kind of family allowed such a thing? That meant . . . that meant . . . "You knew. You knew what he was like. Why didn't you warn me? Why did you let me marry him?"

Dorothy stepped back. "I—I—"

"Why? Why? You could have stopped me. Why didn't you stop me?"

"I thought it was normal."

"Normal? If it's normal, why do they hide it?"

"I didn't—I thought—"

"Did you think I deserved it? For being a cripple? For not being as fun as Betty?"

"Helen!" Dorothy's eyes brimmed over.

Helen pressed her lips together so she wouldn't cry as well, and she crossed her arms over her roiling stomach. "I'm sorry. I know you wouldn't do that."

Dorothy placed a hand over her crumpled face. "I'm sorry. I didn't know how wrong it was until I married Art and went to live with the Waynes. Now I see why Mom and I had to hide it, what Dad and Jim did, because it wasn't normal, because it was wrong."

"It took you that long to figure it out?"

Dorothy's chest convulsed in a sob. "Oh goodness. It was more than that. More. I'm so sorry. You'll never forgive me. I wanted him out. I wanted him gone. That's why I didn't stop you. So—so selfish. I only thought of myself. I didn't think of you at all."

Helen stared at her weeping friend, her emotions in a jumble. How could Dorothy do that to her? But her anger sizzled out under the water of truth—she'd also wanted to get rid of Jim. How could she blame Dorothy for doing the same thing she'd done?

"Dorothy?" she said in the low tone they'd used as children to convey secrets. "I wanted him gone too. I did. I encouraged him to enlist. I wanted him to die."

Her hand lowered from her splotchy face. "I—I understand."

"Do you blame me? Do you blame me for his death?"

"No. I blame the Japanese, I blame him. But not you. Never you." She reached out tentative hands. "Oh, Helen. Can you . . . can you ever forgive me?"

Helen tried to nod, but her swollen throat wouldn't bend. She wrapped her arms around Dorothy, and the women wept on each other's shoulders.

Somehow the tears released another burden from Helen's back. Another person knew, another person understood, another person hated it. Ray knew, but he'd never understand like someone who lived with it.

"I've never," Dorothy said. "I've never talked about this with anyone, not even Art."

"Tell him. Even in a letter."

"When he gets home."

Helen nodded on Dorothy's shoulder. It would be nicer to tell secrets like that in the arms of a gentle man who loved you. "I'm glad you got out."

Dorothy pulled back. "I should have said something when you moved in. But Dad won't hit you, and he'll treat Mom better with you around."

"Maybe, but I'm getting out as soon as I can." Her smile wobbled.

"I wish the Waynes had an extra room."

"It's all right." The war had created a serious housing shortage in California, and no one had extra rooms. Perhaps she shouldn't have been so quick to turn down Vic's marriage proposals—at least she'd be out. But the thought brought up a strange moist giggle. She'd have to be desperate to take the name of Helen Llewellyn. And Vic had stopped proposing anyway.

Dorothy gave her a limp smile. "I should go. Thanks for . . . I'm sorry I . . . Merry Christmas."

"Thank you too, and I'm sorry too, and Merry Christmas to you too." Helen waved good-bye and headed back to the house. She'd tell Ray in a letter tonight. Surely this was progress. She also wanted to thank him for the picture book he'd given Jay-Jay and the journal he'd given her—in case there was anything she couldn't tell him, he'd said. As if she hadn't poured out her entire heart to him—except her love for him, of course.

As soon as she opened the door, Jay-Jay screamed, and an empty box flew through the air and hit Mrs. Carlisle.

"Jay-Jay!"

"It's all right," Mrs. Carlisle said. "He doesn't have any more presents to open."

Shakes traveled through Helen's body. No, she wouldn't allow this to happen to her son. She wouldn't.

She strode over crumpled tissue paper and grabbed him around the waist. "No. Don't ever, ever treat someone like that."

"It's all right," Mrs. Carlisle said. "I understand why he's upset."

"That doesn't give him any right." She clutched her flailing son and headed for the stairs.

"Where do you think you're taking him?" Mr. Carlisle said.

"To his room."

"Oh no," his grandmother cried. "But it's Christmas."

"I don't care." Helen mounted the stairs, careful with her step since her son writhed and her limbs shook. "He needs to learn he can't treat people like that. Ever. I won't let him."

Footsteps thumped behind her. Mr. Carlisle grabbed her elbow and swung her around.

Helen cried out, dropped to her bottom, and clipped her tailbone on a step. Clutching Jay-Jay, she raised an elbow for protection.

No blow landed.

Jay-Jay whimpered, and Helen's breath came fast and hard. In the background on the radio, Judy Garland crooned "Have Yourself a Merry Little Christmas."

"Are you all right, son?" Mr. Carlisle extracted Jay-Jay from Helen's grasp. "Your mother should be careful on the stairs. So clumsy. You could have been hurt."

Jay-Jay's face twisted, and he blinked at Helen.

Her heart slammed against her backbone. Mr. Carlisle blamed her for his actions, and he was teaching Jay-Jay to do likewise.

"Come on, my boy. Let's play with your new toys." Mr. Carlisle took him downstairs, away—away from Helen.

She moaned. Her son. Her little son.

Helen collapsed over her knees, racked by silent sobs. She couldn't let James Carlisle III end up like his predecessors.

27

Bury St. Edmunds Airfield
Monday, January 15, 1945

"A vital target." Jack tapped the pointer at the screen in the briefing room, which made the image shimmer as if underwater. "Lechfeld is a base for Messerschmitt 262 jet fighters and is also a training and research facility, which increases its importance."

Ray studied the slide of a gray field with runways and hangars, bordered on the east by broad black stripes of forest around a silver ribbon. Since H2X radar best showed the contrast between water and land, rivers served as excellent landmarks. The Lech River ran north from the Alps, skirted Lechfeld, flowed through Augsburg, and joined the Danube.

"All right, men." Jack propped his pointer on his shoulder like a rifle. "You couldn't ask for better flying weather. Go knock out some jets."

A low rumble of voices built in the room as the men stood to leave. Despite Jack's assertion of the target's importance, Third Division was only sending 297 B-17s. Within the Third Division, *Ascalon* would lead the fourteen planes of the 94th Bomb Group.

Ray lifted a hand to his brother in farewell. Jack wiggled

his fingers as if playing a piano, and Ray grinned and nodded. Tonight they'd share songs, coffee, and conversation in
the Officers' Club.

Ray followed the crowd outside. His breath caught at the
sight of the moonlight sparkling on the snow. Straight ahead,
Draco's tail curled around the Little Dipper as if hoarding
a jeweled goblet.

"Watch out, Draco," Ray whispered. "Here comes *Ascalon*."

★

"Radio to pilot. I heard from division lead. Head for the
secondary."

"Thank you . . . Fitzgerald. Okay, men. Plot the new
course." Ray frowned. He'd had his new crew for two weeks.
The names should have flowed off his tongue.

Soon Casey, the navigator, gave a new set of coordinates,
and Ray adjusted his heading toward the railroad marshalling yards at Augsburg.

A thousand feet above, P-51 Mustangs flew a zigzag pattern, ready to jump to the rescue if the Luftwaffe came up
to fight.

If only someone had jumped to Helen's rescue.

Ray sighed and adjusted the four throttles. Helen's most
recent letters poured out her guilt over wishing Jim dead. Ray
couldn't blame her—the man had tortured her. Good thing
Jim Carlisle was already dead, because Ray felt capable of
violence for the first time since first grade, when he'd punched
out Bill Ferguson for taunting the Portuguese children.

"We're at the IP," the radar operator said.

"Thanks, Kenton." Ray zoomed his mind back into focus.
The Initial Point signaled the beginning of the bomb run.

"Bomb bay doors opening," said Lieutenant Rogers, the
bombardier.

"Firing two yellow flares," Fitzgerald called from the radio room. The flares and the open doors signaled the IP to the rest of the group.

Over the next ten minutes, Ray concentrated on altitude and airspeed while the navigator, bombardier, and radar operator called back and forth on the interphone, locating Augsburg, which straddled the junction of the Wertach and Lech rivers.

Ahead of *Ascalon*, black blotches stained the sky—moderate flak, but a single well-placed shell could fell a plane.

Ray raised half a smile, which tilted his oxygen mask. Thirty-three missions today, and while he'd never be as cool under fire as Jack, he rested in the Lord's loving and sovereign hands, where fear had no place and courage wrapped like a cloak about him.

Lieutenant Donatelli, the copilot, cursed the flak.

Ray gave him a pat on the back. "A few minutes and we'll hightail it out of here."

"Not soon enough."

"There, I've got it," Kenton called from the waist section where the H2X resided. "What a sweet, sweet target. Let 'em fly, Rogers."

"Bombs away."

"Two red flares fired."

"Okay, fellows," Ray said. "Enough sightseeing. Let's go home."

An explosion at two o'clock high, shuddering, earsplitting. A black belch of smoke. A tongue of red flame. Shrapnel pummeled the plane, rocks on a tin roof.

Ray cringed down. Shrapnel dinged off his flak helmet, his arm.

He wheeled around and gasped. Fist-sized holes perforated the right side and roof of the cockpit, baring fangs of aluminum and Plexiglas.

Donatelli slumped in his seat, his hand clutched to the right side of his neck. Then his hand fell limp to his lap. His red hand. His red lap.

"Donatelli!" Ray cried against the heaviness of knowing his copilot would never speak again.

Ray gripped the wheel, scanned the gauges. He still had four engines. "Damage report. Bombardier? Navigator?"

No response.

The interphone. He'd lost the interphone.

Ray put the Fort into a left-hand turn. He had to follow the rest of the division and lead his group home. "Shreve," he yelled to the flight engineer behind him. "Interphone's out. Go down to the nose, tell the navigator to come up here a minute."

He glanced out the side windows to keep an eye on the formation, since he could no longer get reports from his crewmen in the back.

"Shreve." Ray flung his right arm behind him to get the gunner's attention—and hit air.

Shreve lay crumpled over the platform for his turret.

"Oh no." Ray's stomach lurched at the rusty smell of blood. The flak burst took off the Plexiglas dome for the top turret—and most of Shreve's head.

He whipped back to the wheel, light-headed, but he had to keep his wits. The rest of his crew and his group depended on him. "Lord, help me."

Ray blew out a breath and loosened his grip on the wheel. The controls and engines were in fine shape. All he had to do was follow the division home.

But flak buffeted the plane and Ray's heart.

His eyes stung, and the acrid smell of hot metal hit his nose. White smoke seeped from seams in the right side of the control panel.

A chill raced up Ray's spine. The fire extinguisher hung out of reach on the bulkhead behind the copilot's seat.

After he leveled off from the turn, he flipped on the autopilot switches and adjusted the rudder, aileron, and elevator centering knobs. "Pilot to crew. Can you hear me? I need help in the cockpit. Now."

Ray unplugged the interphone cord and oxygen, and scrambled behind the copilot's seat.

After he hooked up a portable oxygen bottle, he grabbed the fire extinguisher. Yellow flames licked out of the control panel. With shaking hands, he raised the horn of the extinguisher, aimed it at the fire, turned the handle, and pumped the plunger. Powdery white carbon tetrachloride coated the control panel.

Ray stopped. The flames came back, higher now, creeping to the middle of the panel.

Crying out in frustration, he emptied the extinguisher into the flames.

"What's going on up here?" Lieutenant Casey, the navigator, stuck his head up the passageway. "The inter—oh my—" He dropped his jaw and half a dozen curse words.

"Get me another fire extinguisher. Now, Casey. Go!"

Something exploded behind the control panel, warped it, and the flames spread.

Casey ducked and swore. "The oxygen."

Ray coughed. The phosgene gas from the fire extinguisher was poisonous. He'd have to open the windows, but that would feed the fire. And the flames reached toward the wheel and distorted his view out the windshield.

As when Helen's house burned down, he was struck with the impenetrable translucence of fire—and how a life could change in an instant.

He turned to Casey. "Bail out! Go to the nose, get Rogers, and get out of here. I'll go to the back, get the others."

Ray reached down beside the pilot's seat to ring the bailout bell. One long ring to signal stand by for bailing, then three short rings to bail out now. But he couldn't rely on the bell. He'd tell the men in person.

The heat built, but Ray had work to do. After he turned off the autopilot, he strained through the heat to put the plane into a shallow dive away from the formation. He tossed aside the portable oxygen, fumbled in his left thigh pocket for the connecting tube on the bailout oxygen bottle, and attached it to the adaptor on his mask. Then he threw the "flimsies," the mimeographed flight plans, into the fire.

A sick feeling writhed in his stomach as he left Donatelli and Shreve behind. He forged through the bomb bay, gripping the supports for the bomb racks. His seat-pack parachute flapped at the back of his knees.

Today he'd have to use it.

Dread clamped a fist around his heart, but he kept moving.

"Bail out," he told the radio operator at his desk. "Fire in the cockpit. Get out of here."

"But—but—"

"Now." Ray pulled the release tabs on the shoulders of Fitzgerald's flak vest, then remembered to take off his own. "Where's your chute?"

Fitzgerald pulled his chest parachute from under his desk.

Ray pressed through the door to the waist section. "Bail—"

Noise jammed his ears. The floor kicked out from underneath him. He tumbled to the bulkhead, to the wall, banged his shoulder, his back, his head.

He grabbed something—control cables. His legs swung loose and slammed the wall.

Where the tail should have been—nothing but open sky.

"Dear Lord in heaven." Ray grasped the cables with all his might. An antiaircraft shell must have taken off the tail.

Ascalon plunged toward the earth, and Ray stared at the cables in his fists, pulling him down with his plane.

The only way to live was to let go.

✦

Antioch

Helen rolled over in bed and snuggled the chenille bedspread over her ear, but she knew she wouldn't go back to sleep. How could she with the tension in the Carlisle household as taut as her leg muscles when the polio struck?

On Saturday, she'd taken Jay-Jay to a matinee of Roy Rogers in *Red River Valley*, then stayed at Betty's house until Jay-Jay's bedtime. After church, she accepted the Llewellyns' dinner invitation and then spent the afternoon calling on anyone she could think of. But suppertime forced her home, where Mr. Carlisle grumbled about overcooked vegetables in the soup and the profusion of hillbilly music on the radio. Even the Allied progress in the Philippines and the closure of the Bulge failed to cheer him.

Something would happen soon.

Helen sat up in bed, clicked on the lamp, and pulled her Bible from the nightstand. Only at the Lord's feet could she calm her nerves. Ray was so good for her, not just his wise words but his advice to take her concerns to God.

The day before, Pastor Novak preached about the Day of the Lord. The war caused many to fear the end of the world, but Pastor Novak reminded them fear didn't come from God.

The ribbon in Helen's Bible still lay in Obadiah, so that's where she read, until she reached verse 4: "Though thou exalt thyself as the eagle, and though thou set thy nest among the stars, thence will I bring thee down, saith the Lord."

Helen shivered and set aside her Bible. Maybe she'd go straight to prayer. She prayed for Ray among the stars and for Jay-Jay among the wolves. She prayed for Carver and the other men in prison, and for Esther, as alone as any widow.

Restlessness prickled her legs and arms. She stuffed her feet into her slippers and pulled on her bathrobe and coat.

Helen padded downstairs and onto the front porch. Fog blurred the houses across C Street, the thick "tule" fog that clung to the ground in central California and the Delta each winter. Somewhere behind the fog, the sun was rising.

Helen bounced her legs against the damp chill penetrating her pajama pants. She sat in the wicker rocker and set it in motion to warm up, hunching over her crossed arms. Half an hour remained before she had to get dressed and get Jay-Jay up.

The stillness of dawn didn't hold its usual peace.

She wanted out. But how? She had a year to pay off her debt, a year before she could free her salary for rent and necessities to set up house. Papa would never help her. He'd made that abundantly clear. And where else could she stay? Betty was expecting another baby, and her house would be jam-packed come May. All her friends had filled their extra rooms with boarders. She was stuck.

Helen rocked harder.

Motion on the lawn caught her eye. The Scalas' orange tabby strutted along, an affectionate cat. Helen clucked her tongue to get his attention, the sound amplified in the fog.

The cat stopped and turned to Helen—with a bird in his mouth.

Ray had written about a feline gunner who failed to bring down his aerial prey. The Scalas' cat had succeeded.

" 'Thence will I bring thee down.' " Helen tugged her coat against a shuddering chill.

28

Over Germany

Ray let go.

Sky and plane and clouds tumbled around him. In panic, he groped for the security of his plane.

No. It was a false security. He forced his mind to remember his training. He had to clear *Ascalon*'s falling debris.

When clouds appeared in his vision, Ray flung out his arms and legs spread-eagle. His body rocked on the air currents, but now his plane fell faster than he did. Without any reference point, the only evidence of his fall was the frigid air howling past.

Count to ten. He was supposed to count to ten. How could he remember his numbers with nothing but clouds between him and solid ground?

Ten seconds must have passed. He gripped the ripcord on his left shoulder harness and squeezed it tight in his gloved fingers. If the parachute didn't open, he'd be with Jesus in less than two minutes.

A firm tug. The chute whooshed out, snapped open, yanked him hard around the groin and chest. He coughed from the impact. But the wind's whistle ceased.

Ray's vision darkened. How long had he been off oxygen?

He felt around his left thigh pocket, found the green wooden ball on the release cable of the bailout bottle, and pulled it.

He drew deep drafts until his vision lightened. His breath came hard and his heart whammed in his chest, but what did he expect? He hovered four miles high with only a circle of white silk to save him.

Ascalon tumbled in flames into the cloud bank, surrounded by chunks of debris. Two parachutes billowed ahead and beneath him. Two? Probably Casey and Rogers from the nose. But only two? No others?

"Oh Lord." For the first time in his life, words for prayer escaped him. The other men never made it out, never had a chance.

Ray descended into the clouds and took one last glance above, where the silver trail of B-17s left him behind. They'd report the fall of *Ascalon* and the sighting of three chutes.

Only three. Jack would assume he was dead. Dad and Mom would receive a telegram that he was missing in action, but Jack would send a letter with details. Everyone would think he was dead until his name appeared on the prisoner of war list, which often took months.

"Oh no. Helen." She'd mourn him, and worse, she'd blame herself. In her last letter, she wrote that she'd driven Jim into danger and she'd done the same to Ray. But she hadn't. He'd mailed his reply, hadn't he?

Her plea tugged at him. "Please take care, Ray."

His heart felt as heavy as the cloud around him. "Oh, honey, I'm so sorry."

When he broke out of the clouds, he floated over a picturesque landscape of snowy fields, gentle hills, patches of woods, and small towns centered around churches. But this was not the way he wanted to see Germany. Instead of cruising the Rhine, hiking the Alps, and touring Heidelberg and

Neuschwanstein castles, he'd sleep in a Stalag Luft for the duration of the war.

Life in a prison camp. Cold and hunger, captivity and deprivation. He'd have to make the best of it. At least he'd have plenty of men to minister to.

Soon he made out people and vehicles and farm animals. He unfastened one side of his oxygen mask, and it flapped to the side.

People rushed around below. One of the parachutes collapsed as Ray's crewman landed. A German ran up to him, took something from him, then backed up and pointed. A retort, and the airman crumpled.

Ray gasped. They shot him! Shot him with his own pistol.

The other parachute collapsed. A mob surrounded the officer with flailing fists and sticks. They were beating him to death.

Ray's breath came faster, harder. He had to get away. He tugged his parachute cords and shifted his course hard to the left.

"Lord, lead me. Lead me to someone who'll turn me in."

A snow-blanketed field, a barn, a thick wood to his left, and no people in sight. Maybe he could hide in the woods until nightfall, make his way to town, to a church, where he wouldn't be lynched.

Ray raised bent legs and gripped the straps overhead. The ground rushed to him. The jolt shuddered through his body. He fell flat on his face in the snow, knocking out his breath.

For a horrific moment, he couldn't breathe. With great effort, he forced open his ribs like a bellows and sucked in air.

He pushed himself up onto wobbly legs, only to stumble as a breeze caught his billowing parachute. Ray pulled the cords to draw it in.

"Hände hoch!"

Ray obeyed and thrust his hands high. "I surrender. *Ich ergebe mich.*"

An old man in a patched, padded jacket ran to him and brandished a pitchfork. "*Terrorflieger! Terrorflieger!*"

Terror flyer? "*Nein. Ich ergebe mich. Ich ergebe mich.*"

The man jabbed his pitchfork toward Ray's stomach. "*Terrorflieger.*" He spat at Ray, then launched a furious diatribe in rapid speech and unfamiliar dialect. Something about bombs and a house and a daughter.

Compassion and regret flooded through Ray. He never wanted to hurt civilians. He tried his best to avoid it, but here was evidence of what one errant bomb could do.

Ray settled his softest gaze on the poor man. "*Es tut mir leid. Ich meine es nicht böse mit Ihnen.*" He tried to assure him he was sorry and didn't mean for anything evil to come to him.

"*Nicht böse?*" The man shook the pitchfork. "*Sie sind böse.*"

Evil. The man thought he was evil.

"*Ach!*" An elderly lady stood at the entrance to the barn with a brown scarf around her hair and hands over her mouth.

The couple had a spirited discussion, and Ray glanced around—still no one else.

The man motioned Ray toward the barn. "*Bring eine Leiter,*" he called to his wife.

A ladder?

She trotted inside. "*Und ein Seil?*"

A rope?

"*Nein, er hat seinen Fallschirm.*"

He had his *Fallschirm*? *Fallschirm*? *Fallen* meant to fall, but *Schirm*? Ray didn't know that word. *Regenschirm* was an umbrella, however.

Ray's veins froze. His parachute. They planned to hang him with his own parachute.

Voices sounded ahead and a car's motor, and the man's face brightened. He'd have help, probably from the mob that had murdered Casey and Rogers.

Ray spoke the language, though not fluently, and he had the best intentions, but against rage like this, negotiations would fail.

He gritted his teeth. *Lord, guide me. I'm not afraid to die, but I can't bear for Helen to grieve, to blame herself. Dad and Mom, Jack and Walt—I want to live for their sakes.*

Resolution hardened his muscles.

The farmer glared at Ray and leveled his pitchfork at him.

Ray jerked his head to the left as if he'd heard something.

The man snapped his attention—and his pitchfork—in the same direction.

With his left hand, Ray grabbed the pitchfork, and he swung with his right, a hook punch to the man's ear.

The man splayed to the ground, and Ray apologized. *"Es tut mir leid."*

He unhooked his parachute harness and shrugged it off. It'd slow him down.

The voices grew louder, and Ray sprinted for the woods. What good would it do? How far could he go? Could he actually hide?

Ray burst into the woods, dodged trees, leaped over logs, barged through snow-covered underbrush. Shouts rang out back on the farm. They must have found the poor old man, and they'd come after Ray with a vengeance.

Where could he hide? How? He climbed over a recently fallen tree, a large evergreen with long draping needles.

He crawled next to the trunk, wormed under the boughs, tunneled as deep into the snow as he could, and arranged long branches over his body.

Snow prickled his cheek and pine-scented needles tickled

his nose, but he lay still and tried to calm his heaving chest. *Lord, cover me, shield me, hide me.*

The shouts drew nearer. They'd seen where he went, of course.

"*Warten Sie hier.*" Not the farmer, but a man with an authoritative voice, and the crowd listened to his command to wait where they were.

One set of footsteps in the crackling underbrush, straight toward Ray. Footprints. He'd left footprints in the snow.

Ray shrank low, but it was a lost cause. *Lord, let him be a good man.*

"*Kommen Sie hier,*" the man said.

Ray didn't come as commanded. Perhaps he could stay hidden. The man wouldn't order him to come if he knew where he was.

"*Sie sprechen Deutsch, nicht wahr? Das ist gut.*"

Why was it good that Ray spoke German?

Footfalls came closer. The branches over Ray rustled. The man kicked him hard in the stomach. "*Stehen Sie auf.*"

Ray curled up in pain but then struggled to his feet and raised his hands. "*Ich ergebe mich.*"

The man pointed a pistol at him. He wore a Nazi greatcoat, some local official in his fifties with dark, calculating eyes.

Ray tried to look brave, although he'd never looked down the barrel of a gun before. Surely this man would be bound by law to treat him as a prisoner of war. "*Ich ergebe mich.*"

"*Sie haben mit dem Bauer gekämpft.*"

Ray sighed. Yes, he fought with the farmer—because the farmer wanted to kill him. "*Er will mich kühlen.*"

The Nazi's gaze took him in head to toe. "*Sie sprechen mit Akzent, aber Sie sind klug und stark. Gut.*"

Why did it matter that Ray had an accent and was smart and strong? Ray didn't understand. "*Ich verstehe nicht.*"

A twitch of a smile. "Have you a pistol?" he asked in German.

"*Nein.*"

The official gave him a skeptical look. With his gun trained on Ray's head, he unbuckled Ray's life preserver. Then he unzipped Ray's flight jacket and patted down his chest, where many airmen wore a shoulder holster. "No pistol."

Under pressure, Ray struggled with German word order. "Always I tell the truth."

"That could be dangerous." The Nazi jerked his pistol to the side.

With hands overhead, Ray retraced his steps out of the woods.

When he emerged, a dozen people cheered with raised fists. Conversation flew that Ray couldn't pick up, but the Nazi settled them down with a raised hand and a promise to deal with Ray as he'd dealt with the others.

The renewed cheering made Ray's gut twist. They wanted him dead. They wouldn't cheer if they thought the official would turn him in safely to the Stalag Luft.

The farmer's wife held Ray's balled-up parachute. "*Bitte, darf ich ihn haben? Er ist aus Seide.*"

Yes, it was silk. Why shouldn't this poor woman have it? Ray didn't need it. "*Wollen Sie ihn? Ich brauche ihn nicht.*"

The woman's eyes rounded.

"*Nein.*" The Nazi took it in his free arm. "*Er braucht ihn für sein Leichentuch.*"

His shroud. Ray needed it for a shroud.

His heart sank deep into his belly. The pistol jammed his spine, and Ray lifted his hands—they must have sunk as well.

The Nazi marched him to the road.

Soon, not one man from *Ascalon*'s crew would be alive. Ray

could bolt, take a bullet in the back, and die a quick death. Or he could do as told and die a torturous Gestapo death.

No one back home would know which choice he'd made.

Ray gazed up to solid gray clouds. "I'll know, Lord," he whispered, his jaw tight. He hadn't come this far to make a cowardly decision at the end.

☆

Antioch

A thump on the porch, and Helen jumped.

"Sorry, Mrs. Carlisle. Didn't mean to scare you." Down at the curb, Donald Ferguson straddled his bike with a canvas bag slung over his chest.

The *Ledger*. Helen picked it up and waved to the paperboy, who was too far away to see how her smile shook. "Good throw, Donald."

"I wanna play baseball for Antioch High. My dad played for Riverview."

Riverview High, where Ray Novak and Bill Ferguson played ball together, before Ray went to college and Bill somehow ended up marrying Ray's girlfriend.

Helen groaned at how she'd added to Ray's list of failed romances.

She stood and opened the *Ledger*. The headline read "Fall of Manila Expected Soon."

Back in the house, she laid the newspaper on Mr. Carlisle's armchair and headed upstairs to dress for work. With the convicted men imprisoned at Terminal Island in San Pedro in southern California, and with Carver Jones's appeal filed, Victor's job had trickled to busywork. The complaints from black sailors had decreased since the Navy integrated some services and vessels in October, and encouraged promotions on the same basis as for whites.

After she changed into her new wine-colored suit, she went to wake Jay-Jay, but his bed was empty. Helen required him to dress before breakfast, but he loved to sneak down and eat in his pajamas. If his grandmother didn't cater to him, Helen might make progress.

She sighed and trotted downstairs.

"For the last time, where's my paper?" Mr. Carlisle's voice pierced the kitchen door from the inside.

"I—I don't know," Mrs. Carlisle said with a sob. "It wasn't there when I went out."

"Stupid sloth of a woman." A slap. "Lazing in bed while someone steals my paper."

She whimpered. "I'm sorry. You're right. I'm lazy. It won't happen again."

Helen stood frozen in the hallway. Everything warned her to flee, but she alone knew the truth and could stand up for the poor woman. "Lord, give me courage."

She pushed open the door. Mrs. Carlisle cowered by the sink, and her husband loomed over with her hair in his fist.

Helen raised her chin. "Your paper is on your armchair."

Mr. Carlisle released his wife and sauntered over to Helen with eyes of blue-hot flame.

Her soul recoiled at the familiar sight, but she stood tall. "I got up early. I happened to be outside when the paper came, so I brought it in. It's not her fault."

The slap came from nowhere and spun her head with stinging ferocity.

She cried out, clapped her hand over her cheek, and averted her face. That was best. That was always best.

"No one—no one talks to me that way. My paper belongs on the kitchen table at my place. No one reads it before me."

"Yes, sir." Helen hunkered down, turned inside, and

shrank. She caused this mess. She ruined everything. She
deserved the punishment.

The door slammed. Helen looked up through her hair,
and truth wrestled its way to the surface—truth revealed
through opening her memory bin and through listening to
Ray's counsel and the Word of God. She shoved back her hair
and the lie. She'd done nothing wrong and didn't deserve to
be slapped. No one did.

She turned to her mother-in-law. "Are you all right?"

Mrs. Carlisle ran water over the frying pan. "Of course.
I got what I deserved."

"No." Helen laid a hand on her thin shoulder, the twitching
muscles. "Neither one of us deserved it. I made an innocent
mistake, and you had nothing to do with it. And it's never
right for a man to hit a woman, especially the woman he
claims to love."

Mrs. Carlisle spun to face her. "You think you're so high-
and-mighty, don't you? The doctor's daughter with her blas-
phemous thoughts. It's a husband's God-given duty to keep
his wife in line. I'm glad we taught Jimmy right. I'm glad
he hit you."

Helen's eyes stung as she stared into the contorted face.
Over twenty-five years of a warped marriage had poisoned her
mind. Would Helen have ended up like that if Jim had lived?

A fork clanked on a plate.

Helen whirled around. At the kitchen table, Jay-Jay
hunched in his chair with wide eyes.

"Oh, baby." He'd seen the whole thing. She dashed to him
and took him by the shoulders. How could Mr. Carlisle do
such a thing in front of a boy not yet three years old?

"Mama?" He placed a hand on Helen's cheek, making her
wince in pain. "Pease don't make Gampa an-gee."

Her vision swam at his tenderness. She clutched him in

her arms. She needed to get him out before this house sucked away his compassion.

It was time to give up her heart's work. She had to give up the work she loved most to save the person she loved most. Why did life force such cruel choices?

29

Outside Augsburg

"Out of the auto," the Nazi said in German. He spoke no English at all.

With his hands cuffed behind him, Ray swung his legs outside and pitched his body forward to stand up. Before him, a small farmhouse sat far from civilization, devoid of paint, roof bowed with snow under a leaden sky. This might be the last building he saw.

Despite trembling limbs, he squared his shoulders and mounted creaky stairs. In the dragon's lair, cold air smelled of ham and smoke and decay. Scant furniture stood in no particular order, and soot tinged the walls.

The Nazi opened a door, tossed Ray's parachute down the cellar stairs, and removed the handcuffs.

"*Danke schön.*" Ray's hands fell to his sides. He resisted the urge to stretch his cramped muscles.

The Nazi pointed to the cellar. "Put here your *Fluchtausrüstung.*"

"I don't know that word."

"Things. Things for running."

His escape kit? With his eyes on the man with the gun,

Ray leaned down to unbutton his shin pocket and threw the olive drab canvas pouch into the cellar.

"Everything. Your helmet too."

Ray emptied his pockets of flight rations and pocketknife, then removed his steel flak helmet and leather flying helmet with the oxygen mask strapped on one side. This made no sense, but he intended to be compliant within the limits of his orders.

"Give to me your personal things—papers, letters, talismans."

"I have none." All he had was his Bible, but he planned to die with it over his heart.

"Seat yourself." He pulled a chair to the table, sloughed off his greatcoat, and tossed it over a chair, and then tucked his pistol into his holster. "Have you hunger?"

Was it wise to admit hunger? He lowered himself into the chair. "Captain Raymond Garlovsky Novak, serial—"

"*Nein.*" He flapped a hand at Ray and threw sticks into the feeble fire in the fireplace. "You will want food. I have not much, but I give you bread and cheese."

"*Nein, danke.*" Wasn't that a typical interrogation tactic? To start with a show of friendliness to lower a man's guard?

The Nazi pulled two cloth-covered bundles from a shelf, set them on the table, and pulled off the cloth to reveal a dark bread and a pale cheese. "It is not polite to refuse good bread. You will eat. Enjoy Bavarian *Gemütlichkeit.*"

Ray nodded, but the reception of his crewmen didn't reflect the famed Bavarian hospitality.

After the German gave Ray a slab of bread with a sliver of cheese, he sat and rested a booted foot on the table. "I cannot give you much food, but I will a story tell. My story."

Ray stiffened his guard so he wouldn't be lulled into revealing information.

The Nazi took off his cap, revealing gray hair, thick and straight. "After I fought in the last war, I met a beautiful girl in München. Very beautiful. In a month, I married her."

Ray took a bite of his last meal, and the bread crumbled in his dry mouth.

"She gave me three fine sons about your age, I believe. How old are you?"

Ray paused. "Captain Raymond—"

"*Ja, ja.*" Thin lips tilted, not quite a smile. "Three fine sons. Good, strong boys. But their mother grew fat and ugly, and I learned why—she was Jewish. She hid that from me. Then the Nürnberg Laws passed in 1935. I saw opportunity in Hitler's Germany, but not with a Jewish swine wife. I divorced her. They took her away in '38."

The bits of bread and cheese curdled in Ray's stomach.

"*Ach,* you think I am the swine, *nicht wahr?* But I did right. I joined the Party, took many blonde *Mädchen,* and gained power."

Ray studied the face etched deeper than warranted by his age. If he thought he'd done right, where was his peace?

The Nazi got up and poured two cups of water. "No beer. Today it is difficult in Germany." He sat, and the heel of his boot thumped the table. "*Prost.*"

"*Prost.*" Ray returned the dragon's toast.

"When the war started, I became important. My greatest work was to uncover a resistance ring—German race traitors who smuggled Jews out of the country."

Ray took a sip of water, as refreshing as the knowledge that good people stood up against this evil regime.

The Nazi swiped his mouth with the back of his hand. "At the center of the ring stood three men. Three brothers. My three fine, strong sons."

The air rushed from Ray's chest.

Fire crackled in the fireplace and in the Nazi's eyes. "I hanged them. If I hadn't, I would have been butchered. I watched my three fine sons hang to death."

What kind of man could make such a decision? And what kind of world encouraged men to make such decisions?

"For the death of their mother, they could not forgive me or their country." He slammed his fist to the table. "But for my loyalty, what is my reward? The Party does not trust me. They sent me here. Nowhere. I have nothing to live for. My sons are dead. My career is dead. All I have is *Vergeltung.*"

"*Vergeltung?* I don't know that word."

The Nazi waved one hand in a small circle. "*Vergeltung. Vergeltung* weapons. The V-1, V-2."

"I understand." Vengeance. All the man had was vengeance, and Ray's blood chilled.

"Hitler promised good, but he brought death. The folk starve, our cities are bombed, our youth are killed. I see how this war is fought. The Fatherland will be destroyed."

The torture in the man's soul cried out to Ray's ministering spirit. But dragons were known for emotional trickery, and the most dangerous dragons were those who had lost their treasures.

The Nazi sprang to his feet and stoked the fire. "Now I hate the Party more than my sons did. I take vengeance, a life for a life. I have taken two lives, and you will help with the third."

Help? No, Ray would be the third, and he tried not to think how the red-hot poker would be used.

A motor puttered outside. The Nazi looked out the grimy window. "It is time."

Ray's stomach turned. Even one bite of bread and cheese had been too many.

"Fast! Into the cellar." He whipped out his pistol and motioned to the cellar door. "Be entirely still or I will shoot you."

Shooting seemed preferable to whatever waited in the torture chamber, but the cellar contained nothing but a ham and bags of potatoes and apples. The door shut, and a bolt slid into place, leaving Ray in darkness outside and in. What on earth was going on?

He sat on a step with his face to the door, where he could see between warped, mildewed boards. *Lord, get this over with quickly so I can be with you. Thank you that my family and Helen will never know how I died. Be with them, Lord.*

The front door creaked open. "*Guten Abend, Herr Oberleutnant. Heil Hitler!*"

"*Heil Hitler.*" A second man's voice, a younger man. "I seek an American pilot. The folk said you took one away."

"*Ach, ja.* The Luftwaffe collects for the Stalag Luft."

A smile swept up Ray's face. He'd live after all. He'd kiss the ground of that Stalag Luft.

"Come inside. This winter is so cold." The Nazi's voice drew inside. "I have no pilot for you. Today the folk killed three men before I could stop them."

No pilot? Ray reached for the door, but it was bolted, and the Nazi wouldn't hesitate to shoot.

"We must make them understand," the younger man said. "It is not right. Pilots follow the knight's code. A parachute is a sign of surrender. These murders make our pilots fear for their own lives if shot down. It is not good."

"*Ja, ja.* I agree." The Nazi strode to the shelf beside the fireplace. "Would you like a drink? Warm yourself by the fire?"

"Nothing to drink, *danke*, but I warm myself gladly." The officer squatted by the fire and stretched out his hands.

Two steps, a flash of silver. "*Hände hoch.*"

Ray gasped, a sound echoed by the Luftwaffe officer. A gun—the Nazi held a gun to the younger man's head.

"*Hände hoch*. Stand up." He jammed the barrel in the officer's ear.

"I stand. I stand. What is wrong?"

"Undress yourself."

"Undress? Undress? What is wrong with you?"

Ray shrank back from the door. He didn't want to see what would happen next.

"Undress yourself." A click from the pistol.

The officer laid down a string of German words Ray never learned in college or in seminary. Clothing rustled and brass buttons clunked to the floor.

Ray dug the heels of his hands into his eyes. *Lord, protect that man.* The two pilots, though enemies, had fallen into the hands of the same monster. What could Ray do?

"Go out the back door."

More curses, shouts, orders, and the back door opened.

"I can't let this happen. I have to do something." Ray pounded the door. He worked his fingers around a board and pulled. It was decayed. He jumped down a few steps, raised his knee to his chest, and kicked the board. It cracked. Another kick, and his foot punched through.

He extracted his foot, plunged his hand through the opening, and worked the bolt free.

The officer's shouts outside descended to weeping and pleading.

Ray dashed for the back door. At least he'd die defending his fellow man, maybe give him a chance to escape.

He banged open the back door.

A shot, a flash of yellow in the twilight, and a dark-haired man in long white underwear collapsed to the ground.

"No!" Ray cried. The Nazi was insane—he'd shot his own countryman.

The pistol turned to Ray. "Undress yourself."

"What?" Ray cried in English. "Just shoot me with my clothes on."

"*Auf Deutsch.*"

Ray blinked hard, over and over, and held up his hands. His fingers curled into fists. "*Schiessen Sie mich, aber ich ziehe mich nicht aus.*"

The Nazi laughed and tucked his gun back into the holster. "*Nein*, I shoot you not. Already you are dead. And the Oberleutnant lives."

"You are crazy."

"*Nein, nein.* I am smart. He will wear your uniform, and you will wear his. All is clear."

"What? This is crazy."

"When it is full dark, you will leave. If you wear the American uniform, you will be caught, and I will say you murdered the Oberleutnant. You will be tortured and shot. If you wear the Luftwaffe uniform, you might live."

Ray's head spun. "This is—this is crazy. I surrender. Take me to the Luftwaffe."

"*Nein.* You must leave." The Nazi rolled the dead officer toward a dark square in the snow, an open pit partially filled with snow.

Ray's breath chuffed through clenched teeth. This was premeditated murder. The man knew the Luftwaffe would come. Ray was the bait in this man's twisted trap.

The Nazi glanced over his shoulder at Ray. "Put on his clothes and bring me yours. Fetch your things from the cellar. They are useful, and Luftwaffe officers often have American equipment taken from prisoners—or the dead. And give me your dog tags."

"*Nein.*" Ray's hand flew to his chest. As of now, he would be listed as Missing in Action, which would allow his friends and family to hope. If his dog tags went to the dead man, his status would change to Killed in Action. How could he do that to Helen and his family?

The Nazi strolled toward Ray with outstretched hand. "I have done this twice already. I don't know if the men still live, and I care not. I have my vengeance. Germany stole my three sons, and I stole three of hers. But you, Herr Novak, might live."

In Ray's mind, he could see Helen's lovely tea-colored eyes. He had to take the chance, no matter how slim, to gaze into those eyes again.

Ray lifted the tags over his head and dropped his identity—his life—into the Nazi's hand.

In order to live, he had to die.

30

Antioch
Thursday, January 18, 1945

"That's the last of it." Helen relinquished the notebook and all her volunteer work into Allie Novak's hands. Working full time for Vic would leave no time to volunteer.

Allie set all Helen's beautiful notebooks on the Novaks' coffee table, since her lap had gotten too small with the growing baby. "I'll do my best. I know how important this is."

Helen gave a quick nod to stanch her tears. "You'll do well." Allie had proven a hard and efficient worker the last few months.

"It takes both Betty and me to make one Helen," Allie said with her shy smile. "Betty chats with the ladies and motivates them, and I keep her on the agenda."

"Nonsense. Allie does the hard, boring work, and we all know it." In the wing chair, Betty sipped her tea. "But Helen, you'd better relieve us soon. This kind of thing kills me. How long do you have to work full time?"

"Through August, when I can get my own place." Her plan would shave five months off her sentence.

Betty rubbed her rounded belly. "Too bad you can't ask Papa for money, but we know where he stands. We're all grown up. Don't come back begging." She laughed, but she could afford to laugh. She had a good husband and a safe home. "Why the hurry to leave?"

Helen gazed into her empty lap. "I've imposed on the Carlisles long enough. They deserve peace and quiet again."

Betty and Allie nodded as if they understood, but they could never know the real reason Helen was breaking her own heart by sacrificing her work.

But did her heart ache because she was abandoning the purpose the Lord gave her? Or was it a selfish, prideful ache, because the only way she knew how to please people was through accomplishments?

"Would you like some cake?" Mrs. Novak entered the parlor with a single-layer cake frosted in white. "Today is Ray's thirty-second birthday."

Helen inhaled a sharp breath. If she hadn't driven him away, he would be celebrating at home. Perhaps they would be celebrating together.

"Nonsense," Betty said. "You should share with your family."

Mrs. Novak set the cake on the coffee table. "Pastor Novak needs to watch his waistline, Allie isn't supposed to eat many sweets, and that leaves me. Besides, my two little frosting helpers are eating tiny pieces in the kitchen, so why shouldn't their mommies have some too?"

The cake indeed looked as if it had been frosted by Jay-Jay and Judy. Mrs. Novak had spirited them away the moment they arrived. She would be a wonderful grandmother.

"Next year," Mrs. Novak said with a brave set to her chin. "Next year, Ray will be home to celebrate, and Jack and Walt as well. I'll be back with plates and forks."

The doorbell rang, and she smiled. "After I get the door."

Helen stared at the little cake with a wedge cut out. A

year from now, Jay-Jay would be almost four. She'd be in her own place and could resume volunteering. But she would be alone. Surely the war would be over. Ray would come home and find an unbroken woman for his wife.

Mrs. Novak stood in the entry to the parlor, her face as gray as the streaks in her black hair. "There ought . . . to be . . . a limit."

Two envelopes trembled in her hand. Western Union telegrams.

Two years ago, Helen had laughed when she received her telegram, but now her face tingled as the blood drained away.

"This—this is my fourth telegram from the War Department. Once when Walt was injured, twice when Jack was injured, and now . . . there ought to be . . . shouldn't there be a limit?"

One of the brothers was wounded, missing, or dead. Helen clenched her hands on her lap and prayed it wasn't Ray. But it was wrong to hope it was Jack or Walt, especially with Walt's pregnant wife in the room.

"All right, Mom, let's sit down." Allie guided her mother-in-law to the armchair. "Would you like me to go to the church first and get Dad?"

"No, Allie, stay. I'll get Pastor Novak." Betty took off, out the front door.

Helen couldn't breathe or move, but the women she'd written off—one as a useless society girl and the other as a flibbertigibbet—were the only ones of use.

"Would you like to wait for Dad?" Allie said.

"No . . . no. I have you dear girls." Mrs. Novak's eyes glistened, fixed on the envelopes.

Allie knelt beside her. "That one's from Britain, not the War Department. Would you like to open it first?"

Mrs. Novak nodded and worked a finger under the lip of

SARAH SUNDIN

the envelope with a cringing expression. Helen understood. As long as the envelope remained sealed, she could pretend all three sons were alive and whole.

Helen hugged her arms around her stomach, her throat swollen shut.

"I can't. My fingers. Allie, would you . . . is it too much . . . ?"

Allie shook her head, drew her lips between her teeth, and opened the envelope. Then she rested on her heels to read it. "The telegram's from Jack."

Helen took a gulping breath. That meant it was Ray. Walt didn't fly combat missions. The V-1s and V-2s killed thousands of civilians, but no one faced greater danger than the airmen.

Allie rose to her knees and settled one hand on her mother-in-law's arm, her eyes soft but strong. "Ray's plane was shot down over Germany."

Helen slapped a hand over her mouth, clamping off her cry.

Mrs. Novak moaned, pressed both hands over her face, and crumpled over her knees.

Allie rubbed her shoulders. "Jack says there were at least three parachutes. He says we mustn't lose hope. We mustn't."

Hope? At best, Ray was a prisoner of war during Europe's coldest winter on record.

"I know he's safe in a POW camp." Allie hugged her mother-in-law's shoulders. "They'll notify us soon. Jack is writing a letter with more details. We mustn't lose hope."

Weeks would pass while they waited for word, but there would be none. Only three parachutes. Ray would be the last man to bail out, not one of the first. That meant . . .

Her gaze fell on the little white cake, never to be enjoyed, for a birthday that would never be celebrated again.

Helen choked on a sob, but she had no right to mourn. She'd killed another man.

★ 265 ★

★

Along Lech River, Germany
Saturday, January 20, 1945

Ray trudged south in the dark through snowy woods, careful to keep the Lech River in sight to his left. He'd never been this cold and hungry before.

The Luftwaffe uniform was designed for warmth, with a cardigan under a gray blue service jacket, trousers with a buttoned-in quilted lining, and a heavy overcoat, but Ray couldn't shake the chill of wearing a dead man's clothes.

Johannes Gottlieb was his name.

Oberleutnant Johannes Gottlieb, twenty-seven years old, black hair, blue eyes according to his identity card, and a few inches taller than Ray and several pounds lighter judging by the snug fit of the uniform.

Johannes Gottlieb died so Ray could wear that uniform.

He stopped and squeezed his eyes shut against the mental image of Johannes's death. The Nazi official committed premeditated murder three times, but he might as well have killed Ray and the other Allied airmen.

What chance did he have?

Wearing an enemy uniform within their borders was grounds for summary execution under the Geneva Conventions. Even if he made it to Allied lines or the Swiss border, how would he cross?

Ray stepped around a thicket of bushes, a good place to hide during the day, but he wanted to press on for another hour. For Johannes's sake, he needed to press on.

The first night, he'd ridden Johannes's motorcycle and sidecar through Friedberg and across the Lech River south of Augsburg. No one pulled him over. When he ran out of gas, he abandoned the motorcycle in a ditch. He couldn't buy gas with his accent. He didn't even know how German rationing worked.

After he'd gathered his supplies into his parachute, he took off on foot. The Lech led south to the Alps, and then he hoped to head west toward Switzerland.

A futile goal. At least a hundred miles in the dead of winter with little food. His seat-pack parachute held two K-rations with three meals each, and his escape kit contained bouillon cubes, candy, and fishhooks. Poor Johannes had plenty of cash in his wallet, but Ray could hardly saunter into town and buy food.

Ray gazed at the dark overcast sky through the tree branches. "Lord, I don't want to lose hope. I need hope to survive even more than I need food."

Hope kept his feet moving—hope that somehow he'd survive and see Helen again.

Why hadn't he told her he loved her? His reasons seemed good at the time but now felt flat. She'd think he was dead, and he probably would be dead soon. Would it be easier or harder for her to bear the news if she'd known he loved her?

Ray stepped into a clearing. He stopped short and ducked behind an evergreen tree. That was sloppy. The fatigue, horror, and stress were taking their toll. He pressed his forehead to the tree trunk. *Lord, I don't know how long I can keep going. Show me what to do. Give me a sign.*

He peeked around the tree and strained to see through the darkness. Only a clearing, thank goodness, and not a road or a tributary or the end of the concealment of the woods. A chimney rose in the middle of the clearing where the snow lay flat and even.

Ray inched forward. A house once stood there, and a bowl-shaped depression beside the foundation showed a bomb had leveled the house.

Perhaps there was a basement. For once he might get some sleep. He wouldn't have to hide in the brush wrapped in his parachute to blend into the snow, on edge listening for voices and footsteps, any slumber interrupted by bloody nightmares.

Ray hiked over shattered, charred, snow-covered timbers and stomped around in his black leather boots. A hollow sound rang near the fireplace. Under the snow lay a trapdoor. He lifted it and descended a steep flight of stairs.

He groped around in the darkness, over lumpy cloth bags, and he breathed in the earthy smell of potatoes.

For the first time in days, a smile cracked his face. "Food and shelter. Lord, you are good."

Maybe he could stay a few days, rest for the journey ahead. He set down his parachute bundle and went back outside to survey the area.

Nothing to the east but the river, and the south looked clear. Then he headed west. From what he could tell, the woods formed a band a quarter to a half mile deep along the riverbank.

When the trees thinned, Ray crouched low. The land before him lay perfectly flat and empty. He waited and peered ahead until the black of night turned to the gray of dawn.

Far in the distance stood large square buildings.

"Hangars," Ray whispered. Not only hangars, but runways and a couple dozen fighter planes dispersed across the field.

If only Ray could hop in the cockpit of one of those birds and fly away.

A crazy thought, even more so when he saw the triangular form of the fighters. Those were no ordinary planes. They were jets. Messerschmitt 262s.

Ray smiled at the irony. He'd reached Lechfeld, his primary target the day he was shot down, a lifetime ago, when Jack told him to go knock out some jets.

Maybe he could throw some rocks and complete his mission objective.

Ray crawled backward behind the trees, stood, and brushed snow from his uniform. Damp wool. Dew on the fleece. Hadn't he prayed for a sign as Gideon had?

A Luftwaffe airfield. A Luftwaffe uniform.

A new plan swirled in Ray's mind, came into clear view, and brought peace. His uniform wouldn't attract attention around here. He had food and shelter and basic survival gear. Instead of trying to reach the Allies, he'd wait for the Allies to reach him. The dangers of the approaching front couldn't be any greater than the dangers of traipsing a hundred miles through enemy territory.

Ray ran his hand over his thickening beard. If he wanted to blend in, he'd better use the razor blades in his escape kit.

31

Antioch
Saturday, February 10, 1945

"Bumped by a dog."

"Hmm." Helen poked at her ice cream sundae. Listening to her sister's chitchat in the White Fountain's Saturday matinee crowd was difficult enough without the envelope calling from inside her purse.

"Honestly, Helen. You haven't listened to a word I said."

"Of course, I have." She wiped a chocolate smudge from Jay-Jay's protesting mouth. "You were talking about the Le-Roys. First Police Chief LeRoy died in December, and so young. And poor Leon was at sea and didn't even hear of his father's death until he came to port, then when he tries to come home to comfort his mother, he's bumped off his military flight by Elliott Roosevelt's dog."

"The president's son himself. Made *Time* magazine and everything. I wonder if Antioch's ever been mentioned in *Time* before? True, Colonel Roosevelt had no idea his dog was getting the royal treatment, and he was appalled. Oops! Jukebox needs another nickel." Betty sprang from her seat, quite agile for being six months pregnant. Soon Bing Crosby crooned "Swinging on a Star."

SARAH SUNDIN

Little Judy rocked back and forth in her chair, combining Betty's and George's charm. " 'Oo oo eye eye dee daw,' " she sang.

Jay-Jay tapped his cousin's arm with his spoon. "No, Doody. It's 'Woo doo wike do sing a staw.' "

Betty giggled and wiped ice cream from her daughter's arm. "He's turning three next Friday and he knows everything."

Helen smiled, but it hurt. Jay-Jay's hair was trimmed short, reducing his curls to a wave on top. He'd lost the pudginess in his cheeks and arms and knees. Thank goodness he was growing to favor the Jamison side of the family.

"Heaven's sake," Betty said. "Would you go ahead and read that letter?"

Helen's hand tightened around her pocketbook. "This isn't the time. It's Jay-Jay's birthday party."

Betty hitched up an eyebrow. "And you're in such a celebratory mood. Go ahead. It can't make things worse."

Helen sighed and pulled out two pages in Ray's handwriting. January 14. The day before he was shot down. Her last letter from him. Even if he survived as everyone in town believed, in prison camp he'd be allowed to write only a few letters a month, which would go to his parents, not her.

She pulled herself together and read silently:

Today went late and tomorrow will be early, so I'll get to the point.

You've expressed concerns about murderous thoughts toward Jim. Believe me, I've had murderous thoughts of my own. Yours is the righteous anger of a wronged woman.

Please reject the lies. You are not responsible for Jim's death. If all your lovely ways and

★ 271 ★

words failed to persuade him to treat you
properly, you mustn't believe you persuaded
him to enlist.

You have a good heart that belongs to the Lord,
and in time you'll come to forgive Jim. But you
also need to forgive yourself. You fell in love
with a charming man—hardly a sin. The stars
in your eyes blinded you to his controlling
ways and rushed you into marriage—also
not a sin. When his true self emerged after the
wedding, it was too late. The sin is his alone.

The Lord loves you, and he's already forgiven
you as you've asked. Believe him. Trust his
forgiveness.

Please stop apologizing for "burdening" me
with your brokenness. Haven't I burdened you
with my brokenness as well? One thing I've
learned this year is we're all broken and in need
of God's healing hand. Our mutual sharing
has never been anything but an honor.

Helen couldn't finish, not if she wanted to keep her composure.

"Well . . . ?" Betty played pat-a-cake with her daughter.

Helen drew a steadying breath. "I'm going to miss his letters."

"Nonsense. You know he's fine. With our troops at the Rhine, the war in Europe will be over any day now. He'll come home and sweep you off your feet."

Somehow Helen managed the eye roll she used when her sister talked that way.

Betty perked up. "Oh, Dorothy, there you are."

Dorothy Wayne pulled up a chair and set Susie on her lap. "Sorry I'm late. I couldn't bear to wake her from her nap."

Ten-month-old Susie rubbed her eyes with her head on her mama's chest.

"I can't get over how much she looks like Art," Betty said.

"I'm so glad." Dorothy kissed her daughter's straight brown hair. "Art's been in Italy a year and a half. Sometimes— sometimes I'm afraid I'll forget what he looks like, but then Susie gives me an Arthur-look and everything's all right."

Helen's head felt stuffy. Ray didn't have a child, someone with contemplative gray eyes.

"Are you all right?" Dorothy's forehead bunched up.

"Sure." However, Helen couldn't coordinate her smile. "It's just—goodness, the children—how they're growing. Soon they'll be off to school and jobs and getting married."

Betty laughed. "He's turning three, not eighteen."

Helen nodded, but she could see the man inside her little boy.

"So, how are things?" Dorothy's voice was light, but she gave Helen the confidential look they'd shared since Christmas.

Helen returned the look. "Same as always." The Carlisle home rested in the lull between storms.

"How's your volunteer—oh, that's right, you gave that all to Allie, didn't you?"

"Mm-hmm." Helen scraped the last spoonful of ice cream. "Don't let me forget. I found my notebook from last year's spring tea. I need to drop it off on my way home."

Dorothy's brown eyes widened. "You're not going to the Novaks' today, are you?"

"Um, yes." Helen cocked one eyebrow.

"Haven't you heard? It's awful, but Mr. Wayne says it's better to know the worst than to suffer the waiting."

The words buzzed around Helen's head, and she tried to block them and keep them from landing in her ears, in her mind.

"Dorothy," Betty said, her voice firm. "We don't know what you're talking about."

Except deep inside, Helen did know. She'd known ever since the telegram arrived and she couldn't breathe.

"Heavens," Dorothy said. "I guess word isn't out yet. My father-in-law's on the elder board. That's how—"

"What word?" Betty said.

Helen's eyelids fluttered. The glass bowl for her sundae sat before her, white smears marring its clarity. Melted ice cream puddled in the divot where it couldn't be reached, could never be reached.

"Yesterday they heard from the International Red Cross. They received Ray's dog tags."

Ray was dead. His body lay buried in Germany, crushed or burned, all light snuffed, never to smile or speak or write again. How—how could such light ever—ever be quenched?

From deep in her soul, a moan rose and escaped.

"Are you all—oh goodness, I forgot. You dated last year. Oh, Helen, I'm sorry."

Convulsive waves swept her body like the labor pains before Papa gave her ether, not the pains of life straining to light and air, but of death extinguishing her light, choking off her air.

"We have to get her out of here," Betty said. "Remember how hysterical she was when Jim died?"

Betty and Dorothy busied themselves with children and checks and tips, and then pulled Helen to standing. Her left leg wouldn't move, wouldn't move at all.

Betty looped her arm around Helen's waist and half-dragged her out of the White Fountain. "Come on, darling. We'll go to my house."

Helen's contractions pushed out deep and animal sounds that didn't belong on G Street on a Saturday afternoon, but she couldn't stop.

"I can't believe," Dorothy said. "I can't believe I was so thoughtless."

"She had to find out," Betty said. "Better now than in church tomorrow."

Helen gazed up to the sky, gray as Ray's eyes, his closed, buried eyes. How could she ever look at the sky again, the sky he loved, the sky that betrayed him?

☆

Lechfeld
Monday, February 12, 1945

Ray sat cross-legged on the cellar floor in his long underwear and leather flight helmet, with the overcoat around his shoulders. He dog-eared his Bible page at the twelfth chapter of Exodus—the second book for the second month, and the twelfth chapter for the twelfth day. Then he wound Johannes's wristwatch. These two daily habits grounded him in the real world.

The last of the evening light streamed through the slit of a window near the ceiling. Ray flipped to the verse that spoke to him earlier in the evening. In John 4:34, Jesus said, "My meat is to do the will of him that sent me, and to finish his work."

Ray sighed. "Then this is true hunger."

He had no purpose but to survive. He had no one to teach, no one to preach to, and no one to counsel. "Who am I, Lord, if I can't serve you?"

The only thing he could do was pray, which he did with increasing fervency. He set his elbows on his knees and rested his forehead in his hands. He praised God for the sunset and prayed to see the next. He begged God to comfort his family, and he pleaded for Helen with his eyes squeezed shut so hard he saw stars.

"Lord, if there's some way, any way, show her I'm alive and I love her and I don't blame her. More importantly, show her you're alive, show her you love her, and show her you don't blame her."

The light was waning, and Ray needed to finish his evening routine.

He pulled on his light blue shirt and gray-blue trousers, which were no longer tight. Next came the tie, cardigan, and short fitted jacket. After he pulled on the overcoat, boots, and gloves, he exchanged his warm flight helmet for the peaked Nazi service cap. Last he tied Helen's gray scarf around his neck and kissed it, the only item to remind him of home.

He dipped the toothbrush from his escape kit into icy water in his steel flak helmet, and he scrubbed gunk from his teeth.

He stank.

Every night he sponged himself off using a scrap of parachute cloth as a washcloth. On Mondays he rinsed his underwear in the river, and on Thursdays his shirt, but without soap, the smell grew ranker each day.

Ray checked his overcoat pockets for the night's supplies—the miniature hacksaw blade from the escape kit, his pocketknife, his daily potato, and his two remaining matches. If poor Johannes hadn't been a smoker, Ray would have run out long before. He'd never been good at starting fires by rubbing two sticks together, and he didn't look forward to it.

On top of his supplies, he laid the large scrap of parachute cloth he'd use as a white flag on the blessed day he heard American or British voices. In his breast pocket he stowed more scraps to use as handkerchiefs or toilet paper.

Ray settled back to pray and wait.

At nine o'clock he climbed the cellar stairs and slowly

raised the trapdoor. Last week after a heavy snowfall, he could barely lift it.

No platoon of German soldiers met him, and he breathed a sigh of relief and climbed out into the frosty night. No stars shone, nor had they for weeks. Other than the strange whine of Me 262s, he hadn't heard planes overhead since February 5. Was the Eighth Air Force grounded, or were they concentrating on northern or western Germany?

Ray tramped north, careful to step in his own footprints so it looked as if one man had come through one time only.

After he visited his latrine spot, he headed south along the riverbank to the spot where he'd strung fishing line between two bushes on either side of a small cove. From that line, a shorter line hung with his last fishhook.

The line stretched taut, and Ray grinned. He pulled out a silver fish, about ten inches long. Whatever these fish were, they liked the Lech's cold, rushing water and gravelly shoals.

Ray felt like whistling as he headed to his cooking spot, a good distance from the cellar so the sight of smoke or the smell of frying fish wouldn't draw anyone to his hideout. On nights like this, with a good meal ahead, he took pride in surviving on his own in the wild—behind enemy lines, no less. Other nights he felt more like a raccoon than a man.

Under a bush at his cooking spot, Ray pulled out the tripod he'd built from branches lashed together with parachute cord, and the wooden spoon and plate he'd carved. He cleared a spot in the snow and started a fire with only one match, thank goodness, and then he set up the tripod with his flak helmet as a kettle.

After he cleaned the fish, he cooked it in his helmet with the chopped-up potato. His mouth watered. Even if he weren't so hungry, he'd like the taste of this fish—like salmon, with a flavor that reminded him of thyme.

Ray sat on a log and thanked God for his provision. While he ate, he planned out his night.

After he cooled off his helmet in the snow, he'd clean it in the river, then boil the day's drinking water. He'd already run out of halozone water purification tablets, so he had to be careful. Then he'd put out the fire with snow, a hissing and crackling spectacle. Before dawn, he'd return to cover the spot with snow.

For most of the night, he'd traipse in the woods down the length of the airfield. Some of the jets were parked no more than a hundred feet from the tree line. Most Allied airmen saw these birds whiz past at over five hundred miles per hour. Was Ray the first to see one this close?

He grinned. "Wouldn't Walt be jealous?"

He slammed his mouth shut. Silence was his rule, and if he spoke, it'd better be German.

Ray picked up a chunk of wood left from making his dishes. Walt was the carver in the family, but Walt wasn't there.

Ray tucked the wood in his overcoat pocket. If he ever got out of this alive, he'd bring his baby brother a model of an Me 262.

Too bad he couldn't show him the real thing.

32

Antioch
Sunday, February 18, 1945

Wearing a polite, pained smile, Helen wandered around Fellowship Hall as if she had a purpose.

For years she'd faked grief when she felt fine, and now she had to pretend she felt fine when she grieved. She had no right to mourn Ray. Hadn't she wanted to keep their romance secret? If she could have that time back, she'd proclaim to the world how much she loved him.

Someone jarred her left elbow, and Helen gasped and almost spilled her tea. For a moment, the acute pain took her mind off the smothering ache in her soul.

Mrs. Llewellyn set a hand on her shoulder. "I'm sorry, Helen. Are you all right?"

Helen rubbed her arm and forced herself to formulate a sentence. "I'm fine. I slipped in the rain yesterday and banged my elbow."

"You should be careful, young lady," Judge Llewellyn said.

"I—I know." How on earth could she converse with the Llewellyns?

"That was a moving sermon," the judge said.

Mrs. Llewellyn leaned closer. "I don't know how Pastor Novak got up there today. They're both so strong, aren't they?"

On the other side of the hall, Pastor and Mrs. Novak stood talking with the Waynes. The pastor had his arm around his wife's waist, and both wore black suits and brave pale faces.

The space constricted around Helen and squeezed out the air.

"I—excuse me. I need more tea." She set her cup on the first table she saw, grabbed her raincoat, and fled the hall, out into the rain, fumbling with her coat, sleeves all tangled up.

A sob bubbled in her throat, and tears and rain mingled on her cheeks. When Jim died, Helen had concentrated with precision, and everyone thought her strong.

She thought she'd performed grief well, but she'd had it all wrong. Her lips didn't quiver; they twitched. In her true grief, she couldn't think straight, she kept making jerky hand motions, and nothing made it better. Not work, not rest, nothing.

Helen tugged her hood up. The church service made it worse.

Pastor Novak didn't mention his loss. He didn't have to. He spoke with great effort and long pauses, and his hands never left the pulpit.

How could he bear the loss of his firstborn son?

Helen lifted her face to the rain. "Lord, I destroy the men I love. Don't let me destroy Jay-Jay too."

Jay-Jay?

She stopped so fast, one foot slid out beneath her. Jay-Jay had come to church with her while the Carlisles stayed home with colds. He ran around Fellowship Hall with Judy and his other little friends.

Jay-Jay was still at the church.

"Oh no." She broke into a run, a faltering run, her left leg buckling with each step. She slipped on a leaf, cried out, and caught herself on a lamppost. She couldn't afford to have two accidents in two days.

Jay-Jay was fine. He was playing. No one would leave fellowship time for at least another half hour. He wouldn't even notice she was gone. No one would know she'd forgotten him.

No one could ever know.

However, a tiny figure stood in front of the church on the curb, too close to the street. A small boy with blond hair and no coat. And he held his hands in front of his chest, opening and closing them, his gaze sweeping up and down Sixth Street.

Helen gulped out a sob. "Oh, baby. Oh, sweetie."

She ran to him, to his contorted face and desperate cries, and she dropped to her knees on the slippery sidewalk and clutched him to her. "My baby. I'm sorry. I'm so sorry."

His cries changed tone, and he beat tiny fists on her sides. "Bad Mama. Bad Mama."

Helen cringed and bore it because that's what a bad mama deserved.

But no. No. She'd be an even worse mama if she let this pass.

"No, sweetie. No." She took his arms and held him in a firm grip, his wet, red face inches from hers. "I'm sorry, sweetie. I'm so sorry I left you, but I cannot let you hit me. You will not hit me. I love you too much to allow it."

With every ounce of her will, she trained her gaze on him—tender and apologetic but unyielding.

Jay-Jay's arms went limp in her hands. "Mama?" His voice edged high, grasping for forgiveness.

"Baby. My sweet boy." She pulled him to her and buried her face in his rain-sleek, boy-cut hair. Her chest heaved with his, her tears mixed with his, and all her grief ran together into a big muddy pool.

A pool so thick and dark, she couldn't see the surface.

★

Klosterlechfeld
Monday, February 19, 1945

Ray wiped mud from his boots, ran his dry tongue around his mouth, and flexed his fingers over the door handle.

Entering the village shop took more courage than his first combat mission. But he needed to do this. He puffed out a breath, opened the door, and slipped inside.

The shopkeeper talked to a middle-aged woman over the counter and sent Ray a wave.

Ray's heart flopped around like a dying fish, and he wheeled down the aisle. He hadn't looked another human being in the eye for a month. He'd forgotten the power of it.

With long, even breaths, he searched the depleted shelves. He found soap, but it required a ration stamp, and it was nasty, lumpy, and gray. Too bad. The sticky, grimy feel of his skin bothered him almost as much as his empty stomach.

Thank goodness—matches. Ray slid the box open and smiled at the sulfurous odor. The past two nights he'd failed to light a fire. Raw potatoes didn't sit well in his stomach, and dysentery had set in since he couldn't boil water. He could feel every rib.

Farther down the aisle, a sign told customers they could serve the Führer by catching their own fish to eat. Ray scooped up the unexpected bonus of fishhooks and fishing line. Now he wouldn't have to figure out how to fashion more when his supply gave out.

Ray gritted his teeth for the toughest part. He laid his purchase on the counter before the shopkeeper, an elderly gentleman with high, rounded cheekbones. Body odor assaulted him. Maybe with soap scarce, Ray's unwashed body wouldn't stand out.

"*Guten Morgen, Herr Oberleutnant.* How goes it with the Luftwaffe? Every day I hear your little planes."

"*Ja.*" Ray's voice came out raspy from lack of use. He cleared his throat.

"Are you sick? The Luftwaffe does not feed you well?" He tapped the fishhooks.

Ray's mouth dried out even more. Any answer required too many words. He pushed his purchase closer to the shopkeeper. "*Wieviel?*"

The man sighed and rang up the purchase. "How much? How much? Young people always in haste."

Ray handed the man a Deutsche Mark and escaped with his purchase in his pocket.

Outside he took in deep drafts of cool air to settle his heart rate down. He'd done it. Sure, the shopkeeper thought him rude, but he'd done it.

He scanned the white, gray, and yellow buildings with peaked red roofs cleared of snow since a recent warm spell brought an early thaw. Across the street a sign said "Buchhandlung."

A bookstore? Ray's mouth formed a soft O, and a longing as deep as hunger pulled him across the slush in the street. He had plenty of cash. Without a ration book, he couldn't feed his stomach, but he could feed his soul.

He opened the door to the living scent of paper and ink and binding glue.

"*Grüss Gott.*" Behind the counter, a tiny woman with a circlet of white braids sent Ray a beatific smile. Then a look of horror washed over her, and she snapped up her arm. "*Heil Hitler!*"

Poor thing thought she was in trouble for using the traditional Bavarian greeting. Ray smiled at her. "*Grüss Gott.*"

Then he whirled to the nearest shelf. What was he doing? He couldn't say *R*s properly, and a *u*-umlaut? Why not ask her for a hot dog and a paper with the latest baseball scores?

The bookshelf before him burned his eyes with floor-to-ceiling copies of *Mein Kampf*. Enemy territory was no place to be kind and friendly.

Ray sidled down the aisle. So many greats of German literature had been banned as "degenerate," and what remained stank of Nazi propaganda. He picked up a children's book with poetry about animals, which looked safe and pleasant.

How about a biography? Beethoven frowned at Ray, and Ray smiled back and picked up the book, a subtle act of solidarity with the Allied cause. Beethoven's Fifth Symphony served as an anthem for the Allies. The powerful opening chords signaled "dot-dot-dot-dash," Morse code for the letter *V*. Combined with the Roman numeral V, the symphony sang "V for Victory."

Ray headed past the reference section. A dictionary? That would be helpful.

Then his jaw lowered. A German-English dictionary.

He stretched for it, then drew back. Would it brand him a foreign spy? Or an officer expanding his education?

He stroked the binding. A risky purchase, but bad German carried its own risk.

The blood whooshed in his ears, but he added the dictionary to the bottom of his stack and went to the counter before he could change his mind.

"Three books?" The saleslady clapped ancient hands together and lifted her shoulders. "*Ach*, you sweet man."

Despite Ray's vow to be impassive, he smiled. He didn't realize how lonely he'd been.

"*Ach*." She hugged the poetry book. "What a beautiful book. The children will love it. Have you sons or daughters?"

"*Nein*." His smile drooped. He'd almost had a son. If he ever got home, he'd give Jay-Jay this book as a belated birthday gift. Three years old. How much he must have grown since Ray last saw him.

The saleslady's hand rested on the dictionary, and she stared at it.

Every one of Ray's muscles tensed, ready to spring. If she called the authorities, how fast could he run? Should he return to his shelter or flee the area? If he fled, he'd lose all his supplies.

"The Americans come soon, *nicht wahr?*" Her voice trembled.

Ray released his breath. With the early thaw, a spring offensive would come soon and so would the Americans—Ray's greatest hope, but this lady's greatest fear. "*Ja,*" he said softly.

She nodded and raised watery eyes of medium brown, just about the shade of tea.

And she was all the women in his life—Helen, his mother, his grandmother, all mourning half a world away. He couldn't comfort them, but he could reach out to one frightened soul in their place.

He settled his gloved hand on top of her knobby little hand, so much like Grandma Novak's. "*Keine Angst,*" he said, repeating God's great command to fear not.

She raised a faltering smile. "*Ja, keine Angst.* God is with me, and also with you, *nicht wahr?*"

Ray nodded, his heart full.

He paid for his purchase and fled before he said anything more.

Three Luftwaffe officers approached, and Ray slammed to a stop, prepared to run, but the men lifted hands in greeting and sauntered along.

Ray stood still for a minute to catch his breath, and then strode down the sidewalk at a strong pace.

His conversation with the saleslady was too long, too risky. What was he thinking? A month of hiding out, and he almost blew it with a few short words.

33

Port Chicago
Tuesday, February 20, 1945

Helen wadded up the sheet of typing paper and dropped it in the trash can, and then rubbed the bridge of her nose. Somehow she had to concentrate on this letter.

The phone jangled, and Helen groaned. Where on earth could she find a perky secretary voice? "Lieutenant Llewellyn's office, Mrs. Carlisle speaking."

"Hi, Helen. It's Esther Jones."

"Esther." For once, Helen didn't have to fake a warm tone. "How are you? Have you found a job?"

"Yes, with the NAACP in San Francisco. I'm sharing an apartment with some of the office girls. I feel as if I'm helping Carver in some small way."

"How is he?"

"He's holding up, but this is testing his faith. He isn't cut out for prison life."

"No." He was cut out for the lecture hall. Helen twisted her finger around the telephone cord.

"Which is why I called." Esther's voice strengthened. "Lieutenant Llewellyn said we would have word on Carver's appeal by now, but we haven't heard anything. Have you?"

"I haven't. Let me get the lieutenant." Helen knocked on Vic's open office door. He lifted his head from a law book. "Esther Jones is on the phone for you."

His eyebrows hiked up, and then he took a deep breath and picked up the receiver. "Esther, so good to hear from you. How are you? . . . Yes, yes, so you have a new job? . . . I was impressed with the NAACP during the trial."

Helen returned to her desk and rolled a clean sheet of paper in the typewriter while Vic peppered Esther with small talk.

"Yes, the appeal," he said.

Helen's fingers hovered over the typewriter keys.

"Yes. Well, this morning I had word. I wish it were good news, but I'm afraid they refused to hear the appeal."

"Oh no." Helen's fingers curled up, and she lowered her hands to the desk.

"No. No, they didn't. They don't have to give a reason . . . Yes, I know it's wrong."

Helen strained through the silence.

"I wish there were, believe me. But we've exhausted our options. There's nothing else we can do."

Her head hurt with the unfairness of it all. How could Esther bear it? How could Carver?

"If I can do anything for you, anything at all, please let me know. And if something comes up, a new course to pursue, I'll jump on it . . . Yes . . . God bless you too."

Helen couldn't sit and she couldn't type. She rose and grabbed a stack of papers to file, but the print wavered in watery gray.

She rested her forehead on the cool steel filing cabinet. How could the world keep rolling under the weight of so much injustice? An innocent man in prison. A loving wife separated from her husband. A good man stripped from earth far too early. A small boy trapped in a home determined to wreck him.

One woman trying to make order in the chaos.

Helen hugged the papers to her chest. Work didn't comfort her, and it had been a false cure anyway. Only God gave comfort, but Helen was so busy, she didn't have enough time at his feet. Nor did she have enough time with Jay-Jay. But for her son's sake, she had to pay off the last six months of her debt and get out. She couldn't ask Papa for money without blabbing the Carlisle family secret, which wouldn't be right. And Papa was already disappointed in her for marrying young. If he knew the depth of her stupidity, he'd lose all respect for her.

"Are you tired?"

Helen jerked her head up. "Tired? I suppose so."

Vic gave her a lopsided smile and perched on the edge of Helen's desk. "I got more work out of you when you worked part time."

Helen yanked out a drawer and stuffed a paper in a file. "I'm sorry. I'll do better. I promise." She shoved the drawer shut and pinched her finger. She cried out and stuck her finger in her mouth.

Vic crossed his arms across his double-breasted blue jacket. "This kind of work doesn't suit you. You're meant to be some lucky man's wife, running an efficient home, raising clean-scrubbed children, and leading every civic organization in town."

Helen squeezed back tears. "That's not an option."

"Yes, it is." His voice barely reached her ear.

Her hand wrapped around the top corner of the file cabinet, cold and smooth and hard.

He cleared his throat. "The night of the explosion you turned down my proposal very firmly, and I vowed never to bring it up again. However, my offer still stands. It always will. You know how I feel about you."

Helen turned slowly to the escape path opening up before her.

Vic stared at his polished black shoes and tapped his fingers on his crossed arms. His jaw jutted forward.

He'd never beat her—not this man who fought for the downtrodden and threw his body over hers after the explosion. He was a good man, a man of integrity, and a friend. Mrs. Carlisle said all she should look for in a second marriage was support and companionship, and for once she was correct. If she married Vic, she'd have a good husband, a safe home, and she could quit her job and have plenty of time for Jay-Jay and volunteering.

"All right," Helen said.

Vic met her gaze, his forehead puckered up. "Excuse me?"

She swiped moisture from her eyes. "All right, I'll marry you."

His jaw descended. "What?"

"I'll be honest. I don't love you, but I like and respect you. I know you'll treat me well and Jay-Jay too, and I'll treat you well. I'll be a good wife. That is, if you don't mind that I don't love you."

"You're serious?"

Her stomach knotted. "Oh goodness. What am I saying? I can't ask that of you. You deserve a wife who loves you. You should—"

He let out a jerking little laugh. "Don't you back out on me now. I don't mind. Besides, you may not love me now, but you will."

Helen's chest collapsed, and she clamped her hand over her eyes. "You don't want me to. You don't. The men I love get killed."

The desk creaked, footsteps approached, and Vic took the papers from Helen and set them on the desk. He wrapped his arms around her and pressed her head to his shoulder. "Don't worry. I can handle myself. With you by my side, I can handle anything."

Helen pressed her face against the navy wool. He was a better man than she deserved.

He pulled back, hesitation in his iodine-brown eyes. "May I kiss you?"

If Helen was going to be a good wife, she had to start now. She nodded.

Vic pressed his lips to hers, a sloppy kiss, but she kissed him back.

Once they were married, she would give her body to him and let him think she liked it. Why not? She'd made love to Jim when she hated him, feared him, and ached from his blows. Surely she could give herself to a man she felt indifferent about.

She sighed as her life turned from one performance to another.

★

Lechfeld
Friday, February 23, 1945

Claps of thunder roused Ray from his sleep for the second day in a row. Except thunder didn't rattle the ground like an earthquake.

He huddled against the shivering wall of the cellar. Part of him recoiled from the terror that a bomb would snuff out what was left of his life, but most of him wanted to jump up and down and wave his hat to the bombers overhead.

The Allies were on the move. Perhaps Jack was up there, so close Ray could see the silver speck of his plane if he had the guts to go outside and look.

If only he could do something to help. All day long, he burrowed in his rabbit hole, and all night long, he foraged and wandered. He'd helped the Allied cause more when he bumbled around at the Sacramento Air Depot.

Restlessness jiggled his muscles. He'd rather die on his feet than cower underground.

By the time he dressed, with his belt cinched to the last hole, the rumbles had stopped.

Ray cringed from the sunshine and picked his way along the muddy path to the base. Inside the tree line he headed south along the edge of the airfield to survey the damage. A few smoke columns rose from buildings and craters, minor damage at best.

Men crisscrossed the airfield, scrambling to get jets in the air and rushing fire equipment around.

If Ray wanted to explore the base, now was the time.

He squatted behind a tree and huffed out a breath. What a crazy idea. It was one thing to chat with a sweet little lady in a bookstore, another to saunter around a military base.

A new sound built in the north, the throb of fighter planes, the good old kind with propellers, the best kind ever— American P-51 Mustangs.

Ray peered around the tree, his heart keeping beat with those Rolls-Royce Merlin engines. The Mustangs dove, silver birds spraying flashing tracers. Beneath them, chunks of earth shot up in a rippling line, like stones skipped on a lake. An Me 262 burst into flames, another toppled on its side. Neither would harass American boys again.

"Go knock out some jets," Ray whispered. When Jack had given him his last order, neither of them dreamed Ray would be so close. Yet he'd done nothing.

The Mustangs wheeled west, back to their bases in England or France, and Ray got to his feet and strode onto the airfield.

He was dead to his family, dead to Helen, and soon he really would be dead, wasted away from dysentery and malnutrition. Or he'd get caught. If he was destined to be shot as a spy, he might as well act like one.

Purpose ran like an electric current through his veins and drove him into the chaos on the base. Planes burned, smoke blew in acrid clouds, and men ran around or stumbled in a daze. No one gave Ray a second glance. Deeper and deeper he walked, across runways, past huts for mechanics, and right up to a Messerschmitt.

Ray laid a hand on the bird's jet engine, and goose bumps coursed up his arms. Was he the first of the Allies to touch one? So what if he was? No one would ever know.

No matter what he did here, no one would know. That made him smile. His family would never believe mild-mannered Ray would commit sabotage.

Only Helen would think him capable. Only she saw him as a courageous dragon slayer. He'd do it for her because she believed in him, and he'd do it to protect his brother and friends above.

He circled the plane, searching for ideas.

A man lay sprawled on the tarmac, dead.

Ray's heart seized. The man looked so young, still with acne on his cheeks, and his blond hair fluttered in the breeze. He'd fallen midstride as if scrambling for the plane. Beside him lay a brown leather flight helmet and a heavy flight jacket of gray blue cloth with a fake fur collar.

Did this young man also have a family back home and a girl he loved? Ray squeezed his eyes shut. *Lord, comfort them in their grief.*

Then Ray eyed the flight jacket. Sure looked warm. But stealing was wrong. Or could it be his first minor act of sabotage? Any equipment he took would have to be replaced, straining the system.

He stooped and picked up the jacket and helmet. *"Es tut mir leid,"* he said in apology to the boy who no longer needed them. Under the jacket lay a handbook.

"Pilothandbuch: Messerschmitt Me 262 Schwalbe."

The pilot's manual?

Dry paper on the tarmac. Dry fleece on the wet ground.

Ray jammed the handbook under his coat and marched toward the woods, the blood pulsing in his ears.

Now he was officially a spy.

34

Antioch
Saturday, March 3, 1945

Vic smiled across the Llewellyns' lavish dining room table and patted the breast pocket of his service jacket.

Although Helen's insides coiled like the curlicues on the Llewellyn silver, she smiled back and glanced down to slice her roast beef. How had they procured such a roast with the serious nationwide meat shortage?

"Truly a sight for the ages." Judge Llewellyn puffed out his trim chest. "When they raised that flag on Iwo Jima, all American hearts swelled with pride."

Around the table, heads nodded—Mr. and Mrs. Carlisle, George and Betty Anello, Dorothy Wayne, and Jeannie Llewellyn.

"And those poor civilians have been released from the prison camps in the Philippines." Mrs. Llewellyn shook her head, with graying brown curls pinned up in a fashionable manner. "What horrors they endured under the Japanese. Mr. and Mrs. Crawford have been released and their three sweet children. I can't believe citizens of humble little Antioch were caught up in such events. But why haven't we heard anything about when they're coming home? They should have notified us by now."

"Don't worry, Mother." Jeannie shot Helen a mischievous look. "They'll telegraph you before their own families."

Helen sliced her asparagus almandine. Jeannie's disrespect left as sour a taste as her mother's gossip.

"Well, Mother, here's one piece of news you'll hear first." Vic pushed his chair back from the table and got to his feet.

Helen wiped her mouth. Couldn't he wait until after dinner?

He clasped his hands behind his back with a smug smile Helen didn't care for but would get used to. "As you know, when I was younger, I tried to win the hand of the lovely Helen Jamison. I lost to a better man." He dipped his chin to the Carlisles.

Mrs. Carlisle let out a faint whimper.

The knots in Helen's stomach dragged her heart into the tangled mess. Tonight's performance required a wide range of emotions. Did she have the skill to convince such a discerning audience? And why couldn't she and Vic avoid the pomp and get this over with?

"But now," he said in an expansive tone for his closing argument, "I have made a proposal of marriage to Helen, and she has honored me with her acceptance."

The only sounds in the room were soft inhalations of breath and silver tinkling on china.

Helen needed to respond, to bolster Vic. "They need more of an explanation than that, dear."

Someone gasped, probably Betty, but Helen kept her smile on Vic. He would never be *darling* as Jim and Ray had been, so *dear* seemed best, and in time she might mean it.

"Surprised you?" Vic grinned. "Well, no one's more surprised than I am. I've loved Helen as long as I can remember, but it took months of working together and a deadly explosion to show her what a great fellow I am."

"Are you serious?" The judge's gaze dissected Vic as if he were on the witness stand. "Please tell me you're serious."

"You taught me to tell the truth, the whole truth, and nothing but the truth, didn't you?" Vic pulled a small white jewelry box from his pocket. "Most children get in trouble for lying, but Jeannie and I could have been charged with perjury."

Mrs. Llewellyn gasped. "Oh, Victor, my lamb. How wonderful."

"It's about time." Joyful relief colored Mr. Carlisle's voice.

"How wonderful," Mrs. Carlisle said. "I always dreamed our families would be united."

Helen cringed at the fawning but smiled at Vic as he circled the table and dropped to one knee before her. This was necessary for Jay-Jay's sake, and Vic was a good man who adored her. She could do far worse. She already had.

So she accepted Vic's ring, a tasteful arrangement of diamonds in platinum, and she blinked away tears, an appropriate reaction for a fiancée, for a widow.

"Goodness, Helen. This seems sudden," Betty said with a nervous laugh.

"Nonsense. I've known him all my life." Her tone came out defensive, because she knew what Betty meant—it was too soon after Ray's death, a harsh reaction to the loss of the man she loved, and how on earth could she marry a Llewellyn?

When they were alone, Betty would ask if Helen had prayed over her decision. Although she hadn't beforehand, she had since. This was clearly God's way of protecting Jay-Jay. So why did she get a squirmy sensation when she prayed?

Jeannie's crimson lips spread in a smile. "I can't wait for us to be true sisters."

Helen gave a stiff smile to the sister she'd keep at arm's length.

"I'm so happy for you." Dorothy gave her a look full of warm understanding.

Helen's jaw tightened and her eyes stung. She could hold herself together in the face of opposition, but compassion made her crumble.

"This summer's too soon," Mrs. Llewellyn said. "And fall and winter weddings are so unseemly, as if the couple couldn't wait for the proper wedding season. Next spring then, or summer."

Another year? She could get out sooner on her own. "No, it's this year—April 28. We've set the date."

"April? This year? Next month?" Mrs. Llewellyn's smile sputtered. "Why, that won't do. That simply won't do. We have preparations to make. And your parents—they won't be able to come on such short notice."

Vic stood behind Helen's chair and set his hands on her shoulders. "Didn't I tell you Mother would want a wedding extravaganza?"

"But you promised." Helen begged Vic with her eyes. She'd wanted to take the train to Reno this weekend, but Vic had insisted on a church wedding. This was their compromise. Yes, Papa and Mama would be disappointed to miss it, but they would insist upon an understated wedding for a second marriage anyway. The sooner they married, the less time Mrs. Llewellyn would have to fuss over wedding details.

"I keep my promises." Vic patted her shoulder. "Sorry, Mother. We're getting married April 28, and we've written the Jamisons. We want a simple church wedding. If you insist on postponing it or overdoing it, we'll elope."

Helen reached up and squeezed his hand. A marriage built on love and passion had failed her, but this marriage would be built on respect—a stronger, if less thrilling, foundation.

★

Lechfeld
Saturday, March 10, 1945

Evening light streamed through the cellar window and illuminated the Me 262 manual on Ray's lap and the dictionary open on the deflating potato sack.

Translation of technical terms stretched his language skills. Each term required looking up several words and piecing them together. He couldn't write anything down. If caught with the manual, English notes in his American-style handwriting would betray him faster than his accent.

Ray traced a finger over the cockpit diagram and imagined himself behind the stick of a Schwalbe. Some days the idea didn't seem so ludicrous—the hungriest days. He had flown many kinds of planes, and he held the blueprint for the little jet in his hands.

Wouldn't it be something to turn over an intact jet and a manual to Allied intelligence? He could picture Walt's delight, Jack's shock, and Helen's adoration.

"No. It *is* ludicrous." Ray closed the manual. He had no experience with jet engines, and how on earth could he get into a plane undetected and take off without clearance?

He wound his watch and dog-eared Leviticus chapter ten for March 10. The Allies had better come soon, because Leviticus had only twenty-seven chapters. And Ray had only nine more potatoes.

He flipped to the nineteenth Psalm. Carefully he lifted a plum blossom and pressed it to his lips. A year ago today, in another life, he'd pulled the flower from Helen's honeyed hair.

"Lord, I miss her so much." Loneliness surged through him, a pain as raw as the cramps in his intestines.

He puffed out a breath. "No. I'll be thankful, Lord. I have you and I have a plan for tonight."

☆

In moonlight diffused by cloud cover, Ray twisted his arm to read his wristwatch. Midnight.

He waited in the woods another five minutes until cigarette smoke wafted by and shoes swished in the grass.

A lone sentry patrolled the perimeter of the field at night, a boring job. Who would suspect enemy activity deep in the Fatherland?

Ray grinned and marked off another five minutes. The Luftwaffe hadn't counted on the presence of Capt. Raymond Novak—pastor, pilot, saboteur.

He filled his lungs with cool night air and headed toward a plane dispersed to the north.

His sabotage had started with taking tools to slow down aircraft maintenance and to build his arsenal. Each night he hit a different spot with varying acts of sabotage, only a couple a day so they wouldn't suspect a saboteur.

He ducked inside a mechanic's hut and poked around. One blessed night he'd found a tin of flight rations. After he pocketed a box of matches, he caught a glint of glass—a half-empty bottle of brandy. Could be useful for cleaning wounds. He'd used up the antiseptic from his escape kit. He stuffed it in his pocket.

Ray headed two hardstands down to an Me 262. Sometimes he punched holes in the fuel tanks, other times he disabled the electric ignition for the cannons so they couldn't shoot down bombers.

Tonight he ducked under the nose, reached high into the well for the nose wheel, and disconnected the hydraulic line used to retract the landing gear. That would force the pilot to abort his mission. Ray didn't want to hurt anyone; he just wanted to protect Allied airmen.

He crossed the dark, quiet field and chewed his lips as he approached a cluster of buildings. Far down, one of the buildings shone with a faint light. Muffled laughter rose, and men sang "Lili Marlene."

Ray's heart lurched, caught in a tug-of-war between the fear of detection and the longing for companionship. Now he understood why solitary confinement served as effective punishment.

He passed a hangar and held his breath, but no one worked late. The next building, square and squat, held his objective—the scramble siren. His boldest idea yet.

Ray studied the siren about a foot over his head. If he could disable it, the next time the Allies bombed Lechfeld or the Me 262s were called to attack bombers, their response would be delayed. With one act, he could save dozens of American lives or increase the damage when the Mustangs or Thunderbolts strafed.

After he glanced around, Ray dragged over a crate. He dug in the tools in his overcoat pocket, pulled out a screwdriver and wire cutters, and tucked the cutters between his lips.

He removed four large screws and stuck them in the breast pocket of his service jacket. He eased the siren down onto his left shoulder. Wires snaked from the wall. A few snips, and he wrestled the siren back into place and lined up the screw holes. One screw, two screws, three.

The last screw slipped from his fingers and bounced off his boot. *Oh, swell.*

Ray eased his grip on the siren. It stayed in place and looked straight. He scooted the crate aside, squatted, and patted around in the dirt.

A flashlight flipped on, right in his face. *"Was ist los? Was machen Sie hier?"*

Ray froze, his hands splayed on the ground. This was it. Today he'd die. He had a gun, Johannes's gun, but he refused to use it.

Lord, give me strength. He dragged himself to standing, and his left hand bumped the liquor bottle in his pocket. He had a sudden image of King David feigning madness before the gates of Gath.

"Was machen Sie?"

Ray stumbled to the side and offered the bottle to the man. *"Wollen Sie?"* he said with as great a slur as he could muster. He grimaced and shielded his eyes with his forearm.

The man groaned. *"Sie sind betrunken. Gehen Sie ins Bett."*

Go to bed? Hallelujah! King David was brilliant.

"Ja, ja. Bett." Ray set a weaving course past the man. Then he remembered the old German drinking song his professor had taught at Cal.

"Du, du liegst mir im Herzen, du, du liegst mir im Sinn," Ray sang, slurring and mumbling his way around his accent.

He stumbled toward the living quarters. Once he was certain the man with the flashlight was out of sight, he'd head to the safety of the woods.

Tremors raced through him as fear and relief battled for control of his muscles.

Sabotage was not a job for cowards.

35

Antioch
Saturday, March 17, 1945

"Oh, Allie, he's beautiful." Helen held two-week-old Francis Raymond Novak on her shoulder, rubbed her cheek on the soft dark fuzz on his head, and inhaled the smell of milk and talc and baby goodness.

"I can't get enough of him." Allie's face glowed, and she eased herself down onto the couch.

Helen sat next to her and cradled Frankie. He stretched long, skinny fingers and groped the air around his face. One hand smashed onto his cheek. Helen laughed. "I'd forgotten how funny newborns are. Look at his little hands."

"And that serious old man face." Allie scrunched up her forehead in imitation.

They laughed together. Over the last few months, Helen had come to see why Betty liked Allie so much.

Jay-Jay leaned over the baby. "I look like dat?"

"Yes, but you didn't even have fuzz. You were completely bald."

Blue eyes rounded. Jay-Jay patted his head and sighed in relief, then returned to the toy soldiers on the parlor floor.

Helen gave Allie a hesitant look. "Your parents—have they . . . ?"

Allie shook her head and tucked in her lips. "I sent a telegram, but they haven't responded. They can't forgive me, but I've forgiven them, and that's all I can do."

Helen gazed into Frankie's large, wise eyes. "Their loss." Then she raised a smile. "Walt must be thrilled."

"I know. I wish he could be here. But he's where he needs to be, doing his part for the country and being there for Jack."

Frankie's fingers rolled around Helen's pinky as grief rolled around her heart. "How are they doing?"

Allie let out a long sigh. "Walt's holding up, I think, but Jack feels so guilty. He determined the order of the B-17s that day."

Helen frowned. She never thought anyone else might feel responsible.

Allie picked up a receiving blanket draped on the arm of the sofa. "Plenty of guilt in the Novak family right now."

"How so?"

Allie folded the blanket. "Pastor Novak wanted all three sons to follow him into the ministry. Walt was the first rebel when he chose to be an engineer. Then Jack decided to stay in the military, which upset his father. Now the only son who wanted to be in ministry is gone. Poor Pastor Novak thinks he's being punished for his pride."

"Oh no. But that doesn't make sense."

Helen sucked in her breath. Her guilt didn't make sense either.

She wasn't responsible for Jim's death, and she wasn't responsible for Ray's. His internal struggle drove him to combat, and he chose to fly a second tour. Besides, he'd grown in confidence and courage and strength. Maybe he did need to go. At least he died at peace.

Helen stroked the baby's soft cheek. Her shoulders felt lighter without the load of misplaced blame. For Ray's sake—and hers—she needed to continue healing, to find the contentment Ray had. Once she married Vic, she'd have more time to rest at the Lord's feet.

"Good morning, Helen. Hi, Jay-Jay." Mrs. Novak slipped into the parlor and sat in the wing chair. She'd aged several years in the last two months, but a smile brightened her face as she gazed at her grandson. "He's darling, isn't he?"

Helen smiled. "Absolutely precious."

"The Lord knew what we needed." Mrs. Novak gazed to the window where the family service flag hung, with two stars of blue and one of heartbreaking gold. " 'The Lord gave, and the Lord hath taken away; blessed be the name of the Lord.' "

Helen's throat clamped shut.

Mrs. Novak jerked back her gaze and smiled. "And the Lord is giving once again. We're looking forward to having your friend Esther stay with us. She arrives Monday."

"She's so thankful you'll have her. The housing shortage made it hard to find a room in the area, and discrimination made it even worse."

"She's gathering evidence for another appeal?"

"For Thurgood Marshall with the NAACP. He'll take it straight to Washington DC. This job is good for her. She can use her skills and help her husband as well."

Mrs. Novak nodded and gazed around as if distracted. "I—I have something for you."

"Oh?"

"Jack sent a box of—of Ray's things. A while back. I couldn't bear to go through them." She picked her way over Jay-Jay's battlefield to the piano, where a stack of envelopes sat beside Ray's service portrait.

Grief hit Helen in the breastbone and stole her breath.

She'd avoided looking at the portrait until now. Never again would she bask in his smile or graze the stubble on his cheek.

Mrs. Novak faced Helen with her mouth in a puckered line. "These are the letters you wrote him."

Helen drew in a ragged breath.

Allie took the baby out of her arms, and Mrs. Novak set the letters in the hollow, warm space Frankie had vacated.

Helen hugged the letters to her chest. "I loved him, Mrs. Novak." She gasped from the pain, the release of saying it out loud for the first time.

Mrs. Novak's eyes glistened. "He loved you too."

Helen ducked her head so she wouldn't voice disrespect by disagreeing. Ray hadn't loved her in a romantic way, but he'd shown the best kind of love—the open, giving love of a true friend.

★

Lechfeld
Monday, March 19, 1945

"Have you heard whether we're moving?"

"*Nein,* but soon we must."

Ray eased behind two officers as they walked between buildings on the airfield. Something big was happening, with several air raids and missions recently, big enough to coax him onto the base for information, a stony expression on his face to discourage conversation. He felt like Gideon infiltrating the Midianite camp before battle.

"We must move and hide our planes," the taller officer said. "They know we have not enough fuel, and the cowards shoot our planes on the ground."

The shorter officer smacked him in the arm. "*Ach,* we also shoot their planes. And we destroyed the bridge over the Rhine at Remagen."

"That was an Arado 234, not a Messerschmitt, and the next day the Americans built a *Ponton* bridge."

Ray's chest expanded. *Ponton?* Did that mean *pontoon?* Regardless, the Americans were crossing the Rhine, the most German of rivers. But the Rhine lay a good hundred miles to the west. He hardened his face again.

The officers stopped and saluted a young pilot—very young. "*Hallo,* Reinhardt. Are you going to the film?"

Ray stopped and dug around in his breast pocket as if he were a smoker in search of cigarettes.

Reinhardt stood tall under his stiff salute. "*Ja.* Then I can fly the Schwalbe."

A training film for the Me 262? Ray's lips tingled. He spun and followed the teenage pilot at a distance. Every day the idea of commandeering a plane grew in his head, fed by hunger, sickness, and weakness. The night before, he'd eaten his last potato. Now the Lord had delivered this film into his hands.

Ray paused. Would he be allowed in? They'd check identification, and Johannes Gottlieb wouldn't be on the list. Or worse, someone would know Johannes, and it would all be over.

He huffed away the thought and forged ahead. If someone checked Reinhardt's papers, Ray would walk away.

Reinhardt met some buddies, and they jostled each other like American boys, except these men were training to shoot down American boys.

They approached a building, where a guard stood at the door, and Ray sighed and veered to the side. But the guard let the pilots in with a lazy salute. Did the guard know them? Or would someone inside check identification?

Ray marched forward. If they asked, he'd poke in his pockets, look horrified not to find his papers, and leave. The Lord had given him the opportunity, and he had to seize it.

SARAH SUNDIN

At the threshold, his heartbeat accelerated. The guard's gaze rolled over the shoulder boards of Ray's overcoat, golden yellow with silver wire stripes and a single silver star for Johannes's first lieutenant's rank. The guard's arm rose like a drawbridge.

Ray's heartbeat eased down a notch, and he saluted and entered the building.

No check-in table. No man with a clipboard. Just a few dozen chairs facing a screen flanked by portraits of Hitler and Goering. Before he could lose courage, Ray picked an empty row and sat next to the wall behind a large, dark-haired boy who would shield Ray well.

He crossed his arms over his concave chest and put on his least friendly look.

The men's conversation rose through a haze of pungent cigarette and pipe smoke, but not with the nervous exuberance Ray had seen in his trainees in Texas. A palpable mood of fatalism pressed on the room. From Ray's perspective, Luftwaffe losses seemed high, and airmen would know better than the average German about Allied progress.

These boys were so young, teenagers all of them. How many would survive the month, much less the war? How many knew the saving grace of Jesus Christ?

Ray clenched his stick arms. If only he could tell them. But one full sentence from his mouth would label him a spy and wouldn't lead anyone to the Lord.

An officer strode down the center aisle, a captain, and the trainees sprang to their feet, salutes angled high. Ray joined them, and he had a strange sensation of being in a Nazi newsreel.

When the captain told them to be seated, Ray centered his face behind the head of the man in front of him. Thank goodness, the captain gave a quick introduction, and the film rolled.

He strained to tune his ears to the voices in the film. They spoke quickly and used unfamiliar words, though his translation of the manual had expanded his vocabulary.

The film instructor stood on the wing of the plane and showed the student the equipment in the cockpit, then showed him how to start the engines, a complex process. The throttles had to be pushed forward very slowly—that wasn't in the manual—and fuel was injected using push buttons on the sides of the throttle handles.

Ray drank it in, warm and invigorating as coffee. He could do it. He could fly one of these planes. In the chaos of a scramble, he could do it.

He had to try. Sure, he might be caught or die in a fiery crash, but if he stayed, he'd also die. He could be discovered, or shot by the Allies as he tried to surrender, or keep dying this long death of starvation. He'd rather die in an effort to help his country.

Besides, he was already dead to Helen and his family. They had mourned him and were moving on with their lives, which made his heart feel as hollow as his stomach.

Yet out of the hollowness unfurled a flag of liberation. As a dead man, he was free to do things he'd never considered when alive.

In the film, the student hopped out of the plane, and he and his instructor walked into the distance, using the pilot's universal language of swooping arm motions.

The captain dismissed the class, and Ray joined the throng, careful to keep his head down.

When he stepped outside, an air raid siren pierced the air.

A cry rang out among the trainees, and they took off running. Ray ran too, but not with the crowd. They'd seek shelter since they weren't ready to scramble yet.

Neither was Ray. He needed the flight jacket and helmet,

the manual, and a bit more courage. But the air raid gave him a chance to commit his most ambitious sabotage plan.

He ran for the edge of the airfield where a fuel tanker stood. When it had arrived the day before, the men greeted it like children cheering Santa in the Christmas parade. Fuel was the Nazi's main weakness, and knocking out one tanker would be like knocking out dozens of jets. If it blew up in an air raid, no one would suspect sabotage.

A Rolls-Royce Merlin engine throbbed to the north, and the base's antiaircraft guns opened in ear-numbing booms.

Ray scanned the field, but no one looked his way. Despite his shaky hands, he pulled Johannes's pistol from the holster and leveled it at the tanker.

A flash of silver, and a P-51 Mustang streaked past, popping destruction with six .50 caliber machine guns.

Ray fired a shot. He flung himself to the ground, curled up with his back to the tanker.

No explosion.

He groaned and sat up. Swell, he'd missed.

In the distance, smoke rose from a shot-up Me 262. A glimmer caught Ray's eye, a golden line dripping from the tanker.

He frowned and walked over. A ragged hole cut into the tanker, fuel streamed out, and Ray coughed from the fumes. His shot hit square in the middle, a great shot. So why didn't it blow up? It worked in the movies.

He sighed. He had matches, but he could toss one only a few feet. That would be the death of him. If only he could light a fuse. He glanced around and spotted a stack of oil drums and gas cans.

Someone cried out, and he snapped up his gaze. People pointed north, not at Ray, and ran away. To the north, three whirling propellers approached.

If he didn't act fast, he'd lose his chance. He grabbed a

gas can and poured a trail leading out from the puddle under the tanker.

He tossed the gas can under the tanker and pulled out his matchbox. Adrenaline locked his fingers. He struck the match over and over, but it didn't light.

The first Mustang charged down the field and left another jet in a mangled heap.

Ray breathed out a prayer and struck the match again. A spark, and it leaped to life. He touched the match to the trail of fuel.

Orange fire raced toward the tanker. Ray sprinted in the other direction, his weakened legs threatening to crumple.

Behind him, two P-51s roared past. Bullets hit a staccato beat on the ground.

A wall of heat and sound slammed into him, threw him to his face on the tarmac. He wrapped his arms around his head. A searing hurricane blasted over.

Then it was gone.

Ray felt the back of his head. Still had his hair, even his hat. He pushed himself up.

The tanker had been replaced by a raging inferno, a dragon belching out a tower of flame and black smoke.

Ray laughed. What would Helen think? He hadn't slain a dragon. He'd created one.

36

Port Chicago
Wednesday, March 21, 1945

"Mutiny?" the brochure read. "The real story of how the Navy branded 50 fear-shocked sailors as mutineers."

Helen handed the pamphlet back to Esther. "They did a nice job. This will open a lot of eyes."

"That's the NAACP's plan." Esther took a seat across from Helen's desk. "When Thurgood Marshall files the appeal in Washington, the Legal Defense and Educational Fund plans to distribute these, circulate petitions, the works."

Helen scraped a pile of papers from her desk. "Carver must be proud of you."

Esther shrugged one shoulder. "He's glad I'm occupied. When I think of my husband in a prison cell—well, I have to do something. I can't sit still."

Helen opened the file cabinet. "Then you won't mind if I file while we chat."

"I'd hardly expect you to sit still either."

"Lieutenant Llewellyn will be back any minute." She slipped a paper into the W section. "He'll help you track down those documents."

"It's so frustrating. Carver's documents should be at the

Judge Advocate General's office in DC after the lieutenant filed his individual appeal in December. But the staff has been less than helpful, and Mr. Marshall wants to file the group appeal April 3."

"Bureaucratic stonewalling coupled with discrimination. You'll need extra prayer to break down that barrier." Only one paper under Y, none under Z.

"With God and the lieutenant on our side, I know we'll prevail. What a blessing that man is to us. To you as well." She tossed out the words with a playful lilt.

Helen smiled over her shoulder. "Yes, he is."

"He's the best sort of man. He'll treat you and your boy right."

"He already has." Vic had rented a sweet little bungalow on Fifth Street and was paying for Helen to furnish it. Each piece of furniture, each yard of cloth for curtains, each dish made his face glow.

In thirty-seven days she would leave the Carlisle home and come under the protection of a man who adored her, a man she was growing increasingly fond of. The role of Mrs. Victor Llewellyn would be an easy role after all.

The file folders in the back slouched under the forward files. Helen boosted them up. The one in the rear read "St. Jude."

"Oh brother." Helen plucked it out. Vic had a brilliant legal mind but he had no business filing.

The door swung open. "Hello, sweet—" Vic stopped short. "Oh, hello, Esther. I didn't expect you."

She offered her hand and a smile. "Can't a lady visit a dear old friend?"

He shook her hand and grinned. "Old? I feel younger every day." He winked at Helen.

She smiled, rolled her eyes, and glanced at the folder. St.

SARAH SUNDIN

Jude? Unusual. She couldn't remember a client with that name.

"I hope you can help us untangle the red tape tying up Carver's documents in DC."

"I'll do what I can, but no promises." Vic entered his office and set down his briefcase. "Marshall may have taken up a lost cause."

"I disagree," Esther said. "Any logical person looking at the facts can see the injustice."

"Logic has nothing to do with this." Vic leaned against the doorjamb and crossed his arms. "It took me long enough, but now I see this case was never about justice but about politics. You'll never sway the Navy. After race riots in Detroit, Mobile, Harlem, LA—the Navy decided to crack down on the Port Chicago Boys. Justice? They trampled it for the sake of peace."

"They made their point." Esther drew herself taller. "Now on the appeal, justice can be done."

"And admit they were wrong in time of war?" Vic swung his head heavily. "Never. Just last month the Army convicted seventy-five colored troops in that Engineer Battalion on Oahu for refusal to work—also a mutiny conviction. We won't see any movement until after the armistice. The way things are going in the Pacific, that could be years."

Helen sighed and fanned open the folder. Wait. She'd seen these papers before—the appeals brief for George Washington Carver Jones, the medical forms, everything.

"Perhaps," Esther said. "But we're fighting for more than these fifty innocent men, and we're fighting within the system, not with riots. That's why I need the documents."

"These documents?" Helen laughed at the perfect timing and showed the file to Vic. "This is what she needs, right?"

"Oh. Right."

"You found them? Praise the Lord." Esther laughed and removed the papers from the folder. "I'll mail these tomorrow. But I thought—weren't they supposed to be in Washington?"

"Um, forgot about that." Vic rubbed the back of his neck. "When they refused to hear the appeal, they returned the paperwork. Forgot all about that."

Helen arched an eyebrow at him. "And you filed them under—"

He burst out in a laugh. "You know me—barely know my alphabet. That's why I hired you." He settled a kiss on her cheek. "By the way, I forgot to mail this letter at the Post Exchange. Would you mind?"

She took the envelope. "Not at all. I'll walk Esther out."

Esther hugged the papers to her chest as they left the building. "The Lord guided your hand today, didn't he?"

Helen laughed. "Only God could figure out Vic's filing system. I should lock the man out of his own files."

"He needs you to keep him in line." She turned for the depot. "I'll see you in town. Thanks again for introducing me to the Novaks. Wonderful people."

"They are." Her jaw ached at the thought of the most wonderful man she'd ever known, but she headed on to the PX and on with her life. Even if Ray had survived, he wouldn't have returned her love, knowing her as he did. She still would have ended up with Vic.

It was meant to be. And it was necessary, not just for Helen and Jay-Jay, but for Vic too. His incompetence warmed her. At least she'd contribute more than her body and housekeeping to the marriage.

She passed a seaman hauling a trash can outside. Honestly, how did Carver's papers end up under St. Jude, and how did St. Jude end up under Z? "St. Jude?"

"You sick, ma'am?"

"Pardon?" She faced the seaman.

He shrugged thin shoulders. "Sorry, ma'am. Heard you praying to St. Jude, figured you was sick."

"Is he—is he the patron saint of the sick?"

"The sick, the hopeless, all sorts of folk. He's the patron saint of lost causes."

Lost causes? She turned slowly and made her way to the PX, her left foot dragging slightly. Vic called the case a lost cause.

Helen wrapped her arms around her middle. Maybe she did feel sick after all.

37

Lechfeld
Thursday, March 22, 1945

Ray hunched behind a tree in sight of the Me 262 farthest from the control tower.

His breath hitched in his dry throat, but the items tucked inside his flight jacket spurred him on—the manual and wooden model for Walt, the poetry book for Jay-Jay, and his Bible.

In a short time he'd be with his family and the woman he loved, or he'd be with the Lord.

Yesterday the Germans had scrambled, but Ray chickened out when he saw the pilot in the distance. He wouldn't do that again.

Something stirred on the western front. Activity had mushroomed the past week, and Lechfeld appeared to be down to ten functioning Me 262s. Ray's strength fell even faster.

The scramble siren blared in the distance, and his heart lurched. "Lord, this is it. Give me strength, courage, and speed."

He stood, but his gut went into a spasm, and he doubled over, gasping from pain. Then he wrenched himself upright. Dysentery or no dysentery, today was the day.

"Time to be bold." Ray dashed onto the field and hooked a turn for the triangular fuselage of his plane.

By the left wing stood a ground crewman in black coveralls, the first hurdle.

Ray lifted a hand in greeting. He hoisted himself onto the mottled green wing, stuck one foot in the toehold labeled "Einsteigklappe," and swung his right leg into the open cockpit.

"Entschuldigung?"

Ray froze. Time to act like Gideon in battle and break his pitcher, shine his lamp, and blow his trumpet to make himself look fierce. He drew up tall and looked down his nose with what he hoped passed for Prussian arrogance.

The ground crewman adjusted his black cap. *"Entschuldigung,* Herr Oberleutnant. I have not seen you before. You are not one of my usual pilots. Who—who are you?"

Ray puffed up his cheeks as if appalled at the man's nerve and whipped out Johannes's identity papers. Adrenaline tightened his muscles.

"Ja! Jawohl, Herr Oberleutnant." He snapped a salute.

Ray lowered himself into the seat, and his breath tumbled out.

A scan of the cockpit layout—just like the manual. Throttles on his left, electrical switches on his right, and on the dashboard, flight instruments to the left, engine gauges to the right.

In the distance—the Luftwaffe pilot? Ray's stomach twisted. He turned to the ground crewman. He'd better be ready or Ray was dead. *"Bereit?"* he barked to conceal his accent.

"Ja, but I thought Leutnant Schmidt was to fly today?"

"Nein. Bereit? Links." He pointed to the left engine, then flipped on the switches for the battery, inverter, and generators.

The man in black frowned and cocked his head.

Oh no, the accent. Could Ray dispel doubt with fear? He

glared at the crewman and thrust his finger toward the engine. "*Links!*"

The man blinked. "*Jawohl.*" He grasped a ring in the tip of the engine and yanked a cord like a lawnmower. The little two-stroke starter engine sputtered to life.

Ray pulled the cockpit canopy down and locked it. With his right hand on the starter, he wrapped his left hand around the throttle. For the first time ever, he was about to start a jet engine.

He engaged the clutch and pressed the fuel ignition button. A low throbbing noise added to the cockpit sounds. Ray nudged the throttle forward until he reached 2000 rpm, then released the starter.

He pointed the ground crewman to the right engine. "*Rechts.*" At least the turbine's whine would conceal how badly he said *R*s.

About a hundred yards away, the rightful pilot stood with his mouth dangling open. Ray's heartbeat rose with the engine's rotations. He still needed the ground crewman to start the right engine and to remove the wheel chocks.

"*Start rechts!*" Ray yelled, and the man obeyed.

The pilot sprinted to the plane, waving his arms.

"Lord, help me." Ray concentrated on the complex start-up for the right engine.

The pilot ran up to the ground crewman, yelling and gesturing.

The tachometers read 4000 rpm. He had to run both engines up to 7500 then back off to 6000 for taxiing.

The conversation outside intensified. The pilot stomped his foot and hurled down his parachute, a piece of equipment Ray lacked.

He cringed. The ground crewman didn't deserve to get in trouble.

At last, 7500 rpm. After he drew back the throttles, Ray pounded his fist on the window, got the man's attention, and swung his thumb like a hitchhiker to signal for the wheel chocks.

The pilot stepped in front of the man in black and yelled at him, and the ground crewman swiveled his gaze between the two pilots.

Ray had to prevail. He balled up his fear and hunger and desperation and shot a look of fury. He knifed his hand toward the wheels and flung his thumb back over his shoulder.

The ground crewman nodded. He shouldered past the pilot and removed the wheel chocks.

The plane rolled forward. Ray's hands shook from the sudden drop in adrenaline. "Thank you, Lord."

The Luftwaffe pilot tore off his flight helmet, flung it to the ground, and stomped away, spewing what had to be German curses.

Taxiing was the next hurdle. Instead of using rudders and throttles, he had to use the brakes to maneuver the jet.

The plane bumped over the unpaved field. The fume-filled air of the cockpit swirled about him. Every detail stood out—the dark green band of trees where he'd lived for two months, the Me 262s converging on the runway, and the control tower in the distance. He had to take off before the other pilot notified the tower. At first they would think a simple mix-up had occurred, but if they checked their records, Johannes Gottlieb wouldn't be on the roster.

Ray's lips dried out. There was no turning back. His fate would be decided within the next half hour. "Lord, what have I done?"

The runway approached. Five fighters passed. Ray would be the last. His plane bumped up onto the runway. He depressed the right brake, and the Me 262 pivoted to the right. Too far. He tapped the left brake to straighten out.

The next hurdle—clearance for takeoff. Ray plugged the cord dangling from his helmet in to the radio by his right elbow. His headphones filled with static and German phrases, and he picked out, *"Vierundzwanzig? Vierundzwanzig?"*

Twenty-four—the last digits of his plane's serial number. They were calling him, but he wasn't about to respond.

Ahead, a woman in military uniform waved off each plane with a flag. One by one, they sped down the runway. The air shimmered behind their engines, and the blast buffeted Ray's plane. Each one broke free into the sky.

An invisible cord tugged on his heart. "Lord, help me join them."

He hit the brakes and gave the flag lady a smile and a salute to help his case.

She smiled back and gazed up to the tower.

Ray pushed the button to lower flaps to twenty degrees and ran the engines up to 8500 rpm.

The woman frowned and waved at Ray. She tapped her ear and her throat and mouthed, *"Funkgerät?"*

Radio. Ray tensed, but he grinned and tapped his headphones. *"Ja, ja. Alles gut."*

Commands filled his ears. He couldn't make out much except *"Nein"* and *"Nicht."* They weren't clearing him. With good reason. If they knew his identity, they'd torture him to death.

The lady raised a hand to tell Ray to wait and frowned at the tower.

His heart pounded his ribs like a wild animal trying to escape its cage. Time was up. The runway lay clear. He pushed the throttles up to 8700 rpm and checked jet pipe temperature, burner pressure, and fuel pressure.

"Lord in heaven, help me." He released the brakes.

The plane lurched forward. Where was the speed? The power? Was the runway long enough?

Fumes and noise built to almost unbearable levels, and gradually the speed climbed.

At 160 kilometers per hour, Ray pushed the "Ein" button to retract the nose wheel. The nose tipped up.

He grimaced. How many Me 262s had he seen crash on takeoff? "Oh Lord, here we go." Two hundred kilometers per hour, and he pulled back the control stick.

No more bumps. Airborne. Ray pressed the brakes to stop the spin on the wheels and raised the landing gear. Flaps to ten degrees, stick forward a bit. He needed more speed.

At 290 kilometers per hour, he raised the flaps.

A laugh burst out. He'd done it. He'd stolen an enemy jet fighter. Wouldn't Jack and Walt be jealous?

He trailed behind the formation, gaining altitude and speed. He played with his new toy. She responded well, with good aileron control. If only the tower would stop yelling in his ear.

Time for the next step, one he thought he'd never reach. He had to fool the other pilots and break away before the tower figured out this was more than a case of a mixed-up rookie with a broken radio, before the other pilots suspected enough to turn their guns on him.

"Have to play innocent." He picked out the empty slot in the formation and slid in.

The lead plane slipped back to fly level with Ray. Disgust warped the squadron commander's face. "*Was ist los?* What is wrong with you? You weren't cleared for takeoff. Your radio isn't functioning."

Nope, the radio functioned, but Ray refused to push the transmission button on the control stick. "*Nichts ist los. Es funktioniert.*"

"*Nein.* I can't hear you."

"*Ich höre Sie.*" Not a lie. Ray heard him perfectly.

"*Dummkopf.* Return to base. Never take off without permission again."

Ray made a face as if disappointed. "*Jawohl, Herr Hauptmann.*"

The captain grumbled about pilots so new he hadn't met them and so stupid they didn't deserve to fly.

Ray didn't care. His heart tapped a victory dance as he lowered the Messerschmitt from formation and pointed her southeast toward Lechfeld.

At the cruising altitude of two thousand meters, he worked his speed up to 750 kilometers per hour. As soon as the formation disappeared from sight, he wheeled west. The Rhine lay a little more than a hundred miles away, about fifteen minutes at that unbelievable speed. Ray had never been one for stunts, but the exhilaration of the moment made him want to do a barrel roll.

Nope. He'd leave that for some American test pilot.

A smile edged up. Sure. All he had to do was avoid Allied fighters, land an unfamiliar plane behind Allied lines, and convince American soldiers he was one of them. Piece of cake.

Piece of *Schwarzwälderkirschtorte.* The Black Forest and its famous cherry-covered chocolate cake couldn't be far, but Ray headed farther north, where he believed the Allies would cross the Rhine.

A river came into sight, flowing west toward the Rhine, curving through a wooded, hilly valley, and Ray followed it.

A castle flanked one of the hilltops, a large castle that looked an awful lot like the pictures he'd seen of Heidelberg Castle. Wouldn't that be something?

If so, that meant the Rhine was close. Ray eased the stick forward to descend. A plain spread open with plenty of activity, as tanks and troops headed west. German territory.

"Not for long," he said. At one thousand meters, he flew

over a city with streets in a square grid within a semicircle. Like a gumdrop cut out of graph paper.

"Mannheim." Ray had seen it on bombing missions, but he'd never been so glad to see it. On the far side of Mannheim flowed a wide, gray-blue river.

"The Rhine." Freedom lay on the other side. And maybe a good square meal.

Down to five hundred meters, and he lowered flaps to fifteen degrees.

He sailed over the Rhine. Soon the tanks and troops faced east, and cracks of gunfire greeted him.

They were firing at him, but Ray whooped for joy. "Americans! Hey, it's me. I'm one of you." He laughed at his foolishness. But he'd made it. He'd made it to Allied territory.

Almost. He still had to land. Alive.

Speed down to 420. A bit slower and he could lower landing gear, the universal sign of surrender, like a white flag.

He scanned the ground and turned south toward a field.

A crack. The nose kicked up.

"Swell. I've been hit." Could he blame them? They thought he planned to strafe.

Ray hit the "Aus" button for the landing gear, and the nose tilted up momentarily as the wheels threw off the plane's center of gravity.

The ground drew nearer, and he lined up the landing field. Men pointed, but the firing stopped. Either they thought he was damaged or defecting.

A smell rose, sweet but acrid. Last time he'd smelled that odor, he'd ended up in a parachute. "Fire? Not again."

Ghostly tendrils wormed out of the dashboard, and flames licked out, aiming for his hands as if the plane, German to its core, recognized him as an imposter.

"No. Not now." He set his jaw and worked through the

heat to adjust throttles and flaps. His leather gloves didn't help much.

He reached through the flames to lower the nose wheel and screamed from the pain, but a crash would hurt more.

The ground sped up to meet him. He hit hard, banged his head on the window, and stomped on the brakes. "Stop!" Ray shouted, his hands on the heated controls.

Soldiers ran toward him, rifles leveled.

The plane rocked to a stop. Ray closed the throttles and turned off switches to save his trophy. The lever to open the canopy lay deep in the flames. He gritted his teeth, plunged his hand in, and yanked the lever. He cried out and pitched open the canopy to fresh, cool air.

"Stay where you are, Kraut. Hands up."

"*Nein. Feuer. Ich muss aussteigen.*" Ray swung out of the cockpit onto the wing, then hopped to the ground. Wait, why was he still speaking German? To Americans?

He faced a dozen GIs and a dozen rifles. Heat pulsed in his hands, but something better swelled in his chest and sent a smile to his lips. "Boy, am I glad to see you fellows."

"Hands up!"

"I surrender." Ray obeyed. His smile stretched so wide it hurt. "Put out that fire. The flyboys will want that plane intact."

A sergeant stepped closer and tapped Ray under the chin with his rifle. "Say, Jerry, where'd you learn English? Spy school?"

"*Nein.* California." Heat flared in his hands, and the smell of burning leather hit his nose. His gloves. He had to get his gloves off. He groaned, sank to his knees, and tore at the smoking leather.

"I said hands up!" The GI swung his rifle butt and smacked Ray in the left lower jaw.

His head flew back. A shock of pain shot through his skull. Stars filled his vision. They faded to darkest night.

38

Antioch
Saturday, April 7, 1945

Seated on Betty's couch, Helen flipped through her wedding notebook. "Mrs. Carlisle is ahead of schedule on my suit. It's the loveliest shade of cream with a golden cast. The cake, on the other hand—Mrs. Llewellyn insists on taking care of it, and I'm afraid she'll embarrass us with some overblown confection that violates every rationing rule."

"What delicious tea, Miss Anello." Betty knelt beside the little white table Papa had built long ago for Betty and Helen, and sipped from a tiny blue willow china cup.

"Mo?" Little Judy pushed a big hat off her face and lifted the teapot.

"Why, thank you. You're a delightful hostess."

"I don't want tea," Jay-Jay said, his face dwarfed by George's fedora. "I want coffee."

"No." Judy shook her head, and her dark curls brushed the shoulders of her pink dotted swiss dress.

Helen dropped her notebook onto her lap. "Honestly, Betts. You ask about wedding plans, then don't listen to the answer."

"I'm sorry." Betty heaved herself up, not easy with the baby due next month, and she flounced onto the sofa. "I wanted a single sentence, but I should have known you'd read every detail from every notebook."

"One notebook." Helen raised a sheepish smile. "I'm sorry. I know I'm more Martha-like, but we only have three weeks, I'm working full time, and I have so much to do."

"So why the rush? Slow down. Wait a few months."

At the little table, Judy put a graham cracker on Jay-Jay's plate. "Cookie? Dee?"

"Tea's for girls. I want coffee." He leaned back in his chair and crossed his arms, a perfect imitation of his grandfather.

Helen shivered. "Why should we wait? Vic and I know what we want. We know each other well. We want to start our life together."

Betty leaned close, her eyebrows drawn together. "Come on, what's going on? I want the truth. I know you don't love him."

Helen turned pages in her notebook, and her eyelashes fluttered. She ached with the desire to be genuine and open with her sister.

She had nothing to be ashamed of. Jim's beatings weren't her fault. But what was her motive for revealing the abuse? Would she end up as the next gossipy Mrs. Llewellyn? She had no business exposing Mr. Carlisle's shame—not just his, but Jim's, and because of that, Jay-Jay's. What was one more performance for her son's sake?

Helen raised a smile. "You have no idea how crazy I am about Vic." Worded that way, she hadn't lied.

"No tea! I want coffee. Do as I say." Jay-Jay stood over his cousin, his face red, and he lifted a china plate over her head.

"No!" Helen's chest constricted and shoved all the air from her lungs. She dashed to her son, hauled him down the hall to the bathroom, and slammed the door behind them.

She plopped him on the linoleum. Fire snaked up her spine

and stretched her tall over her son, who gaped at her. "Don't you ever," she said through clenched teeth. "Don't ever talk that way to Judy, to a girl, to another human being. Don't ever hit a girl. Ever."

"But she din't—"

"I don't care what she did or didn't do. Gentlemen don't talk that way. Gentlemen don't hit girls."

Jay-Jay pursed his mouth. He'd lived in the Carlisle home almost a year now, forever in his mind. "But—"

"No. The Bible says be kind to others. No hitting."

"But—"

"No." She shook a finger in his face. "You—will—be—a—gentleman. You will be kind. You will not hit. I won't let you."

Jay-Jay squawked and kicked at her.

She stepped out of the way. "Stay in here until you're ready to act like a gentleman."

"Helen?" Betty called from the hallway. "Are you all right in there?"

She left the bathroom and shut the door on her son's cries.

"What a temper," Betty said.

The fire worked its way into Helen's head. She stood toe-to-toe with her sister. "That's why I need to marry a gentleman, quit my job, and spend more time raising my son. So mind your own business."

She turned on her heel and strode down the hallway. Then she groaned. She couldn't leave the house, not with her son in solitary confinement. Now Betty would want to talk, but Helen had already said more than she should.

She entered the living room and stopped short. Esther Jones and Allie Novak sat on the sofa. Helen summoned a smile. "Hello, ladies. I didn't hear you come in."

Betty brushed past Helen and cocked an eyebrow at her. "They came while you were helping Jay-Jay in the bathroom."

Even Betty understood the importance of concealing the family shame, and she didn't know the extent.

Esther stared at an envelope on her lap, her jaw jutted forward. "Helen, may I speak with you alone?"

"Of course."

Betty headed to the kitchen. "Allie, why don't you help me with dinner? You can bring Frankie's carriage. Judy, you come too, sweetie."

They retreated behind the kitchen door.

Esther's knuckles tightened around the envelope, and she raised hard, dark eyes to Helen. "I thought you were on our side."

Helen's lips tingled. "I—I was. I am."

"How do you explain this?" She brandished a Western Union envelope.

"What is it?"

Esther pressed her lips together, and her neck muscles stretched taut, in contrast to the floral fabric of her dress. "When I mailed Carver's documents to Mr. Marshall, I cabled to notify him, so he could stop searching in Washington."

Helen gripped the armrests of her chair.

"This was his reply." The thin paper shook in Esther's hand. "We couldn't find the documents in Washington because they never arrived. Lieutenant Llewellyn never filed an appeal for my husband."

"That can't be. I typed the paperwork myself."

"It was never filed. The Judge Advocate's office has no paperwork for Carver, not since Admiral Wright denied clemency in November. Lieutenant Llewellyn never filed the appeal."

"But he said . . ." Helen's airway clamped shut. They'd gathered the documents, filled out the forms. Why wouldn't he file it? That made no sense. Of course, he had.

Esther's jaw thrust further forward, and her eyes glistened. "I thought I could trust you. I thought you were different."

"But he . . . but he said. He promised. This can't be."

"You didn't know?"

Helen lifted her hands to her temples. Her eyes burned. "This can't be. He said. There must be a mistake."

"Why do you think he hid those documents?" Tears shimmered on Esther's cheeks. "He didn't misfile them; he hid them."

Saint Jude, the patron of lost causes. The burning in Helen's eyes intensified, and she squeezed them shut. No, this couldn't be. Vic was a man of integrity, who fought for the oppressed, who had words of justice stitched on his wall.

"I trusted him." Esther's voice broke. "He promised to do right by Carver. He didn't do his duty to his client. Did you know we can press charges for that? My sweet husband's in jail, convicted of mutiny—mutiny!—and no one fights for him. No one."

Helen pressed the heels of her hands into her eyes until white sparks appeared. Vic wouldn't lie. He wouldn't break a promise. Maybe he forgot, misplaced the forms, or thought she'd mailed them. Yes, there had to be an explanation.

So why did her stomach writhe?

★

France
Monday, April 9, 1945

A nurse circulated among German POW patients in the airfield tent hospital and belted out "Marching Through Berlin" in a Broadway-worthy voice. Most of the men ignored her, but some glared at her—the ones who spoke English.

Ray wanted to smile, but his broken jaw forbade it. The pain and swelling, the wires, and the bandages binding his face prevented speech and smiling, and even made it difficult to suck eggnog and bouillon through a straw.

And with his burned hands swathed in petroleum jelly and thick gauze pressure dressings, he couldn't even write.

He remained Johannes Gottlieb.

Army Air Force intelligence officers had tried to interrogate him, but they never got past the first question, when they asked if he was Johannes Gottlieb and Ray shook his head. "That one may have brain damage," one officer had whispered to his physician.

The nurse set hands on hips and tilted her head of short brown curls. "Okay, boys, time to load you up. I know you wanted to see England from an invasion barge rather than from a C-47 cargo plane. But, oh well. That's what happens when you lose."

Ray had never cared for brashness, but now the very American-ness of it warmed him like one of Mom's sourdough rolls.

"Be nice, Lieutenant La Rue." A blonde nurse carried an armload of blankets past Ray's wheelchair toward the brunette.

"Can't help it. I hate these POW flights."

"You'll have Sergeant Rosenberg with you and an armed MP."

"Still. Gives me the willies."

Something about the blonde struck a familiar chord—the soft voice, the Minnesota accent. Charlie's girlfriend—what was her name? May Jensen. Could it be?

Ray's heartbeat quickened. He'd only seen May a few times. Could she recognize him? How about . . . ? His heart went into double-time. How about Ruth Doherty? May and Ruth served in the same evacuation squadron.

Ray whipped his gaze around the tent. Would Ruth be able to recognize him? He hadn't seen himself in a mirror.

How much had he changed? Between the extreme weight loss and the bandages covering his lower face, could he even recognize himself?

The brunette checked the tag pinned to Ray's bathrobe and scribbled on a clipboard. "Johannes Gottlieb," she said with the *J* sound instead of the German *Y*. "Ugh. Sounds like I've got something stuck in my throat. I'll call you Johnny."

She pushed Ray's wheelchair out onto the tarmac toward a twin-engine C-47. Engines purred, and the warm air carried the delicious smell of aviation fuel, but Ray searched for his future sister-in-law.

Lieutenant La Rue parked Ray's wheelchair by the rear door of a C-47. "Keep an eye on this one, would you?" she called to an MP in his white helmet. "I'll get the next one."

At the plane to his left, a nurse bent over a patient on a cot. When she stood straight, her auburn hair glistened in the sun.

"Ruth!" he tried to scream, but it came out as a loud grunt and sent an electric jolt of pain through his jaw.

She glanced at him, then to the hospital tent.

He waved his arms over his head. If he weren't strapped into his wheelchair, he would have run to her. This whole ordeal could be over in a minute, then Helen and his family would know he lived. *Please, Lord, get her over here.*

"Hey, buddy, you got a problem?" The MP strolled over with his rifle across his chest.

Ray aimed a desperate gaze at him, pointed his giant white oven mitt of a hand toward Ruth, and beckoned her.

She walked over, frowning. "What's the matter?"

"It's one of those Germans, Lieutenant." The MP tapped Ray's shoulder with his rifle butt. "Sprecken zee English, buddy?"

Ray nodded and waved Ruth over until she stood in front of him. He hadn't seen a familiar face in almost three months, and he wanted to grab her and hug her, but he'd probably get shot.

Instead he pointed at his eyes. *Look at me.*

"Are you hungry, sir?" Ruth asked. "Thirsty?"

He shook his head and tapped his cheekbones. Had she seen him often enough to recognize him? Did he look enough like Jack?

"Do you have a headache? Do you have something in your eye?"

How could she see with all the stupid bandages? Ray rubbed his hands down his cheeks and worked the bandages down a bit.

"No, sir. Don't do that. *Nein.*" Ruth grabbed his forearms, but Ray resisted.

A rifle barrel pressed into his chest, and someone grabbed his elbows from behind. Ray sagged back in his wheelchair and groaned. Now he'd never remove the bandages.

A medic tied Ray's arms to the armrests of the chair. "This one making a pass at you, Lieutenant?"

"No, he's—I think he's trying to tell me something." Ruth leaned over and tightened the bandages, her face pale and furrowed.

This was his last chance. He strained forward, lifted his face as close as he could to Ruth's, and spoke with his eyes. *Yes, I'm telling you something. I'm Ray Novak.*

Her eyes widened. Her lips parted.

Ray's heart swelled. *See it? Lord, help her see it.*

She squeezed her eyes shut and shook her head.

Footsteps thumped up. "Oh my goodness," Lieutenant La Rue said. "He looked so harmless."

"I've got him under control." The medic gave the knot a tug, and the cloth restraint cut into Ray's elbow. "But harmless he ain't. Get a sedative."

Lieutenant La Rue put her arm around Ruth's shoulders and guided her away. "Are you all right? You look as if you'd seen a ghost."

Ruth cast a glance back at Ray, her eyes haunted. "In a way, I have. He—he reminds me of someone I used to know."

Ray slumped in his chair. His eyes slipped shut. Fresh pain throbbed in his hands and jaw. How long until he could write or talk? Until he could be Raymond Novak again?

39

Antioch
Saturday, April 14, 1945

On the dance floor at the Forum Club, Helen swayed in Vic's arms as the band played "Stardust." She stretched her eyes wide and sucked hard on her teeth to keep the tears at bay. It had worked on the polio ward during painful procedures, because good little patients didn't cry. It had to work now. The song drew memories that pricked her tear ducts—dancing with Ray in his parents' parlor, Ray humming to the starry sky, his smell and taste and feel.

Helen blinked, and a tear dribbled out. She rubbed it away. Two months had passed since she'd learned of Ray's death, but grief—true grief—had a way of sneaking up and knocking out her breath.

Tonight the grief was even less welcome. She needed courage to find out the truth from Vic. For the past week she had tested excuses for him in her mind. All failed.

He nuzzled in her hair. "Two weeks from today, we'll be man and wife."

Two weeks. She had to know what kind of man he was before then. She and Jay-Jay couldn't afford another marital disaster. "Vic, I need to ask you something."

"Yes?"

Her throat slammed shut as if someone had yanked a noose, and she almost gagged. She coughed to conceal it.

"Darling, are you all right?"

She wrestled her lips into a smile. "I'm fine."

"Good. I've been worried. You've been out of sorts this week. Of course, everyone's upset since President Roosevelt died on Thursday. I assume you have wedding jitters too. At least you're no longer working, so you can focus on the wedding and the house." He smiled, but the tightness between his eyebrows gave him away. He was scared.

A sigh seeped between her lips. He was so close to fulfilling his dream of marrying her, and he was afraid he'd lose her.

The band shifted keys and started playing "Every Time We Say Good-Bye."

Helen couldn't let pity or fear drive her, only the Lord. "I talked to Esther."

"How nice." He pulled her close. "When is she leaving for DC?"

"A few weeks. She has a bit more work."

"That'll be good for her. DC sounds like an exciting place. Always wanted to see the Capitol and the Lincoln Memorial."

She dragged in a breath. "She heard from Thurgood Marshall. The Judge Advocate's office in Washington—they have no record of Carver's appeal."

Vic groaned. "Bureaucrats. Always misplacing things."

"Please don't. They have no record. Not in Washington, not in Oakland. The appeal was never filed. You didn't file it."

"Ridiculous." His shoulder tensed under her hand. "You know I filed—"

"Please don't. Don't make it worse. You lied, Vic. You lied to Carver, to Esther, to me."

"You're not a lawyer." His voice came out stiff. "You know nothing."

That stung almost as much as one of Jim's blows. "I may not have an education, but I know you said you filed the appeal, and I know you didn't."

"You don't understand." His gaze bore down hard. "It's a lost cause. The Navy convicted two other men with documented medical excuses. Carver didn't have a chance. I had no choice."

"That wasn't your decision to make. You promised—"

"Don't you know what I've been through? Haven't you seen?" He kept his voice low, and his gaze swept the dance floor. "I tried to help, you know I did. I had justice on my side. I had the law on my side. But when that conviction came through, I saw the truth. I was just a pawn so the Navy could pretend they'd done the right thing."

"That doesn't mean—"

"It means I'm on the wrong side. The wrong side. You don't know what they've said about me. I've lost friends in the Navy, in the legal profession, because I defended colored men. You don't know. If I'd kept fighting, my career would have been finished."

"Your career?" She blinked back tears. "What about Carver's career? His life?"

Vic squeezed his eyes shut. "His career is already finished. There's nothing I can do. The best thing for him is to lie low and earn an early release. I have other things to worry about."

"Other things? What could be more—"

"You, for example. You deserve so much." His gaze melted, as soft and sweet as molasses. "I can't have you marrying a man with a lackluster career and a tarnished name."

"Tarnished?"

He sighed and tried to pull her closer, but she resisted. "I didn't tell you earlier, because I didn't want to worry you. My dad's gotten letters—threatening letters for being my father, because I took up the Negro cause. He's afraid he'll lose his judgeship, and if I'd kept fighting, that's exactly what would have happened."

Helen blinked at the wavering image of the man in her arms, a man swayed by politics as surely as those men in the jury had been.

Vic rubbed her lower back. "Don't you see, darling? It's all for the best. Filing the appeal wouldn't have helped Carver, not a bit, but it would have hurt my family. That means you too. You don't want to marry into a family with a bad name."

She shook her head. That's what she feared she was about to do.

He wiped her tears with his handkerchief. "Let's forget about this and enjoy our evening."

"I can't." How could she when everything inside her tumbled and twisted? "I need to go home."

"Helen—"

"No." She wrenched out of his arms and threaded her way through the crowd toward the coatroom.

"Helen . . ." His voice pressed up behind her, and he took her elbow. "You can't leave alone. People will talk." With a wide, flat smile, he helped her into her coat and escorted her out of the restaurant, tossing friendly greetings to everyone they passed.

Vic put his arm around her shoulders as they walked down Fourth Street. A stiff wind blew Helen's hair straight in front of her like blinders, and Vic told humorous stories in a voice higher, louder, and faster than usual.

In Helen's abdomen, a rock-hard pain developed.

What kind of man was she marrying? A man who cared—but not enough to follow through. A man who did right—until his reputation was at risk. A man who valued justice—but valued opinion more highly.

A coward.

They turned onto G Street, and the rock of pain pressed up against her stomach, her lungs, her heart. She'd accused Ray of cowardice for avoiding combat. He'd proven her wrong. To the death, he'd proven her wrong, and she couldn't breathe.

The man laughing by her side was a true coward. A moral coward. And he'd lied about his actions. He couldn't even be an honest coward.

He jiggled her shoulder. "Remember that? Sure, you do. I remember you standing in your parents' parlor when my dad brought me in to see your father. You wore a pink dress. I loved you even then."

She mumbled as if too windblown to reply.

"Funny, isn't it?" Vic guided her around the corner onto Fifth Street. "My parents forbade me to swim in the river with my friends, afraid I'd drown, but it backfired on them. They never thought I'd sneak out my window, fall from the tree, and break both arms. They tried to protect me, but I got hurt in a different way. Goes to show some things are out of our control."

"Out of our control," she whispered.

He bounced into another story, but Helen held the other before her, cupped in her hands so she could inspect it.

She was marrying Vic to protect Jay-Jay, but would it backfire? Was she placing her son in a different type of danger? What would he learn from Vic? That truth and justice and courage could be embraced or discarded based on convenience. That some people were more deserving than others. To protect yourself first.

Victor Llewellyn might be a lesser evil than James Carlisle, but he was hardly a good man.

An inaudible moan flowed from deep inside, from the aching stone. *Lord, what can I do? I have to protect Jay-Jay.*

But could she protect him? He was out of her hands, out of her control. She had to trust the Lord to protect Jay-Jay. She had to do what Vic hadn't done—the right thing.

The stone went into a spasm that jolted pain through her stomach. If she didn't marry Vic, she'd be trapped at the

Carlisles. She couldn't work for Vic again, but without a job, how could she rescue her son?

She couldn't. She had to marry Vic. With no money of her own, she had no choice.

Wasn't that Vic's excuse? That he had no choice? But he had. He could have done the right thing no matter the cost.

Shivers coursed through her. God loved Jay-Jay even more than she did. She had to let the Lord protect her boy in his way, a way she couldn't plan or control or even imagine.

Vic rubbed her arm. "Cold tonight. You're shaking like a leaf."

Helen pushed back her billowing hair. Vic's face shone with compassion and love. He adored her. He'd never hurt her. But that wasn't enough.

The stone shifted and forced out her words. "I can't marry you."

"Excuse me?" Vic stopped right in the middle of D Street.

"I can't—I can't marry you."

He laughed, high and staccato. "Wedding jitters. Mom warned me. Just relax. In two weeks this commotion will be over and we can set up our happy little home."

"No, I can't." Her head shook back and forth, every muscle twitching. "You broke your promise. You lied to cover it up. You had a duty to your client and you failed. That's against the law."

His hand tightened on her shoulder. "Carver isn't preferring charges against me, is he?"

Helen squirmed free. "He—he hasn't decided."

"What? Why would he turn on me after all I've done for him?"

"All you've done? But you haven't done. You're nothing but empty promises."

"That's baloney."

" 'Though the world perish.' " Her voice quavered. "That's

what your motto says. 'Let justice be done though the world perish.'"

"That's the ideal. This is the real world."

She clenched her hair at the roots. It hurt. "I can't marry a man who doesn't follow his own motto."

He reached for her, his fingers splayed wide. "Be reasonable. It's only two weeks before the wedding."

"I don't care. I have to do the right thing. I won't marry you." She twisted her engagement ring off over the first knuckle.

"Don't be silly. Let's go to the Carlisles and talk it out."

The Carlisles? A cold wave crashed over her. If Mr. Carlisle found out she broke her engagement, what would happen? Although her security lay in God, she wriggled the ring back in place.

"Oh goodness. Oh no." Shakes pulsed through her, and her vision blurred. "Please, Vic. Please do me a favor. One favor. Please don't tell anyone."

"What?"

She needed to find a job and a place to live. "Please don't tell anyone I broke up with you."

A harsh bark of a laugh. "What am I supposed to do? Act happy? For crying out loud, our wedding's in two weeks. You want me to keep planning and smiling? Are you crazy?"

Helen pressed her hand over her eyes. "Please. A week. Give me one week. If not for me, for Jay-Jay."

"You're talking nonsense."

"I can't tell you why. Please believe me, this is very important. I need a week. Just this one favor."

His upper lip twisted. "You have the audacity to break up with me and then ask a favor? You *are* crazy. What on earth do I get out of this?"

"I know it's not fair. It doesn't make sense. But please believe me. Please."

"Talk to Esther." His voice came out low and hard. "Talk her out of preferring charges. If I were convicted, I'd be discharged and disbarred. I'd be ruined. Talk sense into her."

Helen looked up to his stony face. He knew the consequences beforehand. He knew his actions were illegal. "I'll talk to her, but I can't make any promises."

He glanced away. "You'll try but no promises? Fine. That's what you'll get from me. I'll try to keep it quiet—for one week—but no promises."

"Thank you. I—I'm so sorry."

"Sure you are." He marched down the street.

Helen turned in circles in the middle of the intersection, not sure which way was which. All alone in the dark. Utterly alone. "Oh Lord, did I do the right thing? I'm so scared."

The wind rushed past, tangled up the branches of an apple tree, and a flurry of pale petals danced around her in the starlight.

She reached out. The petals brushed her fingers and cheeks, as they had when she'd fallen off her bike and Ray had helped her up. *"How can I forget helping a pretty girl with flowers in her hair?"*

Fresh tears spilled down her cheeks, but tears of peace. She had done the right thing. No matter the cost.

✫

England
Wednesday, April 18, 1945

Dr. Robinson unwound gauze from Ray's right hand. "Much better. We can leave the bandages off now. Do you understand?"

Ray nodded, his jaws still wired shut. His hands were shiny and pink. Swelling concealed the usual features of veins and tendons and knuckle wrinkles. But today he could finally be himself again.

Behind the physician stood Major Siegel, the Army Air Force intelligence officer who had often tried to interrogate Ray. *"Können Sie jetzt schreiben, Herr Oberleutnant?"*

He nodded, his heartbeat quickening. He could definitely write. Maybe he could see his brothers tomorrow, even today. They could cable Helen and his parents. Wouldn't everyone be shocked and overjoyed?

Dr. Robinson frowned and passed the wadded-up dressings to a German POW medic. "Major Siegel, I've told you. His hands are too stiff, too weak, too unfeeling to write yet."

Ray grunted and folded his hand into the writing position. The physician's jaw dropped. "How . . . ?"

Ray made loops in the air as if writing. Every day when they removed his bandages and soaked his hands in a saline bath, he had discreetly flexed his fingers to the point of pain, preparing for this day. He needed to tell his story.

Major Siegel plunked a notepad on the nightstand and handed Ray a pen. It slipped from his grasp.

"I told you, Major. You'll have to wait."

Ray shook his head, swung his legs over the side of the bed, and reached for the pen. Major Siegel picked it up and held it while Ray bent his pink sausage fingers around it.

With great effort, he scrawled, "May we talk somewhere private?"

The major read the note. *"Sie können auf Deutsch schreiben. Mein Deutsch ist sehr gut."*

Yes, the major's German was very good—better than Ray's. He tapped the note and looked up into the officer's square face.

He narrowed one dark eye. "Private?"

"Important," Ray wrote. The patients were German, and recovered patients staffed the ward. An American MP stood watch, an American nurse supervised the POW workers, and

Dr. Robinson made rounds, but Ray felt uneasy. The other patients debated over him—was he a heroic pilot shot down over Allied lines or a traitorous defector? When Ray's identity was revealed, he'd be moved from the ward, but he didn't want to take any chances.

"All right." Major Siegel picked up the notepad. "Captain Robinson, do you have anyplace I can interrogate the prisoner in private?"

The doctor's mouth bunched up. "He's a patient, not a prisoner."

"He is both, as you are well aware. Someplace private?"

The doctor grumbled. "My office. Down the hall, second door on the right."

"My adjutant and I are armed. We don't need a guard." He waved to a skinny young lieutenant and beckoned to Ray. *"Kommen Sie mit mir, Herr Oberleutnant."*

Ray stuffed his feet into his slippers and followed. The adjutant looked terrified, so Ray offered a smile. With the swelling and pain subsiding, he could manage some facial expressions.

Still the adjutant touched his hand to his holster.

If he could have, Ray would have said, "Howdy, Sheriff."

Instead he followed the major down the sterile hallway. The POWs were housed somewhere in the English countryside in a real hospital building, not a collection of Nissen huts like most military hospitals in England. Presumably, so they could prevent escape by putting the POWs on the top floor.

"Setzen Sie sich." Major Siegel pulled a chair in front of a wooden desk and seated himself in the physician's chair.

Ray sat, motioned for the pen and paper, and forced out letters.

"You are a hard nut to crack, Herr Oberleutnant," the major said in German. "You appear to be a defector with an intact Messerschmitt. But many questions remain."

Ray shoved the notepad before the major. It read: "I am an American. My name is Capt. Raymond G. Novak, U.S. Army Air Forces, 94th Bomb Group."

Siegel's eyebrows shot up, and he blinked several times at the paper. "This is unexpected. So, you're Captain Novak, are you?" He spoke in English this time.

Ray nodded in time to his ecstatic heartbeat.

Major Siegel opened his briefcase on the desk. "That would explain your command of English and your possession of American military issue items—the underwear, oddly enough, and items from an escape kit. And it would explain this Bible."

His Bible! He reached for it longingly. Four weeks without God's Word had been close to unbearable.

"Captain Novak's personal Bible." The major put it back in the briefcase.

Ray's lips tingled. Siegel didn't believe him.

"Do you know when Captain Novak was shot down? Where?"

Ray wrote, "January 15, outside Augsburg."

"Very good. You must have been there. But do you expect me to believe an American airman hid in Germany for over two months?"

The biggest problem with an unbelievable story was when you needed someone to believe it. Ray stretched the atrophied muscles in his hands, already sore and cramped from the few short sentences he'd written. How could he transcribe his lengthy story?

His gaze fell on a typewriter on a small table in the corner. He sprang to his feet.

The adjutant cried out and pulled his pistol.

Ray thrust up his hands and cocked his head to the typewriter, keeping his eyes on the trigger-happy sheriff. Then he brought his hands low enough to mime typing.

"He wants to type," Siegel said. "Go ahead, Gottlieb."

Gottlieb. Finally, Ray could tell Johannes's story and his own. He sat at the typewriter and rolled in paper, fumbling with the sheet, slick in his fingers. Typing required adjustments for his stiff hands, but Ray pounded it out—the lynching of his crewmen, Johannes's murder, his decision to stay at Lechfeld, his translation of the manual and acts of sabotage, and his flight in the Me 262. He wrote in choppy prose and run-on sentences, not striking through his mistakes, avoiding capitalization and punctuation—to get it down before his fingers failed.

After a few minutes, Siegel stood behind him. Ray zipped out the first page and handed it over his shoulder, then kept going, filling three pages in one uninterrupted paragraph.

The major read the pages with a neutral expression, the perfect intelligence officer.

Ray's hands throbbed and flamed as they had the day he landed the Messerschmitt. Had he included the crucial details?

Siegel wiped his hand over his mouth and revealed a slight smirk. "You expect me to believe this?"

Ray spun back to the typewriter. "every word is true to verify my identity please contact my brothers lt col jack novak air executive 94 bg and walt novak a civilian engineer with boeing consulting with 8 af."

Walt was probably inspecting the jet right now and perusing the manual. Perhaps Ray should have penned a personal note inside.

Major Siegel reached around Ray and took out the sheet of paper. "Lieutenant, please escort the prisoner back to the ward."

A sigh rushed out, along with Ray's expectation of an end to his nightmare. At least Siegel would contact Jack and Walt. He only needed one visit to return to his life.

Ray stopped at the desk and scribbled another note: "Please, sir, may I have my Bible?"

Siegel placed the testimony in his briefcase, read the note, and lifted up the little black Bible. "Captain Novak's Bible?"

Ray could almost smell the pliable leather and the tissue pages. He picked up the pen. "My Bible. My grandfather gave it to me on my twelfth birthday. I always carry it."

Major Siegel's face hardened, and the Bible shook in his grip. "How much information did you torture out of Captain Novak before you murdered him?"

Pale pink petals fluttered down from between the pages, the blossoms from Helen's hair. Ray's hopes fell with them.

40

Antioch
Friday, April 20, 1945

Helen handed the job application to the manager at the Hickmott Cannery. A cannery lady. Her parents would be appalled, but it would be good, paying work for the summer.

The manager skimmed the application, then his eyes popped wide open. "Helen Carlisle. I heard you might come by. I—I'm afraid we don't have any positions open."

"Excuse me?" Giant ads in the *Ledger* begged for workers, declaring it a patriotic duty to send canned apricots, asparagus, and tomatoes to the front. "But—"

"Sorry. We just filled the last opening."

Helen's mouth went dry. He'd heard she'd come by? What had he heard and from whom? "If something opens up, please don't call the number on the application. I'm moving. I'll come back later and check. How long would you suggest?"

The manager slid her application away. "We won't need any more help this year."

This year? Nonsense. Cannery work was difficult, and girls quit all the time.

Helen headed up the road toward downtown. What was going on? All week she'd applied for work, avoiding friends of the Llewellyns and the Carlisles. After all, why would Victor Llewellyn's bride need a job? She couldn't openly seek work or a room until the news broke, but she needed both beforehand.

Behind her the San Joaquin River swept water down to the Bay, water as cold as the realization that the news had already broken.

Had Vic told his gossipy mother? Was that why no one would hire her? Was this the Llewellyns' revenge against the woman who broke Vic's heart?

Helen's eyes prickled as she turned onto Second Street. Tomorrow, the week she'd promised him would be over. Without a job, she couldn't rent a room, and if the Llewellyns turned the town against her, how would she find a job? If she left town, she'd be able to find work, but rooms were scarce and who would watch Jay-Jay?

The sweet spring air pressed heavy on her, bowing her head as she passed the businesses closing for the night, desperate to hire anyone but her.

What if the Carlisles had already heard?

Her breath hopped around in her chest. Was it safe to go home? Where could she go? She couldn't sleep on Betty's couch for long, not with the baby due any day. And Jay-Jay was at the Carlisles. She had to get him, get some things.

She picked up the pace to the Carlisle home.

Helen flung open the door. She'd fill a suitcase, grab her son, and go.

"Oh, good, Helen. You're home." Mrs. Carlisle stood outside the dining room door, fiddling with her apron. "Dinner's on the table."

Helen's heart slammed into her throat. "I'm sorry. I'm having dinner at Betty's tonight. Where's Jay-Jay?"

"At the table. You can't go to Betty's. It's pork chop night."

"I don't care for pork chops. Neither does Jay-Jay." She brushed past her mother-in-law into the dining room.

Jay-Jay sat at the table with Mr. Carlisle—and Victor Llewellyn. Helen's veins crackled with ice. Vic had told. He'd broken another promise.

She scooped up her son with shaking arms and returned his smacking kiss. "Hi, sweetie. We're going to Aunt Betty's for dinner."

"Yay! Doody!"

Mr. Carlisle stood. "I wouldn't do that."

"She's expecting us." She inched to the door. While Vic's presence was hardly welcome, it would grant her time to pack.

"You're not leaving this house. We have something to discuss with you."

Helen turned a searing gaze to Vic. "You told."

He snorted. "I didn't have to. They figured it out."

"You said you were working on your new house every day." Mrs. Carlisle sat in her chair next to her husband. "I went by on Tuesday, and you weren't there. Nothing had been done."

Mr. Carlisle sat and slipped a pork chop onto the top plate in front of him. "On Wednesday, Mr. Lindstrom came in to Carlisles' Furniture. He said you applied for a job and inquired about the room for rent above his store."

Helen sank into a chair and clutched Jay-Jay. The Lindstroms and the Carlisles had never been close. She'd thought she was safe.

Mr. Carlisle scooped creamed peas onto the plate. "Strange behavior. Clearly a sign of instability."

Helen gasped. "Instability?"

"One of many. Very troubling." He added a glop of mashed potatoes. "You burn down your house, leave a Llewellyn at the altar, and look for a job and a room when everyone knows we provide well for you. Lots of hysterical behavior. Now this attempt to smear Vic's name."

"What? I haven't—"

"Encouraging that colored girl to press charges."

"I never." She glared at Vic.

His jaw poked forward. "Have you talked her out of it?"

"I talked to her on Monday. That's what I promised to do." She'd let Esther know the consequences and she'd asked about their plans, but she had no right to influence their decision. "Besides, it's Carver's decision, not Esther's."

Red blotches appeared on Vic's cheeks. "First you break our engagement, now you try to ruin my career."

"Me? But you—you're the one—"

"As I thought." Mr. Carlisle passed the plate to Vic. "More signs of instability. Clearly an unfit mother."

"What?" Helen's fingers worked into her son's hair.

Jay-Jay squirmed on her lap. "Mama, I want down."

She held him tighter. Mr. Carlisle dished out food with a calm face, Mrs. Carlisle sat docile as always, and Vic kept his gaze down and his brow furrowed.

"Unfit?" Helen choked out. "I love my son."

Mr. Carlisle fixed a cool gaze on her. "No one doubts your love, only your sanity. That's why we've filed for custody of Jay-Jay."

That punched her in the chest harder than Jim ever had. "Wha . . . wha . . . ?"

"If you show some sense for once and get this girl to see the light, we'll retract it. Under one condition—you continue to live in this house. It's not safe for Jay-Jay to live alone with you."

Helen couldn't breathe, couldn't think. This couldn't be happening.

Vic pushed his chair back. "Thank you for the dinner invitation, but I'd better go."

"How could you?" she cried. "How could you help them?"

"I didn't." He stood. "I found out after they filed for custody. Not that I disapprove."

Her breath came out in hard puffs. To think she'd almost married such a petty man.

Mr. Carlisle dished up another plate. "Jay-Jay needs to stay under this roof where he's safe. As head of the Chamber of Commerce, I notified the town business leaders that you're a bit touched in the head. No one will hire you. No one will rent a room to a penniless, unemployed woman. And don't even think about leaving town. With the custody case filed, the courts would see that as evading justice. The bus and train stations are on the lookout for you."

Every part of Helen felt numb, deprived of oxygen, of life.

"Mama, too tight." Jay-Jay wriggled off her lap.

"Poor baby." Mrs. Carlisle clucked her tongue. "Let Grandma hold you nice and gentle."

The little boy scampered around the table to his grandmother.

Helen's arms remained suspended, frozen, hugging empty air. Her son. They'd stolen her son. They'd imprisoned her in this house. And there was nothing she could do about it.

Vic slithered toward the door, snake that he was, and Mr. Carlisle set a plate in front of Helen.

Pork chops. She hated pork chops, hated everything they represented—rigidity, control, violent enforcement.

She shoved the plate away, bolted from her chair, and caught up to Vic at the front door. "How could you? How could you do this to me?"

He faced her, his lip curled. "First of all, I didn't do it; they did. Secondly, you've got a lot of nerve after what you've done to me."

She stared him down. "I called off a wedding, but you? You're trying to take my baby away from me."

"I'll explain this yet again. I didn't do that. And you heard them—get Esther to back off, and this whole thing's over."

"And if she refuses, they'll—"

"So what? They'll have custody, but you get to live here. Nothing will change, except they'll ensure Jay-Jay's safety. A wise precaution."

"Wise?" she said in a fierce whisper. "It's wise to throw a little boy to the wolves?"

Vic chuckled. "Those doting grandparents are hardly wolves. Aren't you being a little dramatic? A little . . . hysterical?"

Helen wrapped fisted arms around her middle and stepped back. If she weren't careful, she'd end up committed to a sanitarium.

"You know what?" He opened the door and stepped outside. "I'm glad you broke up with me. Last thing I need is a crazy wife."

"You have no idea—no idea what you're doing," she whispered, but she spoke to a closed door.

Helen shivered. All her doors, all her windows were shut, locked, and boarded up. Darkness closed in about her.

⋆

England
Friday, April 27, 1945

Ray walked the length of the ward and returned, determined to beat the previous day's record of sixteen laps. He walked, he stretched, he did push-ups, sit-ups, and arm circles—anything to regain strength.

He stroked his lower jaw, still tender over the break. In a week the wires would be cut, and he could eat solid food again. Although grateful for broth and eggnog, he'd grown as tired of them as he had of fish and potatoes.

Ray passed dozens of men who could use a kind word, but he couldn't minister in any way. He couldn't help the war effort by flying or sabotaging, or even by typing forms in triplicate. For the first time, he didn't mind.

He could pray and read the German Bible the hospital provided. All he had was his relationship with the Lord.

It was enough.

Ray paused at the end of the ward and stretched his arms overhead, to the left, then to the right. *Lord, when I get back to the pulpit, help me remember this.*

"Oberleutnant Gottlieb?" Major Siegel called.

Ray responded to the name now, as he had responded to both his brothers' names when his mother mixed them up. He wanted to talk to the major. Nine days had passed since he'd given his written testimony, but Jack and Walt hadn't come.

Major Siegel ushered Ray into Dr. Robinson's office and handed him a notepad. "Next week when your wires are cut, you'll come into Army Air Force custody," he said in German. "Would you like to change your story?"

"No," Ray wrote in English. "Have you contacted my brothers?"

"If they are in the Army, they are our prisoners or will be soon. The Russians are in Berlin. Soon your government will fall."

Ray sighed. "My brothers—Jack and Walter Novak."

Siegel read the note. "You're standing by that story?" He switched to English.

"I'm standing by the truth. My brothers?"

"They've read your story."

"When are they coming?" He wrote so fast his letters ran together.

"They aren't. They refuse to honor your lies." Siegel crossed thick arms. "The one thing you couldn't torture out of Captain Novak was his personality. He was a mild-mannered man incapable of the feats you described."

Ray felt dizzy. In Germany he'd joked that his brothers would never believe what he was doing. Now it didn't seem so funny.

"Not to mention your handwriting looks nothing like his."

"I just had my bandages off. Show them this." Ray thrust the notepad at him.

He ignored it. "They said your typewritten statement wasn't Captain Novak's style. The grammar, the punctuation, nothing."

"My hands hurt. I wanted—"

"What exactly were your orders, Gottlieb? You flew an Me 262 over enemy lines, conveniently carrying a pilot's manual, wearing a German uniform and American underwear. What did you want to accomplish?"

"I wanted to come home."

Siegel glanced at Ray's response and shook his head. "Tell us your plan and we'll go easy on you. Is the plane booby-trapped? What false information is in that manual to mislead our engineers? If that was your plan, you failed. No one trusts the plane or the manual."

Ray's sigh puffed out his cheeks. So much for his gift to the Army Air Force.

The major leaned over Ray's chair with a hardened face. "The uniform—that's what went wrong, wasn't it? You killed Novak for his identity, but his uniform didn't fit. Your papers say you're several inches taller than Novak. The sleeves, the pants were too short. Without an American uniform, you couldn't deliver the plane, gather intelligence, and slip back behind German lines. But you came anyway with this ludicrous story. Why? Did they hold a gun to your head? To your beloved *Mutter*'s head? They sent you on a suicide mission. See how desperate, how careless, how degenerate your people have become?"

Ray stared up at the major, and his head wagged from side to side.

"You know the penalty for espionage—for espionage, torture, and murder." Siegel spat tobacco-scented words in Ray's face. "During the Battle of the Bulge, German spies tried to pass as Americans. We pulled some of them out of hospitals and shot them. Perfectly legal under the Geneva Conventions. Summary execution of spies."

Ray's fingers went icy cold.

Major Siegel straightened and gave a grim smile. "If you cooperate, we'll see what we can do. Shall we try this again? What were your orders?"

Ray's fingers clutched like icicles around the pen. "To pilot my B-17 over Germany and bomb the Lechfeld airfield or the secondary target of the marshalling yards at Augsburg. If captured, I was to give only my name, rank, and serial number, to try to escape, and to aid the Allied effort. I did this to the fullness of my ability."

"You swear by this nonsense even now?"

"The Lord is my witness."

"The Lord?" Siegel sneered. "You can argue your case before him directly—and soon. May he have mercy on your soul."

41

Antioch
Sunday, April 29, 1945

Helen paused before the door to Fellowship Hall, but she had to make an appearance and show a sane face to society.

She had to prove she wasn't crazy cripple Helen.

With a deep breath, she pushed open the door and stepped inside. Some conversations stilled, others were hushed and shielded behind gloved hands. Pastor Novak's sermon on the evils of gossip wouldn't help. If anything, it would concentrate attention on the rumors snaking through town.

Betty had angrily related what she'd heard—Helen left that sweet Llewellyn boy at the altar, she burned down her house, she talked to herself. Did polio have long-term effects on the brain? How kind of the Carlisles to offer to raise that darling little boy. How sad that they were saddled with an unbalanced daughter-in-law, but her parents weren't in town and they couldn't turn the poor thing out on the streets, could they?

"Oh, Mrs. Carlisle, thank goodness you're here." Mrs. Novak came up to Helen and took her arm. "Mrs. Anello is home sick. Would you please help with the beverages? There's no one I trust more."

Helen's eyes misted over. "Thank you. I'd love to help."

While she now knew better than to use work as a cure, today work would help her look normal.

"The tea's steeping," Mrs. Novak said in an overly loud voice as they passed through the crowd. "The cups are on the—oh, you know what to do. You always do."

"Thank you," Helen said over her thick tongue and plunged into the refuge of the kitchen. She loaded a tray with teacups, set them on the table in the hall, filled two teapots from the urn, and brought them out. No sugar or coffee, so she only had to refill teapots, replenish cups, wipe spills, and clear dirty cups.

"Good morning, Mrs. Jeffries, Mrs. Lindstrom," she said with a measured smile.

"Oh yes. Good morning." They gave her nervous glances as they retreated with their tea.

Although Helen's heart faltered, she made sure her smile didn't fade.

"I'm grateful for today's sermon." Mrs. Llewellyn's voice rose from the line. "How Victor's suffered from gossip. He's so brave coming to church. Yesterday was supposed to be his wedding day, the poor lamb. How that girl could have the nerve to show her face. Well, it goes to show her mind isn't quite . . ."

Mr. Peters stepped aside with his tea, Mrs. Llewellyn reached for a cup—and caught Helen's eye. The woman gasped.

"My mind, Mrs. Llewellyn?" Helen managed to speak, to smile, though her jaw set like rock. "My mind is at peace knowing Pastor Novak wasn't referring to *me*." She spun away into the kitchen, her heart battering her rib cage.

She opened the cupboard door, which smacked into the cabinet, and she lined up thick ceramic cups on the metal tray. Her hands shook.

The kitchen door swished open and shut. "Do I have permission to slap that horrible Llewellyn woman?" Esther stood by the door with her arms crossed.

Helen's chuckle caught on the way out. "As much as I'd love that, it wouldn't be wise."

"Someone has to defend you. What's this I hear about the Carlisles filing for custody of your son?"

"I'm afraid that rumor's true." Helen turned teacup handles to face the same way. "But I talked to Matthew Ward, my father's attorney, and he says I have a good case. All the Carlisles have is rumors and opinion. I just have to show everyone I'm a good mother."

"Who's hearing your case? Judge Llewellyn?"

"He—he's the only one in town, but Mr. Ward will try to get the venue changed."

"That Victor Llewellyn. I know he's slippery, but I had no idea how mean and vengeful—"

"It's not him. Really."

"You don't think he advised the Carlisles? Gave them the idea?"

"I don't think so. All I know is he won't stop them unless . . ." Oh no, she didn't want Esther to know about the Carlisles' condition. She whisked the tray off the counter and swept past Esther into the hall.

"Unless what?"

Helen laid fresh cups on the table and loaded the tray with dirty cups. "Mrs. Jones, would you please check if the teapots need to be refilled?" She dashed back into the kitchen.

"Unless what? What's that slimy lieutenant up to?"

"Nothing." Helen reached for the teapot in Esther's hand.

She held it back. "I won't let you refill this until you tell me what's going on."

Helen set the dirty cups in the sink. "I didn't tell you for a reason. You need to make your own decision."

"Me? What do I have to do with it?"

"Absolutely nothing. That's my point. Vic, the coward, wants me to talk you out of filing charges against him. I refuse. You have every right. He failed in his duty and he should face the consequences."

Esther set the teapot on the counter. "What's this have to do with you and Jay-Jay?"

Helen glanced out the window over the sink. Children played tag on the lawn, and Jay-Jay chased Donald Ferguson, who faked a slow run so the younger boy could catch him. Pain cinched around her heart. "It has nothing to do with us whatsoever. Mr. Carlisle says he'll drop the custody case if I talk you out of it. He says it's a sign of sanity. Utter nonsense."

Esther released a long, low sigh and leaned against the counter. She touched a scar on Helen's forearm. "Your husband beat you, didn't he?"

She looked her friend in the eye. She'd never admitted it to anyone other than Ray and Dorothy. "Yes, he did."

"Did he learn from his daddy?"

Helen's stomach folded in on itself. She nodded.

"And if they raise Jay-Jay . . ."

The thought wrenched through Helen and ripped out a sob before she could stop it. She clapped one hand over her mouth.

"We can't let that happen." Esther marched to the kitchen door.

"Where are you going?"

"To find the lieutenant and put an end to this." She shoved the door open.

"No! Esther, don't." Helen followed and took hold of Esther's arm.

She didn't even slow down. "It's bad enough Carver's in prison. We can't let them snatch away your baby boy."

For the benefit of the crowd, Helen plastered on a smile and lowered her voice to a stage whisper. "They won't. I have a good case."

"Do you? Have you heard the rumors? They've turned this town against you. You don't stand a chance."

Helen spotted Vic chatting by the front door, and she tugged Esther's arm. "God will protect Jay-Jay. I know he will. Even if I lose, he'll protect him. But we have to do what's right. We have to have the courage to stand and fight."

Esther looked deeply into Helen's eyes. "Sometimes the Lord wants us to fight, but sometimes he wants us to surrender. Surrender can require a lot more courage than fighting."

"But you shouldn't. You have every right—"

"I'm giving it up." Esther pried Helen's hand off her arm and glided up to Victor with a wide smile. "Good day, Lieutenant. May I speak to you outside?"

Vic's gaze darted to Helen, and surprise melted into relief. "I'd be delighted." He held open the door for Esther.

Helen recovered in time to follow them outside to the oak tree at the edge of the church property. She couldn't let this happen.

Under the tree, Esther turned on Vic and stuck her finger in his face. "I have lost all respect for you. You're willing to sacrifice a woman and child to save your career."

He drew back his shoulders. "How dare—"

"You deserve to be reprimanded, maybe even disbarred, but I won't let you hurt Helen and Jay-Jay in the process."

Helen gripped Esther's arm. "Please don't. This isn't your concern."

"He made it my concern." She snapped open her handbag and pulled out a form folded in half. "Carver asked me to bring this to church and pray over our decision. Looks like the Lord answered my prayer."

Vic's cheeks went white. "You won't prefer charges?"

"No, we won't." She held the form high and ripped off little pieces right into Vic's face. "I leave you in the hands of the Almighty. I suggest you repent of your sins and pray for mercy."

"You . . . how dare . . ." Vic brushed paper scraps from his face and uniform.

Esther cocked her head and gave him a sweet smile. "The words you're searching for are 'thank you.'"

His mouth contorted. "Thank you."

"You're welcome. And I forgive you. I refuse to let you drag me into the gutter of bitterness. Now, get rid of this custody case and tell your mama to turn off the gossip mill."

He gave a single nod. "I promise."

Helen clamped her tongue between her molars so she wouldn't say what she thought of his promises.

Esther took Helen's arm. "Come along. You can have Sunday dinner at the Novaks with me while the good lieutenant has a little talk with the Carlisles. He will, won't he?"

"I will."

As Esther led her away, Helen glanced behind her. Vic narrowed his eyes and raised the thinnest smile, the smile of victory. But the victory was hers. She hadn't married him.

★

Helen hung up the gold jacket that matched her gold and green plaid dress. She bent down to help Jay-Jay.

"Where have you been?"

She tensed at Mr. Carlisle's harsh tone and draped a little blue jacket on the coatrack. "We had dinner with the Novaks and supper with George and Betty. Didn't Dorothy tell you? I couldn't find you after church, and I asked her to tell—"

"Tell? You don't tell—you ask!" His hand sliced up and slapped her across the cheek.

She cried out and pressed her hand over her sore cheekbone. "Ask? I don't have to—"

"Everything's changed. You can't take away my grandson without permission."

"But—but that's only if you win . . . wait, didn't Vic come by?"

Mr. Carlisle's face stiffened. He turned and walked into the living room and sat in his armchair with *Time* magazine.

Helen took two dragging steps closer. "Didn't Vic come by? He promised he would."

"He came."

"Did he tell you the Joneses aren't preferring charges?"

"Yes." He turned a page in the magazine.

Helen's leg muscles quivered. "So you'll drop the custody case."

"No." He gazed down his thin nose at the magazine. "That would be unwise. You're an unfit mother. Today's behavior confirmed it—ranting like a madwoman to Mrs. Llewellyn, failing to ask permission, and Victor said you tried to talk that Jones woman out of her decision, the opposite of what I told you to do."

"But . . . but . . ." She felt her son lean against her leg, and she groped for his warm little hand.

"Only a precaution. You can live here as long as you behave, but I can't let you take my grandson away to live in a dangerous home."

She couldn't think of a more dangerous home than this one. Everything inside her screamed. His promise meant nothing. Esther's sacrifice was in vain. But she clamped her mouth shut. As Esther and Ray had shown, courage came in many forms—surrender, peacemaking, fighting—or in Helen's case, escape. "Come on, Jay-Jay. It's bedtime."

Thank goodness, he didn't argue as she led him upstairs.

She had to think, to plan, to act. Mr. Ward said the Carlisles couldn't force her to reside there before the trial or afterward if she won the case. If she stayed, the violence would escalate. She had to get out tonight.

Help me, Lord. She closed Jay-Jay's bedroom door. "What a good boy you are. Let's get your pajamas on."

She sang a song while she helped him, and her mind whirled over plans. "For story time tonight, let's do something different." She pulled *Mother Goose* off the shelf. "You point to a rhyme and I'll recite it."

"Okay, Mama." Jay-Jay sat cross-legged on his bed with the black-and-white checked book. "Miss Muffet."

"'Little Miss Muffet sat on a tuffet,'" Helen said in a singsong voice and pulled a suitcase from the closet. She recited "Wee Willie Winkie" and "Old Mother Hubbard" while she filled the suitcase with Jay-Jay's necessities, leaving room for her own.

Later that night, when everyone was sound asleep, she would sneak out with the suitcase and her little boy, who slept like the dead. She'd go to Betty's house tonight.

Then she'd do the unthinkable.

She'd beg for help. The thought burned behind her eyes. She would admit failure and cable her parents for money. They might refuse, but if she told them of the custody case, they might relent. She needed rent for the room over Mr. Lindstrom's store. She'd look for work in Pittsburg, the next town down the river.

Tears dribbled down her cheeks, but she kept chanting Mother Goose rhymes. This wasn't the life she'd planned on.

The bedroom door swung open, and Mrs. Carlisle walked in. "There's my angel. Your mommy didn't let me see you all day." She stared at the suitcase on the floor. "What's this?"

Helen sprang to the door and shut it, then grasped her

mother-in-law's hands. She had to appeal to her as a woman, as a mother, as a fellow victim. "Please. Mr. Carlisle hit me today. You know what it's like. It'll get worse and worse until he beats me senseless. I need to leave. I promise I won't leave town. I just have to get out of this house."

Mrs. Carlisle looked down at the suitcase with a sad longing Helen had never seen before.

"Please." Helen squeezed her bony hands, trying to convey her compassion, her necessity, her pain. "You know what it's like. Please let me go."

Mrs. Carlisle's gaze shifted to Helen. "If you go, and he finds out I knew . . ."

Her mother-in-law would get beaten and hard. Helen's mouth drifted open. The blood sucked from her face, and the hope sucked out of her heart.

Tonight one of them would get beaten. In the flat brown of Mrs. Carlisle's eyes, something sparked. Control. For the first time since her wedding day, she had control.

The older woman yanked her hands free and flung open the door. "James! She's running away! She's stealing our baby!"

"Oh no!" Skeletal hands clawed at Helen's throat. She dumped the suitcase contents into the top dresser drawer, scrunched them down, tried to close the drawer, but what did it matter? She couldn't get out, could never get past the man thundering up the stairs and into the room.

"She tried to leave, but I stopped her." Mrs. Carlisle pointed to the suitcase splayed open on the floor.

"What's this?" He shook the suitcase in Helen's face.

She backed up, and cold, white fingers closed around her throat. She had no defense, no excuse. "I won't—I won't leave town. I promise."

"You won't leave this *house*!" He swung the suitcase and struck her in the head.

Blazing white pain erupted in her skull, and she fell, curled into a position she knew well, knees to her chest, arms over her head.

The blows pummeled down on her—her side, her arms, her legs—until the suitcase fell apart. Then he cursed her and kicked her, and Helen cried out for him to stop, to please stop, and Jay-Jay wailed and begged him to stop, and Mrs. Carlisle stood in the corner, clutching her sides, her eyes cold and lifeless, and she didn't say one word to stop him. As if she could.

As if anyone could stop him.

When he tired, he dragged her into her room and locked her in from the outside and said if she ever tried to take Jay-Jay out of the house, he'd have her arrested for kidnapping.

Helen lay coiled up on the hardwood floor, salty blood and tears mingling in her mouth. She'd never get away, never get out. The Carlisles would win custody, and this would happen over and over until he killed her.

No Japanese torpedo would save her now.

A sob convulsed her, and pain shot through her chest. He must have broken a rib or two. She hugged herself hard to brace against her tears, her searing grief.

Then a thought formed. The Carlisles didn't care if she lived or died, stayed or left. They only cared about Jay-Jay. Mr. Carlisle would never beat him, just as he'd never beaten Jim.

A black thought, but it shone in its blackness like obsidian.

She couldn't save her son, but she could save herself.

And she grasped it in all its gleaming, cold, hard blackness.

42

England
Monday, April 30, 1945

Dr. Robinson snipped the last wire, and Ray's jaw sagged open. With effort, he closed his mouth, but it flopped open again. He massaged his jaw muscles, both stiff and weak from six weeks' immobilization.

"Can he talk now?" Major Siegel hovered behind the physician.

"Yes," Ray croaked. He cleared his throat. "Yes, I can talk." His voice came out thin and unrecognizable.

Dr. Robinson smiled at Ray. "You can have soft foods. Are you ready for your first meal?"

"You bet."

"His last meal, actually," Major Siegel said. "And we'll take care of it. Come, Herr Oberleutnant."

Dr. Robinson stood and faced the major. "He's still my patient. I haven't written the discharge order."

"Then write it, Captain. He has an appointment."

Yeah, an appointment with the firing squad. Ray's heart settled into the void of his stomach.

The physician bent over the chart, muttering about how

soldiers should stick to their work and keep their noses out of doctors' work.

Ray ran his hands over his lap down to the worn knees of Johannes's Luftwaffe uniform, which smelled a lot better than the last time he'd worn it.

"Well, Gottlieb, does it feel good to wear your uniform again?"

"It never felt good to wear the uniform of the enemy."

The major let out a dry chuckle and handed Ray the flight jacket and Helen's scarf.

Ray fingered the soft gray wool, wound it around his neck, and clutched it in both hands. If only he could have sent Helen a letter to say how much he loved her. His family too. But it was better this way. Everyone had mourned his death. If his brothers found out they could have prevented his execution, the guilt would be unbearable.

"Is that from your *Mutter*?"

"No. The girl I love in California."

"Still won't give up? Stubborn man."

"A Novak trait."

Major Siegel held up a pair of handcuffs. "Get your jacket on."

Ray sighed and put on the flight jacket. The uniform still fit loosely, but he'd gained a few pounds on his liquid diet. For what good?

Siegel handcuffed Ray behind his back. "Let's go." He nodded to two MPs and his adjutant.

Ray turned to his physician. "Thank you, Dr. Robinson. I appreciate your care and kindness."

The doctor glared at the major. "Sounds like an American accent to me."

"He's good, isn't he?" Siegel led Ray out of the ward, down the stairs, and outside.

Ray lifted his face to a cool breeze and a flock of cumulus sheep. This was the first time he'd been outside in weeks, and his last time ever.

What irony. An American pilot who had flown over thirty combat missions and committed acts of sabotage behind enemy lines was about to be executed as a spy.

And no one would ever know.

At least he'd die knowing what he was made of and at peace with the Lord.

When they reached an Army truck, Major Siegel tied a blindfold over Ray's eyes, and Ray said good-bye to the blue.

☆

Antioch

Past midnight, in pallid gray moonlight, with the obsidian thought before her, Helen lurched into action.

She untucked the top sheet and laid it flat on her bed. Then she piled in necessities—work outfits, undergarments, nightgown, shoes, gloves, and a beret that wouldn't be squashed.

The blackness of her plan oppressed her. She was abandoning her child. What crippling pain and smothering guilt she'd bear the rest of her life. But what a horrific choice she faced—stay until Mr. Carlisle killed her, or leave and lose everyone she loved.

She wanted to live.

Her window looked down on the overhang above the back porch. She could toss her bundle onto the lawn, climb onto the overhang, and ease herself down. What were a few more injuries?

The rest of her plan floated in a nebulous haze. Walk to Pittsburg, use her little bit of cash for a train ticket to San Francisco, stay at the YWCA until she found a job and a room. She could get lost in the city.

Her throat tightened, but she blinked away the haze of doubt. She had to regain control.

From the dresser, she grabbed her manicure kit, cosmetics case, and hairbrush. Then she opened the top drawer.

Ray's stack of letters, tied with a ribbon. Fresh pain jabbed her.

She clutched the letters to her chest and sank to her knees. What would he think of her plan? He always understood, but who could understand this?

She gripped the letters in one hand and her aching side with the other. She'd lost him, killed him, and now she'd leave everyone else she loved. But it was for the best. A cripple girl who injured herself and killed the men she loved. She'd destroy Jay-Jay too. He'd be better off without her.

She had failed as a wife, a mother, a woman. She deserved the beating. She deserved to lose her son. She deserved pain and shame for the rest of her life.

One envelope slipped from the stack.

Helen groped for it. The envelope felt thick and uneven, and she removed the leaf Ray had sent, silvery gray in the moonlight.

Waves of grief buffeted her. Ray had courage. He hadn't cared about his life, only about doing the right thing. He had slain his dragons.

Helen was fleeing hers.

A sob bobbed to the surface. "Oh, Lord. What can I do?"

She cradled the leaf in her hand, as fragile as her son. If she closed her hand, the leaf would crumble to pieces. What would happen to Jay-Jay if she left him?

A new thought formed, soft and white and lustrous as a pearl. What if she had it backward? What if leaving Jay-Jay would destroy him? Had she ever hurt him? No, not once. She took good care of her son.

What harm would come to him if she left? He'd be raised by the Carlisles, taught that a man should be cruel to his wife, taught that his mother didn't love him, and never taught to control his temper. He'd turn out like his father. Maybe worse.

Hadn't God given Jay-Jay to her? Yes, to Helen. Would he do that if he thought she would destroy him? Perhaps if God trusted her, she should trust herself.

The pearl of truth expanded, glowed, and shattered the obsidian lie.

She struggled to her feet. "I won't—I won't leave without my son."

That overhang ran under Jay-Jay's window as well as Helen's. And while her door was locked, his wasn't.

She stashed Ray's letters in her purse and tied the corners of the bed sheet together. Her window slid open without a sound. Helen took off her espadrilles, tied the ribbons together, and hung them around her neck.

Wincing from the pain in her side, she climbed onto the overhang, the shingles rough under her bare feet. She sidled over to Jay-Jay's window, gripped the frame, and pushed upward. It didn't budge.

She groaned. If his window didn't open, she'd have to drop to the ground and come through the front door, increasing the chance she'd be caught.

"Please, Lord." Another push, and it wiggled, squeaked in protest, and banged open.

Helen ducked below the windowsill, but no sound rose other than the blood whooshing in her ears.

She retrieved her bundle, pushed it through her son's window, and climbed through.

Jay-Jay lay on his stomach, his rump in the air, his middle two fingers in his mouth, a baby habit he'd outgrown. A dark circle fanned around his face on the pillow. It was damp.

The poor thing had cried himself to sleep. For her. She had to rescue him before his compassion turned to callousness.

After she added his belongings to the bundle, she unbuckled the leather belt around the waist of her dress, looped it under the knot of her bundle, and strapped it to her back, passing the belt over her uninjured right side.

With more care than usual, Helen lifted her son and his blanket, cooing as she had when he was a baby. His limp weight molded to her body.

She rested her cheek on his damp hair. How could she even think of abandoning him? He was part of her, and she could no more leave him than she could leave her own heart.

Helen stepped toward the door. The extra weight of boy and bundle made the floorboard creak.

Her heart wild, she paused and strained to listen through the stillness. She made her way to the door, testing each board underneath and walking the firmest ones like balance beams.

She turned the glass doorknob, hating each click, and opened the door.

The Carlisles' bedroom lay across the hall. Mild snores issued from the other side of the door. If those snores stopped, Helen would take off running.

She probed each board until she found a quiet one, walked its length, and used her ballet training to keep her steps light and long.

Down the stairs, working through her feet—toe, ball, heel to lessen the impact.

Silence upstairs. Was she too far away to hear the snores, or had Mr. Carlisle woken up? The front door stood before her, and Helen picked up her pace, her steps muffled by the hall rug. At the coatrack, she grabbed Jay-Jay's jacket and her own.

The front door made a nasty clunk when she opened it and a nastier one when she shut it behind her, but she stepped outside into free air. She dashed down the walk, down the sidewalk. Pebbles pricked her bare feet, and she stubbed her toe. Her legs threatened to buckle, she stumbled, she kept going.

At the corner of Sixth Street, her legs gave way, and she fell hard onto her knees. She couldn't go on. Too much weight, too much pain, and she was too weak from the beating.

Jay-Jay lifted his head and whimpered. He brought his eyes to focus on Helen. "Mama?"

"Shh, sweetie." Helen glanced behind her, breathing hard. Was that a light in the Carlisles' window or the reflection of the moon? The angle was bad and trees stood in the way.

"Where are we?"

Helen clapped her hand over her son's mouth. "Quiet, sweetie," she whispered. "Can you walk?"

"Wanna sleep," he mumbled under her hand, and he laid his head back on her shoulder.

The air pressed on her, cold and clammy and stifling. She couldn't carry both him and the bundle. Training her gaze on the Carlisle home, she fumbled with the belt buckle. Her fingers shook and wouldn't cooperate. At last she unfastened it, and the bundle thumped to the sidewalk.

Helen struggled to her feet and down Sixth Street. One house, two, three, no sign of Mr. Carlisle, and she pounded on the Anellos' door until the light flipped on.

George opened the door in his bathrobe, his hair mussed up. "What—Helen? What are you doing here? What happened to you?"

She hadn't seen herself in the mirror, but the taut pain in her left cheek meant an angry welt and drying blood.

"Please let me in." Her knees buckled, and George caught her by the elbow and guided her inside.

"Helen? Oh goodness! What happened?" Betty rushed to her side, her bathrobe no longer closing over her pregnant belly.

"Take Jay-Jay, please." He'd fallen asleep again.

Betty did so, and Helen slumped to the sofa.

George took her chin and frowned at her. "What happened? Who did this to you?"

In the warmth of the Anello home, fear evaporated and resolve took its place. For years, she had concealed the Carlisle shame. No longer. She'd kept it secret to protect Jay-Jay, but her protection had backfired. "Mr. Carlisle beat me. He found out I was leaving with Jay-Jay."

"Oh my goodness!" Betty sat next to her with Jay-Jay in her arms. "How could—how could he do such a thing?"

George strode into the front hall. "I'll call the police, a doctor."

"No, don't. The police won't help. They know about the custody case. Mr. Carlisle will say I fell down the stairs, threw myself down in a fit of madness, staged it to get custody. I know how this works. And don't wake the doctor. It can wait till morning. Believe me, I have experience."

"Poor thing," Betty said. "You've had so many accidents."

"So many beatings."

"What?" George marched back to the living room. "He's beaten you before?"

"No. Jim did. All the time." The truth at last, and freedom lifted her.

"Jim?" Betty said in a tiny voice, and she held the sleeping boy tighter with one hand over his head as if to shield him. "But he—he loved you."

"Jim's idea of love was nothing but power and control." Helen traced a scar on the back of her hand. "These aren't from cooking accidents. Jim liked to burn me. He kicked me and threw me around and punched me and smashed furniture over me. He caused two miscarriages. Then he blamed my injuries on my clumsiness."

"Dear Lord, no." George lowered himself into the armchair and ran his fingers into his hair. "No. I knew Jim all my life. We were friends. Sure, he had a mean streak but . . . I had no idea."

"All this was going on and you never—you didn't tell me?" Betty's eyes filled with tears.

Helen sighed. Why had she expected condemnation instead of sympathy? She'd been blinded by the lies—that she needed to be perfect to be loved, that she had failed, that she deserved what she'd gotten. "I didn't want to admit I'd made a mistake. Everyone told me to wait to get married, but I didn't listen because I was afraid I'd lose Jim. And I hated to admit I was stupid enough to fall for such a man. I thought you'd think less of me."

Betty choked on a sob. "Oh, darling, I never would have thought that."

No tears remained, but her sister's compassion made her chin quiver. "I know now, but back then . . ."

"You should have told us. We could have helped."

"How? I had no grounds to divorce him. He never cheated on me."

"But after he died . . . why didn't you tell me then?"

Helen reached over and stroked her son's hair. "A boy should look up to his father. I didn't want him to know what Jim was like. But it backfired. He saw firsthand what his grandfather's like."

George sat up straight. "He'll come after you. If he finds out you left. And he'll look here first."

A chill rippled through her. "Oh no."

"You can't stay here. It isn't safe." He strode to the front hall and slipped his coat over his bathrobe.

"I'm sorry. I didn't mean to put you in danger."

"Nonsense." Betty pointed to Helen's shoes around her

neck. "Get your shoes on, darling. George will take care of you."

He took Jay-Jay from his wife. "Lock the door behind us and don't open it for anyone but me. Call the police if you need to."

"Of course, darling. Be careful." Betty folded Helen in a hug, damp with tears. "I'll pray for you."

"Thank you." Helen extracted herself from the painful embrace and noticed bloodstains on her dress. Her jaw tightened. She was sick of removing bloodstains.

Helen and George headed down Sixth Street. "Where can we go?" she whispered.

"The Novaks."

"Oh no. We can't wake them. It's past midnight."

"We need to take you to someone with standing in the community. Pastor Novak is on your side. He'll protect you and stand up for you. No matter where we go, we'll wake someone, and I'd rather wake someone I know."

Helen sighed in resigned agreement.

They walked at a brisk pace. Mr. Carlisle must not have come searching because her bundle remained at the corner of C and Sixth. When George picked it up, Helen held her breath, but no movement came from the direction of the Carlisle home.

George pounded on the Novaks' front door. Dizziness swept through Helen. The walk had taken the last of her strength, and she sagged against the wall.

"Coming." Pastor Novak opened the front door. "How may I—George? What's wrong?"

"It's Helen. Mr. Carlisle beat her up. She needs someplace safe to stay the night."

Pastor Novak leaned outside. His face stretched long. "Oh no. I never thought . . . why didn't I say anything?"

He looped his arm around her waist and led her in. "Edie!" he called, but Mrs. Novak was already gliding down the stairs, tightening the belt of her bathrobe. Allie and Esther peered down from the top of the stairs.

"Oh dear," Helen said. "I didn't mean to wake—"

"Allie, get the first aid kit," Mrs. Novak said. "Esther, would you please take Jay-Jay, put him down in Ray's room?"

Ray's room. Helen collapsed onto the sofa.

"I'll call the doctor," Pastor Novak said.

"No. I'll see him in the morning."

"I trust her judgment," George said.

Mrs. Novak knelt in front of Helen and took her hand. "The doctor's daughter should know."

Helen raised a grim smile. "Jim Carlisle's wife should know."

Mrs. Novak's eyes widened. "Oh no. Did he . . . ?"

"All the time, and he blamed me. But I refuse to protect him any longer." The strength and calmness of her own voice surprised her. She'd always thought confession would break her, but it freed her.

Pastor Novak sank into the wing chair and rested his forehead in his hands. "Like his dad. I should have known. I should have warned you. But you were in love, and Jim had never given me cause to worry. I had to give him the benefit of the doubt."

"I understand." His pain and guilt proved what the Carlisles denied—that their actions affected anyone but themselves.

"When you moved in with the Carlisles, I should have said something. I didn't think it was my place. I didn't think—I thought you'd be fine. He never beat his children that I could tell."

"Only his wife."

He looked up with a haggard expression. "I've confronted

him countless times over the years, but he tells me to mind my own business."

Helen's eyes drifted shut. Now she understood why the Carlisles hated the Novaks. Finally the feud had a source.

Allie returned with a first aid kit. "Let me clean that cheek. This may hurt." She dabbed at the welt with a damp cloth.

Helen winced, but it didn't hurt as much as the original blow.

Esther sat on Helen's other side. "That boy sleeps like a rock."

"It's the only way I was able to escape. I sneaked out my window and into his, then out the front door."

"Oh my goodness." Allie dabbed stinging iodine on Helen's cheek. "What will you do now?"

"I don't know." Helen's mind fuzzed over. "He controls my money. I'm not allowed to leave town because of the custody case, but I can't find a job because of the rumors. I don't have anywhere . . ." Her throat clamped shut.

"Of course you do. You can stay here as long as you like." Mrs. Novak gave her a soft-eyed smile, a smile like Ray's.

"I—I can't—"

"Nonsense. We'd love to have you. I once had a houseful of boys, and now I'll have a houseful of girls."

"Thank you," Helen said with a choked sob. "But I still have to figure something out."

"Not now." Allie fixed a bandage over the welt. "Now you need to rest."

"You can figure things out tomorrow," Esther said. "Remember, we're here for you."

Pastor and Mrs. Novak, George, and Allie nodded. The Carlisles and the Llewellyns didn't have the power to turn true friends against her. Gratitude swelled her throat shut.

"Come on, let's get you to bed," Esther said.

She and Mrs. Novak helped Helen to her feet and up the stairs. "Would you be fine sharing a bed with Jay-Jay, or should I make up a little bed for him?"

"We can share."

Mrs. Novak opened a door. "This was Ray's room. I haven't had the heart . . ."

The room still smelled like Ray, like books and grass and leather. An ache grew under the sore spot on Helen's ribs, a fresh sense of loss, not only for herself but for his family.

After Mrs. Novak left, Helen changed into her nightgown and crawled under the covers. She wrapped her arms around her son and pulled him as close as her pain allowed.

On the far wall hung a watercolor, dim in the moonlight, a pastoral landscape with a broad open sky.

Ray used to gaze at the sky with a contemplative look. She missed him so—his soft eyes, his deep words, his passionate kisses.

Helen burrowed her face into the pillow. The smells of Ray and Jay-Jay mingled in her nose and in her memory.

The two men she loved most.

43

England

The blindfold came off. Ray blinked as his eyes adjusted.

Major Siegel led him down the aisle of a small courtroom. "Although you deserve summary execution, you'll receive formal sentencing."

Ray drew a long breath. Either way he'd be dead. How much would it hurt? How long would he be conscious of pain? He wouldn't care once he was at Jesus's feet, but he wanted to get over the hump with dignity.

A dozen men sat in the audience facing the judge, a thin-faced man with a skimpy gray mustache. His nameplate read Col. Elton Maxwell.

The colonel studied a paper. "Lt. Johannes Gottlieb, the court has reviewed your testimony. Do you have any additions or amendments?"

An officer stood by the judge's side. "Oberleutnant Johannes—"

"Excuse me, sir," Ray said. "I don't need a translator."

"Very well," Colonel Maxwell said. "I repeat my question."

"First of all, sir, my name is Capt. Raymond Novak," he said, although he didn't recognize the scrawny voice. "My testimony is complete and true."

"Lieutenant Gottlieb," the colonel said in a plodding voice. "You may wish to reconsider. This court has enough evidence to convict you of espionage and of involvement in the murder of Captain Novak."

Ray's mouth twitched. No, this court would be involved in the murder of Captain Novak.

Colonel Maxwell glared. "You laugh at this court?"

"No, sir. I apologize for smiling, but I'm a man at peace. 'The body they may kill. God's truth abideth still.'"

The judge's gaze hopped to the audience then back to Ray. "'A Mighty Fortress.' Good German hymn."

Everything condemned him. "Yes, sir. Written by Martin Luther."

"Do you have anything to say to this court?"

"No, sir."

"Very well. Have a seat while I review your paperwork." He indicated a chair to his left.

Ray perched on the chair, his hands cuffed behind him, and he closed his eyes. The hymn marched through his head. He could see Mom playing the hymn on the church piano while Dad led the congregation and Ray shared a hymnal with his brothers.

Darkness threatened his peace and bowed his head. Ray would never see them again in this world. His life was finished. It felt incomplete. So much work remained. How many of the men in this courtroom knew Jesus?

Why not make the most of his final hours? Why not preach until the bullets silenced him? With renewed purpose, he lifted his head and opened his eyes. "'God commendeth his love toward us, in that, while we were yet sinners, Christ died for . . .'"

A dozen men sat in the audience, six U.S. Army Air Force officers and six civilians. He had seen only their backs as he entered the courtroom, but now he could see their faces.

Two of them he knew.

His vision, his mind tumbled around and around. "Jack? Walt?"

"Excuse me?" the judge said.

"My brothers." Ray leaped to his feet and stumbled from disorientation. "Jack! Walt!"

"Guards, restrain the prisoner."

Two MPs grabbed his arms, but Ray laughed, his head spinning into dizziness. It was a lineup, nothing but a lineup. His brothers stared at him, jaws dangling.

"You recognize me? I know I've changed, I'm skinny, my voice, but you see, don't you?"

"Which men are you referring to?" the judge asked.

His life whirled back into existence, and Ray struggled to focus. "Second man from the right—no, left—second row. That's Jack Novak. Third man from the left is Walt. They're my brothers. My brothers."

Walt's face jerked into a smile, and he moved to stand up.

Jack swung an arm in front of Walt to stop him. He frowned at Ray. "It can't be."

"It is. It's me, Jack." Ray fixed his gaze on his younger brother as if his life depended on it, which it did.

"Remember the instructions," the judge said. "Questions only your brother would know."

Jack nodded, his expression softer. "Tell me what's on the piano top at home."

Ray laughed. Stupid tears dribbled down his cheeks, and he couldn't stop them. It was over. The ordeal was over. He was going to live. "Three photographs—all three of our ugly mugs in uniform. Mom's doilies. And the ink spot."

"Tell me about the ink spot." Jack blinked too many times.

Ray grinned, the first time in months, and it hurt. "I did it."

Walt laughed, wiping his eyes. "Are you crazy? I did it."

"Stop it. Stop lying, both of you," Jack said with a deep laugh. "You know it was me."

Major Siegel rose from his seat. "Let the court recognize the prisoner did not know the correct answer."

Jack stood. "With all respect, Major, let the court recognize we've had this argument for over twenty years. That's my brother. My brother. Would you get those blasted handcuffs off him?"

The judge nodded, and the guards freed Ray.

He lurched to his brothers, now standing in the aisle, and they locked in a mass hug, all laughing, all trying not to cry, all failing.

"You lunkhead." Jack whapped Ray on the back of the head. "What do you mean getting shot down, letting us think you were dead?"

Ray whapped him back. "Who's the lunkhead? Why didn't you visit me in the hospital? They were about to execute me."

Jack and Walt eased back and frowned. "Sorry," Jack said. "We read your statement. It didn't sound like you. I can't believe you did that stuff."

"Neither can I."

"Wow." Walt's jaw dropped. "So that manual is real?"

"It got me here."

"You flew a jet. From the manual."

"And a training film."

Jack and Walt stared at Ray, and then Jack erupted in a laugh. "Walt beat me to the altar, and you beat me in the adventure department. What's this family coming to?"

"Excuse me, gentlemen." The judge tapped Ray on the shoulder. "Captain Novak, a dozen intelligence goons want to interrogate you. I told them you boys need time together first. Would you like to sit in my chambers? I'll have food brought in."

"Food." The word thumped into the hollow pit of Ray's stomach. "Yes, please."

The judge's face twisted. "Sorry to put you through that, young man. Intelligence runs this show."

"I understand." Ray scanned the courtroom for Major Siegel, but he was no longer present. Not the type to apologize.

The judge led them into his office. "I'll stand guard and I won't let in a soul unless he bears food."

"Thank you, sir." Ray flopped into a wooden chair in front of the desk, exhausted. He was going to live. He was going home. He was going to eat. "How are Mom and Dad? Grandma and Grandpa?"

Walt sat on the metal desk, his face serious. "They're . . . they're grieving. They're strong, you know, but it's tough on them, on all of us. We thought you were dead, for heaven's sake."

"When they get this news, they'll be as good as new." Jack leaned back against the wall, ankles crossed.

Heaviness drifted down in Ray's chest. Grief aged people irreversibly.

"The baby's helped a bit." Walt flipped open his wallet and pulled out a snapshot. "It's a boy. Francis Raymond—Frankie. Frank for my friend who died, Raymond for—for you. But you're not dead. Wow."

Ray gazed at the little black-and-white face. His nephew. "Have you seen him?"

"No." Walt's voice deepened. "He's two months old now. Smiling, Allie says."

"You'll go home soon. We all will," Jack said. "War's almost over in Germany. Any day now. We flew our last strategic mission April 16, our last tactical mission April 25. No targets left."

Walt's feet tapped against the desk. "Say, that jet's legitimate. We'll ship her over to Wright-Patterson Army Air Base in Ohio, study her."

"What a swell plane." Jack turned to Ray, a hundred questions in his eyes.

Before discussing planes, Ray had one more inquiry. "How's Helen?"

"Helen? She took it hard, Allie said." Walt paused, a blank look on his face. "Uh-oh."

"Oh boy." Jack groaned.

Ray sat forward. "What is it? What's the matter with Helen?"

Walt's face scrunched up. "Nothing's the matter. It's . . . well, she's getting married."

"Married?" Ray whispered.

"No, got married. It was Mom's birthday, April 28. Two days ago."

"Victor Llewellyn," Jack said.

Married? Two days ago? To Vic? Ray felt his blood draining away, as if he'd been riddled with bullets by the firing squad after all.

For months a tiny dream had hovered on hummingbird wings, a dream that Ray would return and make Helen his wife.

The wings stilled. It was never meant to be.

44

Antioch
Friday, May 4, 1945

Helen stood by the newspaper rack at the corner of Third and G, where the *Ledger*'s headlines read "250,000 Nazis Give Up in North Reich" and "Two German Armies Only Troops Left to Oppose Allied Arms."

Mrs. Kramer passed and stared at the bandage on Helen's cheek. She gave her a shocked look and a flustered "Good morning," and ducked inside Della's Dress Shop.

Just what Helen had waited for. She steadied herself on the newspaper rack. She'd talked this over with the Novaks and the Anellos and had prayed about it. Now she had to do it. "Lord, give me courage."

With her chin high, she entered the store. The bells on the door jangled.

Mrs. Carlisle smiled. "Good morn—Helen! Oh my." She scurried to the back curtain. "James, Helen is here."

Mr. Carlisle barged out with an expression of restrained alarm. "How good to see you. Come to the back. I have something to show you."

"No, thank you." She gave him a sweet smile. "I'll stand by the window where I can be seen." Pastor Novak had offered to come along for protection, but Helen declined. She needed to stand up for herself.

He came to her with a fake smile. "Where have you been? I've looked all over for you. I've been worried about you."

Although she faced the dragon, she refused to be the damsel in distress. "Why? Afraid I was seriously hurt when you beat me up?"

"Keep your voice down." He grabbed her arm.

His touch seared. "Let go," she said in a low voice with a pointed look toward Mrs. Kramer, who flipped through the rack of summer blouses.

He let go, but his fingers remained hooked like claws. "Don't say such things in public."

"Yes, let's keep the family shame hidden—but only for Jay-Jay's sake. That's why you'll drop the custody case today."

His hands folded into fists.

Helen stepped back and glared at those fists. "Dr. Dozier examined me, and Officer Mandeville took a police report. I can charge you with assault."

"What?" he said in a harsh whisper. "You have no right."

"I have every right."

"No one can dictate what I do in my family."

"Legally I'm not family. I can charge you, but I won't if you drop the custody case."

His face grew as red as the welt on Helen's cheek. "You think you can blackmail me?"

"It's not blackmail. I'm protecting your family's reputation. If the custody case goes to court, I'll be sworn to tell the truth, and I will. I'll testify how you beat your wife, how Jim beat me and you beat me, and how Jay-Jay would learn cruelty if he grew up in your house."

A sneer. "Your word against mine. Who will believe crazy cripple Helen?"

She pulled herself tall and straight. "You've forgotten. There's another witness, someone who grew up in your home and knows what happens there."

Mr. Carlisle's face went as white as Helen's many scars. "She wouldn't."

"Dorothy's already agreed. She doesn't want Jay-Jay to turn out like you and Jim."

He stared at her, chest heaving as if he could smite her with fire.

But she'd doused his flames, and she had one more bucketful of truth to throw at him. "Even if you won, even if you were awarded custody, your behavior would be exposed. That would be bad for business, especially a business that caters to women." Helen inclined her head toward Mrs. Kramer. "Drop the case today."

"Fine," he spat out. "But when they lock you in the loony bin, I'll get my grandson."

The way she saw it, she had escaped the loony bin. "Since I no longer live with you, Jay-Jay and I will need our monthly living expenses, as you promised your son. I'll take two months' worth today."

"Two?"

Helen held out one gloved hand. "For the medical and legal expenses you inflicted on me. Two months. Now."

He stomped behind the cash register. "I don't have that much."

"Yes, you do. You always do."

His gaze scorched her from across the store. "Come and get it."

"No, thank you. I prefer it over here by the window. Such lovely warm sunshine we've had lately. Don't you agree, Mrs. Kramer?"

"Yes, lovely." She glanced between Helen and Mr. Carlisle.

Even if she hadn't heard a word, tension crackled in the store. "A beautiful summer collection. I'll be back."

She headed for the door, but Helen stepped in her way. "It's so nice to see you. How's Evelyn? She's a senior this year, isn't she? Such a sweet girl."

Mrs. Kramer beamed. "Thank you. She can be a silly thing, but aren't all girls like that?"

"Yes, they are." Helen beckoned with her fingers for the money. "Does she enjoy her job at El Campanil?"

"A little too much. Don't you know Larry Parker works in the ticket office, and she can't keep her eyes off him."

A wad of bills landed in Helen's hand, and she curled her fingers around it. "Make sure Evelyn gets to know him well before she gives him her heart. One needs to be very careful whom one marries." She smiled at her former father-in-law. "Good day to you, Mr. Carlisle. And to you, Mrs. Kramer."

Helen stepped outside, and her breath turned heavy and ragged. She stopped on the corner of Fourth and G to steady herself. She'd done it. She'd stood up to him and met her goal.

She stuffed the money in her handbag and counted it inside—twenty dollars less than she asked for, but a hundred dollars more than expected.

Enough to get her and Jay-Jay to Washington DC. She'd wait until Monday to be certain the case was dropped and to have a few more days to heal.

Helen continued on her way. She'd never see another penny from Jim's life insurance, and she'd have to beg her parents for help, but Washington had plenty of jobs. The NAACP had found an apartment for Esther, which she'd offered to share with Helen and Jay-Jay.

Nursery care remained a concern, but Helen had called her parents the day before, and Mama thought one of the ladies from her church might help.

With long-distance calls restricted to five minutes, Helen hadn't told them why she was coming, but as soon as she arrived in DC, she'd swallow her pride and tell them everything.

Helen glanced behind her, down G Street to the river. Pain tightened around her middle. She loved the river and the grassy hills and rugged Mount Diablo. She loved the buildings and the people and the tomato soup smell during canning season. She loved the bittersweet reminders of her childhood, her marriage, and her romance with Ray.

In a few days, she'd leave it all behind.

<hr />

Over the Arctic Ocean
Sunday, May 6, 1945

Jack leaned forward in the bucket seat in the cabin of the C-54 cargo plane. "Okay, boys, let's get the plan straight."

Ray smiled. "Only you could turn a homecoming into a combat mission."

"Dead right." Jack held up one finger. "Tuesday morning, Allie meets us at the bus stop with the baby. She's the only one who knows, and she thinks Walt's the only one coming."

Walt snuggled lower in his heavy flight jacket. "I wonder if she figured out my telegram: 'ACCOMPANYING RARE EXOTIC BIRD HOME.' She has to know it's a jet. Wait till she hears how we got it."

Ray pulled the blanket tighter around him. The cabin temperature hovered below freezing, and he didn't have extra body weight for insulation, despite having gained another seven pounds the past week. At least the intelligence officers fed him well while they grilled him.

"Allie won't blab because she'll want time to neck with Walt. Only the Lord knows why." Jack held up a second finger. "Walt and Allie go in the house first. Five minutes later, Ruth and I surprise them. Five minutes to meet Ruth, five to catch up, five to lay the groundwork for Lazarus. Ray waits on the porch until we open the door. Open it wide so Mom's river of tears will have somewhere to flow. Sound good, boys?"

"Great," Ray said. "Let's synchronize our watches."

Ruth Doherty came from the back of the plane with an armful of Thermoses. "Coffee for Jack and Walt, and broth for my patient, the only reason they let me work this route."

"Thanks." Ray never thought he'd want to taste broth again, but today he craved the combination of warmth and nutrition.

Ruth set hands on hips well padded by a flight suit. "Your plan sounds like *The Three Stooges Come Home*. You'll mess this up like you messed things up for Ray. Didn't I tell you I saw a man who looked like him at the airfield in Melun? Then intelligence said they had a man claiming to be Ray, and you didn't put it together. Keep your plans on the air base, flyboy."

Jack's grin flipped up the corners of his mustache. "What about my plans to marry you?"

She smiled and shook her head at him. "You should have sent your parents a telegram."

He reached for her with one hand and patted his lap with the other. "What would the telegram say? 'RAY ALIVE STOP REALLY HE IS STOP SERIOUSLY STOP LONG STORY STOP.' They wouldn't know what to think, and we'll get home faster than a letter would."

Ruth ignored her fiancé's lap invitation. "You'll give your parents coronaries."

"That's why we're bringing a nurse."

She looked down at Ray. "You're fine with this?"

"My idea. They won't believe it until they see it." Ray had another reason for not cabling—to allow Helen more time to settle in as a bride. The deeper into the honeymoon, the less she'd regret her marriage if she harbored any romantic feelings for him. He doubted that, considering how fast she'd fallen for Vic. He wrestled back his resentment. Vic would be a good husband and stepfather, and Ray needed to wish them well.

Too bad they wouldn't be away on a wedding trip, but Vic belonged to the Navy. Hitler was dead and German soldiers surrendered in droves, but the war in the Pacific trudged along. The way things were going on Okinawa, the Japanese wouldn't surrender easily, if ever.

His brothers laughed.

Ray blinked and brought his eyes back into focus.

"Finally get to see what makes that Messerschmitt tick," Walt said. "Can't wait to get to Ohio with my wife and son, and my personal jet expert." He gave Ray a wink and a nudge.

Ray flicked a smile at him. Ohio lay a blessed far distance from home and from Helen.

"While you boys play with your little toy plane, I'll be at the controls of a B-29 Superfortress," Jack said. "Can you imagine 8800 horsepower?"

"Then off to the Pacific." Ruth frowned and wrote on a clipboard.

"Marry me now, and I'll get you stationed near me."

"You pulled enough strings getting all three of you on this flight, getting me assigned to the same flight, and then ten-day furloughs. Pull any more strings and you'll unravel the entire fabric of the Army Air Force." Ruth sent Jack a sidelong glance and headed down the aisle. "I need to take vitals."

Walt backhanded Jack's arm. "You should have pulled those strings a few days earlier. I could have been home for my anniversary."

Walt and Allie had married a year ago today. The day that propelled Ray into this adventure.

"I'm going to walk, try to warm up." Ray stood and rearranged his blanket. If he'd known what the year would hold, he wouldn't have made the same decision. And that would have been a mistake. Sure, he might have held on to the woman he loved, but as half a man, never knowing what he was capable of with God at his side.

The C-54's four engines rumbled through his booted feet as he walked down the aisle past patients in seats, then men on litters stacked like four-tiered bunk beds.

At the rear of the plane, he leaned against the fuselage wall and gazed out the window. Jagged black peaks knifed through creamy glaciers. Greenland. Still so far from home.

Ray had begun to dread going home. He looked more like himself with a good haircut and an American uniform, and he sounded more like himself. But who was he now?

He'd done things he never thought he would. Everyone at home would expect the same old Ray. Even his brothers, who knew the life-altering effects of war, didn't completely understand.

"Hi there. How are you doing?" Ruth hugged the clipboard to her chest.

"Think I'm strong enough for this big emotional scene?"

"You are, but am I?"

"You're not worried about meeting my folks, are you?"

She shrugged. "I shouldn't be, but still—Chicago slum girl meets small-town pastor, wholesome wife, and society girl daughter-in-law."

"They'll love you. And Allie—she's probably worried about meeting Jack's gorgeous fiancée. She has a good heart. You'll get along great."

"I hope so." She tilted her head and studied Ray. "How about you? You're quieter than usual. Being alive again isn't all it's cracked up to be, is it?"

Ray turned, and his sigh fogged the window. "No, it isn't."

45

Antioch
Tuesday, May 8, 1945

Jay-Jay jumped up and down on the church lawn. "Victee!"

Helen smiled and led him by the hand up the church steps. Despite Jay-Jay's enthusiasm, Antioch's Victory in Europe Day would be subdued. The schools and most businesses remained open for V-E Day, and only the taverns had closed to prevent carousing.

Since the Japanese seemed determined to fight to the last man, celebration felt premature. Regardless, today Americans would thank the Lord for peace in Europe.

Mrs. Novak stood in the foyer, straightening piles of fliers. "Hello, you two."

Jay-Jay hugged Mrs. Novak's legs. "Hi, Gamma Nobak."

She leaned down to hug him. "I like it when you call me that. You look so handsome in your suit."

"Fank you." He galloped back to Helen and grabbed her hand in both of his. He'd clung to her since the beating, and he hadn't asked to see his Carlisle grandparents once.

"You're early for the service," Mrs. Novak said.

"On purpose. I don't want to draw attention."

She patted Helen's arm. "Things are quieting down now that the case has been dropped."

"I know." But she couldn't wait to leave. Traveling yesterday when Germany surrendered or on V-E Day would have been foolish, so she planned to leave tomorrow.

In the sanctuary, sunlight streamed over dark woods and creamy walls, and lemon oil scented the air. On the wall over the pulpit, a banner declared "Victory," but at the front of the sanctuary, over two dozen stands held portraits of men in uniform, each draped in black.

Antioch's fallen.

Her heart spilled molten lead down to her toes, but Helen dragged her feet down the aisle. The dead were arranged alphabetically. James Carlisle Jr.'s portrait stood near the left, and Helen studied his face, handsome and charming and cruel.

"Dat's Daddy."

"Yes, sweetie." Helen squeezed the hand of the best part of Jim Carlisle. For the marriage, she bore no shame. For his death, she bore no guilt.

Gazing into his smiling, cold eyes, she felt neither love nor hate. "Good-bye, Jim."

She walked past portraits, including those of former schoolmates, and stopped in front of Ray's. Now she felt love, heart-crumpling love.

"I seen him," Jay-Jay said.

"Oh?" He couldn't possibly remember Ray from the year before.

"Gamma Nobak's."

The portrait on the piano. "That's Ray Novak, their oldest son. He was a kind and good man, and he liked you very much."

Jay-Jay turned a smile up to her. "He did?"

"Yes. He called you munchkin."

He giggled. "Dat's silly."

"Yes, he could be silly and thoughtful and—and he was a very good man."

"Why's he wearing a scarf?" Jay-Jay touched the black draping.

"It means . . . it means he went to be with Jesus."

Footsteps sounded behind her. Helen looked back to see Esther.

Her friend tucked her arm in Helen's and looked around at the portraits. "Such a terrible cost, this victory."

Ray's image swam into a blur. "Terrible indeed."

★

The Greyhound bus rumbled to the corner of Second and G, an intersection Ray thought he'd never see again.

"There she is!" Walt jumped from his seat.

On the sidewalk, Allie held a baby wrapped in a blue blanket. She bounced on her toes, grinning and waving.

"That's my wife, my son! I'm a father." Walt charged down the aisle of the bus. As soon as the doors whooshed open, he dashed out, threw his arms around his wife, and kissed her hard enough to knock her hat loose.

Ray stood and slipped on his waist-length "Ike" jacket, buckled the waist, and fastened the concealed buttons.

Walt broke off the kiss to hunch over the baby. His hand hovered beside Frankie's head, as if his son were a delicate piece of machinery. He gazed at Allie with a look of wonder and kissed her again.

Ray headed down the aisle after Jack and Ruth. He'd never know that thrill, but at least he'd have nephews and nieces to enjoy. The way Walt was kissing Allie, he'd have lots of them.

Jack helped Ruth off the bus, but Ray lagged behind.

Allie exclaimed in surprise and hugged Jack, then exchanged shy smiles with Ruth. When Allie showed Ruth the baby's face, the ladies' smiles warmed.

"Excuse me, sir?"

Ray startled and looked behind him to the petite brunette at the wheel. He still wasn't used to female bus drivers.

"You getting off?" she asked.

He wanted to say, "No. Take me to Ohio—now." Instead, he said, "Yeah, it's my stop."

Ray stepped off the bus but didn't approach the laughing, living group. For almost four months he'd been dead, separated from humanity, and now he wondered whether he belonged.

Walt turned to him. "Say, Allie, look who we found."

Allie gave him the unblinking, fixed smile of someone who knows she should recognize a person, but doesn't. Then her eyes rounded, and she glanced at Walt. "It can't be."

"That's what everyone says." Ray gave her a smile. "But it's me."

"Ray? Oh my goodness. We thought . . . how on earth?"

"Can we wait until we get home? It's a long story, and I only want to tell it once."

Jack laughed. "Fat chance."

Ray held out his arms to Allie. "Not much left of me, but I still want a hug."

Her eyes shimmered, and she hugged him with her free arm. "Oh goodness. How on earth . . . ? Your parents—they'll be so happy. So happy. This day just gets better and better."

Ray pulled back and admired his nephew, and Frankie flashed Ray a quick, gummy smile.

"Look, he's happy his uncle's alive. Everyone will be thrilled." Allie wiped away tears, and her smile broadened and softened. "And Helen—how happy she'll be."

Why would she connect him to Helen? "It'll be good to see her, to see everyone." The words tasted like dry oats in his mouth.

Jack wrinkled his nose. "The newlyweds off on a wedding trip, I hope?"

Allie blinked. "Newlyweds?"

"Vic and Helen."

"Oh, that's right. You couldn't have received my letter yet. You don't know."

Ray's heart went into a holding pattern. "They got married on the twenty-eighth, right?"

"A lot has happened the past few weeks." Allie's smile rose as slowly as the sun. "No, they didn't get married. Let's just say something came up."

With a swift wind, the clouds swooshed out of Ray's life. The wedding was postponed. He had time to tell Helen he loved her, to have a chance with her. "Where is she? Where is she right now? Do you know?"

"At the church, of course." Allie held Frankie up to her shoulder and patted his back. "You're just in time. Thank goodness. Another day and it would have been too late."

"The church? Too late?" Why would it be too late? Her wedding? Had she postponed it to . . . today? What day of the week was it? Monday? Tuesday? Odd choice for a wedding, but maybe they'd grabbed the first available date. "What time's the ceremony start?"

"Eleven. Why?"

Ray glanced at his watch. Already eleven, and weddings only took about fifteen minutes. He had to act fast. No thinking, no planning.

A cab sat at the curb, waiting for the lot of them to stop chatting, load the luggage, and settle the baby in.

Ray didn't have time. This was the scramble for the jet all

over again. "I'm going to the church. Take your time, get the luggage. See you later."

He took off running with his head down. He didn't have time to be recognized and rejoiced over.

The postponed wedding was a gift, a sign that God wanted him to act. Not necessarily that Helen would ever love him, but that Ray had to declare his love.

Amazed at his strength and stamina, he turned onto Fifth Street, down two blocks, across the church lawn, up the steps, and into the foyer.

All his life he'd been a man of words, but now he knew he could also be a man of action. Ray flung open the sanctuary doors and charged down the aisle. "Stop the wedding! Stop the wedding!"

Two hundred heads swiveled to him. Dad glared from the pulpit. Mom peeked around the piano.

Emotion surged up, grabbed him around the middle, and he ground to a halt halfway down the aisle. He hadn't seen them for a year. And he was about to turn their grief to joy.

But before the reunion, he had a wedding to interrupt. "Stop the . . ."

Something was wrong. Where was the bride? The groom?

A banner spread across the wall behind Dad. What kind of man was arrogant enough to display his name at his wedding?

No. It read "Victory," not "Victor."

This wasn't a wedding.

It was a service for V-E Day.

Ray's engines sputtered. His plan stalled. And he drifted alone in a sky of familiar faces.

"Excuse me, sir," Dad said. "May I help you?" He didn't recognize his own son, not that Ray blamed him.

Ray pulled off his cap and raised a sheepish smile. "As

Mark Twain said, 'The reports of my death are greatly exaggerated.'"

Dad stared at him, his eyes searching, doubting, questioning, believing. A murmur rose in the congregation, whispers, gasps, his name repeated, building to a crescendo of crying, laughing, and shouting. People stood, leaned, strained to see, heads bobbing to get a better view.

Of the dead man back from the grave.

Of the father lurching to him.

Of the mother crying out and stumbling down the aisle.

Ray's chest sank under the full weight of his parents' grief, only imagined beforehand, now visible, etched on their faces.

He met them halfway and almost fell from the impact. Mom grasped his shoulders, his face, exploring like a blind woman. "Ray? Ray? You're alive? My baby boy."

He winced from the pain in his jaw and pulled his mother into a hug. "I'm back, Mom. I'm alive. Sorry you had to go through that."

Dad's arm clasped Ray's shoulders. "My boy's alive," he said with a throaty laugh. "My boy. Praise God! Praise the Lord!"

Grandpa and Grandma Novak approached with faltering steps and tear-stained faces, and Ray hugged them with his left arm, because Mom wouldn't leave the space under his right arm. She burrowed into his chest, shook with tears, and clutched his uniform.

"Excuse me? May I have your attention?" Mr. Wayne rapped on the pulpit with his fist.

The church hushed except for random muffled sobs. Ray took advantage of the shift in attention to search for Helen, but he didn't see her.

"Pastor Novak," Mr. Wayne said. "I assume you're in no shape to continue this service."

Dad gave a big, damp laugh. "Absolutely not."

"As chairman of the elders, I have a request for Ray Novak. You must have quite a story, young man, and I can think of no better way to celebrate V-E Day than to hear it." He beckoned Ray to the pulpit.

Ray hung back, but the crowd urged, and the idea of telling his story only once appealed to him. He ducked to his mother. "I need to go. Dad, I may need some help."

With a little coaxing, Mom dislodged from Ray and locked onto Dad. Ray headed up front, where Mr. Wayne greeted him with a handshake.

Ray faced the pulpit and ran his hands over the varnished wood, along the dark, furrowed curves of the grain. The Lord had stripped everything from him, but now he had given it back—identity, family, and ministry.

He folded his hands around the rim of the pulpit and gazed upward. *Lord, thank you for restoring my life. Let me use this experience to serve you better.*

He gazed at the congregation.

Helen sat in the third row on the right, gloved hands over her mouth, her eyes enormous.

Pain wrenched through him—deep, visceral pain over what he'd lost.

Who was he kidding? He'd lost her a year before, and she loved another man. She had to know what he meant when he screamed about stopping a wedding. Could he have made a bigger fool of himself?

The sooner he got to Ohio the better.

Ray huffed off the pain. He had a story to tell, not about him but about the Lord. "Ladies and gentlemen, this past year has brought great change, and not just in my body weight."

The laughter encouraged him and poked up a smile. "I've done things I never thought I'd do and realized things about myself I'd never thought possible. Through this, I've learned much about God's love and strength. He's changed me."

For a split second, he met Helen's gaze. The Lord had changed her too. She'd grown and healed in ways he loved on paper but had never witnessed in person. And what had happened the past four months? How much more had she grown through Vic's love?

Could he honestly say he knew this woman? That he loved her?

Ray threw himself into his story, editing in mind of the small children present. He shook his thoughts off what he'd lost with Helen to what he'd gained with Christ.

46

Paralysis was the most unnerving sensation.

For months, Helen had lain in the county polio ward. No matter how hard she'd concentrated, her legs wouldn't do what she asked from them, demanded from them, pleaded from them.

Now she sat paralyzed in the pew, her hands plastered over her mouth, and her eyes strained to dryness, afraid if she blinked he'd be gone again, dead again.

Yet he stood there and told his story, his raspy voice a soothing ointment. When he smiled, the same bittersweet pain thumped behind her breastbone as when she watched Jay-Jay sleep.

Ray's story proved him a hero of the conventional sort with bold action in great danger. But he was also—had always been—a hero of a deeper sort, a better sort, who stood up for good and right no matter what.

Even though he was skinny, she couldn't imagine a more attractive man.

But he rarely looked at her. Their romance had ended in flames, and a deep friendship had risen from the ashes, but so much had happened since. Had he heard about her engagement, how it ended, the custody case, and the rumors of insanity? If he hadn't, he would soon.

If only she could move her muscles. If only she could take Jay-Jay and slink out of church. She needed time in private to pull herself together. Ray was alive. Now what? Would he want to renew their friendship? But she loved him, and he'd see it. Her love lay on the surface where no performance could hide it.

When Ray finished his story, he stepped down from the pulpit into a swarm of family and friends.

Betty gripped Helen's arm, which disengaged her hand from her mouth. "Aren't you thrilled?"

Helen's lips felt numb from the pressure. "I—I'm happy for his family."

"For his family? What about you?"

"Me? It's too late," she whispered.

In the center aisle, Ray hugged Mrs. Anello, but his gaze swept the congregation and locked on Helen.

"See?" Betty said. "Didn't you hear him say, 'Stop the wedding'?"

Helen turned to her sister. She had a vague memory of an officer yelling about a wedding, but when she realized it was Ray, all that washed away. "That . . . that has nothing to do with me."

"Baloney. Who else had a wedding planned? He wanted to stop you from marrying Vic. Just like in the movies. Isn't that romantic?"

"Couldn't be. It must have been a joke." Ray wasn't the type to barge in on a wedding . . . but he also wasn't the type to play practical jokes. Of course, she didn't think he was the type to steal an airplane either. Who was this man?

"Well, he's coming this way. You can ask him yourself."

He crossed to the side aisle, his gaze locked on her.

Not now. She had to get away and compose herself, pray

about this, and figure out what to do. Helen stood and grabbed Jay-Jay's hand, but Betty blocked her escape.

"Ray! Over here." Betty waved him over and drew him into a hug. "Goodness, your mom needs to fatten you up."

"I'll say." He turned to Helen, one arm slightly extended in a subtle invitation for a hug, but he didn't step forward.

Neither did Helen. She was a porcelain vase, rapped and cracked. One touch from Ray and she'd shatter.

His soft smile threatened to shatter her as well. "Hi, Helen."

"I can't . . . I can't . . ."

"I can't believe it either," he said with a quick shrug. "So, I hear congratulations are in order."

"Congratulations?" She searched his face, but his polite smile revealed nothing.

"You and Vic? When's the date?"

Her eyes opened and closed, over and over, as she tried to comprehend. He thought she was still marrying Vic. Was Betty right? Was that why he barged in? To stop her wedding?

"You didn't hear," Betty said. "She broke up with Vic, thank goodness. You wouldn't believe what he did."

Helen snapped her gaze to her sister. "We mustn't gossip."

Betty slung her purse over her shoulder. "She never loved him anyway. She only agreed to marry him to get out of the Carlisle house, and who can blame her after what Mr. Carlisle did?"

"Betty, please. No gossip."

"It's not gossip. It's the truth."

"Oh, Helen." Ray stared at her cheek, his voice low and husky. "Did he do that?"

Her hand flew to her cheek, but she lowered it. No more performances. "That's why I moved out. I'm leaving for Washington DC tomorrow. I would have gone today but . . ."

One corner of his mouth crept up. "So that's what Allie meant by 'just in time.'"

"Excuse me?" Helen said.

Jay-Jay tugged Ray's trouser leg, and Ray squatted. "Hello, munchkin. You've sure grown up."

Jay-Jay gasped. "You're right, Mama."

"Your mama's always right and don't ever forget it," Ray said. "I brought you something from Germany. I'll give it to you later."

Helen's mouth flopped open. "You brought souvenirs?"

Ray's laugh scrambled up her insides. "That's the only one. Well, and the plane, the manual, the Luftwaffe uniform. Though I want to get the uniform back to Johannes's family somehow."

Jay-Jay balanced on one leg like a flamingo. "Why din't Jesus want you?"

Ray shot Helen a quizzical look.

"I told him you—you went to be with Jesus." Her voice cracked.

He gave her the longest look, full of knee-buckling compassion, and then lowered his gaze to Jay-Jay. "Sorry, munchkin. I didn't get to see Jesus. He still has plans for me here on earth."

He looked up to Helen. His eyes shone with hope, but questions tugged at the edges.

Helen couldn't breathe, and she grabbed the pew back for support. Goodness, he still cared for her.

Mrs. Novak came down the aisle in a flurry. "Ray, how could you boys—all three of you home, and Ruth too, and not one telegram to warn us."

Ray stood and put his arm around his mother's waist. "And miss seeing the look on your face?"

She swatted him on the stomach. "You rascal. Good thing I already had a reception planned at the house after the service. We have so much more than victory to celebrate."

The reception? Just what she needed. Work—not to cure her or make her worthy, but to help her sort out her emotions. "Mrs. Novak, if you'd like, I could set things up."

"Would you? You're such a dear."

Helen took Jay-Jay's hand and headed up the aisle.

"Helen," Ray called. "I need to talk to you."

She waved and smiled. "I'll see you at the reception."

Betty asked her to wait up, but Helen forged ahead at a speed her heavily pregnant sister couldn't maintain. Betty would ask blunt questions Helen couldn't handle, not with Ray's dreamy look fogging her mind.

Yes, dreamy. The look of a man who didn't want to renew their friendship, but their romance. Thinking of his kindness woven through with a new thread of boldness, thinking of the man she loved returning her love—it wreaked havoc with her heart.

47

Grandpa Novak shifted on the couch in the living room. "So, boy, tell us again how you blew up that tanker."

The retired gentlemen gathered around Ray nodded in agreement.

Ray launched into his story. So much for only having to tell it once.

The house throbbed with activity. In the parlor, Walt and Jack took turns pounding out tunes on the piano while children danced. Sometimes Jay-Jay's squeal rose above the crowd. He probably didn't say *daff* anymore.

Helen burst out of the kitchen with a tray, exchanged it with one on the dining room table, and returned to the kitchen with a cute bump of her hip to the door.

She was avoiding him. Either he'd made his love too obvious and she didn't welcome it, or she was using work to deal with her feelings. Ray had to find out which and soon. He wouldn't let her leave town tomorrow unless he was certain she had no interest in him.

Something in her eyes when they talked in church said some interest remained.

He finished his story with a ka-boom, and the men grinned

and laughed and slapped knees. Any one of them would have enjoyed his adventures more than he had.

Ray scooted forward in the armchair. "Excuse me, gentlemen. I need more coffee."

Allie passed by with a stack of plates. "I'll bring you a fresh cup."

That's how it had been for the past hour and a half. Everyone brought him food and drink and trapped him in storytelling.

No more. Ray stood. "Need to stretch my legs."

He entered the kitchen and groaned. Helen and four other women bustled about. How could he get her alone?

Helen gasped. "Oh dear. Did we run out of something?"

"No. I thought I'd—I'd like some milk." He pulled a glass from the cupboard and opened the icebox. How could he get the other women to leave?

"You should rest. Go sit down. I'll bring you some." She reached for the bottle.

Ray poured milk into the glass. "I'm a big boy. I can do it myself."

She leaned her hip against the counter and smiled. "You can't avoid the party in here forever."

He took a sip and raised his eyebrows at her. "Neither can you."

Her lips parted, and she squinted at him. "Ruth dear, why don't you escort your patient back to his seat of honor?"

Ruth took him by the elbow and guided him out of the kitchen. "That's her polite way of saying you're in her way. She's a busy one, isn't she?"

"Oh yeah." Busy avoiding him, but he grinned. Something remained between them, and he planned to stir it to life.

Ruth led him to the armchair. "Sit and rest. Nurse's orders."

"Yes, ma'am." Ray sat, gulped down the milk, and got up again. "That was good. I'll get some more."

"No, you don't. I'll get it."

"Wait. It's your first day here. Shouldn't you be with Jack, meeting his friends? Send Helen out with it."

She studied him with a little smile. "I thought Jack was the manipulative one in this family."

"He is. I'm the nice one."

"Oh brother. You're all hopeless. I'll send her out."

Ray settled into the armchair and listened partway to the men's discussion of last week's prison riot on Alcatraz that required Marine intervention. As if the Marines didn't already have a war to fight.

Helen emerged from the kitchen with a bottle of milk. She stood in front of Ray's chair, eyebrows arched. "You rang?"

"Yes, ma'am. May I please have some more?" He held his glass low, so she'd have to come closer.

"Thirsty, aren't you?" She leaned over to pour, and blonde curls spilled over her shoulder.

"Mm-hmm." He wanted to weave his fingers into her hair and pull her down to his lap for a long kiss. "Martha, Martha."

She paused and looked at him with those delicious eyes. "Martha?"

He didn't want milk anymore. He wanted tea and lots of it. "Sit and talk with your brother Lazarus."

Helen straightened up and tilted him a smile. "No, thank you. Remember what Martha said after Jesus raised her brother? Lazarus stank." She waved her hand in front of her pretty little nose and whirled away.

All the men laughed and joshed Ray and slapped his scrawny shoulders.

Ray smiled like a fool, but he didn't care. Something remained, all right, and he intended to claim it. He stood and set his milk, untouched, on the coffee table. "Excuse me, men, but I have an important mission."

★

Helen's hands trembled as she set a handful of strawberries on the cutting board. The banter with Ray rattled and drained her.

Her chest heaved, and she muffled a sob, mindful of the other ladies in the kitchen.

It was too much to handle, too much for one day—Ray alive and home and interested in her. The mutual attraction hummed with life, and she could practically taste his kisses. But if he touched her, she'd turn into a blubbering idiot.

What next? She didn't want to leave town now, but Ray would reclaim his room, and where would she live? And if she stayed, wouldn't everyone think she was pining over Ray? What if he wasn't interested in her romantically? What if she'd misinterpreted everything?

But no. He wanted to stop her from marrying Vic. The way he looked at her, the way he teased her, the way he sent for her—it was too wonderful.

Helen lifted the knife over the strawberries, but it shook in a silver blur, and she set it down. She was in no state to use a knife.

The kitchen door swung open. Oh goodness, Ray again.

"Excuse me, ladies." He strode through the kitchen, pushed open the door to the backyard, and faced Helen. "Since you won't sit and talk, we'll go outside. In the fresh air you won't notice my odor." He dropped her a wink.

Under the force of his humor and determination, she had to clutch the counter for support.

"Go, Helen." Esther nudged her from behind.

Betty put one hand where her hip used to be. "If you don't go, we'll drag you out there."

"No need for violence." Helen fumbled with her apron, untied it, and set it aside. She headed for the door as if this would be a casual conversation, an everyday occurrence, but as she brushed past Ray's warmth in the doorway, she crossed another threshold—from the claustrophobia of expectations and performances to open, verdant, genuine life.

She forced breath over tingling lips as she walked with Ray across the yard, weaving among trees in full leaf, blossoms shed and replaced with embryonic green fruit.

At the back fence, Ray turned to her—tender, amused, and silent.

Helen ripped her gaze away to the trees wagging their branches over her head. "It's beautiful out here."

"Beautiful." But he didn't look at the trees or the sky, only at her.

This couldn't be happening. How could he be alive? How could he look at her like that? How could he stand so close? Close enough to touch.

"Everyone wants to talk to the dead guy. Everyone but you. But you can't avoid me forever."

"I'm not . . ."

He tipped a smile.

Her breath rushed out, not quite a laugh. "All right, I am. But it's so much, so emotional. I think—I think joy can be as nerve-wracking as grief."

"So you're happy." His gaze asked much more.

"Very much. But—but I still can't believe you're alive."

"So take time to get used to it. Don't go to Washington." His gray gaze held her with the softness of flannel and the strength of steel.

"I won't." Her voice fluttered out.

"Good." He moved closer, and something ignited in that gray, a fire she'd never thought she'd see again. He ran his fingers into her hair, behind her head, and tilted her face up. "I want you here with me. Always."

The warm touch of his living flesh coursed through her. Her knees buckled, but he embraced her, pulled her close, held her together, and pressed his lips to hers, his warm, living lips. All the old passion returned, lit by a new flame of longing fulfilled and life reborn.

Everything spun in Helen's head, all her emotions and plans, all she thought she knew about Ray and about herself. He cared for her as much as before, if not more.

New strength surged inside and braced her legs. She caressed his back, his shoulders, his face—thin but alive. And hers. He was hers.

Ray pulled back, and the steel came to the foreground of his eyes. "I love you. I love you so much, and I won't let you get away. You're going to Ohio with me. You and Jay-Jay. Walt and Allie will be there too. We'll find you a room and a job, and maybe Allie can watch Jay-Jay while you work. Until you're ready to get married."

With those words he rubbed out her dreary future, and a new future zoomed into rainbow-hued focus, brilliant in the light of his love. His love! He loved her. "All right."

"No arguing. I love you, and I won't let you get away."

"You weren't listening, darling." She stroked the contours of his face. "I said yes."

"You said yes?"

"I said yes."

"Yes, you'll go to Ohio, or yes, you'll marry me?"

"Both." She brushed a kiss over his lips, stiff from confusion. "I am deeply in love with you, Raymond Novak, and I have been for a long time."

His eyelids fluttered. "You have? Since when?"

She looped her arms around his neck and laid a series of kisses along his cheekbone. "Since you plucked blossoms from my hair last year, since you rescued me after the bike accident when I was ten, since you played checkers with me when I had polio—it's hard to tell. For all I know, you smiled at me when I was a baby, and it started then."

"Wow. I can't . . . I can't believe it."

"Hmm. Sounds like you need some convincing." She pulled him down for a long, deep kiss. "Now do you believe me?"

He raised that sloppy grin she loved. "A few more like that and you might convince me."

She laughed, and he joined her, and he kissed her, and their kisses and laughter knit together like a silver scarf, swirling around them and binding them together.

Ray burrowed in her neck. "When do you want to get married?"

His kisses made her too warm and woozy. "Soon."

"Today then. Tomorrow if you insist on a long engagement."

She laughed, but the eager rumble in his voice kicked up her heart rate. "I know a preacher. Maybe he's available."

He chuckled, his face in her hair. Her hair would be a mess, but who cared? "I have some influence with him. Maybe I can talk him out of those long engagements he endorses."

"Then again, what about Jay-Jay? Maybe we should wait a little while to give him time."

"Yeah, you're right. And I need to put some meat on my bones. You don't want to marry a scarecrow."

"I'm not." She worked her fingers through his soft black hair. "I'm marrying Sir Raymond, my hero and the love of my life."

He swallowed hard, his eyes smoky. "I never thought I'd say this, but it was all worth it."

Helen snuggled close and breathed in the scent of him. The pain of the past year didn't evaporate in the warmth of his love—and she didn't want it to, because it made that love possible. "Yes, it was worth it."

48

Antioch
Saturday, September 8, 1945

Dad set his hand on Ray's shoulder. "Are you sure you want to be a pastor?"

Ray chuckled and ladled two cups of Mom's wedding punch, one for him and one for his bride. "All my life."

"You don't have to if you don't want."

Grandpa Novak picked an apple out of a bowl on the dining room table. "Heavens alive, John. First you want all your sons to be pastors, now you want none—"

"I want him to do what he wants to do."

"I want to be a pastor." Ray gave his dad a dark glare. "Don't stand in my way. Especially not on my wedding day."

Dad laughed and clapped Ray on the back. "Go find your wife."

"My wife." He savored the words, headed into the living room—and stopped short.

"I'm a jet. Can't catch me." Jay-Jay ran in front of him, arms spread wide. Little Judy Anello and Susie Wayne trailed behind in echelon.

"Whoa, there." Ray smiled at his stepson. His son. He couldn't have been prouder if the three-and-a-half-year-old were his own. Ray was glad God had called him to a church in Martinez, less than twenty miles away, so Jay-Jay could grow up near family.

The Army Air Force uniform sat comfortably on his shoulders, but he wouldn't miss it after his discharge. Now that the Japanese had surrendered, his discharge would come any day.

"Too bad you can't stay longer. You just got back from Ohio." Betty Anello scowled at Allie Novak seated on the living room couch beside her.

Allie bounced Frankie on her lap on his little fat legs. "Boeing wants Walt in Seattle."

"And we needed to spend the last few days in Riverside." Walt slung his arm around his wife's shoulders. "Finally got to meet Allie's friends. Cressie and Daisy—what characters."

"I got to meet Eileen Kilpatrick too."

Ray nodded to Walt. "Your friend Frank's widow, right?"

"Right. She's doing well. She worked the assembly line at Lockheed Vega, fell in love with her foreman. They're getting married next month."

Betty put her new baby girl to her shoulder. "I love these happy endings. Even with Allie's parents."

Allie and Walt exchanged a smile. "I don't know if I'd call that happy," Allie said. "But it was improvement."

Walt made a funny face at his son. "You don't need an olive branch when you have the cutest baby in the world."

Ray smiled. "Who could slam a door in that little face?"

"Not even my parents." Allie wiped drool off Frankie's chin. "Our reception was chilly, but we were received. It was a good start."

Laughter from the parlor drew him. "Excuse me," Ray said. "I want to find my wife."

"Your wife?" Walt said. "Really? She's your wife? You've only said that phrase a thousand times today."

Ray winked at his brother. "The day is young and my *wife* is waiting." He carried the cups of punch into the parlor.

Jack sat at the piano playing "Till the End of Time," and Ruth sat on the bench beside him in her wedding dress. Since both Helen and Ruth wanted small weddings, they'd chosen a double service to limit the fuss.

"Say, Ray," Jack said. "Sure you don't want to stay in the military, come to the desert with me, and test jets?"

Ray rested his elbow on the ink spot on the piano that earned him a spanking but saved his life. "Sure you don't want to stay in the ministry and write sermons with me?"

Jack laughed. "Yeah, I didn't think so."

Ruth leaned on her new husband's shoulder, now adorned by silver eagles. "I'll have my work cut out keeping you in line . . . Colonel."

"That's for sure. Still can't believe they promoted me even though I never got to fly a B-29 in combat."

Ray clucked his tongue. "Stupid surrender—ended the war and spoiled your fun."

"Oh, I'll have plenty of fun at Muroc Army Air Base."

"The Mojave Desert. I'm so excited. You think there'll be cowboys and Indians there?" Ruth's youngest sister, Maggie, a leggy girl of thirteen, danced with Jay-Jay. Since Ruth's other siblings were in the service or in Chicago, only Maggie represented the Doherty family.

"Flyboys, not cowboys," Ruth said.

"Too bad." Maggie couldn't stop talking about leaving Chicago to live with Jack and Ruth. She hugged Jay-Jay. "Can we take him with us? He's so cute."

"Sorry. He's coming with me," Ray said. But the adoring look on Jay-Jay's face said he'd rather be in the California high desert with Maggie. "Don't get any ideas, young man. Two weddings in one day are enough."

Jack laughed. "Say, he can double up with Charlie and May in December."

"Nope. I refuse to consent until he turns five." Ray glanced around. "Speaking of weddings, anyone seen my wife?"

Ruth grinned. "Checked the kitchen?"

"Mom and Grandma banished her. It's been tough." Ray wandered out of the parlor. Despite the teasing, Helen had developed a beautiful balance between Martha busyness and Mary-like faith. His new church had a moribund ladies' group, but not for long. Helen would spark them to life.

Dr. Jamison's deep voice rumbled from down the hall, and Ray followed it into Dad's study. "Too bad your friend Esther couldn't be here. Wanted to meet her."

"I know. But her latest letter brought good news. The Navy reduced the men's sentences to two to three years, with one year already served. We think they'll be quietly released soon, now that the war's over." In the study, Helen sat in Dad's leather armchair, lovelier than ever in a cream suit and with his ring on her finger.

Ray's throat felt thick. He'd given up his dream of wife and children and ministry, and now the fullness of that dream spread before him, richer and more vibrant since it was lost and then restored.

"Darling!" Her face lit up. "There you are."

Could his smile get any bigger, any goofier? Probably not. "Brought you some punch."

Punch dribbled down the armrest, and Helen sprang to her feet. "Oops! Where's your handkerchief?"

"My fault. Distracted by my bride." He set the cups on Dad's desk, pulled out his handkerchief, and wiped up the spill. "Why not use your hankie?"

"Never." She clapped her hand over her breast pocket, which contained the square of parachute cloth Ray had hoped to use as a white flag, now hemmed and embroidered with their initials and wedding date.

Ray sat in the armchair and pulled Helen down to his lap. "Special?"

"Very." She stroked the gold "Caterpillar Club" pin on his service jacket for "hitting the silk" in combat.

She gazed down at him with such dreamy eyes he wanted to kiss the breath out of her and haul her upstairs.

Mrs. Jamison stood. "Come along, Henry. Let's give the newlyweds some privacy."

Dr. Jamison took Helen's hand and glared at Ray. "Treat her well," he said with a growl.

"I'll love her with my life, sir."

His face relaxed. "I know you will, son." Then he entrusted his daughter's hand to Ray, her heart and her life.

Helen's strength showed in the set of her chin, Ray's to enjoy, and her vulnerability showed in her glistening eyes, Ray's to protect.

He brought her hand to his heart. "With all my life."

Acknowledgments

The more I write, the more I realize a novel is a group project. For some reason, mine is the name on the cover, but many others belong there as well.

My husband, Dave, keeps the business side of the household running, and his love inspires me to keep writing. Our children, Stephen, Anna, and Matthew, have adapted to the oddity of having an author in the house—leftovers, late school pickups, and friends' mothers asking for autographs—how embarrassing! Love you guys.

Special thanks go to my parents, Ronald and Nancy Stewart, and to my sister, Martha Groeber, for a lifetime of encouragement and love. And writing this novel made me appreciate all the more my wonderful, godly in-laws, Carl and Diane Sundin.

For growth in writing, I'm indebted to the faculty of Mount Hermon Christian Writers Conference, and the membership of American Christian Fiction Writers, Christian Authors Network, and Diablo Valley Christian Writers Group (Kathleen Casey, Ron Clelland, Carol Green, Cynthia Herrmann,

Rebekah and Ruth Kronk, Susan Lawson, Marilynn Lindahl, Georgia Sue Massie, Paula Nunley, Evelyn Sanders, and Linda Wright). My deepest thanks to my stellar critique partners—Judy Gann, Bonnie Leon, Marci Seither, Ann Shorey, and Marcy Weydemuller. And special thanks to Marcy, my sounding board with full slap-me-upside-the-head privileges.

I am deeply grateful for help in research. The staff of the Antioch Public Library has helped with research questions and has patiently explained—more than once—how to use the microfiche machine to read the Antioch *Ledger*. Many thanks to Rick Acker and Nicklas Akers for help with the military legal system. Any errors are mine alone. And I apologize for maligning your noble profession. Special thanks to Sam Allen for lending his military aviation expertise and skilled eye for reviewing this manuscript. I also want to recognize the Collings Foundation and the Experimental Aircraft Association. Without the opportunity to walk through their restored B-17s, my stories would have been poorer.

El Campanil Theatre is featured on this book cover. You can learn about the theater's restoration and programs at www.elcampaniltheatre.com.

Prayer—my oxygen tubing. Thank you to my friends from church and small group for holding me up.

It still gives me a thrill to use the phrases "my agent" and "my editor," and I couldn't have asked for better ones. Rachel Kent at Books & Such Literary Agency guides me in writing and career development, and I'll always be grateful to Vicki Crumpton at Revell for taking a chance on an unknown writer and for her insightful editing. The team at Revell makes the publication process a joy. Thanks to the wonderful people in editorial, marketing, publicity, cover art, and sales for supporting a debut author so well.

Highest thanks go to the Lord, who teaches me to push

back fear and to forge ahead in his strength. May you also find courage in his presence.

Thank you, dear reader, for joining me and the Novak brothers on this journey. Please visit my website at www.sarahsundin.com to leave a message, sign up for my quarterly newsletter, see a diagram of a B-17, or read tips for book clubs. I'd love to hear from you!

Discussion Questions

1. Helen says she "performs grief." Why does she do it? What would you do in a similar situation? How does her true grief contrast with her performed grief?

2. Ray is a natural peacemaker. How is this good? Any negatives?

3. Helen and Jay-Jay have an evening routine of dancing to the radio. Any sweet parent-child rituals in your family?

4. As a noncombatant during wartime, Ray feels people look down on him. Why do you think he feels this way? Do you agree with his decision after the fire?

5. Jay-Jay, like many children his age, has a temper. How does Helen deal with his tantrums at the beginning? At the end? Have you known the joy of raising a tantrum-throwing child?

6. Helen's "heart's work" is leadership and volunteering, and Ray's is ministry. How do you see this? Do you have an area where your talents and gifts combine into something useful and enjoyable?

7. Circumstances keep both Ray and Helen from their "heart's work" during the story. How does Ray handle it? How about Helen? Have you ever been kept from something you enjoy, and how did you handle it?

8. Discuss Jim and Helen's marriage. What clues did you see? How did Helen's childhood experiences as a polio patient and as a ballet pupil set her up for this relationship?

9. At the Sacramento Air Depot, Ray feels he hinders the war effort. How is he not suited for this job? Have you ever had a position you weren't suited for? What did you do?

10. Victor Llewellyn just can't take no for an answer. Do you think this stems from arrogance or from insecurity? Why do you think he made his decision about the appeal?

11. During World War II, many women were single mothers due to widowhood or their husband's deployment, and 19 million women took jobs outside the home. These women faced many modern issues. How do you see this in Helen's life?

12. How do Ray's past experiences with women affect his relationship with Helen? Do you think he moved too fast? Why? What was the result?

13. Helen deals with rationing and shortages on the home front. Do you have any personal or family experiences of World War II home front life? How would you have handled these difficulties?

14. Ray flies his combat tour at the peak of strength for the U.S. Eighth Air Force. Still, conditions were difficult due to German fighters, flak, extreme cold, collisions, and crashes. How does Ray cope? How about his crewmates? How would you cope?

15. Do you think Helen volunteers because of her personality and gifts? Patriotism? Dealing with pain? Pleasing people? Pleasing God? Some combination?

16. By the end of the story, Ray is able to do things he couldn't do before. Do you think he was always capable, or did his experiences change him fundamentally?

17. How would you describe the relationship between Helen and Betty? Between Ray and his brothers? Between Jim and Dorothy? How did their early roles affect them as adults? Do their relationships change during the story? If so, how?

18. The Port Chicago Explosion was the largest home front disaster of the war, and the aftermath of the mutiny trial eventually led to the desegregation of the U.S. armed forces. While Carver is fictional, two men with medical excuses were convicted. What examples of racism and segregation do you see in the story? Were you surprised?

19. Ray is frustrated when Major Siegel doesn't believe his testimony. How does he deal with this? Have you been in a situation where people didn't believe you?

20. If you read *A Distant Melody* or *A Memory Between Us*, did you enjoy the updates on Walt and Allie and on Jack and Ruth?

Sarah Sundin is the author of *A Distant Melody* and *A Memory Between Us*. She lives in northern California with her husband, three children, a cat, and a yellow lab prone to eating pens and manuscripts. She works on-call as a hospital pharmacist and teaches Sunday school and women's Bible studies. Her great-uncle flew with the U.S. Eighth Air Force in England. Please visit her online at www.sarahsundin.com, www.facebook.com/SarahSundinAuthor, or www.twitter.com/sarahsundin.

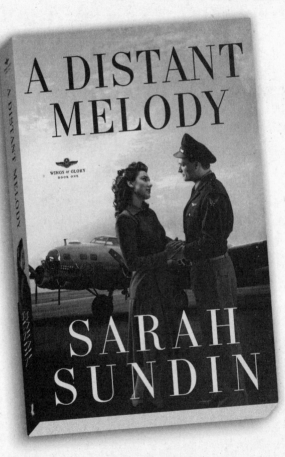

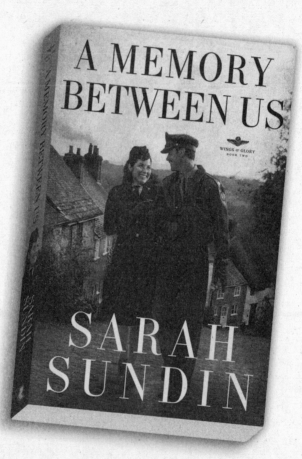